ABSOLUTELY
TRUE LIES

RACHEL STUHLER

TOUCHSTONE

New York   London   Toronto   Sydney   New Delhi

Touchstone
An Imprint of Simon & Schuster, Inc.
1230 Avenue of the Americas
New York, NY 10020

First Touchstone trade paperback edition May 2015

TOUCHSTONE and colophon are registered trademarks of Simon & Schuster, Inc.

For information about special discounts for bulk purchases, please contact Simon & Schuster Special Sales at 1-866-506-1949 or business@simonandschuster.com.

The Simon & Schuster Speakers Bureau can bring authors to your live event. For more information or to book an event, contact the Simon & Schuster Speakers Bureau at 1-866-248-3049 or visit our website at www.simonspeakers.com.

Interior design by Kyle Kabel

Manufactured in the United States of America

10 9 8 7 6 5 4 3 2 1

Library of Congress Cataloging-in-Publication Data is available.

ISBN 978-1-4767-6302-6
ISBN 978-1-4767-6304-0 (ebook)

To my grandmother, Lorraine, for giving me a voice;
to Ms. Marcia Habecker, for teaching me how to use it;
and to my husband, Jake, for making me unafraid to roar.

ABSOLUTELY
TRUE LIES

CHAPTER 1

People are always asking for my advice on how to break into this business. "It can't have been easy," they tell me, "landing your first TV show at the age of ten." Nothing about show business is easy, but my path is not anyone else's. I didn't ask for fame and I didn't ask for that first television show. One day I was going to school with my friends, worried about boys and how I'd do on Friday's math test, and the next I was memorizing sixty script pages and trying to fit in photo shoots after tutoring. I've always felt it was God's plan, to make me an ambassador for other people my age.

The day I graduated from Sarah Lawrence with my degree in creative writing, my mother told me, "Holly, in a few years, you'll be so famous they'll be asking *you* to give the commencement address."

She was wrong.

Four years after graduating from college, I was twenty-five and writing for a magazine in Los Angeles that was so tiny they practically had to pay people to read it. It was supposed to be an insider view of celebrity life, but TMZ and Radar Online can pay top dollar for their inside scoops and we had an operating budget of about seventy-five cents. Meaning that no one wanted to talk to us. Not to mention, the readers Kragen Publishing so desperately sought were not the ones who routinely scoured newsstands for celeb gossip; everything the teen and twenty-something set wants to know about the latest scandals is up in fifteen minutes. Our site was perpetually down for maintenance, which was perfect for our sixty-five-year-old readers, who didn't know the first thing about computers, anyway. My boss once told me that our magazine was purchased most by widowed housewives who also happened to be buying the *National Enquirer*.

So I was reduced to writing blurbs on museum exhibitions, doing "interviews" by e-mail with famous people's agents, and writing reviews of movies that had already come out. Despite my having graduated magna cum laude and applying for hundreds of jobs all over the country, this was one of only three job offers I received. The first was at my hometown newspaper, and the second was for a farming magazine in Montana. Both paid more than double what I was making now, but *Westside Weekly* was about *Hollywood*. How could I say no to that? I did, however, have to lie to my mother and tell her *WW* was my only job offer; if I had admitted that I was offered double to basically live down the block from her, she would have died of happiness. And I would have committed myself by the end of the year.

When I took the job in L.A., she sighed and whined that I was abandoning her, but she actually managed to let go of the car as I drove away. And every month since, she's demanded to know why she can't find the magazine at the grocery store. She lives in Syracuse, New York, a city of about 150,000 people. *I* couldn't even find my magazine in Los Angeles, so I have no idea why she thought the Syracuse Wegmans would be flush with copies, but she was continually outraged. I finally got the assistant editor to send her a few courtesy issues, but I'm pretty sure by that point my mother thought I was really unemployed and had fabricated the entire thing on my computer.

My job did exist, although just barely. My paycheck showed up in the mail only sporadically and often not for the amount promised. But I lived in a studio apartment the size of a postage stamp, so my overhead wasn't terribly high. Even so, I couldn't afford to go out very much, and my cat, Smitty, had to settle for whatever food was on special that week.

I'd lived in L.A. for more than four years and my social life consisted of an ornery cat and the occasional pint of Ben & Jerry's on my Goodwill couch. I had a few close friends, but they all had jobs on film crews and worked twenty-hour days, so I only saw them between projects. And since I refused to accept a date with anyone whose opening salvo was "I drive a [insert Mercedes, Jaguar, BMW, Ferrari, Lamborghini]," I hadn't been out on a date in almost a year. Despite this dismal reality, everyone back home assumed I was living the high life. Whenever I visited, I was lauded for being the "big L.A. writer," the one who hung out with celebrities until all hours of the night and then slept through the day until it was time to do it all over again. I once saw Steve Martin at the car wash, but I don't really think that's anything to write home about. I really did try to tell my friends and family the truth, explain to them that I lived in a suspected gang neighborhood with zero vegetation and a "no cruising" city mandate, but they just wouldn't listen. And because my family is truly unimaginative, they all started calling me Holly *Wood*. Hilarious.

Yep, I was well on my way to . . . moving back home and writing gardening blurbs for the Syracuse *Post-Standard*.

Every once in a great while, though, I scored an assignment that gave me a glimpse of just how cool a career in celeb writing could be. When an actress from the CW started her own clothing line, they gave press credentials to pretty much anyone who asked, and I snapped mine up and found myself sandwiched between Perez Hilton and the editor of the Garden Grove High School newspaper. I tried to remain as calm and cool as the sixteen-year-old yawning apathetically next to me when Britney wandered past, but inside, I was jumping up and down. What was the matter with these people? Didn't they know where we were, what we were doing? It was dark and I couldn't be sure, but I think Orlando Bloom may have spilled a martini down my dress. It was the pinnacle of my career to that point.

But for every high moment, there were about fifty humiliating letdowns. The assistant editor knew someone who was second cousins with George Clooney's personal hairstylist, and said that she could get me into the premiere of his new movie. It was Oscar season and the film had a lot of buzz surrounding it, and the magazine just happened to go to press one day before the movie's release, so—for once—we would be in the thick of things. I didn't have the money for a red carpet dress, so I went to Goodwill and bought an old quinceañera dress and some shoes, then spent three days meticulously pulling rhinestones off the hem and repainting the scuffed pair of heels. I'm sure I looked like a thrift store prom queen, but I was so excited I couldn't eat for three days. When the assistant editor saw me, she was congratulatory and asked if I was finally taking an interest in my appearance (I'm five-ten and a size 8—in this town, that's practically the giant blueberry girl from *Willy Wonka*).

So there I was, dressed to the nines and on my way to the premiere in Westwood. I couldn't afford a chauffeured car, so I had to park almost a mile away and walk the distance in my cheap bridesmaid's shoes. By the time I got to the theater, I was sweaty and had put a stiletto hole through the back of the dress, plus my shoes were a size too small and my feet had gone numb in the first five blocks. None of this dampened my elation as I got in line with the rest of the critics who were here to review the film.

The first thing I noticed was that I was the only one clad in evening wear. The rest of the reviewers looked like refugees from the MTV movie awards, with hipster haircuts and asymmetrical hemlines. They all gave me dirty looks, but I didn't care—I still listen to bad eighties pop, and not even ironically. I shot a few dirty looks back at them, thinking, *Heaven really* is *a place on earth, and you can all suck it.*

As we reached security one by one and were asked for our publication names, everyone got through—except me.

"I'm sorry, *what* magazine did you say you were from?" the security guard asked.

"Westside Weekly," I repeated for the third time. A gaggle of the hipster mafia who'd already made it past the checkpoint chuckled quietly.

"Doesn't that come out once a month?" weird emo-girl with purple-streaked black hair asked me.

"Yes," I replied quietly, trying to steel myself against hurt feelings. They were once fresh-faced, small-town newbies, I reminded myself. And despite the fact that their paychecks dwarfed mine, not one of those poser, Diablo Cody wannabes was any better than I was. At least, that's what I told myself. "I have no idea why they call it a weekly."

"I'm sorry, you're not on the list," the security guard told me. Despite his words, he didn't look particularly sorry.

"But—" I sputtered. But—what? I didn't have the name of the second cousin or the hairstylist, and it wasn't like I knew a single person associated with the event. I tried desperately to think of a way to prove who I was, that I deserved to be on that list.

"I'm sorry, ma'am, but I'm going to have to ask you to step out of line," the guard said, starting to get a little irritated. "I've got a lot of real press to get through."

Real press. "Oh," I practically whispered. "Okay."

With my cheeks on fire, trying to hold back tears, I turned around and stepped out of line, forcing myself to avoid eye contact with the now raucously laughing hipster critics. If I'd had any doubt where I rated in this town, I was sure I was a nobody now.

My eyes trained on the sidewalk, I staggered the mile back to my car. I tried to ignore the pain in my feet, even as they started to bleed, making the cheap satin heels slippery. I was only two blocks away from the parking garage when I turned a corner and the back of the dress caught on something. I didn't notice the ripping sound until the entire skirt pooled around my ankles and I realized I was nearly naked from the waist down.

After that night, I never bothered asking for better assignments. I took what they gave me, even if it meant the movie I was reviewing was already out of theaters by the time my article was printed. And when my mother complained that I was getting too old to be the "ingenue writer," I just turned on the vacuum cleaner and told her the connection was breaking up.

I lived like this for another year, barely getting by, going out with my friends twice a month, and pretending I was happy. I was getting paid to write about Hollywood, wasn't I? Wasn't this all I said I ever wanted? As for my dream of one day writing a novel, well . . . Everyone wants to do that, but no one really gets around to it. Again, that's what I told myself.

But my tenuous hold on life came crashing down one Tuesday afternoon, about five hours after I'd submitted my latest article, a review of a Korean day spa in downtown L.A. I was already in a bad mood because the spa hadn't comped my facial and I'd been forced to pay the seventy bucks out of my own pocket. They hadn't told me this up front, and so I'd had to hand over my grocery money just to leave the building.

I spent the entire ride home repeatedly calling the assistant editor and leaving voice mails about reimbursement, but no one answered or called me back. I'd just pulled up in front of the demilitarized zone that was my apartment building when Lacy, a colleague of mine at the magazine, called me.

"I'm waiting on a call from Susan," I told her. "I can't talk long."

"Susan got *fired*," Lacy said. "That's why I called you."

"Oh," I replied, feeling sorry for her. Susan was incompetent, rude, and had the IQ of a housefly, but hey—everyone needs a job. "Who'd they hire to replace her?"

"No one," Lacy said, like I was missing some big piece of information that should have been staring me in the face.

"Does that mean her job's open?" I hated working for the magazine, but I was practically making twelve cents an hour; any salary increase would have made a difference in my life.

"Are you deaf, Hol? There's *no* job. Not for any of us. Kragen Publishing is shutting down the magazine."

Too shocked to reply, I sat in my car and watched as a ten-year-old sold marijuana to an old man in a fedora and cardigan on the front steps of my building. My job—my shitty, humiliating, barely-minimum-wage job—was gone.

"Are you still there?" Lacy asked.

"Um . . . I gotta go feed Smitty. I'll talk to you later."

I hung up the phone, knowing that if Lacy said one more word, I was going to throw up all over my steering wheel. And in my fifteen-year-old car, there were already enough noxious odors without adding vomit to the list. So I flung my cell into my purse and got out of the car, ignoring the drug deal ten feet in front of me and heading into my building.

My mind raced, trying to figure out what to do. I couldn't throw in the towel and get a job at the Coffee Bean, I just couldn't. It would mean the end of everything I'd worked for. I wasn't even sure which was worse—getting a retail job or going back home and taking that job at *The Post-Standard*. And I knew that half the kids I went to high school with, who still lived in the same zip code and married the guys they'd lost their virginity to, would be smugly elated to welcome me back. I'd seen it in their eyes when they bought me good-bye drinks four years ago—they wanted me to fail, *needed* me to fail to justify their own choices in life. I couldn't let that happen. I had to find another writing job, and soon.

My rent was only eight hundred a month, but I had no savings. Zero dollars minus eight hundred equaled living on a park bench at the Santa Monica Pier. And I've been down there plenty of times—all the good benches have already been claimed, and I'm not so keen on shivving people. My family was pretty much right out of the trailer park, so it was futile asking for help from them unless I needed a skinned possum overnighted to me, and even then, I'm not sure any one of them could figure out how to properly mail the package.

So I was screwed. And not even in a good way.

Four hours later, I'd eaten an economy-size bag of M&M's, four boxes of Girl Scout cookies, and every frozen pizza, Hot Pocket, and burrito I had ready for the next week's lunches. I was also drunk off my ass, having gone through all the daiquiri and margarita mixes hours ago, and was now down to doing shots of chocolate syrup and peppermint schnapps. I was in my own minty hell when Susan finally called me back at eleven o'clock that night.

"I'm sorry I didn't call you sooner," she cooed. "But I didn't know if I was authorized to tell you or not."

"'Ssssss okay," I replied, a split second before I burped into the phone.

"Are you drunk?" she asked, her tone laced with irritating self-righteousness. I mean, who the hell was *she*? My mother? Unemployed or not, how was it her business if I was plastered before midnight on a Tuesday?

"Maybe." I shrugged, as though she could see me. "What's it to you? You're not my boss anymore."

"I'm just concerned, that's all. It's a stupid little magazine, Holly. I think Starbucks pays more than you were making."

Suddenly, I reached that moment where you slide from "everything's cool" to "morose drunk girl." "At least I was making something. Someone was paying me to write."

"Haven't you always wanted to write a novel?" she said cheerfully. "Why don't you take your savings and spend six months doing that?"

Was she fucking serious? Did Susan Baker think I was a fucking Rockefeller? Thanks to the money I'd unwillingly spent at the Korean spa, I now had less than a thousand dollars to my name. And it was the twenty-first of the month—I had five weeks until I turned into a pumpkin. The only writers I knew who could crank out a book in that time were coked out of their minds. And I was *way* too poor to take up a drug habit right now.

"Yeah . . . yeah, maybe," I told her, too embarrassed to admit the truth. "What about you?"

"Oh, I knew this was coming," Susan said, sounding pretty damn pleased with herself. "I've been putting out résumés for months. I start my new job on Monday."

Months? She knew about this for months?

"Again, sorry I couldn't tell you sooner, but I was told not to worry anyone."

Bitch. "Yeah, I totally get it," I said. "Well, good luck to you. I gotta go. I'm . . . out with some friends."

From the far end of the couch, Smitty meowed at me and I prayed to God Susan couldn't hear it through the phone.

"Ohh-*kay*," she answered, clearly calling me a liar. "I'll call you next week, maybe we can do lunch."

"Sure," I said, knowing I would never, ever, ever see her name on my caller ID again. "Take care and good luck in your new job."

"Thanks, babe," Susan said. "Talk to you later."

I hung up the phone and then stared at it for a moment.

"Liar," I said, wishing I'd had the nerve to actually say that to her. But then, I was just as big a liar, who was I to judge? As if to verify this, Smitty meowed again, batting his declawed paw at me.

"Whose side are you on?" I said, now slipping into angry drunk-girl mode. "Do you work for Susan now?"

In response, Smitty came over and settled in my lap. I was momentarily touched by his affection until he began licking the chocolate syrup off the sides of my glass. I almost swatted him away, but I didn't really care enough to do it.

"I guess we'll both end the night by puking."

That's the last thing I remember until about eleven the next morning, when I woke up to find Tito, my neighbor, staring at me from just outside my patio. I guess I'd fallen asleep with the blinds open, and since my legs were splayed across the couch, I'm sure he got a pretty good show. At least someone should have been enjoying the view.

Too depressed to think straight, I stood up and walked to the blinds, flipping Tito the bird before shutting them. I then collapsed into my tiny bed and went to sleep. For days. And I do mean *days*. By the time my mother called to make sure I hadn't been gang-raped and strangled to death, the hair on my legs could have been French-braided.

"What, Ma?" I said from beneath the covers, lest I accidentally let any light enter my dungeon of despair. "I'm not in the mood."

"You haven't called me in a week, Holly. I thought you were dead."

No, I just wished I was dead. "I'm fine," I lied, yawning. "I'm just tired."

"Why are you tired? You go to the movies and write five hundred words about it."

This was an argument we had all the time. My mother works for city government and feels that her forty hours a week at a desk is much more grueling than my forty hours a week at a desk. I didn't know how to tell her that I no longer even had a desk.

"I'm sick, okay?" I shot back, about ready to throw the phone at the wall.

"Were you making out with someone last night?" my mother asked, chastising me like I was twelve years old and caught with the boy next door. "You don't know where those men have been, Holly."

The only creature who'd attempted to make out with me in months was Smitty, and even that only happened when I was eating something that smelled appetizing.

"No, Mom, it's just something that's going around at work." Yeah, it's called unemployment. "I'll call you back in a couple of days when I feel better."

"I just wanted to let you know that Uncle Bob is going to be calling you—"

"Great," I said, "Love you, Mom. Bye." I hung up quickly, before she could say anything else.

Then I opened up the back of the phone and yanked out the battery, tossing all three pieces on the floor next to the bed. I had no job, no boyfriend, and very few friends—who the hell needed to talk to me? If I were found dead in this apartment a week or so from now (the manager always bangs on the door and lets himself in when the rent is even six seconds late), who would really care besides the local news? I'd even be willing to bet that I'm worth more to this world as a tragic, twenty-five-year-old dead Hollywood wannabe than a living, breathing, aspiring novelist. And my mother would finally have an emotional wound big enough to top everyone else in her bridge club, including Debbie Paul, whose son was born with a cleft palate and, according to my mom, never shuts up about it.

So I went back to sleep, half of me hoping that this was all just a really cliché insecurity dream and the other half praying that God, Allah, Zeus, or whoever would just strike me down in my sleep and save me from having to wake up again.

But I did wake up eventually. By the time I actually did get out of bed long enough to take a shower and change my clothes, Smitty was in the kitchen, chewing through a cardboard box of cereal. I had a sudden pang of guilt as I saw the row of hastily opened cans of cat food I had just tossed on the floor each night before crawling back into my den of self-pity. Apparently, I had forgotten to even do that the night before.

"I'm sorry, Smits," I said, bending down to pet him. But Smitty just gave me a look of contempt and abandoned the cereal box, sashaying his way into the living room without so much as a backward glance. Great. Now even my cat hated me.

I didn't know what day it was, and it was only by the sun peeking through my blinds that I guessed the microwave clock read 2:00 P.M., not 2:00 A.M. Against my better judgment, I walked the ten feet from my kitchenette back to my bed and knelt down, gathering the pieces of my cell phone. The only thought running through my mind was that I had had this phone number for four years now; four years and I was likely about to have my phone shut off for nonpayment.

As the screen blinked to life, I saw that it was now the twenty-ninth. I had been asleep for eight days. I waited anxiously for my phone to register any texts or voice mails, hoping to discover that Kragen had reconsidered and saved the magazine, even though I'm fairly certain they made about eleven dollars an issue.

I was even more hopeful when my phone politely dinged and said I had nine new voice mails. But my excitement quickly faded as I discovered that the first five were from my mother.

At least number six was a surprise. "Hey, kid, it's your Uncle Bob-O. I just wanted to let you know that I gave out your number to a friend of mine in the L.A. area. He said something about needing an entertainment writer and I told him I had just the gal. His name is Jameson Lloyd and he used to jam with me back in high school. Not really sure what he does now, but maybe you can clear some extra cash. Talk to you later, Holly."

I pressed delete. You might think I was excited by this message, or at least the teensiest bit encouraged, but I wasn't. Not even the slightest. That's because in this town, people promise you Tiffany and can't even deliver Taco Bell. Everyone I've ever met in L.A. has told me what a fantastic, talented, brilliant, genius writer I am, and how they plan to catapult me to the top of the literary world. No one has ever gotten me a job, read a single word of what I've written, or even bothered to call me back a second time. Even my "agent,"

Gus, who I met through the aunt of a friend of a boss's sister-in-law, who guaranteed me he'd tear the throat out of any client who tried to screw me, never met with me again after I hired him. Though he does dutifully collect his ten percent of my measly earnings every month. When my paycheck from Kragen is late, it's Gus who notices first, not me. Oh, and he didn't even get me that job—I applied over the Internet and was stupid enough to tell him about it.

So when I listened to the next two messages, I wasn't expecting a thing. My best friend, Camille, called to say she was worried about me and that my mother had been obsessively texting her for information, and was I alive and available for a drink? As I thought back to my drunken mint stupor, the bile rose in my throat and I quickly pressed 7 and moved on. I resolved to abstain from alcohol for six months or until I had hung myself in despair, unable to wash the stench of failure off my skin, whichever was sooner.

The eighth was from a local congressman, hoping for my vote in the special election. I was not aware we were having a special election, and to be perfectly honest, I'm not altogether sure I'm registered to vote in the state of California (I've always had a misaligned sense of civic duty). I sighed and expected that the last would be from a Chinese food hellhole telling me about their latest egg foo yong special, but I was unfamiliar with the voice speaking back at me through the phone.

"Heya, Holly, my name is Jameson and I got your name through Bob Riker."

I sat up straighter in astonishment. I think I may have even glanced at Smitty to make sure he wasn't talking to me, as somehow, *that* would have seemed less strange.

"I have a client who's looking for a good ghostwriter, and Bob recommended you. I'd love you to come out and meet with us next week if possible, and you two can chat and see how things go. I can't promise you anything beyond that, but give me a call and we'll see if we can work something out. My number is 3-1-0—"

I heaved myself off the floor and ran for a pen. Not finding a piece of paper, I wrote the phone number on the wall with a Sharpie. Hey—I already lived in a shitty apartment, how much more damage could I do to the place? I then replayed the message to double-check the number and make sure I wasn't hallucinating. But it was real, all of it. I had no idea who this client was or how much the job might pay, but if it could get me through even another month, it might be enough to keep me afloat until I could find something else.

My grandmother always says that God never closes a door without opening a window. For twenty-five years, I was pretty sure she was full of shit, but right about now, I was ready to throw open every one of the barred and double-paned windows in my postage stamp. Hallelujah, praise Jebus—there was a chance that I was back in business.

CHAPTER 2

You'll be surprised to know my life is actually pretty normal. I live in a house with my mom and dad, just like other teenagers. I failed my driver's test twice (I can't believe I just admitted that!), and even now, my mom doesn't really like me to drive after dark.

I probably don't get as much sleep as other teens, though. With work on the show and my next album, sometimes I only have two or three free hours a day, during which time I curl up with my three dogs and try to get a little bit of shut-eye!

Four days later, I was driving aimlessly around Holmby Hills, a part of Los Angeles I'd only just discovered existed. It's an absurdly rich section of West L.A. sandwiched in between Bel Air and Brentwood, and given that we do still technically live in a desert, I found it bizarre and more than a bit offensive that every lawn I passed looked like Technicolor Astroturf. I once saw a weed growing resolutely from a crack in a sidewalk in my neighborhood, and even the weed was a mousy brown.

You might think I was driving in endless circles because I was lost, but that's not the case at all. I just had no idea where I was headed. When I first returned Jameson Lloyd's phone call, I received a laundry list of instructions that provided not a single clue as to (a) where I was going, (b) who I was meeting, or even (c) what the job was.

"My client is very private," Mr. Lloyd had told me over the phone. "And so you understand why I can't give you the address."

"Of course," I lied. "And what does the specific job entail?"

Lloyd inhaled sharply through his teeth like he'd just stubbed his toe. "Wow, *Hols*—I can call you Hols, right?" He didn't wait for an answer before rushing on. "I think we're getting ahead of ourselves. Just head out to Holmby Hills around noon on Sunday and give me a call. I'll give you the turn-by-turn directions to get up here."

By this point, I was fairly convinced my uncle Bob had sold me into white slavery and I was about to be kidnapped and shipped to Abu Dhabi. Especially when I tried to locate Holmby Hills on a Google map and was informed that no such city existed. But after a few more online searches, I finally realized it was a neighborhood—a very tony neighborhood with residents like Gwen Stefani and Hugh Hefner. I still thought I was about to become the concubine of a wealthy Middle Eastern oil magnate, but at least then I wouldn't have to worry about making rent every month.

So as Sunday approached, I was terrified. But not just at the possibility that this job could all be some sort of a scam where I was asked to mail a check for a thousand dollars to Christian aid workers in Nigeria; I was also just as scared that this might be a real job. I had never ghostwritten anything before and had zero idea what the hell it really meant. I mean, I knew that I was supposed to write down the words and let someone else take the credit for them, but nonfiction has never been my strong suit. I'm a lazy researcher, and most of the time I find the truth about as exciting as instant oatmeal. I would much rather offer my ill-informed opinion or, even better, make up a story entirely. But I had just written my rent check and now had two hundred dollars to my name, so this wasn't the moment for me to be picky.

At 11:55, I called Mr. Lloyd from the parking lot of a golf course on Sunset.

"Excellent," he said. "My client should be getting up any time now."

My eyes shifted to the clock in my car. It was noon, right? I know this is a strange town, but who gets up at noon? I shook my head and remembered that I had to keep an open mind. Maybe he or she was sick, or had been down for a nap with their newborn . . . There were plenty of reasons—other than idle waste—that someone might sleep into the afternoon. It's just that, given the inherent hedonism of my adopted hometown, I was inclined toward the latter explanation.

Now that I had reached the general vicinity, I expected Mr. Lloyd to give me the actual street directions to the house. Again, I was wrong.

"The paps would just die if they had this address," he told me. "And besides, it's really only another mile from where you are, I can totally talk you through the turns. Get back on Sunset going west, and let me know when you see a street to your left that's shaped like a thong."

I'm sorry, a *what*?

"Um . . . sure," I replied, once again illegally talking on my cell phone. I turned back out onto Sunset Boulevard and wondered what the hell a thong-shaped street was supposed to look like. "A thong, you said?"

"Yeah, yeah," he replied quickly. "Off to your left, just a couple streets up. Wide mouth for a residential street."

I caught sight of the street and moved into the turn lane, cringing as I realized why he thought it looked like a thong. So far, this guy seemed like a real class act.

"Now you're going to follow that road for the next three quarters of a mile, almost until it ends. You'll be able to see the split, but don't go that far—turn in to the last house on the right. The guard knows you're coming." And without his saying good-bye, there was an audible *click* as he hung up the phone.

"Okay," I said to myself as I wound past houses several times larger than my entire college. Just in case I actually got this job and

had to come back, I made a mental note that I was on Charing Cross Road. I wondered if Lloyd, in keeping the address from me, thought I was truly so stupid that I wouldn't—or couldn't—read the street signs. Me . . . a writer.

I drove past several more estates that looked far too large for any single human being or family to reside in, before seeing the end of Charing Cross a hundred feet in front of me. I slowed down and anxiously turned in to the gate for the last house on the right, noticing that it was one of the biggest in the neighborhood.

And when I say I slowed down, I mean I *slowed down*. Whenever I start something new, I find the most frightening part is walking into an unfamiliar place and meeting your new bosses and coworkers. I'm never really that nervous in interviews or even the morning of a new job, but that last couple of minutes before I'm thrown into the mix makes me want to turn tail and flee to a cantina in Oaxaca and spend the rest of my life as a beach bum. I imagine my first morning of preschool had to be sheer hell for all involved.

But the entry to the driveway was only about thirty yards deep, so I couldn't avoid the inevitable for very long. By the time my front tires touched the driveway, a burly guard had already sprung out of his little brick station and was halfway to my car. In the three seconds before he actually spoke to me, I realized that in my ancient and sputtering vehicle, he might mistake me for the maid. And I wouldn't blame him one bit.

"Holly Gracin, here to see . . . er . . ." I hesitated, wondering how I was supposed to announce myself to the unnamed and unknown big shot who lived in this palace of capitalist greed and waste.

"They're expecting you." The guard nodded. "Just drive straight up to the house and Mr. Lloyd will meet you."

He turned and walked back to the guard station, typed a code into the computer, and then the heavy iron gates began to swing open. For a split second, the theme song to *The Real Housewives of Beverly Hills* popped into my head and I craned my neck to see if some superfamous restaurateur I'd never heard of was painting her nails on the front veranda. But who was I kidding—no one does that in front of the house in plain view of the street. They have backyard infinity pools for that.

I drove around the small, circled driveway and wished like hell I didn't have to park my car in front of this house. Couldn't I have hidden it down the block and walked the rest of the way? If I had to negotiate a project price, I knew I wouldn't have much leverage once the client caught sight of the heaping pile of fiberglass and rust baking in the sun.

But if I was worried that Mr. Lloyd would make a snap decision upon seeing me climb out of the car, I didn't need to be. Contrary to what the guard had told me, there was no one waiting for me. In fact, just from looking, I wouldn't have guessed there was anyone home. No open windows, no cars in the driveway . . . The place might as well have been a movie set.

I waited another minute or so, then climbed up the steps and walked to the front door and rang the bell. No one answered, but immediately, I heard what sounded like thirty yappy little dogs begin barking from somewhere inside the house. When I rang the bell a second time, I could hear them skittering toward the door, their collective miniature paws scraping the bare floors.

"Belle, Jasmine, *Ariel*," exclaimed a high-pitched girlish voice with a distinct southern drawl. "I swear to God, y'all are giving me a headache!"

A moment later, the enormous front door swung open and I found myself staring down at a teenage girl so slight I was pretty sure she could fit in my pocket. It was roughly five more seconds before I realized *who* she was, this face that I'd seen plastered on magazine covers and movie screens for the last several years (not to mention the endless tawdry tabloids I glanced at in line at the grocery store).

Her beauty in person was nothing less than profound, and I completely understood why men and women alike stopped and stared. With golden blond, wavy hair that fell to the middle of her back, a heart-shaped face that completely lacked guile or pretension, and eyes the color of clear Bermuda water, the girl looked like she had been crafted by an artistic genius instead of born from a normal, living, breathing human being. If I pricked her, I thought she might have bled Cristal.

The midget screen princess blinked up at me with those enormous Caribbean eyes and broke into a dazzling grin. "Are you Holly?"

"Yes." I nodded nervously, glad I still retained the power of speech.

"I'm Daisy Mae," she continued, smiling brighter. "But I'm sure you already know that."

Of course I did. You'd be hard-pressed to find someone under the age of seventy who didn't know the name Daisy Mae Dixson, the veteran Nickelodeon child star who had moved seamlessly into both blockbuster movies and pop music, and whose adolescent crushes were the subjects of entire articles in *Star* and *In Touch Weekly*. She was such big news that this time last year someone had devoted a website to the countdown to her eighteenth birthday, for those men who felt their attraction was acceptable once she passed the age of sexual consent. As though this gave them any chance of getting within a mile of the Christian pop princess who still went to church with Daddy on Sundays and wore a promise ring on her left hand. And yes, it frightened me that I, a twenty-five-year-old woman, knew this many details about the life of an eighteen-year-old stranger.

In my defense, part of my stuttering, starstruck reaction was simply that I did not run in these circles. I'd never been to any of the hottest clubs or had lunch at the Ivy; as stupid as it sounds, since I had not crossed over into the celebrity world, they still seemed a little like mirages to me. Logically, I knew that famous people were real, tangible humans who went to the grocery store and the movies just like everybody else, but it just wasn't something I really thought about. And to find myself at Daisy's front door, I suddenly realized just how much I was out of my element. I didn't belong here, and in whatever capacity she wanted to hire me, I knew I was drastically underqualified. Even still—this was pretty damn cool.

"Nice to meet you," I finally managed, reaching out and shaking her hand. I looked down just as her three pocket-size dogs began leaping up at me. I wasn't sure if they were trying to protect Daisy or just say hello.

"I'm so sorry about these three," she sighed, her drawl more pronounced on *sorry.* Daisy watched, shaking her head, as her fluffy beasts continued to maul me, the Pomeranian nosing his way up my skirt. "I've had a gazillion dog trainers over here—I even hired that Dog Whisperer guy—but no one has made a lick of a difference."

The actress said this like it had all happened in the past tense, as though I wasn't furiously trying to keep the irritating yellow dog out of my underwear. I kept waiting for Daisy to pull the dogs back, either physically or with a few sharp commands, but she just watched and continued to shake her head. She also seemed not to notice that I was still standing outside the house in the hot sun.

At that moment, a woman I instantly recognized as her mother (same gorgeous face and tiny figure, plus twenty years in age) came into the foyer, wiping her hands on a dish towel.

"Is that the writer?" She said it like *wryyy-terrr,* her accent decidedly thicker than her daughter's.

"No, Mama, she's a Jehovah's Witness tryin' to save my soul," Daisy teased, rolling her eyes for my benefit. "Of course it's the writer. Holly, this is my mama, Faith Dixson."

"Pleasure to meet you, Mrs. Dixson." I smiled back. I would've shaken her hand, but I was still standing awkwardly on the front porch. Daisy hadn't waved me in or even stepped aside, and I wondered if I was supposed to have this interview in the ninety-plus-degree heat. Maybe in this business, you didn't get to come inside until you actually had the job.

"Call me Faith. And Daisy Mae, haven't we taught you any manners? Don't leave the child outside like that. Come on in, Holly, and I'll pour you a glass of my famous sweet tea."

"Sorry about that," Daisy said, blushing, for the first time really seeming like a normal teenager. "Please come in." She pulled away from the door and nodded for me to enter.

As I stepped inside the enormous mansion, I realized my thoughts about *Real Housewives* were mistaken—this house was more classic, like a syndicated rerun of the original *Dallas*. I followed Daisy through the antebellum foyer with a winding staircase and wrought-iron banisters, and then abruptly into a modern kitchen that took my breath away. Stainless steel Bosch appliances, real cherry cupboards, and slate countertops with a microtile backsplash. It was a virtual culinary heaven.

"What a gorgeous kitchen," I said. I can't help it; I'm a sucker for gourmet kitchens and appliances. Sometimes I like to hug the Maytag front-loading washers at Best Buy, just so they know I'll be back for them when I can finally afford it. At the moment, I've accomplished nothing greater than an Emerson microwave with a dedicated popcorn setting. But a girl can dream.

"That's all Mama," Daisy said, smiling. "I can barely turn on the coffeepot."

"It's true." Faith giggled, her laugh like the tinkling of a wind chime. "But I couldn't cook when I was Daisy's age, either. It all comes to us in our own time."

I was instantly charmed by these two, happy to see that Daisy's good-girl image was real, instead of some corporate facsimile of the ideal teenage girl. I was also more than a little in love with their home and easy, flowing relationship. The Dixsons looked and acted like the quintessential American family, and I was immediately jealous. Don't get me wrong; my mother and I love each other, but the woman can make me crazy and no one would ever mistake us for friends.

"Sit down, Holly." Faith waved as she poured me a glass of iced tea. "Jamie'll join us in just a minute, he's just hammering out a deal with De Niro's people."

As I sat down, I looked at Daisy in astonishment, but the caliber of the name seemed to have no effect on her.

"We ran into him at the Tribeca Grill last month," Daisy said, taking a seat next to me at the table. "He has a script Jamie wants for me. I don't get it—way too artsy and talky, but Jamie says it could get me an Oscar, or at least a Golden Globe. The working title is 'Alley' something, I think."

"Back Alley?" Though he refuses to pick up the phone and attempt to get me a real job, my agent does e-mail me all of the scripts that were sold that week, along with their sales figures. He claims it will help me learn what producers are looking for, but as I have never had any inclination to become a screenwriter, I think it's really his way of showing me how much money I'm *not* making him. I'd read "Back Alley"—twice, actually, because it was highly convoluted.

"I think that's it," Faith agreed. "So dark and mysterious, just what the academy looks for. I swear, I didn't even understand half of the scenes."

"That's because they don't make sense," I said before I could stop myself. I am perpetually in need of a verbal shoehorn. I was pretty sure I'd just lost this job, but just in case the situation could be salvaged, I quickly added, "I didn't . . . *hate* the script. . . . It's just that the source material is so much better."

Like twins, Daisy and Faith stared at me with huge, blank eyes. "What do you mean?" Faith asked.

Neither of them had ever heard the term *source material* before? Daisy had been in this business since her bike had training wheels. "Um . . . the book," I said, trying to hide my disbelief. "It's based on the memoir of a pregnant prostitute. I just didn't think the script did the story justice."

I could tell Daisy was listening to what I had to say, but Faith was already back at the kitchen counter, waving me away dismissively with a dish towel. "We're not one of you egghead types. Jamie decides those things," Faith answered quickly. She almost seemed insulted that I thought she might have an opinion of her own.

"Oh . . . okay," I said, nodding and trying to gauge the level of damage I had done here. I needed a paycheck, it didn't matter anymore where it came from. "I'm sure he'll pick what's best for your career."

"It's really about time I started getting these offers," Daisy said, the weight of the world clearly pressing down on her shoulders. "I've been trying to break into drama for years."

"It's all happening," Faith said, bringing over the glass of tea and setting it in front of me. She leaned down and kissed her daughter on the top of the head. The mother looked at me and said, "I'm just so impressed with her drive and talent. Believe me, her father and I resisted letting her get into acting, but Daisy was absolutely determined. You just thank the Lord that you have no idea what it's like to be ambitious. It's quite the burden."

I stared up at Faith Dixson for a moment, trying to figure out if her last words were a slip of the tongue or an intentional dig at me, but I chose to go with the former.

Before I had too much time to think about it, Jameson Lloyd came into the room. He was in his mid-forties and ruggedly handsome; I could see why the Dixson ladies liked having him around. Then I thought of my balding, pudgy, and belching Uncle Bob, and suddenly knew why he'd never made it out of suburban New York.

"Hols, glad you found the place," Jameson said, grabbing my hand and practically crushing it. "My directions were okay?"

Barely sufficient, actually, I thought.

"Just fine, thanks."

Jameson pulled out a chair and swung it around so that it faced the opposite way, then plopped himself down backward. He offered me a stunning, toothy grin that made me a little dizzy. "So how's the meet-and-greet going?"

"Great," Daisy said, smiling at me. "I really like Holly."

"I knew you would," Jameson replied, ruffling Daisy's hair like she was an adorable six-year-old. "She and I haven't had nearly enough time to work out the fine print, but I was struck by how well she got you, Daise. I just knew you'd be two peas in a pod."

I stared at Jameson, dumbfounded. We'd spoken on the phone for maybe five minutes, and he'd never once mentioned Daisy's name. I didn't even know what kind of writing I was expected to do. He must have seen the confusion in my face, because he winked knowingly, then briefly gave me a thumbs-up. I had no idea what that was supposed to mean.

"So . . . can we pull the trigger on this deal?" he asked, looking back and forth between Daisy and Faith.

I assumed Jameson was talking about the De Niro movie deal, but a beat later, I realized he was referring to me.

"Yes, yes," Daisy said, tugging on Jameson's shirt. "You said we could have this done for my birthday!"

Jameson turned to me, shrugging. "What do you think, Hols? You up to the task?"

"Of course," I said, wondering what the task was.

"Isn't this just the greatest birthday present ever?" Daisy gushed, kissing Jameson on the cheek. "You're the best, Jamie."

Faith took the last seat at the table, smiling and shaking her head. "I just don't know how your father and I are going to compete with Jamie having your autobiography written. We'll have to launch you into space or something."

Ohhh . . . So I was ghostwriting her autobiography. This simultaneously answered and created a whole host of questions. I'd never written a book before, even though I'd spent a lot of time thinking about it. I was used to writing one- to two-page articles. Books needed to be three to four *hundred* pages. At most, I'd thought I was being hired to write some celebrity's guest piece for *Cosmo* so she wouldn't have to. But a *whole book*? I hoped the terror wasn't evident on my face.

As the others laughed at Faith's joke, I joined in, just so that I didn't start crying in panic. Ha, ha, *launch Daisy into space, how ridiculous,* we all seemed to be saying. But a moment later, I realized how ridiculous my entire world had just become.

"Oooh, could we really do that, you think?" Daisy cooed. "I mean, everybody is taking that stupid Richard Branson space plane, but that's just up and right back down. What if I went to the space station? I could sing for the astronauts." She looked first to her mother, then to Jameson. "I bet I'd even get the cover of *Vogue* for that!"

"I'll call NASA. I'm sure they can use the publicity." And just like that, he stood up from the table, pulling out his cell phone.

"Jamie, do you really think this is a good idea?" Faith said, cringing. "I don't like the idea of sending a teenager into orbit. Sounds awfully dangerous." She turned to me, her expression that of any mother concerned about the welfare of her child. Her child, who could afford to have herself launched into space. "What do you think, Holly?"

"Er . . ." I stalled, trying to come up with a suitably noncommittal and inoffensive response. "I don't think NASA would put a civilian in danger." Daisy was a civilian, right? I was fighting hard not to hyperventilate. Everything I'd ever hoped for had just been dropped into my lap . . . and I simply wasn't ready.

Jamie held up his hands for calm. "I'm only going to put some feelers out, nothing concrete," he said. He then snapped his fingers and pointed at me. "You can stick around for another few minutes, right? We'll work out a price and get you a retainer check."

"Sure."

Retainer check. As far as I was concerned, the two greatest words in the English language. Who knew that they had the power to create the wave of excitement that rippled through my entire body. My first thought was, *Smitty's getting gourmet cat food tonight.* My second thought was, *God, my life is depressing.*

Daisy yawned, her mouth making a perfect little sleepy O that didn't even crease her face. Seriously, was this girl made out of clay?

"Do we have to start today? This meeting has worn me out."

I didn't point out that I'd only been there for fifteen minutes. "Of course not," I said. "I can come back tomorrow, if you like."

Faith clucked her tongue and shook her head. "Can't do tomorrow," she said. "We've got that photo shoot with *Elle*. And we'll be on vacation in Nice next week. How about the week after?"

"Sure. You said you wanted the book done for Daisy's birthday? When is that, exactly?"

"Four months and six days! Magic Mountain is shutting down for the day to host my birthday party . . . Ooooh, you'll come, right?"

"Sounds like a lot of fun," I replied, barely paying attention. Did she just say four months? I had to write an entire book in four months? Even with three extensions, I still hadn't finished that library book I took out *six* months ago.

Jameson appeared in the doorway and waved for me to follow him. "You're up, Hols." Did he really just get NASA on the phone in three minutes?

"It was lovely to meet you, Holly," Faith said, giving me a hug.

"I'm sure we'll be the best of friends," Daisy told me, waving.

I smiled and waved at Daisy and her mother and then followed Jameson into the hall, wondering what the hell I had just gotten myself into.

"You're good with a standard thirty-five/thirty-five, right?" Jameson asked me as soon as we stepped into his office. Even though he was her manager, I still found it creepy not only that he had an office inside Daisy's family home but that the walls were plastered with publicity shots of an eighteen-year-old girl. Some of them in very suggestive poses.

And surprise, surprise, I had no clue what a 35/35 was.

I blinked back at him, trying to reason out what he might be talking about. Money, percentages, the number of cattle being bartered in this deal . . . Luckily, Jameson mistook my confusion for calculation.

"Okay, okay." He laughed, holding up his enormous hands. "I'm sorry I lowballed you, but hey, I'm a businessman . . . I had to try."

I laughed back, more out of relief than anything else. I wagged a finger at him jokingly. "Did you think I wouldn't do my homework?" I hoped it wouldn't occur to him that I couldn't possibly have priced a job I knew nothing about.

"Forty-five?" he tried, raising his eyebrows.

I studied Jameson's face for a few seconds, trying to read his expression. I still didn't know what game we were playing here, but I sensed that I had more wiggle room on the number. "Fifty," I replied, sounding as firm as I could manage. "Fifty/fifty."

He didn't even pause. "Done." Jameson sat down at the giant mahogany desk and pulled out a checkbook. "Should I make out the check to you, or do you have a corporation?"

"Just make it out to me," I said, trying to keep the excitement out of my voice. "My agent will take care of the rest."

Jameson nodded, filling out the check. Over his shoulder, he asked, "I can hook up with your agent later today, if you want. I'd like to have the contract signed by close of business tomorrow."

"Oh, I can take care of that," I added hastily. "He's looked into you."

Again, Jameson laughed. "I like you, Hols, I really do." He signed the check with a flourish, then tore it off and passed it to me. I had to resist the urge to read the amount right then and there; I couldn't risk being betrayed by my reaction. "But the most important thing is that Daisy likes you. We've interviewed so many writers, and she's hated every one."

"Really?" Our meeting hadn't seemed like much of an interview to me, and they hadn't requested a single sample of my writing. Not to mention, I'd barely spoken . . . I wasn't sure how they could have taken a liking to me.

"You're our sixteenth writer this month," he said, shaking his head. "She's vetoed every last one, until you. Now get on out of here and cash that check, missy. I'll have the contract messengered over this afternoon."

He shook my hand, again with enough force to break a few bones. "Welcome aboard, Holly."

CHAPTER 3

I've heard people call L.A. "Hollyweird," and this hurts my feelings. It's been my home for almost half my life, and I swear, it's not all that weird. We work and live and love, just like everywhere else. It might be a little different than what you're used to, but it's the world we know. And the fancy cars and nice clothes may make us seem superficial, but they're just things. Deep down, most of us are good, honest people, just like you.

An hour later, I was sitting in my apartment, staring down at the check. I knew I needed to go to the bank—I'd promised Jameson as much—but when I had finally pulled out of the Dixson compound and glanced down at the amount, I was so distracted I could barely find my way back home, let alone run errands. I had just made it into the apartment when a messenger appeared at my door with several copies of my contract.

Ten thousand dollars. My retainer for this four-month job was ten thousand dollars. And if my limited understanding of the contract was correct, my fifty/fifty deal was for a total of *fifty* thousand, double my salary for last year. In fact, if I could finish this job, I'd finally be above the poverty line for the first time in my adult life. It was another ten minutes before I could inhale properly and continue reading the endless document. I then quickly realized the other "fifty" was a percentage.

I read those lines of the contract four times before the realization finally sunk in and I began to hyperventilate, convinced I was one shallow breath away from a blackout. *It couldn't be,* I thought. I couldn't possibly be reading the contract correctly. But right there, in black and white, it said that I was guaranteed fifty percent of the book's royalties. *Half* of every dollar that Daisy Mae Dixson, a girl who once sold out Staples Center in twenty-four minutes, made with this book.

I'd love to tell you that my next thought was about the work, about the possibility that I could carve out a new career for myself and make some good money at the same time. But those things never once crossed my mind, at least not at that point. I wasn't qualified to do this job, not in any way, shape, or form, and I guessed it was just a matter of time before Jameson discovered this and canned my ass. So my first real concern was how much money I could get out of the deal before they realized I was a talentless hack.

I dutifully signed the contract and headed back out of my apartment; I was surprised to see that the messenger had waited all this time. I immediately felt like a jerk because, despite having a ten-thousand-dollar check burning a hole in my wallet, I didn't have a single dollar with which to tip the poor kid. I apologized profusely, offering him a glass of water or use of my bathroom, but he just waved me away. Which was probably for the best, as I didn't have a washed glass and I hadn't cleaned my bathroom in a month.

"Mr. Lloyd takes care of me," he said, taking the envelope back. Of course he does.

I followed him back out to the street and was dismayed to discover that this kid, who couldn't have been a day over twenty, drove a Mercedes.

"Nice car," I told him, purposely not moving toward my fifteen-year-old heap of scrap metal.

"Eh. I should've gone for the S-Class."

Clearly, I had been working with the wrong people.

One of the strangest things about this town is the erratic work schedules. Sometimes people work fifteen-hour days, six days a week, and other times, those same people are off for an entire month. It's not really unemployment, at least not the way the rest of the country thinks about it—my best friend, Camille, likes to call it *fun*employment. They go off to do a movie, fall off the face of the earth for six weeks to three months, then reappear with money to burn and endless free time. Rinse, repeat.

On that particular Sunday night, I was in luck. Camille had just gotten back from shooting a Fox reality show in Mexico and could stay up for nine days straight if she wanted. We'd met my first month on the job at *Westside Weekly*, when I was writing an article about one of her earlier reality shows, *Man vs. Sea*. My boss had tried valiantly to get me an interview with the show's "star," but Camille was as close as she could get (and I have been forever grateful). As Camille's always had the better job, our friendship's largely made possible by her generosity. For the first time in the entire four years since I'd met her, I was beyond excited to take *her* out to dinner. She readily agreed to this, with the stipulation that we take a cab—partly so we could both drink, and partly because she was embarrassed to be seen getting out of my car. I swear to you, Camille's not really as shallow as I'm making it sound, these are real-live networking concerns in a town as glossy and superficial as L.A.

We started off at Il Sole, an upscale Italian restaurant on the Sunset Strip. I'd promised myself that Camille could choose the place and I wouldn't worry about the bill—in fact, I wasn't even going to look at the prices on the menu. It had been months since I'd been anywhere that didn't have a kids' meal, an early-bird special, or require their servers to wear the appropriate amount of "flair." And I'd certainly never been able to afford a place like Il Sole before. For the first time since I'd gotten to L.A., I felt like I belonged to the special little club that is the Hollywood elite. I almost passed out from the excitement.

As we settled in over a glass of Cab Sav and I excitedly told Camille about my new job, she didn't react quite the way I'd hoped.

"You took the job?" she asked, dumbfounded.

"Yeah, why?" I asked, confused. I'd expected a squeal of glee and maybe an over-the-table hug. Not a blank stare and obvious incredulity.

I noticed that Camille took a deliberately endless sip of her wine before responding. "It's just that, well, you never take *any* job offers."

"What is that supposed to mean?" This night was quickly going downhill, and we hadn't even ordered yet.

"Oh, babe," she rushed on, reaching across the table and squeezing my hand. "I didn't mean anything by it. But when I got you in for that story editor job last year, you canceled the final interview."

"I was sick." I'd woken up that morning with a migraine. It had disappeared shortly after my original interview time, but that wasn't my fault. Besides, I didn't want to be a story editor, no matter how much it paid. I'd seen Camille get sucked into the cushy, miserable life of reality TV, and I didn't want to join her.

"And when that recruiter from *LA Weekly* asked for samples of your writing?" she pressed on, eyebrows raised.

"I . . . I just forgot to send them," I said. I had forgotten, right? "And he wasn't going to hire me, anyway. He was just being nice."

Camille's expression was dubious, but she didn't push me any further. Instead, she broke into a sympathetic smile. "You know what? It doesn't matter what happened last year or even yesterday." She raised her glass. "Today you are the new personal pet of Daisy Mae Dixson, and that is definitely something to celebrate."

Uncertainly, I raised my glass and allowed her to clink it with hers.

She seemed determined to move on from the sensitive subject. "She's an uberbitch, right?" Camille giggled. "Please tell me she's a brain-dead, oversexed, stuck-up bitch."

I wanted to be mad at her, but I couldn't. After all, there wouldn't be many nights as good as this one and I didn't want to waste it by pouting.

"Sorry to disappoint you." I shrugged. "But Daisy was pretty nice. Her mom, too. They're a little odd, but what teenage gazillionaire isn't just a bit warped?"

"Nice?" Camille cried, throwing up her hands. "Nice? I can't sell 'nice' to TMZ. They'll want the real dirt."

"No selling anything to TMZ," I warned her. "You have to keep your mouth shut."

Camille groaned, then drained the rest of her glass and promptly refilled it. "But that's boring. Why do you get to have all the fun?"

I rolled my eyes. "You just came back from shooting *STD Island,* or whatever this one's called. You can't tell me that wasn't an adventure."

Camille is a producer for a reality show company that specializes in ruining people's lives and making them look like whorish morons on network TV. She started as a production assistant right out of college and found that her ability not to have sex with any of the contestants was the elevator to success. Though she loathes every minute of every day, it pays alarmingly well and there never seems to be a shortage of work.

"One of the wives tried to lure me into the hot tub at the hotel. . . . Said she'd always been bi-curious, and with me around, she knew the cameras wouldn't be rolling." Camille shook her head slowly. "I told her I'd been propositioned by much hotter women and none of them had succeeded. I swear to God, I don't know what it is about reality TV and casual bisexuality."

"Boredom?" I suggested.

"I dunno." She shrugged, sighing. "But it's making me nuts. It's bad enough having to fend off the men, but the women just don't give up."

"Cam, those people didn't sign up for reality shows because

they're fabulously well adjusted." I've never believed that claim that people are doing it "to make a little extra money." If you feel the need to have your face plastered all over prime-time TV for the number of bugs you can eat in sixty seconds, there are deeper psychological issues at work.

"I suppose you're right." In the space of two minutes, Camille had drained another glass of wine and was reaching for the bottle. The persistently casual bisexual must have taken a toll on her. She looked up me, crestfallen. "But really, Daisy Dixson is pretty normal? I mean, you can't even lie to me and say she has a hidden tail or something?"

I laughed loudly. "I didn't say she was *normal*. For her birthday, she wants to be launched into space. Honest to God, outer space."

A tiny spurt of wine escaped Camille's surprised lips as she started to giggle. "Oh, that's more like it. Please tell me there's more."

Little did I know there would be oh so much more.

By 1:00 A.M., Camille and I were staggering out of the bar at the Chateau Marmont, where, if I hadn't been drunk off my ass, I might have sworn that we were standing about twenty feet away from Adele. I could have just walked up and talked to her if I'd really wanted to be sure, but you learn quickly to ignore the celebrities in their natural habitats. That, and I'm just too chicken. It's probably why, after four years, I didn't have a single really juicy celebrity story.

Cam and I stumbled out onto Sunset Boulevard and got all the way to the curb before it occurred to either of us that we hadn't called a cab. She pulled out her phone and loaded Uber, squinting at the swirling cars in the area. It's one of the perks of living in a big city that you can find a local cab in the middle of the night just by pressing a few buttons. At least, you can on a smartphone. Mine only makes phone calls and you have to press the two halves together tightly to get that to happen.

"Do we pay more for a taxi or use UberX? I'm sure there are lots of people out tonight looking for a few extra bucks."

"Taxi. I'm not getting in some rando's car." I couldn't help but think how many torture porn movies start just this way, two girls alone on a dark street, climbing into an anonymous car. Not that Sunset is ever particularly dark or empty, even in the middle of the night.

"Shit," Camille said, rubbing her eye tiredly and smearing eyeliner down her face. "I told Donovan I'd be home by midnight at the latest."

Donovan is Camille's fake producer/poser/live-in boyfriend. He's forty-two, his real name is Donnie, and the only thing he's produced in the last ten years is a tuna fish sandwich. But like most people in L.A., he's always got some "big project" in the works and wants to attach me as the writer. Every few months, he corners me in their apartment and tells me about what he's supposedly working on, and each time, the roster of producers and so-called investors changes. I'm never sure if these are guys he met down at the Laundromat or if he's just randomly picking names off the Internet. And though Cam refuses to believe it, Donovan's been trying to knock her up for the last year, just so he knows he'll never be alone. The guy's a real winner.

"Oh, what does he care? He's just on the couch watching infomercials and eating Hershey's miniatures." The man has an unnatural obsession with child-size bars of chocolate.

"He doesn't like to be alone at night," Camille whined, sympathy creeping into her tone. "And you know Donovan's had a lot of trouble with his weight the last couple years. He says he feels more in control of his snacking with the miniatures."

"He's not in control if he's eating the whole bag," I replied, leaning on a streetlamp to keep from falling off the curb.

"I know, I know," she said, shaking her head with a level of empathy I couldn't understand. "It's just that the financing on his latest project fell apart and he's very depressed. He says we can't afford to get engaged this year because he just doesn't have the money for a ring. Like I care about a stupid diamond."

They've been together for five years. Every year he tells her they can't afford to get engaged, even though Camille makes well over a hundred grand. Usually I can keep my opinion of that bottom-feeder to myself, but on this night, I was too far into Jäger country to keep my mouth shut.

"What is it with you and that loser? There are like four million eligible men in Los Angeles and you can't get away from a guy who thinks leather pants are appropriate funeral attire."

Understandably, this riled her up a bit. "Four million eligible men? This from the woman who hasn't gotten laid since Obama's first term? Where are all these eligible men? Huh?"

She had me there. I paused for a moment and put on my most serious, contemplative expression. "Well . . . I'm sure they must be around here somewhere." I turned my head to the right and left, but all I saw were similarly inebriated Angelenos leaving the bars and clubs, most of them laughing or shouting obnoxiously. It wasn't doing much for my cause. "If you'll just give me a minute, I'll find one for you."

I spun around just in time to see a forty-year-old guy with slicked-back, thinning hair pull up in a Bimmer. He lowered the passenger window and leaned over to talk to us. "Marmont's played out for the night. Get in and I'll take you to this after-hours in Silver Lake."

"Is that the guy you were looking for?" Camille asked.

"Clock's ticking, ladies." No lie, the guy even held his wrist out and tapped the face of his watch. I think it was a Rolex, but for all I know, it was a fake—either good or bad. Fifty bucks or fifty thousand, they all look the same to me.

"No one's getting in your car, asshole," I told him.

Camille took things one step further, moving to kick the guy's passenger door. As drunk as I was, I had the presence of mind to pull her back, lest she put us both on the receiving end of an arrest warrant. "And come on, loser, you're forty! What are you doing at after-hours clubs?"

"Screw you," Bimmer Man said. "There are plenty of hotter girls than you out tonight." He gave us the middle finger before swerving back out into traffic.

There was a long moment as we watched him go before Camille gave me the annoyingly smug look I knew was coming. "Please, go on, Holly. You were telling me about these four million eligible men?"

"Shut up and pick a taxi."

CHAPTER 4

With a schedule as crazy as mine, one of the most important things is having good people by your side to make sure all of the arrangements are made. It's easy for things to slip through the cracks when you have a last-minute appearance scheduled at a store or on an awards show. Is the hotel room booked? Does the airline know you need a vegan meal? Is there a car to meet you at the airport? Do you have enough time to get through security or from the hotel to your appearance?

My parents are the most important people in my life, but my manager and his helpers are a close second.

Faith Dixson promised that we'd get started on the memoir in two weeks, after the family returned from Nice. So I didn't worry when I didn't hear from anyone right away, and used the time to try to figure out how the hell to do my new job. I called every writer I knew, asking about the rules and the tricks—and the no-no's—of working with stars. I spent a fortune at Staples buying supplies and digital tape recorders and then bought out the celeb tell-all section at Barnes & Noble. And owing to Daisy's obsessive fans and the lax stalker laws on the Internet, I was able to compile almost an entire life history for her. I followed her on Twitter, Facebook, Instagram, and Pinterest, slogging through endless tweets about the best BB cream and how "totally amazeballs" her friend Teri was in that latest

ABC Family movie. If I was going down on this job, I was going down fighting.

I was gratified to discover that most celeb autobiographies are basically insipid chronicles of bad behavior, and told in an entirely linear way. There didn't seem to be much stylish language or heady writing technique, which made me less afraid of the immediate road ahead. I did notice that even though the celebs in question hadn't written a word of their own books, every line sounded like it came directly out of their mouths. I had no idea how to pull off that kind of feat; I could only hope that as I spent more time with Daisy, her voice would become second nature to me. Which was scary in another way entirely.

Once I couldn't read another word of rock-star drivel, I went to Target and spent eighty dollars purchasing all four seasons of Daisy's current show. The writing and acting were so terrible I only made it through about five episodes, but the behind-the-scenes footage turned out to be a gold mine. Despite the fact that all of my friends work on film sets, I had remarkably little idea what they did. Seeing this enormous crew working like cogs in Daisy's teenybopper machine was fascinating. Everyone talked about how rewarding it was to spend fourteen hours a day working on something so fun and family-oriented. Now, I don't know much about jobs like script supervisor or wardrobe stylist, but I can't imagine anyone being happy and excited at the fourteen-hour mark. It had to be a lie, but it was definitely a lie I could print. I also instantly noticed that Daisy's movie-set home had most of the same furniture as her real home. I wondered which came first.

And because I was now flush with cash, I got cable for those moments when I just couldn't work anymore. I'd never had cable in my life, but I immediately wasted four days watching something called WE TV for reasons unknown. One night I found myself watching a show called *Rehabilication,* where an "addiction specialist" with dubious credentials tried to stop various celebrities from snorting anything they could find—all while on a fabulous vacation. It was a terrible name for a show, but it was also apparently the name of the actual rehab center. First I wondered if Camille knew anyone who worked on the program, then considered who would routinely watch such garbage. And lest I be casting the first stone, I quickly turned the channel to History's *The Nostradamus Effect*. Yes, it was equally suspect, but at least it was the History Channel.

It was a great two weeks. For the first time in a very long time, I was happy and relaxed. I went out with friends when they called and didn't worry about having to chip in twenty-five bucks for dinner. I started to think this middle-class thing wasn't too shabby after all.

But by the third week, I still hadn't gotten a single phone call from the Dixson entourage. I wasn't too concerned on Monday, but by Wednesday night, I started to panic. Had I missed some deadline I wasn't aware existed? Was *I* supposed to call *them*? The clock on my microwave said it was past ten, but around here, business gets done pretty much twenty-four hours a day, so I wasn't worried about calling Jameson. My thoughts were validated when he answered on the first ring.

"Hols?" he asked, concerned. "Everything all right?"

"Yeah, of course," I said. "I was just checking in with you, seeing when I can start working with Daisy."

"Oh, *right*," he said like he'd forgotten to pick up the dry cleaning. "We've been swamped. . . . You understand." Jameson paused for a moment, but I didn't respond, even with the normal platitudes. I *didn't* understand Daisy's life—that's why I needed to meet with her. I heard paper rustling before he continued. "I suppose we have a few hours tomorrow afternoon. How's that sound?"

"That's just fine," I replied, nodding like an idiot as though he could see me through the phone.

"Great, we'll see you then, Hols." And then he hung up.

While I really liked the Dixson ladies, I wasn't altogether sold on Jameson. Maybe I was judging him too harshly, but to me, he seemed like one weird dude. He'd hung up on me after five sentences without telling me where to meet them or at what time. I assumed he meant the house, but how could I possibly know that? I was waiting for him to tell me that he'd been sending me messages telepathically since our first phone call, and that it was my fault I hadn't received them.

Hey, in this town, you never know.

At six the next morning, there was a loud knock at my door. I briefly thought it was the first and my landlord had come screaming for the rent, but then remembered it was the middle of the month. While it always seemed like I just wrote my rent check and it was still miraculously time for the next, for once, I was off the hook for another couple of weeks.

I sat up, groggy and confused, and tried to decide if I should answer the door or just pretend I wasn't home. But the knocker didn't give me much of a choice; the banging just went on and on. I got up and threw on a sweatshirt, knowing the Vietnamese woman who lived two doors down would come out swinging a rolling pin in a matter of seconds.

I was surprised to find Jameson's messenger on the other side of the door. Especially since my building has a security door that someone had clearly forgotten to close—again.

"Hi," I said, bewildered.

"Man, sorry I'm late," the kid told me, rubbing his eyes tiredly with one hand. The other was occupied with a large manila envelope that I guessed he was coming to deliver to me. "The traffic coming out of Bev Hills is already a real bitch."

He held up the envelope and shook it before passing it to me. I stared at him for a second, trying to make sense of the weirdness that seemed to be taking over my life in the last few weeks. He was *late* coming over here? Unless he was supposed to show up last night or at 2:00 A.M., I wasn't sure how that was even possible.

The kid looked me up and down quickly. "You're going like that?"

Clearly, I was missing a major part of this equation. "The only place I'm going is back to bed, and I assure you, it's a really relaxed dress code."

He looked at his watch, then up at me, smirking. "You do know your flight leaves at nine A.M., right?"

The kid was joking. He *had* to be joking. "Flight?"

He nodded toward the envelope. "Mr. Lloyd said you'd need the tickets by five A.M., but I forgot you lived in the tenth level of hell." He yawned loudly. "It took me over an hour to get here."

I'd been awake for three and a half minutes and today already sucked.

"Dante's Inferno only has nine levels."

"Who's Dante?" he asked.

Confused and a little irritated, I closed the door in his face. Then I promptly ripped open the top of the envelope and shook the ticket into my outstretched hand. I felt like I was playing some strange lottery where I switched places with a crazy person and took over their life for a few days. I inhaled deeply to restore my inner calm before I could dare look down at the ticket.

And the winning city was . . . I squinted at the small print— Miami? I was flying to Miami and Jameson hadn't bothered to tell me? I was shocked enough by the realization that I had to fly to my meeting with Daisy, but I assumed I was going someplace like Vegas or San Francisco, only a few hours away, where it just happened to be more convenient to fly than drive. But no, I was apparently traveling three thousand miles to have a conversation.

As I read through the information, I also noticed that there was no return ticket. Not only did I have to leave for the airport twenty minutes ago, I had no idea what—or how much—I was supposed to pack. For a few seconds, I was really, truly irritated with Daisy Dixson and her publicity machine for their lack of consideration. Then, just as quickly, I realized that the oversight may not have been intentional. When you have millions of dollars, maybe this is just the way you roll. Bored with your everyday life? Head to Miami for a couple of days and see what happens. I could either spend the day cursing my new employers or just shut up and deal . . . and perhaps have a good time doing it.

I spent the next ten minutes showering and packing at tornado-like wind speeds, throwing everything I could grab into a duffel bag I used to use for the gym. As it had been two years since I'd actually bothered to go to the gym, I figured I should find some new use for the bag. I was in such a hurry that as soon as I was finished, I had absolutely no idea what I'd even packed. For all I knew, the contents could include an evening dress, no underwear, and a parka. But none of it would really matter if I couldn't make the flight on time, so I tossed the bag over one shoulder, left Smitty with a neighbor, and drove the 10 freeway like a bat out of hell.

I was lucky in that rush hour had barely begun and traffic wasn't nearly as horrific as it would have been an hour later. All it took was a little reckless driving and illegal use of the carpool lane and I some-how made it to LAX in twenty minutes, and with only four people swearing at me or giving me the finger. That I noticed, anyway.

By 8:30, I was happily in my first-class seat, drinking a mimosa and having already forgotten the insanity of the morning so far. I was even starting to look forward to my impromptu work trip to Miami. After all, I was traveling with the rich and famous—how bad could it be?

The flight landed just before 5:00 P.M., and by 5:15, I found myself weaving through throngs of travelers in cheap Hawaiian shirts and flip-flops to get to baggage claim. I was still so Zen from five hours of expensive champagne that I didn't pause to consider the practical elements of this trip. The first of which were, where was I going from the airport, and how was I supposed to get there?

In light of who I was working for, I think I assumed that a car would be waiting for me at the terminal, but I waited nearly an hour and no one appeared. After a while, I must have looked like quite the idiot, sitting at the curb, watching as people came and went. Eventually, even the airport police began circling me suspiciously, perhaps thinking that my pink Nike workout bag held some sort of explosive device. Just as three cops huddled together and stared at me, whispering among themselves, I pulled out my cell phone and called Jameson.

"Hols!" He answered on the first ring. The guy must have had his Bluetooth surgically implanted in his ear. "How was the flight?"

"Just fine," I told him. My champagne buzz was wearing off, and the ninety-five-degree, sticky heat was starting to get under my skin. "I'm at the airport now."

"What are you still doing out there?" he asked me. "Get yourself a car and come play with us."

"And where exactly would I be going?"

"We're at the Fontainebleau, in the Presidential Suite. Just come on up when you get here."

And, as always, Jameson just hung up. I pulled the phone away from my ear and stared at it for a second, willing some sane, normal person to call so that I could have a sane, normal conversation. No one called. I wasn't even sure I knew someone who fit that description.

I heaved myself off the curb, then started back toward baggage claim in search of a car rental agency. It would be fine, I told myself. Surely they would pay me back for the car. What was a few hundred dollars up front?

It was seven o'clock by the time I reached the Fontainebleau and I was starving. I'd considered pulling into a convenience store along the way, but I thought better of arriving at the Presidential Suite with Cheetos breath and neon orange fingertips. Besides, I figured the Dixsons had to eat dinner at some point.

While I thought it might be a challenge to even get to the Presidential Suite (we've all seen those movies where a starstruck teenage girl tries desperately to break into her idol's hotel room), the Fontainebleau knew I was coming and whisked me upstairs before I could so much as utter the name Daisy Dixson and start a panic in the lobby. And I assure you, there would have been a panic. I was barely able to pull into the valet stand without accidentally running over some paparazzi. And the tween girls just "hanging out" in the lobby, pretending to read, weren't working too hard to hide the real purpose of their visit. So I was appreciative when my name alone was enough to get things moving.

I was promptly assigned a personal attendant named Minka, who looked to be about my age but acted like a German efficiency specialist and didn't appear to particularly like me. As she barked orders at a frightened bellman, she kept throwing me less than cordial looks. A few times, I think her nostrils actually flared. I had no idea what I'd done to incur her wrath, but I couldn't wait to get away from her. As my duffel bag was spirited away, Minka prodded me toward the elevators with a firm hand pressed to the small of my back. I wasn't sure if I was being handled or about to be taken hostage.

"We've placed you in an oceanfront balcony suite in the Versailles building, per the request of your . . ." She threw me a look, faltering in her businesslike façade for the first time. "Your . . . *fellow guest.*" The woman cleared her throat and continued resolutely. "I hope you know that privacy is very important to us here at the Fontainebleau. Your party absolutely will not be disturbed by either photographers or fans."

"Oh . . . thank you," I replied, figuring that's what I was supposed to say. I was expected to worry about these things, right? I was starting to wish there was a manual to consult for these kinds of questions, just so that I wouldn't get caught looking stupid. After this experience, perhaps I'd write one: *Diving into the Celebrity Pool, a How-to Guide*.

"Should you need anything at all, please do not hesitate to contact me," she charged on. Despite her words, I got the feeling she had no interest in ever hearing from me again. We approached the elevators, but Minka shook her head and steered me to the left, down a small hallway. I was almost blinded by the Florida sunshine streaming through the windows and glinting off the hotel's endless marble surfaces. I found I had to shade my eyes just to keep them open. "We will have an attendant or concierge on duty twenty-four hours a day to *service* your needs."

Her last sentence was enunciated so strangely, I couldn't help but throw her a look. *Service* our needs? I had a feeling there was more implied in her words than I wanted to know. Maybe that was her issue, I thought. If celebrities stayed at this hotel all the time, maybe their bad behavior caused all sorts of problems for the staff. But Daisy was an eighteen-year-old born-again Christian; aside from failing to curb her dog, I couldn't imagine her trashing a hotel suite.

We reached a smaller elevator and Minka nodded for me to enter. She placed a key into a slot at the top of the row of buttons, then turned it. The elevator doors had barely begun to slide closed when she snapped her head to the left, *Exorcist*-like, to stare me down.

"Are you related to Miss Dixson?" she asked, being far more forward than I would have thought proper for such a "private" hotel. I could feel her appraising my relative worth, measuring it against her own. Suddenly, I was a little afraid to be alone with her.

"Um . . . no, I'm working with her," I replied politely, hoping we could leave it at that.

Minka looked me up and down and frowned, apparently finding me unworthy to have such access to a person as famous as Daisy. "Well, you're not her personal trainer," she said with mild disapproval.

"Maybe I'm her personal *psychic*," I shot back, perhaps a bit too defensively. "What does it matter to you?"

"Of course," Minka responded snidely. "I'm sure you're quite . . . *indispensable* to Ms. Dixson."

If we hadn't reached our floor at that very moment, I might have slugged her. But the elevator dinged and the doors glided open, and I stepped out into the hallway, hoping to soon be rid of my shadow. Minka dropped my room key into my palm, unwilling to make actual physical contact with my bare hand. I wondered if she was germaphobic or just a bitch.

"You will need to swipe your key card in the elevator to reach both this floor and your own," she told me, continuing on to the suite door and knocking loudly. "It's Minka from the hotel staff," she called. "I have Ms. Gracin here for you."

I could hear Daisy's yappy little dogs begin to chirp long before I heard footsteps approaching. Jameson flung the door open.

"Well, hello there, Minka," he said, offering her a wink. The three dogs swirled and yapped at his feet, but Jamie didn't acknowledge their presence.

"Hello, Mr. Lloyd," she replied, blushing and looking away.

Jameson threw me a look and nodded in a way that made me feel he was calling attention to his prowess. "Thanks for taking such good care of our girl."

Minka flushed a deeper shade of red, then giggled. Honest to God, she actually giggled. "My pleasure. Let me know if there's anything else I can do for you."

I was pretty sure I knew what she was willing to do. It also explained her immediate and intense dislike for me, but little Miss Minka needn't have worried.

"Yep, thanks for your help," I said loudly, pushing past Minka and stepping into the suite. "You've been fantastic. Bye." I deliberately closed the door, waving as her scowl disappeared into the hall.

"Hols, glad you made it," Jameson said, shaking my hand. He frowned. "You really look like shit."

"Thanks," I said, looking around him to take in the largest hotel room I'd ever seen. It was beautifully decorated but in a way that didn't lend itself to any particular style. There were couches and lounge chairs that didn't appear to be the slightest bit comfortable, but which I'm certain were designed by someone of note. Someone who could charge the GDP of a small country for his or her services.

"Oh my God, oh my God, you're heeeeeere!"

The squeal came from the balcony as Daisy dashed inside and made a beeline for me. Although it was nearing seven-thirty, she was clad in a bikini so tiny a gynecologist could have done an exam around it instead of having to take it off. She bounded toward me, and I tried really hard not to get an eyeful of her enormous boobs as they shimmied and bounced with each step. I'm totally not into women, I swear, but at that moment, she was almost more boob than woman. It was hard to look anywhere else.

"Thank you soooooo much for coming!" Daisy exclaimed, throwing herself at me. I tried to hug back gingerly, but she just pressed herself more firmly into me. I was creeped out not only by her relative nakedness but also because this was the most flesh I'd encountered in the last eighteen months.

"She's been talking about it nonstop," Jameson said, smiling. "I'm so glad we decided to bring you out."

"Glad to be here," I responded. "Don't get me wrong, I'm *surprised* to be here . . . but glad. I certainly wouldn't have imagined this yesterday."

"I'm sorry we all have to stay *here*," Daisy said, throwing her agent a dirty look.

"Daise," Jameson chided, "the Fontainebleau is a five-star hotel. You love it here."

The scathing gaze he got in return clearly said, *You don't know me as well as you think you do, buddy.* "No one stays here anymore," she replied petulantly. "It's *so* wasteful, Jamie, and so over." Daisy turned to me and explained, "These hotels are all about decadence and luxury, and regular people just can't afford to live like this anymore."

Anymore? I didn't need to ask the price of this particular suite to know that no one in my family, even if they'd saved up for five years, could have *ever* afforded to stay here. Although it was slightly moving that Daisy was at least trying to be socially conscious. It wasn't her fault that she was bargain-challenged.

"Very thoughtful of you."

"Nowadays, everybody's into bungalows," she continued, nodding. "Mariah totally won't stay in a hotel unless there aren't any available bungalows."

That made more sense. It wasn't that she actually wanted to develop a social conscience; she just wanted to look like she had.

"Maybe I care more about your security than Mariah's people do," Jameson said, shrugging. "I just wanted you in a place where a shooter couldn't get a good line of sight. Sue me for being concerned."

Call me crazy, but I was concerned that *he* was concerned about shooters and their lines of sight. Who wants to shoot a teenage girl who makes high school comedies and sings about puppy love and buying your first car?

Daisy rolled her eyes but offered him a little smile. "You're always so worried, Jamie," she teased him. "It's very sweet, but really . . . I can take care of myself."

"Of course you can," Jameson said, his tone dripping with condescension. It was so pronounced that I quickly looked to Daisy, worried about her reaction. But if she took any notice of the subtext of his words, she sure didn't show it.

"Anyway." Daisy giggled, turning back to me. "Are we gonna start working now? I've been making notes about all the stories I want to tell you, and I just can't wait. We are going to have so much fun, I swear."

I was exhausted, starving, and in desperate need of a shower. The last thing I wanted to do right now was listen to Daisy endlessly talk about herself. But I knew I couldn't refuse; my only consolation was that she'd been tired and bored fifteen minutes into our first conversation, so this session probably couldn't last that long.

"Sure," I said. I wondered what the bathtub was like in my room. And if (with a big enough tip) room service would deliver bathside. "I just need to run to my room and grab my notebook and recorder."

I hadn't even taken two steps toward the door when Jameson stopped me. "Oh, that's not necessary. Go on and get started with Daisy and I'll have Minka bring up your things."

When Minka had said she was here to do whatever we needed, I doubt that meant rifling through my haphazard luggage for a digital tape recorder. But if Jameson was the one asking, I knew she'd climb thirty-seven flights of stairs if the elevator took too long.

"Let's go talk in the bedroom," Daisy said, already leading the way. "It'll be like a slumber party."

I reluctantly followed, hoping this slumber party would involve a few more articles of clothing.

CHAPTER 5

People make a big deal about celebrity feuds, but I swear, there's rarely anything to them. The tabloids have been saying for years that I'm "at war" with the girls from that ABC Family show, but really, we couldn't be closer. Just last year we went on a joint charity mission to Uganda and helped build a school for underprivileged kids.

Don't think of us as stars. We're just young women trying to find our way in this crazy town. How can I hate the only other people who understand how strange and difficult my everyday life can be?

By 11:00 P.M., I'd heard every story about Daisy's ongoing friendship with the buyer from Fred Segal (important because she always knew about a change in inventory before anyone else) and the 48,000 other teen celebrities she hated because they copied her signature look, didn't invite her to their premieres, or, occasionally, just looked at her disrespectfully.

As for the actual story of her life, she remembered hardly anything. All of the autobiographies I'd read had detailed stories about every stage of the person's life, from childhood through the writing of the book. The most detailed story Daisy told me was about her obsession with Julien Macdonald's clothing line, starting with his journey replacing Alexander McQueen as creative director at

Givenchy, going off on his own as a designer, through every piece that walked during his latest runway show. I didn't have the first clue how I was supposed to translate these nonsensical words into a memoir people might buy. Also, she never put on another stitch of clothing for the entire conversation.

"So tell me about grade school," I asked her at one point, trying to steer things back toward a useful subject.

"What about it?" We'd been talking for an hour and she was tying dozens of pink bows in Ariel's fur. The other two dogs had smartly run for their lives when she pulled out the doggie brush and I hadn't seen them since. If I'd known what article of furniture they were hiding under, I might have joined them.

"Well . . . people will want to know everything about you, including where you went to school, when you first decided you wanted to act . . ."

"I don't know." She shrugged, brushing out a knot near Ariel's right ear. "I went to school for a few years, and then I got my first show. I'm not sure how it happened."

I tried something easier. "Okay . . . where did you go to school?"

Daisy shrugged again. "Somewhere in Savannah, I think." The dog yelped and tried to jump off the bed, but Daisy held the pet's writhing body tight against her and kept brushing. "Can't you ask my mom this stuff? She's got all that crap."

"Sure." I nodded, making yet another note for Faith. After just an hour, I had nearly a full page. So far, Daisy had forgotten the names of every director she'd worked with and everything they'd ever said to her. As far as Daisy was concerned, only her acting and vocal genius were responsible for her rise to fame, and everyone else was just there to make money off her. She referred to the executive producer of her show on Nickelodeon as "the hot dog guy" because he'd once told her he liked Pink's. Everyone in L.A. likes Pink's.

"Great," Daisy exclaimed. "Did I tell you about the Grammy after-party in Hollywood last year?" She didn't wait for me to answer.

"I was wearing Stella McCartney and those girls from E! were *so* jealous because they were clearly wearing off-the-rack . . ."

And so it went, for more than three hours.

By eleven, I could tell her interest was waning, and I was so hungry I was ready to take a bite out of one of her yelpy dogs. When Jameson peeked his head in and said, "You ladies about done for the night?" I nearly leapt off the bed and ran screaming back to my room. My room, which I had yet to see.

"Totally." Daisy sighed. "We've put in a real day's work."

We really hadn't, but I wasn't about to argue. "I'd say I've gotten enough for today," I told him and nodded. I stood up and stretched, stifling the urge to yawn.

"Perfect," Jameson said, checking his watch. "I was worried we were going to be late."

"Oh, *shoot*," Daisy said, wiggling off the bed. "Is that club thing tonight? I thought it was tomorrow."

"I told you three times it was tonight." The more he insisted on talking to her like a kindergartner, the more irritated I was with him. Granted, Daisy wasn't exactly a Rhodes scholar, but he certainly wasn't helping things by talking down to her all the time. "And Sharla and Axel have been here and ready to go for the last half hour."

"Do they want me to wash my hair?" Daisy asked, frowning.

"No, just go on out to Axel and he'll take care of you," Jameson replied, snapping his fingers at her. "Now scoot."

I didn't want to seem too excited, but all I could think about was room service food. A hamburger and French fries, and maybe a giant piece of chocolate cake for dessert. I didn't know anything about Sharla, Axel, or a club opening, and to tell the truth, I couldn't have cared less.

But Jameson was getting very good at thwarting my planned escapes.

"You can head to Sharla first," he told me.

"I'm sorry?" I asked, looking behind me to make sure he wasn't talking to someone else in the room. But the only eyes looking back at me were Ariel's.

"Axel will do Daisy's hair first, then you two can switch." Jameson seemed to survey my appearance and then frowned. "I hope the dress will fit. A six was the biggest they had."

He said *six* like it was a plus size.

"I'm going with her?" I asked, still a few steps behind. I was ignoring the implied disapproval of my weight, and also trying not to think about how many pairs of Spanx it would take to get me into a size-six dress.

"Of course," he said, eyeing me strangely. "We didn't fly you across the country to leave you alone in your room all night."

"Oh . . . thanks."

"Now get on out there," he said, patting my ass lightly.

I think I jumped about a foot when Jamie touched me. "Um . . . I'd appreciate it if you didn't do that."

"Do what?"

"I'm not a Playboy bunny or a pro football player," I responded. "So please don't pat my ass."

Jamie laughed, obviously missing the point. "Oh, Hols . . . I *know* you're not a Playboy bunny. I've dated a few, believe me . . ." He continued to laugh, even wiping a tear away from his eye. "Now get out there. Sharla's waiting." As I left the room, he still couldn't stop laughing. It was great for my self-esteem.

Maybe now is the time to mention that I hate clubs. Not just hate—loathe and abhor. I can handle the occasional bar when it's not too loud or crowded, and I'm all about nice restaurants and charity events. But stick me in a small room with four hundred drunk people swaying to music I can feel vibrating up through my legs and I want to kill myself. I would seriously rather swallow jagged pieces of glass than spend hours getting liquored up to grind against some greasy guy I don't know. And don't tell me the guys are different in Miami; it doesn't matter where they're from, they're always greasy, and they can never keep their hands to themselves.

I thought about arguing these points to Jameson, but I knew they would fall on deaf ears. This was the job I had signed up for, and I had to be willing to make a few sacrifices. Besides, maybe there would be food at this club. If not, I could make do with a bucket full of maraschino cherries.

I walked out into the living room, where a gorgeous, model-thin black girl and a man in skinny jeans were animatedly talking to Daisy. After only thirty seconds, the man (who I immediately assumed must be Axel) already had Daisy's hair portioned out and was curling it at lightning speed.

Sharla spotted me and waved me toward the chair. "Come on over, Holly."

The last time I'd had my makeup done was for my senior picture, and that woman had made me look like an unemployed Cher impersonator, so I was a little nervous about this whole situation. Of course they made Daisy look amazing—she was naturally stunning, and at eighteen, no matter what you do to your body, it pretty much looks the same.

"Hi," I said shyly, climbing into the chair next to Daisy. Before I could say "nice to meet you," Sharla was attacking my face with all sorts of brushes and powders I'd never heard of. I had to stifle a feeling of claustrophobia as she leaned so close that I could make out each and every one of her pores—a huge feat, since they were tiny and well disguised.

"Glad to have you aboard, Holly." Sharla smiled, revealing an enormous set of teeth that bordered on horsey.

"Thanks for doing this," I said. "I really appreciate it."

"Are you staying with us the whole time in Miami?" Axel asked, speaking for the first time. There was something that seemed intentionally haughty about his tone, and while that should have made me dislike him, I had this sudden desperate desire to earn his approval. This almost certainly meant that he was gay, as I never have this kind of visceral reaction to straight men.

I looked to Daisy, unable to answer that question on my own.

"She totally is," Daisy answered quickly. "Holly will be so much fun to play with."

I have never felt more like a Raggedy Ann doll in my life.

"Then please—pretty, pretty *please,* let me teach you how to pluck your eyebrows. We all love Frida Kahlo, but she would have been more successful if she didn't look like a Cro-Magnon peasant girl."

"Sure," I replied, trying hard not to blink as Sharla practically tore one of my eyelids out of my head to apply eyeliner. "I've never been very good at it."

Axel laughed. "You didn't need to tell me that, sweetie. I have eyes."

We left the hotel just after midnight, and despite the late hour, the paparazzi were still hanging around the entrance. I wondered if Jameson had made them aware of Daisy's schedule, or if there was always someone from each tabloid waiting for pictures, should she happen to go out. It didn't seem like an efficient system to me, but I also didn't understand why people wanted pictures of her eating dinner at a restaurant in the first place.

I will say this for Axel and Sharla—I looked amazing. I was corseted so tight inside the tiny dress that I could feel my heartbeat in my liver, but seeing my nearly unrecognizable figure in the lobby's mirrors was worth the pain. I've never thought of myself as particularly heavy, but I was a little too pleased with my unnaturally narrow waist and enormous cleavage. The instant I saw myself, I decided that this designer was someday making my wedding dress. That is, if he or she knew how to work with more than a yard of fabric.

As we took our first few steps outside, Daisy was immediately flanked by two enormous bodyguards she seemed to know quite well but whom I'd never seen before. I couldn't even tell when and where they'd appeared, it happened so suddenly. One minute, our little group was just five, and then a moment later, we were seven. The ridiculousness of this teenage girl's entourage was starting to dawn on me. I spend most of every day completely alone; I suddenly realized Daisy was probably only by herself when she slept.

And if I thought the level of media attention was absurd before, once we reached the club, it was *insane*. There were throngs of people, packed together like sardines, as far as I could see in any direction. And since everyone seemed to have a camera, it was almost impossible to tell who was a fan and who was paparazzi. If any one of us spoke on the walk from the SUV to the club, I wouldn't have heard it. It's also unlikely that I would have seen it—or anything—with the endless flashes bursting in front of my eyes. From where I was standing, the club might as well have been pink-and-purple speckled.

Three steps inside the door, so many things happened at once, I could hardly process them all. On stage, the DJ gave a loud shout-out to Daisy, prompting the crowd to go wild. At the same time, our group was herded up to a VIP level above the dance floor, and before we reached the room, all of us but Daisy were banded with red paper strips and she had a black X scrawled across the back of her hand. This relieved me somewhat, as I hadn't been able to figure out why an underage girl was parading into a club in full view of the cameras. I figured no one would stop her from actually drinking, but I just couldn't imagine she'd be dumb enough to do it while people were filming her.

"What is this place?" I yelled loudly to Daisy as we settled into a large red velvet couch.

"New club, just opened," she shouted back. Jameson walked by us and handed her a large plastic cup with MOUNTAIN DEW on the side. "They paid us fifty grand to show up."

"Fifty grand?" I asked incredulously. No wonder she could afford to hire a biographer—she could cover my salary with one night's work. If you could call this work. "What do you have to do?"

"Nothing much," Daisy said. "We just need to hang out for an hour or two, I'll walk over to the balcony a couple of times and pretend to dance, and then we can go home." She seemed to remember something, snapping her fingers for Jameson, who handed her a cell phone without a word. "Oh, and one more thing."

Daisy set down her cup and turned so that her back was to the main part of the room. She raised her phone and put on a bright, fun smile. I'm sure there was a photo click during some portion of this, but I certainly wouldn't have heard it. "Selfies!"

I hate the word *selfie*. It's a tween's word, rammed into our cultural consciousness and now spoken by everyone from the president to the Dalai Lama. I know it's a perfectly legitimate word these days, but I refuse to utter it out loud. "Who are the pictures for?"

"My tweeties," Daisy answered, never taking her eyes away from her phone. She tap-tapped for all of one second before passing the phone back to Jamie. It was lightning-quick.

"You already got that up on Twitter?" I asked. "You're fast."

At this, Daisy and Jamie turned to each other and laughed, sharing their first moment of true camaraderie in front of me. "I don't handle my own social media. What am I, a hobo? Or a reality star? I have people who handle these things."

Jamie crossed behind me, leaning in to my ear. Despite the level of background noise, I heard him pretty clearly. "We don't even give her the passwords. Trust me, it's for the best."

Her "work" now done, Daisy picked up her cup and leaned back on the couch, yawning. I used to feel sorry for celebrities who couldn't take two steps without a bodyguard and a camera in their faces, but my sympathy died in that Miami club. In fact, I was pretty angry. I practically lived in gangland, and she was getting paid to sit on a couch, drink soda, and fake-smile for her millions of fans on the Internet. Suddenly, I didn't feel so obligated to waste my night keeping her company.

Axel and Sharla, already with drinks in their hands, ran over to me.

"Dance?" Sharla shouted, holding out her hand to me. Axel hadn't waited for us; he was twirling right there in the VIP section.

"No, thanks," I answered her. I thought I had refused loud enough, but Sharla grabbed my hand and yanked me up off the couch. Either I was screaming for nothing or it didn't matter what I wanted. I looked back at Daisy. "You coming?"

"Can't," she said. "Security issues. No one in their right mind would put a celeb in the middle of a dance floor."

Perhaps some tiny bit of sympathy should have returned, but it didn't. Maybe Daisy was forced to be bored out of her mind for a couple of hours, but it was for money. And I was stuck in a smelly, sticky, hundred-degree club where I didn't know anyone and I hadn't eaten in twelve hours. I seriously wouldn't have cared if cleaning the toilets was a requisite for Daisy collecting her fee.

So I made my way downstairs and out onto the dance floor, completely sober but wishing I was blackout drunk. I was tempted to grab a drink—Axel and Sharla sure seemed to be mixing business with pleasure—but I didn't really know the rules for this sort of thing. If there *were* any rules. I was also afraid of getting wasted and calling Jameson a weirdo or, worse, telling Daisy I was starting to think she was a moron.

I was dancing for less than five minutes when a sweaty guy with a ponytail and a shirt open to his navel sauntered up to me and starting grinding against my leg. I resisted the urge to vomit on him, but the floor was so packed, I really had nowhere to go. It was even hotter out on the floor than upstairs, and as my body swelled a bit, I suddenly couldn't catch my breath. People began looking wavy and out of focus, and their crazy gyrations didn't help.

Axel spotted me trying to squirm away from Mr. South Beach and fought his way over. Without a single look to the other guy,

Axel wiggled between the two of us and began dancing with me. He had just put an arm around my waist when everything went black.

"O-M-F-G, we are already on TMZ."

These were the first words I heard, and while I recognized it as human speech, I had no idea what it meant. I slowly opened my eyes and discovered that I was on the couch in Daisy's hotel room, completely encircled by the group. The second I moved, all four people leaned in and stared down at me intently.

"She's awake," Daisy said.

"Thank you, Daise, we can all see that," Jameson replied.

I struggled to sit up, but Jameson shoved me back down. And I don't mean that he gently moved me back to the cushion, he literally thrust me down.

"You shouldn't move," Jameson told me, in what was possibly the worst bedside manner I'd ever seen. "The club's medic said we had to keep you lying down."

I opened my mouth to speak but didn't get a chance.

"I can't believe that photographer managed to get the whole thing," Sharla said, shaking her head. "I thought they weren't allowed into the club."

"There's always some vulture with a cell phone pic or hidden camera," Axel said.

"Oh, come on." Sharla snorted. "*You're* the one who's always trying to get pictures with those MTV kids."

"You look *so* thin in this picture," Daisy said, holding up her tablet for me to see.

I moved my head around so that I could get a good look at the screen. I did, in fact, look quite thin, but I also looked like a strung-out inebriate being carried off the dance floor. It took only a moment longer before I saw the headline: SOMETHING ROTTEN IN DAISY'S ENTOURAGE???

"I am so sorry," I said, certain that I was about to be fired. So much for staying out of trouble.

"Why?" Daisy asked, laughing. She put the tablet back in her lap and started looking up other websites. "This is *awesome*. I want to see if X17 has the pictures yet."

I struggled to sit up but only made it about halfway. I was still strapped into the tiny dress and felt breathless and dehydrated. "I don't understand," I said, shaking my head. "How is this a good thing?"

Before anyone could reply, Jamie's cell phone chimed and he answered it in the middle of the first ring.

"Yeah," he said, his tone clipped. Jamie stared off, listening to the voice in his ear. I think Bluetooth devices are ridiculous, anyway, but it's times like these that I really hate them. If Jamie just had the phone pressed to his ear, chances are we would have been able to hear at least *some* of the conversation. Instead, the four of us leaned in closer, waiting for some clue as to what was being said, but pretending we hardly even noticed the call. "Sure. . . . Of course not."

"Perez Hilton is saying you're my alcoholic cousin," Daisy whispered to me. "Is this like the coolest thing that has ever happened to you?"

"Ugh, Perez is over," Axel said. "No one reads him anymore."

I know I lead a pretty sheltered life, but I've still had plenty of experiences that rate above passing out in a sweltering Miami nightclub and having the pictures plastered all over gossip websites. Call me crazy.

"Uh-huh," Jamie continued. He rolled his eyes, but I couldn't tell if it was for our benefit or his. "Yeah, I'm on top of it. . . . I'll start making calls at nine A.M. . . . Talk to you tomorrow." He hung up the phone and then sighed, throwing Daisy a look of irritation. "Your mother is a pain in the ass."

"That's not nice," Daisy said, not moving her gaze from the tablet screen. "I've asked you not to talk about her like that."

"The day she earns a single goddamn dollar of her own money, she can tell me what to do," Jamie shot back, grabbing a remote control from the coffee table. "Until then, Faith can shut her mouth."

If anyone else was shocked by this exchange, they didn't show it. In fact, Axel yawned broadly and leaned his head on Sharla's shoulder. When Jamie flipped on the television, I used the screen as an excuse to look somewhere else.

"B-T-dubs, we made it on to CNN," Jamie tossed out as he reached the channel. "Faith saw the teaser about five minutes ago."

Axel snorted. "And how would your mother know what's happening on the Communist News Network?"

Daisy shrugged. "She likes to know what lies the lefties are telling."

I was momentarily distracted by Jamie's idiotic text-speak, but it took me only a few seconds longer to realize what was going on. Pictures and/or video of me passing out in the club were about to be splashed all over the giant plasma screen. And watched in millions of homes in America—including my mother's. The dizziness washed over me again and I had the urge to vomit on Daisy's lap.

"I have to go," I said, struggling to sit up. I attempted this a few times before I realized that the corset was too tight to allow me to bend at the waist, so I was forced to roll off the couch. "I can't watch this."

"Sweetheart, you shouldn't be standing," Sharla said, getting up and putting her arms around my shoulders.

On TV, CNN came back from commercial and a well-coiffed reporter smiled blankly at the camera. I tried to move quickly, maneuvering out of Sharla's grip, but I was sick, exhausted, and trussed up like a pig—and about as fast as a Christmas ham.

"As we reported before the break, a member of Daisy Dixson's entourage passed out tonight at a club in Miami, and we have the exclusive footage."

I felt the bile rising in my throat and just made for the door, somehow having the sense to grab my purse on the way out. "I'll see you in the morning," I managed to say between hyperventilating breaths.

"Do us a favor and don't die in your sleep," Jameson called after me. "This level of publicity helps us, but a death would really cramp Daisy's Oscar chances."

CHAPTER 6

Dating in Hollywood can be tough. We all work insane hours, but that isn't even the hardest part. It always seems like everyone wants something from you. So when you find someone who really likes you for you, it's important to hold on to them. I look at my mom and dad's marriage, which has weathered twenty-three years, and I have hope!

My cell phone started ringing at seven the next morning. I had been asleep for barely four hours and hadn't thought to turn off my cell when I collapsed into my wonderfully comfortable bed. I knew who the caller was even before I glanced at the phone; there was only one person who couldn't care less if I was tired or sick.

"Hi, Mom," I said, pulling a pillow over my face to block out the sun. I hadn't had a drop of alcohol last night, and I still felt like I was completely hungover. It wasn't fair.

"Holly Ann Gracin," my mother said. Her disappointment was audible. I immediately pulled the phone away from my ear and pressed the speakerphone button. The last thing I needed was Mom's Western New York accent boring another hole in my already throbbing brain. "You have thirty seconds to explain yourself."

"It's not what you think—"

"You do know that I have to show my face at work Monday?"

Mom continued, sounding very sorry for herself. "Do you know what people are going to say? *Hmmmm?*" This time I didn't even bother; she wasn't asking my opinion. "They're going to point and whisper behind my back that I have the druggie Hollywood daughter who got carried out of a nightclub in Florida!"

I wondered if she was more concerned about drugs or about the possibility that I might have gone "Hollywood." "Mom, if they're talking behind your back, they're not really your friends."

"Excuse me, young lady? Do you think this is *funny?*"

Actually, I did. "Of course not," I reassured her. "But I swear to you, I'm not on any drugs. I wasn't even drinking. I was just overheated and wearing a really tight corset."

"That'd better be true," she said, still all kinds of wound up. "Because if you've fallen in with those weirdo L.A. types, I will hire the best deprogrammer money can buy."

No, she wouldn't. My mother won't pay extra for guacamole at Chipotle.

"You have nothing to worry about," I told her. "If you want to blame anyone, blame the rich people who didn't let me eat dinner last night. Listen, Mom, I have to go."

"You have to *go?* Because you have better things to do than talk to your own mother? Honey, if these people don't even let you eat—"

Oh, geez. "Mom, I always love to talk to you but I do have to work," I lied. "Busy day ahead of me."

"Fine," she sniffed. "You just remember that I'm the only one who cares about you, Holly. Those famous people are only using you for your brain."

"Yes, Mom." I sighed. "I'll talk to you later."

"You'd better believe you will—"

I like to think I hung up on her at that moment, but I suspect that's not the truth. Though she never mentioned it again, I think I fell back asleep.

That's the last thing I remember until noon, when my room phone rang. I rolled over and picked it up, yawning into the receiver.

"Hello?"

"I hope I'm not calling too early" came the cool reply from the other end of the phone.

"No, Minka, not at all." I could hear the judgment in her voice, and it made me want to push her smug little face into a brick wall. "What can I do for you?"

"I was thinking I could perhaps be of assistance to *you*," Minka said. "I would be happy to send up Tylenol and a glass of orange juice or Gatorade. Or maybe you'd prefer an eye-opener? We make a lovely Bloody Mary."

"No, thank you," I replied, my voice dripping with saccharine sweetness. Of course she'd seen me on the news; she was probably monitoring every gossip site for news about Daisy and her precious Jameson. I resisted the urge to call Minka a sanctimonious bitch, though it was a close one. "What I would love is a cheeseburger. With fries and a chocolate milk shake. And *loads* of whipped cream."

There was a long pause on the other end of the line. I was pleased to think I'd momentarily stymied Frau Minka.

"Of course," she said finally. "I'll have the kitchen prepare that straightaway. I've just put in an order for Miss Dixson; I'll have everything sent up to the Presidential Suite when it's ready."

"That's not necessary," I added quickly. I desperately needed some time alone before heading back into the Dixson Dramarama, just to watch twenty minutes of some awful *CSI* rerun and collect myself. Not to mention take an hour-long bath and scrub the funk off my skin. "Just have my food brought to my room."

"It was Mr. Lloyd's suggestion," Minka stated, intimating that I had no choice in the matter. I could choose to stay in my room, but going upstairs was the only way I would ever see my food.

"Fine." I threw off the covers and reluctantly got out of bed, knowing that—for the second morning in a row—I hated the day just minutes after it began. "Thank you for your help, Minka."

"Of course, Ms. Gracin." She hung up.

I sighed and headed into my amazing bathroom, ready to longingly admire the tub from my view inside the glass-enclosed shower.

Twenty minutes later, I stepped into the Presidential Suite, the room service cart about a foot behind me.

"Yay," Daisy cheered, jumping up from the couch. "Holly *and* yummies!"

I was immediately dismayed to see that she was wearing practically nonexistent cutoffs and a bikini top. Did this girl have an aversion to being fully clothed?

"Any fallout from last night?" I asked, cringing.

Daisy shook her head. "No, we took care of it. Jamie issued a statement and it seemed to shut everybody up. Don't even worry about it." She ran up and hugged me tightly, before turning around and bounding toward the tray. "I thought you were never going to get here, Holly, I totally missed you!"

"She really did," Axel said from the couch, painting his toenails black. "The first thing Daisy said when she opened her eyes was 'Do you think Holly's up yet?'"

While I was fast growing accustomed to the epic weirdness, I still did a double take. "I'm sorry, do you sleep with Daisy?"

As she sat down at the dining room table and somehow managed to cross her legs Indian-style on the chair, Daisy giggled again. "Of course he does! I'd get so lonely if I slept by myself!"

"Don't you have three dogs?" I asked.

"*Yeah*"—she nodded—"but it's like, a monster bed. It can fit six people."

I didn't bother to ask how she knew that. I approached the table and sat down, trying not to bite the bellman's hand off as he arranged the food at an infuriatingly slow pace. The silverware had barely left his grasp before I snatched up the utensils and removed the plate cover. As soon as the mouthwatering cheeseburger was revealed, Daisy gasped.

"What is *that*?"

"A cheeseburger," I told her as I crammed a handful of French fries in my mouth.

Daisy lifted the cover from her meal, and I tried not to choke as I saw what she'd ordered. Or didn't order. All I can say for certain is, nothing on that plate resembled food. From the couch, I heard Axel *tsk* obnoxiously in my direction. This prompted me to pick up my burger and take the largest bite I could possibly manage without choking.

"Holly, I just cannot believe you," Daisy exclaimed, seemingly truly upset. "Who eats *beef* anymore?"

"It's so 2004," Axel agreed.

"I love beef," I said with my mouth full. "I pretty much worship steak."

Daisy began picking at her own plate, clearly disgusted by my lack of enlightenment.

"You're a vegetarian, then?" I asked. To be honest, I didn't really care, but I realized this was good fodder for the book. Since she wasn't interested in talking about any other part of her life that didn't involve shopping or celebrity vendettas.

"Yes." Daisy nodded. "But I'm also insulin-resistant."

"And gluten-resistant," Axel chimed in.

I took a long slurp of my heavenly milk shake while absorbing this. "So you don't eat sugar . . . or bread."

Again, Daisy nodded. "And soy does funky things to your thyroid, so I avoid that . . . Mom and Daddy prefer I stay away from nuts, just in case there's an issue there. And *nobody* should be ingesting dairy." She looked pointedly at the milk shake clasped tightly in my hand. I took another long, loud drink.

"What is that you're eating?" I asked, nodding toward the red, soupy concoction on her plate. I'd been staring at it for the last few minutes and I still hadn't figured out what it was supposed to be.

"Tomatoes and onions." Daisy grinned, smacking her lips. "I'm so lucky I'm not allergic to nightshades."

Lucky wasn't the first word that came into my mind. "Did a nutritionist recommend that for you?" I asked.

Daisy shook her head like I was being absurd. "No, it's like a really famous diet."

"From who?" I didn't want to admit this out loud, but I've tried every diet known to man. I've eaten nothing but cabbage soup for three weeks, tried only bananas and milk, and subsisted on eleven pounds of Atkin's-approved bacon slices. And I'd never heard of the tomatoes-and-onions diet.

"Um, only that gorgeous Brazilian model that died of starvation," she told me. "It was all over the news. It's a great diet, but obviously, she wasn't eating enough of it."

There were so many things I could have said in response to that, but I knew I'd be wasting my breath. "Did you order anything, Axel?"

He waved me away dismissively. "Today isn't my day to eat."

Since I was now devouring my carnivorous feast mostly to prove a point, it didn't taste quite so good anymore. And knowing that Daisy and Axel were undoubtedly thinking about what a big, fat tub of lard I was made each bite a little more forced than the last. I finally gave up halfway through the burger, but I refused to abandon my milk shake. No dessert left behind.

Jameson and Sharla walked in the door, both talking rapidly. At first I thought they were arguing with each other, but then I realized Jamie had his Bluetooth in his ear and Sharla was talking into those iPhone headphones. These days, it's so much harder to tell when someone's a crazy person talking to their invisible Martian friends.

"Six dozen pink teacup roses—"

"The makeup trailer had better be fully stocked by the time we get there—"

"I did not say tonic water, I said *club soda*—"

"I cannot use a *brush* on her face, I don't care what brand it is—"

Across the table, Daisy clapped her hands. "Oooh, today's going to be so much fun!"

"So, what are we here for?"

I was standing on the beach in Biscayne Bay, watching as production crews put the finishing touches on a stage just feet from the ocean. Cameras were being set up at every conceivable angle, and I hadn't seen Daisy, Sharla, or Jameson in over an hour. It didn't seem safe to have so much electrical equipment that close to a huge body of water, but what do I know?

"Nickelodeon Kids' Something Kick-Ass Awards," Axel said with a yawn. He'd disappeared for forty minutes, but once Daisy's hair was done, he was bored and looking for someone to cause trouble with.

"Really? That's what it's called?"

Axel gave me a look like I was missing a chromosome. "I don't know what it's called, but they're all something like that. I bet Daisy doesn't even know. She just knows she has to sing her latest song, blow kisses to the tweens, and hug Ryan Seacrest a couple of times."

I was also starting to get the sense that Daisy spent most of her days sleepwalking through events and asking as few questions as possible.

Jameson walked toward us and snapped his fingers at me like I was a misbehaving puppy. "Hols, get over here."

I was so irritated by his attempt to control me that I remained motionless and waited for him to come to me. The rebellious part of me likes to think he was subconsciously put in his place, but to tell the truth, I doubt any part of his Neanderthal brain noticed the slight.

"Am I going to have a chance to work with Daisy today?" I asked.

"Aren't you working with her right now?" Jameson asked me, waving his hands around at the frenetic preparations. "You're getting unfettered access to her life. You can't buy that."

It was also completely useless without concrete personal information. I wasn't so much writing a book *about* Daisy as writing a book *as* Daisy. And watching her from across the beach wasn't going to make learning her voice any easier. "So that's a no?"

"That's actually what I wanted to talk to you about," Jameson said, smiling tightly.

My stomach dropped and I almost barfed hamburger bits all over his thousand-dollar shoes. I was going to be fired, I just knew it. Last night, Jameson had held on to me in case they needed me to make a statement, but now that he'd handled my nightclub debacle, he was sweeping me under the rug.

In the three seconds before he spoke again, I tallied all of my worldly possessions, thought about what I could sell, and tried to add up how much of the original ten grand I'd already spent. What can I say—I can worry at light-speed.

"I was thinking you could spend the day with one of our execs from Nick," Jameson continued, scanning nearby groups of people. "They've worked with Daise for years, and I think I've found you a producer who isn't as easily distracted by shiny objects as our precious pop star."

My first thought was, *Phew*. My second thought was, *What a prick*. How Jameson got away with talking about his only client this way, I didn't understand. "Okay," I agreed, shrugging. "Whatever you'd like."

Jameson spotted who he was looking for and waved the person over. I couldn't decide if I thought this exercise would be a colossal waste of time or the best idea Jamie'd had to date. Plus, if this producer guy or girl was really boring, I could always slip away and have the night to myself. It was unlikely anyone would notice over the throngs of teenagers screaming and jumping up and down.

"Hey, Jamie," came a voice from behind me.

I turned and saw a blond guy a few years older than I was, with dark-rimmed glasses and wearing a *Doctor Who* T-shirt under a blazer. He looked like he belonged at Comic Con, instead of on this beach with the world's prettiest perma-teens. It made him instantly likable.

"This is the writer I was telling you about," Jameson said, putting a hand on my shoulder.

"Does this writer have a name?" the blond guy asked, winking at me.

"Holly Gracin," I said, reaching out to shake his hand. "And you are?"

"Vaughn Royce," Jamie answered. Vaughn's mouth was open to speak, but when Jamie responded for him, the producer's face relaxed into a smile. "You kids good? Great. I'll see you later." The agent jogged off down the beach, his eyes already on his phone.

"Does he always speak for you?"

Vaughn shrugged, still grinning. "Jamie seems to think everything in the world is addressed to him. Why would you ever bother speaking to me?"

If I liked him before, I *really* liked him now. Axel, on the other hand, didn't seem to feel the same way. "I'm bored," he announced. "You're boring me. I'm going to go flirt with the cute soundboard guy." He promptly marched away from us.

"He'll be disappointed," Vaughn told me, shaking his head. "The cute soundboard guy has a very sweet—and very large—husband."

"How long have you worked with Daisy?" I asked.

"I started on her first show with Nick about six years ago," he said, sighing and shaking his head. "Six years and she still thinks my name is John."

"You're kidding me," I said, laughing.

"No," he replied. "Daisy always does remember my last name, though. . . ." I looked at him questioningly. "The Rolls-Royce is her favorite car."

"I see." I racked my brain, trying to figure out if I had any idea what a Rolls-Royce looked like. After a few seconds of thought, I came up blank. "Daisy seems to know my name all too well. . . . We've only met a few times and I'm already her new favorite person."

Vaughn laughed, his mouth going a little bit sideways with the motion. "Of course you are. You've been hired to let her talk about herself all day. I'm surprised she hasn't requested you be surgically attached to her hip."

"It's not a good look," I replied. "I'd probably make her butt look big."

I found myself relaxing into the conversation, marking the first time my shoulders weren't tensed up to my ears since I had landed in Miami. "I have to know—does Daisy parade around set half-naked?"

Vaughn looked at me, horrified. "What? Ew, no. We would never let that happen, it's a family network."

I was pleased that the thought of Daisy barely clothed earned an "ew, no." This guy was all right. "I swear to God, I've had more contact with her breasts in the last few days than my own," I exclaimed.

Vaughn's head whipped back toward me. "Excuse me?"

"Hugging," I added. "She keeps hugging me in weirdly tiny bikini tops. . . . That's what I meant."

"Right." He chuckled.

Daisy walked onstage, fully made-up but still in her cutoffs. She approached the microphone and said sweetly, "I'm ready for sound check whenever y'all are."

I nodded toward her clear state of undress. "See, I told you. Imagine those things bouncing toward you every couple of hours."

Vaughn shook his head. "You're the envy of seventy percent of men in America." From the stage, we could hear Daisy quietly singing scales. "Listen, do you want to get out of here? As much as I'd love to hear 'Date Night' for the millionth time, my work here is pretty much done. We can grab a drink and have an actual conversation."

"Sure." I nodded, suddenly desperate to get away from this place. "Sounds like a plan."

CHAPTER 7

Sometimes you look at gossip sites and think, When did those
two start dating? *It seems like all of our relationships, romantic
or friendship, move at the speed of light. And you'd be right. We
don't work with people for a few hours a day and go home to our
friends and family. Working on a film set is a family, and you see
those people a whole lot more than the ones you're related to.*

*We're up before the sun to get ready for work, and we're
usually together long after the sun sets. A typical day can run
fourteen or fifteen hours and you can have all three meals with
your cast and crew. So when it seems like two people are suddenly thick as thieves, it's because they've spent so much time
together. Think about it this way—if you go out on five dates
with a guy, you've spent far less time with him than I would with
a guy I work with, just over the course of one week. It's called
compressed time.*

Vaughn drove to the Titanic Brewery, a cute little restaurant and
bar just a few minutes from the beach. I couldn't help but wonder
if it was bad luck to name an establishment—so close to a major
port—after the *Titanic*. On the way, we chatted about Daisy's career
and her strange habits and stranger family. I learned that despite
being the star of the show, Daisy couldn't make any set call time
before 11:00 A.M. and how if she didn't have the very last line in each

episode, she ad-libbed one. Badly. I found out more in ten minutes than during the last twenty hours.

"Are you hungry?" Vaughn asked as we were seated in a back corner.

"I had a burger about two hours ago," I told him. "Though I wish I was hungry. . . . I have a feeling I won't get many judgment-free meals on this trip."

Vaughn snorted. "Let me guess . . . the queen of tomatoes and onions doesn't approve of solid foods?"

"It's apparently very 2004 of me to eat beef."

He flagged down the waitress, smiling a little to himself. "Come on, it's totally hot when girls eat."

"You should become a life coach and preach this to all of the emaciated girl-children in Hollywood," I told him.

"Does life coaching come with dental? I'm told I grind my teeth. It's a very expensive problem."

Our cute, blond waitress stepped up to the table, offering a smile to both of us. "Hi, my name is Danielle, and I'll be your server today." After looking at me, she did a double take, her eyes going wide.

"Is everything okay?" Vaughn asked.

Danielle nodded, never taking her eyes off me. "Yeah," she replied, seeming a little starstruck. "Ummm . . . can I get you something to drink?"

"I know it's still a little early," I said sheepishly, "but I would love a strawberry margarita."

"A Fat Tire, please," Vaughn told the waitress, who still hadn't looked at him.

In fact, Danielle didn't even scribble anything on her notepad. She just continued to stare at me, now looking more than a little disgusted. I almost wanted to ask her if a strawberry margarita killed her mother.

"Is something wrong?" I said finally.

"Are you *sure* you want a margarita?" she asked.

Vaughn and I exchanged looks of confusion. "I'm well over twenty-one, I assure you," I replied, in case that was the problem.

This earned me an even dirtier look. "Look, if you want to drink, I can't stop you," she said. "But I don't have to be happy about it."

Danielle turned on her heels and marched back to the bar, leaving me and Vaughn bewildered. "Did I miss something?" I asked, laughing.

"Maybe she's Mormon and doesn't drink?" he suggested.

I shook my head. "Then she shouldn't work in a bar. Plus . . . she didn't seem to care about your beer."

"Touché," Vaughn replied, shrugging. "Does it really matter? The only consequence of Danielle's words is her ever-shrinking tip."

"I suppose you're right," I agreed. But I was still bothered by the waitress's behavior; I know I shouldn't care what someone else thinks of me, but I always do. I'm perpetually that weird, desperate little girl who's willing to pull up her dress for attention.

"Can I ask you a question?"

"Shoot," Vaughn told me.

"Have you met Daisy's father?" I asked. I hadn't really thought about the peculiarity of his absence until just now. Not that I'd spent a lot of time with Daisy until Miami, but part of me was starting to think her father didn't really exist. Even though Faith hadn't traveled with them to Florida, she was still referenced quite a bit. No one talked about Daisy's father at all.

Vaughn smirked and made a face I couldn't read. "Yes, I've met Deacon." He nodded slowly, still with that same expression plastered on his face. "Many, *many* times."

"His name is Deacon? Deacon Dixson?" At this, Vaughn nodded. "So they're Deacon and Faith. . . . That's a little too perfect for my taste."

"Nothing about them is perfect," he said.

Before he could say any more, a man walked over with our drinks. Surprised, I looked around for Danielle, who was watching us nervously from behind the bar. When she caught my gaze, she quickly looked away.

The man set Vaughn's beer in front of him but continued to hold my margarita. "You ordered the margarita, right?" he asked.

"Yes," I replied, now even more confused.

"And you *are* aware of the dangers of alcohol?"

Again, I looked to Vaughn, wondering what this was about. I was starting to feel like we'd stumbled into some weird religious sect. Why run a bar if you have so much trouble serving alcohol? "Acutely," I answered, irritated. "As are most people."

"All right, then," the man said, setting down my drink. "I hope you enjoy it." From his tone of voice, I think he really hoped I'd choke on a chunk of ice and die.

As soon as he left the table, I stared at Vaughn in astonishment. "What the hell was that all about?"

"You know, I wouldn't peg you as one of L.A.'s infamous ghost-writers," Vaughn told me two hours later as we sat on the beach. We had long since stopped talking about Daisy and her entourage.

"I'm not," I freely admitted. The prevailing wisdom in Hollywood is to "fake it till you make it," meaning that I should have gone to the ends of the Earth to pretend I was some unknown literary hotshot, even if that meant lying outright. But I am a terrible liar under any circumstances. "I'm an unemployed movie critic for a now-defunct magazine no one's ever heard of."

Vaughn stared at me for a moment. "Hmm," he said finally. "I wouldn't peg you as one of those, either."

"Is that a fact?" I laughed. "Do you see me as a secretary or a biochemical engineer?"

"A novelist, actually. I can totally see you on some author panel, dazzling your sycophantic fans with your dry wit and pretty hazel eyes."

No one ever notices that I have hazel eyes; they're so dark everyone just thinks they're brown. You have to look at them really closely to see that they're green around the edges. More than once, I'd gotten pissed at some long-term boyfriend who thought it was cute to croon "Brown Eyed Girl" to me. I'd given up thinking that guys ever noticed things like that.

"That's the dream. Now I just have to write a novel. Except that when I have the money, I don't have the time, and when I have the time, I'm too worried about money to be creative."

"At least you're writing." Vaughn shrugged and turned to stare at the preparations down the beach. The number of people had tripled since we'd left for our drink. "Not all of us get to do the job we set out to."

"You mean, as opposed to producing a show for preteens and watching as the IQ-challenged star makes millions for warbling songs about her boyfriend's convertible?"

Vaughn still didn't turn back to look at me, but he smiled ruefully at my question, the grin not making it all the way up to his eyes.

"If it's not producing, what is it you want to do?"

I couldn't be sure, but it looked like Vaughn reddened slightly. He finally glanced back toward me, his expression that of a little boy who'd just been caught doing something embarrassing. "Promise you won't make fun of me."

Since I'm not that in control of my emotions, it would be a promise I couldn't possibly keep. "I won't laugh as long as you don't tell me you want to be a trapeze artist or rodeo clown."

That earned a real grin. "What, you don't think I could pull off the floppy shoes?"

"A bright red nose wouldn't go with your complexion."

I expected him to laugh, but instead, he inhaled deeply. "I went to college to be a director," Vaughn blurted out. He made it sound like some deep dark secret.

I stared at him for a brief second, trying to figure out what was so embarrassing about that. "Unless you want to direct snuff films, I can't imagine why you would hide that."

"Because everyone wants to be a director. In L.A., that's the next worse thing to saying you want to be an actor."

We both stayed silent for a few beats, watching the warm bluish green waves wash up onto the shore. It occurred to me that I never go to the beach in Los Angeles, maybe because I'm terrified of being mugged at knifepoint. "I'm willing to bet thousands of people would kill for your job."

"I'm sure I could find tons who want your job, too."

I shrugged, acknowledging he had a point. "I'm sure there *are* thousands of tweens who would die for my access to Daisy Mae Dixson. And men of all ages, if she continues to wear her underwear to work."

A gust of wind blew my hair directly into my mouth, and before I could reach up and brush it away, I felt Vaughn's hand gently pull the strands from my lips. The move made me both uncomfortable and a little flushed. Good God, I needed a date—of the nonfeline variety. Worried my red face betrayed my thoughts, I stood up as soon as his hands were clear from my face.

"Listen," I said, smiling politely. "I really should go. I need to start transcribing and maybe even write a few pages."

Vaughn looked openly disappointed. "Sure, you're right. I should probably get back to the stage, anyway. I don't really have any work to do, but I should at least pretend."

I brushed the sand from my clothes, trying to act as though I wasn't in a hurry to escape. I was just about to start walking back toward the street when I remembered I had come here with Daisy's entourage and my rental car was back at the Fontainebleau. Damn. "Would it be too much for me to ask for a ride back to the hotel? I think I need a night off from the Dixson clan."

"No problem," Vaughn said, standing up and taking his keys from his pocket. "Are you going to be around tomorrow? We don't fly back until Sunday."

"Maybe," I told him. "I don't really know what the plan is for the rest of this trip."

"I'll take maybe," he said, smiling.

As we headed back toward his car, a question popped into my head. "If you don't have anything to do, why are you here?" I asked, partly out of curiosity and partly as a writer trying to grasp the inner workings of this odd little circle.

"Nick is doing the awards show in conjunction with several of our sister stations and crossover shows," he answered, as though that explained anything at all. "I'm not here officially working so much as acting as a show rep. Gotta protect your brand."

Maybe because I'm just one person or maybe because I live in a single tiny, perpetually messy room, I didn't know the first thing about branding. I also didn't know what a crossover show was. "Does that mean you're here for free?"

Vaughn laughed, actually throwing his head back a little. "Oh, God, no. I wouldn't show up unless I was being paid. Believe me, I'd much rather spend the weekend in my apartment, playing video games, than hugging a thousand people I can't stand. Most of whose names I don't remember, anyway."

"So . . . you don't have anything to do, but the show is still paying you to . . . just be here and talk to people?"

"Yes." He nodded. We reached the car at that moment and Vaughn turned to look at me, noticing the strange look I was giving him. He chuckled. "I guess it sounds pretty bad."

"You are never allowed to complain about your job again."

As I knew very little about filming and even less about awards shows, I had no clue how long the Kick-Ass Somethings would take. My hope was that the Dixson gang would be tied up all night and I could enjoy a blessedly quiet evening. I know I hadn't been in Miami long, but it already felt like an eternity.

I did sit down with my digital recorder and my laptop, but I didn't get much work done. After thirty minutes of listening to Daisy ramble on about absolutely nothing worth putting onto paper, I knew I was correct about being unqualified for this job. Even if I could get her to open up to me, I didn't know the right questions to ask. The instant they asked to read pages, I was dead.

As I was puzzling over my uncertain future with Daisy, my room phone rang. I glanced at the clock and saw that it was just after ten. Crap. Was there another opening tonight? A photo shoot? A séance? I considered pretending I wasn't there and letting it ring, but this was my job, not a vacation.

"Hello?" I asked, trying not to sound too forlorn.

"Have you had dinner yet?" The voice was Vaughn's. "Because I haven't."

I smiled. "I had a cupcake from the bakery downstairs at about five o'clock. Does that count?"

"It does not."

I looked down at my current clothing, a pair of *Sailor Moon* pajamas I've had since college. Definitely not appropriate for dinner. "I need to change first."

There was a polite but firm knock on my room door. "No, you don't. I don't care what you have on."

"Come on, Vaughn—"

The knock came again. "Uh-uh. You're not making me wait. These bags are very heavy."

I heaved myself off the bed and grabbed the first sweater I saw. I couldn't do much about the pants, but at least I could cover my tank top. I opened the door and found Vaughn in the hallway, holding two enormous plastic bags. "Are several dozen more people joining us for dinner?" I asked him.

Without waiting to be invited in, Vaughn moved past me and went for the open balcony door, straight to the small table overlooking the water. There wasn't much to see in the dark, but the sound of the ocean was soothing. "No more people, please. That beach was like a rave by the end." Vaughn quickly went to work, setting a little dinner scene in my hotel room. He glanced up at the half-moon that hung low over the water. "Nice view."

"Do you not have a view?"

"I'm a few floors up and my balcony wraps around the corner," he said, busying himself laying out utensils. "So yes. I'm just never in my room long enough to enjoy it."

"Tell me about it." I looked around the room, realizing my things were scattered everywhere. I'd managed to make a five-star hotel suite look like a dorm room. "Are you sure I can't change? I'll be quick."

"No. Sit." He shot a quick look to my pajama pants and grinned. "There's no need to hide *Sailor Moon*. You're among friends."

No one I'd met in L.A. knew *Sailor Moon*. But then, I also didn't know many people who walked around in *Doctor Who* T-shirts. "You're a fan?"

Vaughn shrugged. "I always found Usagi a little whiny. Sailor Mercury is more my speed." He gestured for me to join him on the balcony.

I walked over and sat down, feeling enormously out of place, even in my own room. I wasn't sure why Vaughn was there, and I've never been particularly fond of uncertainty.

He opened the containers of food, revealing breaded chicken and mashed potatoes. "Sorry if it's not fancy. You can't be too choosy this late at night."

"The only takeout I've ever had at ten P.M. came from a drive-through window. No worries." I didn't want to tell him that fast food was pretty much my entire diet. By this point, I wasn't even sure my body would recognize a green vegetable.

As uncomfortable as I was, Vaughn seemed right at home. He relaxed back into his chair and took a bite of his potatoes. We'd only met eight hours ago and he was already acting like we'd been around each other for years. I didn't know what to make of it.

"So tell me how you came to the Monkey House." Vaughn went to work opening a bottle of wine. I wanted to tell him that I think wine tastes like turpentine, but I appreciated the gesture. And isn't drinking wine something adults do?

"I'm sorry?" I'd never heard that expression before. I wasn't sure what it meant or if I should be offended.

"My first day on a set was right out of college," he told me. Vaughn grabbed a couple of plastic cups and filled them with wine. "And I walked on, all terrified and nervous that I was going to fall on my face. No one talked to me for ten minutes, until I found the second AD—second assistant director. And as we walked to the production trailer to get started, he said to me, 'Welcome to the Monkey House. It'll be crazy and infuriating and you'll love it more than you'll hate it.' He was right."

"Really, you love it?" I asked. "I watched the behind-the-scenes footage and everyone kept saying that. But you work crazy long days, right?"

Vaughn shrugged. "Yes. But most of my friends work on film sets, too. I wouldn't really know what else to do with my time."

"I don't know. Muay Thai. Knitting. Whatever." I was confused by the thought that an industry literally built by creativity was populated by people who couldn't come up with a nonwork hobby.

"You still didn't answer my question. What brought you here to play with us? You don't seem anything like the other ghostwriters Daisy interviewed on set."

There was that word again. Daisy had also referred to our work as "play." Maybe I needn't have worried so much about my geek-culture pajamas; it was seeming more and more like no one here wanted to behave like an adult, anyway. "It's a great opportunity," I said. "Why wouldn't I take it?"

Vaughn stared at me for a moment. Then he laughed. "Of course. Great opportunity." There was definitely more behind that moment of hesitation, but I didn't know him nearly enough to guess what that was. He raised his plastic cup. "Let's toast to new opportunities. And new friends."

"Cheers." I touched my glass to his and forced myself to take a sip. I was glad the cup was giant and red, as it hid my inevitable grimace. Why didn't more people toast with margaritas? "I have a million more questions for you about the show and Daisy and . . . just about everything."

"Later." Vaughn grinned at me and I again noticed how lopsided he smiled. It was adorable. And I really didn't want to let myself think of him as adorable. This was my job, and one I desperately needed. "For now I want to hear more about you."

Me? There's nothing interesting about me. Unless he wanted to hear about the weekly marching band practice at the school near my apartment, I didn't know what to tell him. "Um . . . I'm from Western New York. Which is not the city and also not upstate."

"That's a start." Vaughn's grin grew wider, and I knew I was in trouble.

I worried we wouldn't have anything to talk about, but somehow, Vaughn and I stayed up chatting until nearly 3:00 A.M. He told me a little bit about working his way up to producer, but the story sounded all too brief. I didn't even know it was possible to become a producer by the age of thirty-one, and he'd already been working with Nickelodeon for six years.

He seemed just as engaged by learning about me, but I couldn't figure out why. My story is as terrestrial as they come. I told him about Sarah Lawrence and growing up just my mom and me, how I'd needed my scholarship and several jobs to pay my tuition. I talked about Camille and Donnie, and my tiny little jerk, Smitty. It was nice to meet an L.A. person who actually cared what I had to say and not just about what designer made my shoes.

I finally kicked him out when I saw the last lights start to flicker out across the beachfront. Not because I necessarily wanted to, but because I knew it was already tomorrow and I had run out of things to say. When Vaughn paused at the door, I found myself tangled up in a few dozen knots as he leaned in to my face. He sweetly kissed my cheek, which might not sound like much, but which I found a hell of a lot more appealing than if he'd gone for my lips.

Under any other circumstances, I would have been giddy over this turn of events. But all I could think was, *Crap.* This was going to make things just that much more complicated.

"Tell me about you and the yummy professor," Axel said, pouncing the instant I walked into the Presidential Suite.

"It's so crazy." Daisy giggled. Today she was clad in a minuscule, partially see-through sundress that may have been a bathing suit cover-up. "I swear, Mama and I thought John was gay."

"Vaughn," I corrected her. The rest of the world could treat her like some adorable little idiot, but I wasn't about to. I just didn't have the energy.

"He sure talked about *you* an awful lot last night," Axel said.

Daisy made a sound of disgust. "God, I know. How old is Holly, how long have you known her, what kind of music is she into . . . I was finally like, man, nobody cares about Holly."

How touching.

"Did he come find you last night?" Sharla asked. "He asked for your room number. I guess the hotel wouldn't give it to him."

From the end of the couch, Axel kicked Sharla with one foot. "You didn't tell me that."

"I forgot." When Axel didn't seem mollified by this, she held up her hands apologetically. "I was busy!"

I watched the exchange, hoping it would sufficiently distract them from noticing I hadn't yet answered the question. It didn't. It only took another two seconds before all three turned to stare at me expectantly. They looked alarmingly like Daisy's three dogs, lined up in a row and waiting for a treat. Unfortunately, I was the treat.

"Well?" Axel demanded.

"He did," I replied, keeping my tone as noncommittal as I could manage. "He's helping me. Giving me information about the show, how it works. You know."

Axel and Sharla yelled at me at the same moment, while Daisy yawned. Axel called out, "Boo!" while Sharla shook her head and said, "Well, that's no fun."

The door to Daisy's bedroom opened and Jamie walked out, clad in sweatpants and a T-shirt. I instantly forgot about Vaughn as I was now focused on the rumpled man heading toward us. I was shocked, but when I looked around at the others, no one reacted or even seemed to notice. Though I managed to hide my outrage, internally I was on fire. It was bizarre enough that Daisy slept next to her makeup artist and gay hairstylist, but her forty-five-year-old *straight* agent? This was starting to seem all kinds of messed up.

"We need to be ready to leave by one," Jamie said brusquely, grabbing a LäraBar from the table.

The others seemed to forget about Vaughn, too. Daisy turned to me and frowned. "I don't know what we're going to put you in," she said, disgusted.

I was wearing shorts and a tank top with a hoodie. I didn't think there was anything wrong with my appearance, but apparently, I was Godzilla in thrift-store discards. Not all of us could look like we were getting ready for a spread in *Playboy*.

"You're right." Jamie winced. "We can't put her in a bathing suit."

If I wasn't offended before, I certainly was now. I was starting to experience all sorts of body issues I'd never had before. Bulimia was beginning to make sense to me.

"What would you like me to wear?" I asked.

"They need you to hide your tummy," Axel whispered loudly.

"Why?" I asked, unconsciously putting a hand on my stomach. It felt pretty flat to me, but who was I to judge my own worth?

"Oh," Daisy said, waving a dismissive hand in the air, "when you passed out the other night, Jamie told the press it was because you were preggers." She turned to her agent thoughtfully. Well, as thoughtfully as she was capable of. "You know, maybe we should put her in a bikini. She could totally pass for three or four months along."

Suddenly, I knew why the waitress at the Titanic had been so upset with me. She'd thought I was pregnant and still ordering hard liquor. Awesome.

"No," Jamie said. I wondered if people constantly overestimated his level of intelligence because he said everything so purposefully. "Let's put her in a baggy sweatshirt. The paps will think she's trying to hide her stomach."

"But I don't look pregnant in the pictures from the club," I pointed out. In fact, I'd venture that the corset pushed so much of my body fat back inside me that I could have caused internal damage.

Daisy smiled up at me sympathetically. "That's open for debate, sweetie."

Jamie looked me up and down, then took a fifty out of his wallet and slapped it into my hand. "Go to the lobby and buy a sweatshirt big enough to hide your Amazon warrior princess frame and meet us at the car in half an hour."

It took me a full five seconds to process the instructions and actually move. Nothing about this job was playing out the way I'd expected, and it was keeping me perpetually off-balance. I couldn't begin to guess what would happen next.

As we drove the streets of the city in the Escalade, I found my mind drifting to Vaughn again. To our odd late-night dinner and what it meant, if anything. As the group chattered away about some model named Knox and an accident with a tongue ring, I mentally replayed the conversations from the night before, looking for meaning I may have missed.

I was so lost in my own head that I didn't notice where we were going until we pulled up outside of a marina. A cadre of old men in hideous canvas vests lined one side of the pier, their fishing poles cast out into the Atlantic. Wait a minute . . . Daisy didn't believe in eating anything but tomatoes and onions, but she was cool with spearing fish through the mouth and gutting them?

"Um, I don't handle live bait," I said nervously as everyone piled out of the SUV. "No offense, but I really hate worms."

Daisy looked at me strangely. "Oh my God, do yachts run on worms?" she cried. "That is so barbaric."

Without missing a beat (or even looking at Daisy), Jamie replied, "No, Holly, we're not going fishing."

"We're going out on a yacht?" I asked, feeling stupid. I hadn't been on a boat since a whale-watching field trip in the fifth grade.

"Not just any yacht," Daisy said. "Christos Oradon's yacht."

"The Greek shipping magnate?" It astonishes me how many gazillionaires know each other. Maybe there's some kind of social club we normals aren't allowed to know about.

"Yep," she said. "We dated when I was like fifteen, but that was forever ago. We're cool as friends now."

Christos Oradon, if I wasn't mistaken, was thirty-three and twice-divorced. Which meant that the then fifteen-year-old Daisy had dated a twenty-nine-year-old man who owned his own chain of islands. Faith was clearly a top-notch parent.

"But don't put that in the book," she added.

Of course not, I thought. The parents of her fans would be outraged.

"Yeah, people don't really like it when celebs date foreigners."

Sure, because that was the only thing wrong with that statement. And since when was dating a foreigner a taboo subject? I could name literally dozens of A-list couples from opposite sides of the world. I couldn't imagine where Daisy was getting her erroneous information about public perception, but it did explain a lot of her actions. "So Christos was okay with your no-sex thing?" I asked, looking down at Daisy's purity ring. I figured I already knew the answer, but I had to ask.

"I want you to tell the world that sex is meaningless without commitment," she answered, tapping the metal of her ring. "My parents have always said I should make my own decisions in life, but I'm a big supporter of their work with abstinence programs."

"Really . . ." I mused, trying to formulate an opinion on her words.

"Not really." Daisy snorted. "I'm a total nympho, I just know better than to get caught."

Axel leaned in to my ear. "Sugar, this bitch could show you some things."

"Awww," Daisy responded, starting to skip up the walkway. "You're so sweet."

I would love to tell you that I enjoyed my first yachting experience, but I was so far into my own head that I barely paid attention to where we were. We could have been spectators at the Space Olympics and I might not have noticed. As I sprawled out on a deck chair that cost more than my entire wardrobe, I heard Sharla loudly whooping from the stern of the boat and Daisy call out, "Axel, make out with me for a little while!" On a normal Saturday, I would have been very interested to watch how a flamboyantly gay man makes out with the world's girliest girl, but I didn't have the mental bandwidth just then. The yacht was also blindingly white and shiny; even with sunglasses on, looking at it was like staring into a supernova. I had a headache inside the first ten minutes.

Christos approached me, in all of his baby-oiled, bronzy goodness, and offered me a glass of champagne. "You like the champagne?" he asked. "My family own the company."

"I'm sure they do," I replied, taking the glass. I'll admit, I was slightly amused by his bastardized English. Especially since I guessed he'd learned the language long enough ago that he should have mastered it by now, but no one had wanted to correct the world's youngest trillionaire.

"Daisy say you print book about her life?" he asked, leaning back and striking a weird, greasy, Adonis-like pose. "Must be I am whole chapter to myself. Very much we were in love. I buy her racehorse."

I stared at him, trying to decipher if he meant he had bought her a racehorse, or if he had purchased one from her. But I doubted he would try to impress me with the latter, so I chose to go with the gift theory. The most expensive present a man had ever given me was a hundred-dollar Zales necklace. I'd never even gotten flowers that didn't come from the grocery store.

"Daisy doesn't like to kiss and tell," I replied. "She wants to keep those memories just for herself." Even with my limited exposure to Daisy, I knew this was a total lie. I wasn't convinced she could have a thought without saying it out loud.

"Oh," Christos responded, looking a little puzzled. I'm certain he was trying to decide if he was flattered or disappointed. "I understand. I no tell the press about the many mothers of my children."

I made a mental note to ask Axel later to properly quantify the mothers and children. This guy was more fun than I'd had in weeks. "That's very noble of you," I said.

He nodded toward the galley, where Sharla was drinking some frozen concoction right out of a blender. That girl could really drink. "We have many foods for you to enjoy. Whatever the baby need to be happy, my chef make."

Yes, my imaginary baby with my imaginary lover. I was also a little disturbed that he thought I was pregnant and had no qualms about offering me champagne. I wondered if Dom Pérignon was a pregnancy craving of his many baby mamas. "I'm fine, thanks."

At that moment, Daisy came stomping up from the galley, Jameson following quickly on her heels. I noticed she was carrying the oversize Mountain Dew cup again. Didn't that conflict with her no-sugar policy?

"But I *want* to *go* to *Havana*. Christos says we can be there in four hours. And everybody says they have the best clubs in the world!"

"We are not going to a Communist country, and that's final! If anyone gets a picture of you—"

"And who's gonna take a picture?" Daisy asked, taunting him. "Don't Communists think cameras steal your soul?"

"Cubans aren't tribal African pygmies, you fucking idiot," Jamie roared in her face. Though I'd witnessed his wrath on a number of occasions, it was nothing compared to this. The agent's eyes were as close to murderous as I'd yet seen, and his fists were clenched at his sides. If Daisy had been an eighteen-year-old guy, I bet Jamie would have slugged her.

The party atmosphere of the boat ground to a halt and everyone drifted toward the argument.

"You treat me like I'm a stupid baby," Daisy screamed back, tears springing to her eyes. "You tell me what to say, what to wear, what projects I should and shouldn't take, and I'm sick of it!"

"I tell you what to do because that's my job," he yelled back. "You pay me to keep the work coming and keep your parents' grubby little fingers off your money. Which I've managed to do quite well these last ten years, no thanks to you and your pea brain."

Daisy shoved Jameson as hard as she could, but the effect was a little like a marshmallow hitting a wall. "You all act like you made me," she spat back in a singsong tone. "But I'm the one keeping all of you in your fancy Bentleys and Alfa Romeos. You'd be a damn window washer without me!"

Hearing this, Jamie barked with laughter, throwing his head back. "Yeah, your lovely singing voice and unparalleled acting ability have kept us all employed. We'd be lost without you," he continued. "You know what, you dumb little bitch, go ahead and find a way to weasel out of our contract. Hire Faith to represent you. That way you'll be broke and addicted to crack by twenty-one."

For the second time, the mention of Faith seemed to be Daisy's dividing line. She yanked the top off the Mountain Dew cup and threw the liquid in Jamie's face. He immediately yelped in pain and doubled over, covering his eyes with his hands.

Sharla dashed over and grabbed Jamie, pulling him back toward the galley. "We need to rinse out his eyes with water," she cried. Axel and one of the bodyguards quickly joined her, half-dragging, half-carrying Jamie down the stairs. Even when they disappeared from sight, I could still hear him sobbing in pain.

Daisy, on the other hand, didn't look the slightest bit upset. She tossed the empty cup at her other bodyguard and waved him away. "I'm going to lay out for a little while," she said, yawning.

As she headed to the front of the yacht, I was again left alone with Christos. "Is Mountain Dew corrosive or something?" I couldn't figure out if Jamie was actually hurt or if he was just being melodramatic. I thought it would be kind of awesome if he turned out to have Munchausen syndrome or acute hypochondria.

"What you mean?" Christos asked me, confused. His reaction didn't immediately raise any red flags for me, as I got the feeling that he was confused by a great many things.

"I mean, why's he crying over Mountain Dew in his eyes?"

Christos looked at me like I was simple. I recognized the look because I'd been giving it to him all afternoon. "Mountain Dew? You think there was soda pop in the cup?"

"Yes . . ." I said. Daisy carried that thing around like a baby blanket. Maybe it was her one real vice (next to sex, of course), and in her infinite anorexic wisdom she didn't recognize it as sugar.

Christos started to laugh. "Oh, no, Holly . . . there is no soda in the cup. . . ." He chuckled so hard he had to bend over a little. "Daisy like the vodka."

I stared back at him, sure he was mistaken. "Vodka?"

The greasy Greek continued to laugh heartily. "Yes." He leaned over and ruffled my hair, and I reached up and swatted his hand away before I could stop myself. "Daisy almost always drunk off her butt. You can't tell?"

I flashed back to the night at the club, when I'd wondered about the propriety of her presence in a twenty-one-and-over establishment. Compared with the inebriated messes that were Sharla and Axel, Daisy really had seemed perfectly sober to me. Either I was more of a prude than I thought or Daisy was just so desensitized to alcohol that a boatload of vodka barely altered her at all.

Christos finally stopped laughing and wiped the tears away from his eyes. He squinted off toward the water, then looked back at me. "So what you think? Jamie let us go to Cuba or no?"

CHAPTER 8

It's true that not many people my age have employees, and I've seen plenty of celebs abuse their assistants and stylists. But I could never do that. My mom always made sure I knew how hard my team was working and how we're all in this together. So when they need something, if it's money or a recommendation or even just a sympathetic ear, I make sure I'm always available. I want my team to enjoy the time we spend together. They're some of my favorite people and the only ones I want along on this crazy adventure.

I have a great life because of these folks, so I think it's important that I give them great lives, too!

We didn't go to Havana. I'll admit, I was half-relieved, half-disappointed. I was curious to see what the fuss was all about. There was something exciting about sneaking into the harbor of a so-called illicit nation and then back out again with no one being the wiser. I felt like one of the femmes fatales from James Bond.

Despite the copious amounts of water Sharla and Axel poured into Jamie's eyes, he was still in a lot of pain, and they worried he might have burned his corneas. So we turned the boat around and went back to dock, with Daisy crying alone in the corner about how no one ever thought about her feelings. She screamed that no one really cared what she wanted, and I have to say, she was probably right. But not in the way she thought.

This pampered, spoiled little princess truly believed that she was getting the raw end of the deal. She was so out of touch with reality she refused to see that the entire world rearranged schedules, dates, and lifestyles to give her what she wanted. Or thought she wanted. But because she didn't recognize—or couldn't be bothered to notice—any of these massive efforts, she made those same people hate her. So ultimately, I doubt they really did care. And that was entirely her fault.

When we arrived back in Miami, the ever-silent bodyguards (I never did learn their names) escorted Daisy to the hotel, while Sharla, Axel, and I took Jamie to the Mount Sinai Medical Center emergency room. I thought Jamie's status would get us in faster, but we still had to wait nearly two hours alongside surfing accidents and raging cases of the flu. By the time Jamie was released with a bottle of eye drops and fugly-looking blue-blockers, it was almost midnight.

The four of us slumped into a cab, and I assumed everyone else was as tired as I was. Jamie started snoring even as we pulled away from the ER. But as I sat in the front seat, Axel leaned forward and tapped me on the shoulder.

"I heard a rumor about an underground club at the Port," he whispered. "You wanna come with?"

I turned back and saw Sharla nodding in encouragement. I didn't know what an underground club was, but it sounded like one of my worst nightmares. "I think I'm going to go to sleep, but thanks."

"Just because you wear old lady shoes doesn't mean you can't dance like an idiot."

"Next time. I promise." It was a lie, but when would there be a next time? I thought Axel and Sharla were fantastic, but I held no illusion that they'd want to hang out with me back in our real lives.

"Fine." I waited for Axel to lean back into his seat, but he tapped me on the shoulder again. "But you do wear old lady shoes. Just saying."

"Got it."

Now it was Sharla's turn to lean forward. "Does this mean we're going shoe shopping?"

It wasn't until I fell into bed at twelve-forty-five that I thought to check my messages. I was still waiting for parental fallout from the fake baby announcement. Barely able to keep my eyes open, I dialed my voice mail.

"Hey, Holly. This is Vaughn. Some of the show's crew is headed out to this amazing restaurant tonight and I wondered if you wanted to tag along. Give me a call back."

I moved to erase the message, but stopped myself at the last second. Instead, I pressed 9 to save it. Though I felt weak doing it, I wanted to hear his sexy growl on loop. So I saved it, pledging to never tell anyone.

Then I fell asleep.

At 10:40 the next morning, the room phone rang. I struggled to open my eyes, but mostly failed and had to find the receiver by blindly smacking my way across the nightstand. I finally answered it, hoping in vain that it would be Vaughn.

"Good morning, Sleeping . . . um . . . Lady," Minka said.

Why did this woman have to ruin all my days within seconds of my waking up?

"Morning, Minka, what can I do for you?" I rolled over and finally managed to pry my eyes open and check the time.

"Well, I was wondering if you were planning to stay longer than the rest of your party," she replied, her tone again laced with acid. "We expected you would be checking out today."

"Oh . . . okay."

I scrambled out of the bed in panic. We were leaving today? No one had bothered to tell me that. Of course, they rarely told me anything, but I would have thought someone might mention having to take a cross-country flight today. I dimly remembered Vaughn saying the crew left today, but I didn't know that applied to Daisy and her entourage.

"Then, yes, I'm leaving, too, I guess," I replied, angry that she was catching me so thoroughly off guard.

"Checkout is in twenty minutes," she told me dubiously. "You clearly just woke up. Are you *sure* you'll be able to vacate the suite by then?"

"As sure as I am that you'd weep with joy if I fail," I shot back. I'd been a slob while staying at the Fontainebleau. My clothes were strewn across every piece of furniture and I didn't even remember where I'd put my duffel bag. I had no idea how to get ready before I turned into a pumpkin at 11:00 A.M., but I wasn't about to tell her that. "I'll be down in a few minutes."

I dropped the phone, very likely just onto the nightstand and not anywhere near the receiver. At that moment, I couldn't have cared less. Much like the morning of my trip out here, I raced through the rooms, grabbing anything that looked remotely familiar. Then with armfuls of tank tops, sandals, and toiletries, I found my bag and dumped everything inside.

I made it to the lobby at exactly 10:58, and was chagrined to discover Minka waiting for me, her eyes expectantly glued to her watch. I swear she looked disappointed when she saw me dragging my bag across the marble.

"I'm impressed," Minka said coldly, turning and walking back to the front desk. "I thought I'd have to send the bellhops to help you pack."

"Well, I made it just fine," I said breathlessly, abandoning my bag somewhere near the middle of the floor. I approached her and dropped my purse on the counter. "Where are the others?" I had the forethought not to use Daisy's name in the lobby, recalling all the paparazzi insanity whenever we came or went. I looked around and noticed that the lobby was quieter than it had been over the last few days, and wondered if people had tired of Daisy. I know I was certainly beginning to.

"Oh, the rest of your group checked out hours ago," she said matter-of-factly. "They had an eight A.M. flight back to Los Angeles."

My heart had one of those roller-coaster moments where it dropped into my stomach like a fifty-pound chunk of concrete. "They left?" I asked, now not just breathless but also having chest pains. "They just left and didn't even tell me we had a flight?"

Minka stopped typing into the computer and stared up at me. She looked completely unsympathetic, and perhaps even a little sorry she wasn't already rid of me. "Your name wasn't on the list of boarding passes I printed out for Mr. Lloyd," she told me and smiled tightly. "I assumed you had a later flight."

They wouldn't have just forgotten about me . . . right? Maybe their flight was already fully booked and they had to put me on another one. And maybe they'd just forgotten to tell me about it. They were pretty unreliable people. But I had to have a flight home . . . right? Or was I supposed to book it myself and bill them later?

If I felt nauseous before, it was nothing compared to the near-blackout ripples of consciousness that occurred when Minka handed me the checkout form.

"Will you be paying by credit card?" she asked sweetly.

I looked down at the paper and saw a number that was so large it couldn't possibly have been real. It had to be some sort of a confirmation or registration number. This couldn't be my bill.

"I'm sorry," I choked. "What is this?"

"You do have to *pay* for the room."

"I was a guest of Dai—Mr. Lloyd," I corrected myself quickly. "I am his hired employee."

I put the piece of paper down on the counter and slid it toward Minka, almost afraid to touch it. I had the irrational thought that if I maintained contact, it would somehow burn me. She immediately pushed it right back to me.

"Then you will certainly have to submit the bill to him for reimbursement," she replied cheerfully. "But he didn't say anything to me about paying for your room."

I glanced down at the bill, still unwilling to touch it. I knew that if I did, if I admitted that the hotel suite the size of Rhode Island was my financial responsibility, I was screwed. The total due to the Fontainebleau was $4,800, nearly half of my original retainer fee. And I still didn't have a ticket home, nor had I paid for the rental car I'd only used once. Adding that to the fact that I'd already spent more than two grand of the money on my monthly bills and other expenses, I was now almost back where I'd started. I'd gotten this big job and I was officially nowhere.

I didn't argue with Minka. I knew there was no point. Had I refused to pay the bill, I'm sure she would have delighted in calling the police. I remembered what happened to that famous couple who'd skipped out on a hotel in Santa Barbara. And I wasn't famous; no one would care if I went to jail.

I just took my credit card out of my wallet and numbly handed it over to her. I shouldn't have even had a card with a limit that high, but for once, I was thankful that a lot of banks like to hand out irresponsible lines of credit. And I couldn't give her my debit card because the bill exceeded my daily limit. By a *lot*.

Minka ran the card and then handed me a pen to sign the sales slip. I no longer cared that she was giggling inside at my misery. If she wanted to be the wicked bitch of Miami, I was all for it.

"Is there anything else I can do for you?"

"Yes," I sighed, taking my credit card back and instantly handing her my debit card in exchange. "Can you please book me a ticket home?"

The earliest flight Minka could find was a 5:00 P.M. that stopped in Atlanta for some reason. I spent my entire afternoon trying to call Jameson, but his phone was—of course—off while he was in the air. I knew that they had a direct flight and had landed by the time I made it to Hartsfield-Jackson, but he still didn't answer. I wondered if he was avoiding me. As though I wasn't eventually going to bring this up, even if it involved driving to the house and banging on the front door.

My second flight didn't take off until after 9:00 P.M., and with the time difference, I landed just after 10:00 P.M. Pacific time. I still had no return call from Jamie, and I'd just realized I now had to pay to get my car out of long-term parking, at a bargain price of sixteen dollars a day.

Depressed, I tried to call Camille on my drive home, but Donnie said she was still at a casting session for *STD Island 2: Hot, Wet, and Dangerous* (it wasn't really called *STD Island,* but I'm sure you've guessed I can't say the name). He tried to talk to me with food in his mouth, presumably his favorite Hershey's miniatures, but he gave me the heebie-jeebies even over the phone, so I quickly ended the conversation.

I thought about calling Vaughn, but I knew I shouldn't. He probably thought I'd stood him up yesterday, not to mention that the act of calling him for a pick-me-up at this hour was all-around inappropriate. I barely knew the guy, despite our late-night balcony dinner.

So I drove back to my tiny shack of a studio apartment with the sudden—and unwelcome—realization that nothing had really changed in my life. In the last several days, I'd glimpsed a flashier, more glamorous existence, but it wasn't mine. In most ways, I was grateful for that. God knows I had no interest in spending my days with vapid Hollywood hangers-on . . . but I would have appreciated keeping just a tiny bit of that sheen on my everyday life.

Despite the new job and my new friends, I was still going home—alone—to a neighborhood the local grandmothers liked to call Diablorado Street. By the time I dragged my suitcase up to the second floor, my neighbor's apartment was already dark and I had to accept the fact that I would have to spend the night without my Smitty.

It was all I could do to put on my pajamas and crawl into bed. I was exhausted, but I wasn't really sleepy. I felt defeated, like I'd just wasted weeks of my life on an enterprise that no one would believe, anyway. My last thought before the blessed blackness of sleep was that at that moment, I didn't care so much about being a writer anymore. I'd built it up in my head as this magical profession that made all your dreams come true, but it wasn't magic at all. It was just as harsh and real as anything else in life . . . and I desperately needed to believe that the good would come right along with the bad. I needed to believe it would eventually balance out.

CHAPTER 9

I once read in a tabloid that Harley-Davidson was gifting me the new model of their motorcycle six months before it was shipped to their showrooms. Aside from the fact that I don't even ride motorcycles, I would never expect anything for free. When you see that every girl has the same purse I bought a month ago, you might think I carried it around because I had a sponsorship deal. But that's not true. I love the things I love and I'm happy to pay for them. If my fans like and admire my taste, there's really no better compliment!

"You're going to ask them for the money, right?" Camille asked me the next day.

I was three bites into an enormous chocolate chip cookie and ice cream sandwich, so I shrugged rather than talk with my mouth full. We sat at a little table on the street in Westwood, watching all the lucky rich kids from UCLA go about their business. I had checked my bank account on the way over to make sure that I could still afford to eat my way through Diddy Riese's homemade cookies if I so chose.

"Seriously, I invoice people all the time. Just give Daisy's manager copies of all of your receipts, and include an itemized list. That way he can't claim he 'missed one.'"

I nodded like I was processing information, but I wasn't really listening. I mean, I heard what Cam had to say, but the words just existed as free-form syllables floating through my broken brain.

"Sure," I said confidently, hoping she would mistake it for real understanding. Of course, she didn't.

"Don't just shake your head at me," Camille shot back. "I can see that you're about to turn this into a twenty-pound-weight-gain depression about how your life and career are going nowhere. So stop it now. It's not your fault that Los Angeles is chock-full of morally challenged, worthless jerks who only care about themselves."

I gulped down a mouthful of chocolate chip goodness by way of an answer.

Camille just sighed. "Really, Holly. I'm here for you—you know that. But I'm not going to be a guest at your pity party. Things aren't great, but I bet they're really not as bad as you're acting like they are. Break out your contract, threaten a war of the agents, and get your ass paid."

"Have you seen my agent?"

"No." She shrugged.

"Neither have I in over a year. So I don't think he's going to rush to help me, especially since he already cashed his commission check." I was in full-on pout mode, my lower lip even protruding slightly. This felt like the end of the world, and I didn't want to talk to anyone who wouldn't help pack the bunker and prepare for the coming Apocalypse.

"Okay, little Miss Melodrama . . ." Camille leaned over and used her spoon to swipe some of the ice cream from the center of my sandwich. Greedily, I pulled my bowl away. I needed all of my consolation calories, and she couldn't have them. "You don't need your agent for anything other than his name and job title. Threaten Jamie Lloyd with Gus the Grave Robber and he'll fold. But let him walk all over you now and you'll never see the rest of your commission or any royalties."

Camille was right but I didn't want to hear it. I immediately registered the sense in her words, but I was too far in my funk to really care, so I filed the wisdom away for later use and focused on the board inside the ice cream shop. I couldn't decide if I wanted a sugar or peanut butter cookie next. My only certainty was that I wouldn't leave until my jeans were tight enough to constrict blood flow to my brain.

"And while I'm dispensing unwanted but necessary advice, you should call Vaughn." She gave me her all-business stare-down, which had often silenced even the most wanton whorish reality show contestant. I glared back at her, just to let her know I wasn't intimidated.

"And what would I say?" I asked, burying my face in the all too quickly disappearing ice cream. "I don't even know what that was about. I'm sure he was just being friendly and I was reading too much into it."

At this, Camille finally gave in to her irritation with me and rolled her eyes. "If you insist on acting like a fucking infant, at least go home so that the rest of the world doesn't have to put up with your attitude. No one wants to go to your pity party."

Like a straight-A student reprimanded by her favorite teacher, I instantly felt guilty. It wasn't enough to pull me out of my funk, but I did finally get the message to tone down my theatrics. I stayed silent, but offered her a contrite, if wan, smile.

"All right, then," Camille said, taking a swipe of her own rainbow sherbet. Even when she's being bad, it's in the healthiest possible way. It's revolting. "Another minute and I was going to smack you across the face."

The next morning, I nervously put the finishing touches on my invoice and receipts and drove over to Kinko's to fax them to Jamie. I'd been up all night adding and re-adding the numbers in my bank account, willing them to somehow come out in my favor. This is my particular brand of mental disease; I can wake up at 4:00 A.M. to pee and then spend the next three hours counting how many times I thoughtlessly went out for lunch when I should have had a three-dollar frozen meal.

I got back home around 11:00 A.M., knowing I should actually start to write Daisy's autobiography. I had enough to at least begin, but to be honest, given the Dixson's recent financial shenanigans, I wasn't terribly inclined to do any work. So three seconds inside the door, I was bored out of my mind. I could've turned on the TV and watched one of my two hundred new channels, but the very idea made me feel guilty. Maybe I had been rash ordering cable in the first place; I should've just borrowed some more B-movies from the library and called it a day.

My cell phone rang and I had to force myself not to answer it on the first ring when I saw that the caller was Jamie. Trying to seem sensible (and not at all desperate), I waited until the third ring to pick up.

"Oh, hey, Jamie," I said. As soon as I spoke, my teeth began chattering furiously, and I had to keep my mouth deliberately open to keep them from clanging into the speaker.

"Hols, I just got this invoice you sent over," he said.

Oh, crap. He sure didn't sound like someone about to apologize for his thoughtlessness. "Uh, yeah . . ." I answered, still feigning nonchalance. "Sorry I didn't get that to you yesterday."

"No prob," Jamie replied. "Most people let these things go for so long I forget about the bill to begin with."

I exhaled so deeply I'm pretty sure I lost a couple of pounds. "I just wanted to keep on top of it." I felt a little bolder, but it still took every ounce of my nerve to continue. "But since the next installment of my fee is due on Thursday, you can just write one check if it's easier."

"Awesome," Jamie said quickly. "Can you come out to the house on Thursday to work with Daise? Then we can kill two birds with one stone."

"Absolutely," I replied, now having the opposite problem of trying not to sound too eager. "What time should I be there?"

"Let's say noon," he answered. "And if she's not up by then, the two of you can have a little slumber party."

I shuddered at the thought but said, "Looking forward to it."

"Awesome," Jamie said again, immediately hanging up on me. It had happened so many times now, I wasn't even offended anymore.

Now that things seemed more secure, I should've broken out my laptop and gotten to work. Instead, I took a decadently long, carefree nap. I deserved it. I still had plenty of time to start writing.

On Thursday, I presented myself at the Dixson estate promptly at twelve. Unfortunately, no one was home. The guard looked perplexed as I pulled up to the gate.

"Maybe you were supposed to come by on Saturday?" he asked.

"No," I replied, shaking my head. "I talked to Jamie two days ago. He told me to come to the house today."

The guard shook his head right back at me. "Maybe you heard him wrong. Did he tell you to go to the studio?"

"Um . . . no," I repeated. I knew perfectly well what he'd said. I have the memory of an autistic savant. I can remember whole sections of dialogue from episodes of *Beverly Hills, 90210* I haven't seen since 1993.

"I think that must be it." The guard nodded, like I was simple. "I'm sure Mr. Lloyd told you to go to the studio, and you just forgot. Happens to all of us."

"And what studio would that be?" I asked. With Daisy's random schedule, she could be working on anything from a music video to a Neutrogena commercial to an abstinence PSA. How the hell would I know where she was shooting? L.A. has more soundstages than fake blondes with barely legal boob jobs.

"Sunset and Vine," the guard said. "I know security down there. I'll call and let them know you're coming."

"Thanks."

The guard winked at me. "And don't worry, I won't tell anyone you accidentally came here first."

On my ride down to Hollywood, I tried to let go of my growing irritation with the Dixson entourage. I was being paid to join in this madness, which meant my personal time was irrelevant. I had to accept that inconvenience and frustration were par for the course. Just as I'd successfully brought my blood pressure back down to normal, my phone rang. Zen was not to be found today—it was my mother.

"Hi, Mom." She was the last person I wanted to talk to right now, but I wanted one of her rambling messages even less.

"Holly Ann. Sweetheart." Her tone was measured, even. Slightly disappointed. Which meant I was about to get a lecture. At least it wasn't one of her angry, what-is-wrong-with-you moods. "You're not pregnant, are you?"

"No, Mom," I told her. I nearly sighed into the phone, but caught myself. This wasn't a question of whether or not I'd had a few too many drinks, this was the rest of my life. Though I hated to admit it, she had every right to be concerned. "Again, just the people I'm working for. I guess they needed to say something to the press, though I don't know why they picked that."

There was a pause on the other end of the phone. It was never a good sign when my mother wasn't prepared with another comeback or line of questioning. "Because they weren't thinking of you," she said.

I laughed. "What do you mean?"

"I'm glad you're having fun with your job—Uncle Bob says this Jamie guy is a lot of laughs—but please be careful."

There were a million things I could have said to this, not the least of which was that these are people who either directly or indirectly employ hundreds. They may have been weird and thoughtless, but I highly doubted they would intentionally try to hurt me. "I will be."

"I mean it, Holly," my mom said, sounding less than convinced. "Like I said before, these people are not your friends."

My ego deflated. I didn't try to hide my sigh this time. "I'll be careful, Mom."

"Good. I love you, sweetheart."

"Love you, too, Mom." She had the ability to make me crazier than anyone else in the world, but I really did love her. Even when she managed to destroy my self-confidence in a two-minute phone call.

By the time I reached the studio at Sunset and Vine, the temperature gauge on my car was dangerously close to the red. In anyone else's car, this might be a sign of impending doom, but my rust bucket has about a ninety-minute drive time limit and I had just traveled from one end of the city to the other . . . and back again.

Daisy's guard was as good as his word, and the gate security gave me a day pass and politely pointed me in the direction of the visitor parking lot. It was a cute little studio, with several soundstages and warehouses, made up to look like a tree-lined small town. The sidewalks were lined with benches, and there was a small commissary with a window for takeout and ice cream.

Had I not been in quite such a mood, I'm sure I would have been charmed by the studio. After all, I didn't get to spend a lot of time in places like this. Camille's "reality" programs were always shot during the off-season at some exotic resort hotel, and most of my other friends never invited anyone to visit them on set. As one told me when justifying his refusal to bring his mother to the major TV show he was lighting, "Everybody works. Production is a tough game. I don't want my electricians chatting up my mom and accidentally starting a fire." After hearing that, I made the decision never to ask. So this should have been more exciting.

In front of the commissary, I recognized a couple of tween stars doing stunts with their skateboards. I wasn't sure what show they were from, but I knew my little cousin had their poster plastered to her bedroom wall. It instantly struck me as odd that these kids, who could buy and sell me a million times over, were actually playing out in the street. They were acting like real live, normal kids. It was like watching chimps do long division.

Because the lot was relatively tiny, it took me less than five minutes to find Stage 3. I knew I was in the right place when I spotted Axel smoking up a storm in front of a trailer. He spotted me and blew a kiss.

"Since when do you smoke?" I asked, giving him a hug.

"Ugh, since I gained two pounds," he replied. "I looked in the mirror the other day and I'm *totally* getting a tummy." He reached out and patted my stomach. "You know what I'm talking about."

"I'm not really pregnant, remember?"

Axel eyed me strangely. "Of course I remember. I'm the one who made it up."

Okay, so he was just calling me fat. Whatever. I was growing impervious to their digs about my body. "Do you know if I'm supposed to work with Daisy today? Jamie told me to go to the house, but then the guard told me everyone was here."

Axel shrugged. "I don't know . . . but I would be careful around Daisy Mae if I were you. Kitty has her claws out today."

Perfect. "Do you know where she is?"

Axel nodded toward the enormous, hangar-like stage in front of us. "She has her own little bungalow behind the stage. Last time I saw her, she was crying about how Steve Jobs wouldn't give her the newest version of the iPhone."

"I thought that didn't come out until fall." I'm not really a techie, but I've wanted—and been unable to afford—the iPhone since it was first released. So every year I lie and tell myself I'll get the next model. Some year I'm bound to be right.

"It doesn't." Axel rolled his eyes. "I love the bitch, but sometimes she gets out of control."

Sometimes? From where I stood, it looked more and more like Daisy lived in an entirely alternate universe from the rest of us. "I suppose I should go see her."

At this, Axel laughed. "Good luck, sweetheart. When you're done, I have a bottle of Jack in my trailer—you might need it."

I could hear the exaggerated sobbing before I reached the front door of the bungalow. It didn't even sound exactly like crying; it was more like a dying animal's caterwauling.

"I hate you, I hate you, I hate you," Daisy screamed. Just as I put my hand up to knock, I heard something shatter. I thought about turning around and walking away, but my curiosity got the better of me. I couldn't wait to witness Daisy's freak-out, so I went ahead and knocked.

"Come in," responded a voice that was altogether too calm for the scene playing out inside the room.

I slowly opened the door and peered in. Daisy was balled up in an armchair, sobbing hysterically, the shards of what had once been a coffee mug (and its contents) in pieces on the floor. My heart skipped a beat as I realized that the two men with her were the show's executives—and one of them was Vaughn. He winked, nodding for me to enter.

"The crew will be back from lunch in forty minutes, and they have nothing left to shoot today but your scenes," he told her, maintaining an even temper.

"Now, we have calls in to Apple headquarters, but this will take longer than a day to resolve," the other man added. It sounded like he was talking to a three-year-old; then again, Daisy was behaving like one. "But I promise you, we'll let you know as soon as we hear anything."

This earned a new wail of despair from Daisy. "Call my daddy. He played golf with Steve Jobs a few times when I was a kid. Tell him he *needs* me. When the paparazzi take pictures of me with the phone, everybody's gonna want one!"

The unnamed exec snickered, throwing a look to Vaughn. "Like Apple needs help selling those things."

I've often thought that having TiVo in everyday life would be useful. We've all had that moment when we wish we could hop back eight seconds and say something other than the rampant stupidity that came flying out of our mouths. This was one of those personal TiVo moments; the instant the words escaped from the man's lips, the consequences were apparent. Vaughn's face immediately went white, and it took Daisy about two seconds to screech, "*WHAT* did you say to me?"

She leapt out of her chair and somehow managed to avoid slivers of coffee mug in her bare feet. Daisy barreled toward the door, running right past me without even acknowledging my presence. "You are fired, you stupid son of a bitch," she shouted venomously. "John, you're the only one I'll deal with. This asshole is *done*."

Daisy flew through the door and slammed it shut, leaving me alone with the two men.

"Derek, this is Holly. She's writing Daisy's autobiography."

Despite having just been fired, Derek waved to me genially. "Hello, Holly."

"If this is a bad time . . ." It didn't matter if they wanted me to leave, I clearly wasn't going to get any work done with her today.

"Oh no," Derek said, shaking his head. "Daisy fires me at least once a month. Luckily, she really doesn't know or care who most of the producers are, so she'll forget in a couple of days."

I grinned at Vaughn. "I see she still thinks your name is John. I tried to correct her in Miami, I swear."

Vaughn broke into a wide smile, rolling his eyes at me. "You are so wasting your breath, but I do appreciate it."

The other man looked back and forth between the two of us, as though trying to figure something out. He finally gave up and started for the door. "I've got calls to make. I'll see you on the stage."

"Um . . . does she really not know that Steve Jobs has been dead for, like, years?" I asked.

"Oh, God, no." Derek laughed. "We don't let her anywhere near the news. Gossip sites are fine, but real-life concerns. . . . It's better for everyone if we control her access to the outside world."

The exec continued to chuckle as he walked outside. And though I know it was stupid, I got nervous the instant Vaughn and I were alone together. We were still across the room from each other, but even this proximity to him was making me a little hot and sweaty. I hadn't talked to him since Miami, and I still didn't know if his interest in me was merely friendly or something more. It sure felt like something more.

He unclipped a walkie-talkie from his belt. "I suppose I should call a PA to come clean this up." He sighed. Vaughn looked around the cute little room that was bigger and nicer than my entire apartment. But instead of calling for help, he walked over and sank into the couch. "Eh, it can wait a few minutes. Come sit with me for a little while."

"Are you sure Daisy's not coming back?" I asked, eyeing the door. I didn't think she'd appreciate finding us just hanging out in her dressing room. If that was what this cool little house could be called.

Vaughn made a face and waved me over. "When Daisy's in this mood, she goes to find her mother. She won't be back until she's absolutely certain she's ruined our production day and someone else has cleaned up her mess."

Feeling my temperature rise with every step I took toward Vaughn, I made my way to the couch and took a seat. It wasn't very wide, but I made sure I was as far from him as humanly possible.

I felt more in control of myself with that couple inches of space between us.

"Where is Faith?" I asked. "Does she have her own bungalow?"

"No, but she does have an office in the main building," he told me. "Faith may not be that bright, but she is a hard worker."

I suddenly recalled Jameson's multiple tirades about Faith. "That's not what Jamie thinks."

Vaughn shrugged. "That attitude's not about work. Jamie and Faith had a . . . less than professional relationship, once upon a time."

Gross. I like to think of myself as fairly enlightened, but can't any of these people keep it in their pants? "Oh man," I groaned. "I didn't need to hear that. Especially now that Jamie's sleeping with Daisy."

My revelation caused Vaughn to sit up with a start. "I'm sorry, what did you say?"

"He came out of her bedroom one morning in Miami," I answered honestly. "I know, it's disgusting."

Vaughn suddenly looked relieved, exhaling deeply. "Okay, I'm sorry, I misunderstood you. I thought you were saying they were . . . you know . . . sleeping together, minus the actual sleeping."

I stared back at Vaughn, feeling lost. "He was in her bedroom. Presumably all night. You really think they were just sleeping?"

He offered me one of his wry, wicked little grins and ruffled my hair affectionately. "I know it sounds bizarre. It is bizarre, really. But that girl is majorly screwed up. She really can't sleep alone. And believe me, if she were involved with Jamie, we'd all know about it. Daisy can't keep her mouth shut. It's been a real challenge keeping her behavior out of the press."

I didn't care how much they were paying me, I was never getting into bed with Daisy. Not without Cipro and a hazmat suit. "But really, Jamie and Faith?" I figured I didn't need to, but I asked, "Isn't she married?"

"God, you're cute," he said, laughing (although I tried not to react, I know I must have blushed). "Acting like we live in a society of morals instead of this empty celluloid wonderland."

"Forgive me for believing in the sanctity of marriage," I replied, sticking out my tongue.

"I don't think fire-and-brimstone Deacon minds," Vaughn said. "In fact, I'm sure he's completely happy to have someone else deal with his wife."

"Oh, the book I could write if I could actually tell the truth." We'd done almost no work at all yet, and already I had enough to publicly crucify Daisy Mae Dixson and her entire, messed-up entourage.

"Except that you've signed an ironclad nondisclosure agreement and if one word got leaked to the press, you'd be sued within an inch of your life. It's a powerful incentive to stay quiet."

Not that the Dixsons or Jamie had been astute enough to recognize this when they hired me, but they'd never have to worry about me turning on them in the press, no matter how many lies they told about me. As revolting as I found this life of Daisy's, it was hers to lead. But that didn't mean I understood it.

"This town," I said, shaking my head. I laughed a little, but it wasn't because I found any of this funny. Quite the opposite. My miserable mood suddenly returned with a vengeance, and I felt a little hopeless. "I don't know why we all live here. It's not real. It's not . . ."

"It's not life," Vaughn finished quietly. "It's a blockbuster movie. All flash and drama, and very little substance." We both mulled this over quietly for a few seconds before he added, "You know what I don't understand? Why does anyone live here if they're not in the entertainment industry? I mean, we're trapped here by our ambitions, but why the hell does L.A. have a single plumber or mechanic?"

I considered this for a moment. "Because they have this awesome, groundbreaking script that would be just perfect for Channing Tatum?"

This caused both of us to break into a fit of giggles that lasted far longer than it should have. It was the first time I'd really heard Vaughn laugh, and it was quite endearing. His laugh was loud, deep, and sounded one hundred percent sincere. I was really going to have to start searching for things to dislike about him.

When we finally calmed down, he sighed in frustration and reluctantly picked up the walkie-talkie. "I suppose I've avoided my job long enough."

"I'm sorry to distract you." I wasn't sorry. Not even a little bit.

Vaughn shook his head, giving me another dazzling, genuine smile. "Please. This is the best conversation I've had in months."

"So our marathon confab in Miami wasn't up to snuff? I apologize, I'll have to brush up on my late-night talking points."

At this, Vaughn blushed and I knew for certain that he wasn't just being friendly. My heart gave a great big thump in my chest. "Let me rephrase. I meant that this conversation with you—in the larger sense—was more fun than with anyone I've talked to in months."

I knew what he'd meant the first time. "All right, then."

"Hey," Vaughn said, touching my knee briefly as he stood up, "I was going to call you. What are you doing tomorrow night?"

Wearing sweatpants and a ratty T-shirt while eating ice cream from the container and watching a terrible MTV reality show? "I don't think I have anything planned," I replied. "Why?"

"There's a new female action comedy screening over at the Fox lot, if you're interested. I'm allowed a plus-one."

"That sounds great." Not that I planned to turn down any invitation from Vaughn (the first normal person to ask me out in forever), but I was relieved it was an action comedy. Some guys seem to think women want to watch drippy romances on dates. Personally, I'd rather watch a guy get his arm blown off than see two people canoodle in Central Park with autumn leaves falling everywhere, hinting at the lovers' inevitable demise.

"Awesome. I'll call ahead and give them your name. Just meet me on the lot around six-thirty." Then someone called for him over the walkie, and Vaughn instantly shifted into work mode. "Copy that, on my way," he responded. He patted me on the shoulder as he headed toward the door, saying, "See you tomorrow night."

So . . . I was going with him to a screening but he wasn't picking me up. *Was* this a date or just two friends hanging out? I truly hated elementary school, but at that moment, I would've loved a little piece of paper with one question and three possible answers. *Do you like me—yes, no, or maybe?*

CHAPTER 10

My mom really is, and always has been, my best friend. She was young when she had me, so we've always had a bond that was closer than your average mom and daughter. But this isn't to say that she lets me get away with everything. Faith Dixson knows me better than anyone else, and she's the first one to call me out when I'm doing wrong. I feel it's made me a stronger, better person, and if I can be half the woman my mom is, I'll be able to take over the world!

After leaving the bungalow, I asked for directions and made my way to Faith's office, where I found a surprisingly happy Daisy playing a game on her apparently outdated iPhone.

"You're not mad anymore?" I asked, wondering if she had perhaps already forgotten and I was going to be labeled an idiot for bringing it up again.

"Whatevs." Daisy shrugged, her eyes trained on the screen. "Even if that dumb-ass producer can't fix things, my daddy will. He always does."

From her desk, I saw Faith silently make a sour face. Apparently, she didn't share the same opinion of her husband. I suddenly realized just how off I'd been in my initial assessment of this family. As lovely and perfect as they seemed from the outside, in reality they had the market cornered on dysfunction.

"So do you want to work a little bit today?" We needed to work *a lot,* but I didn't want to scare her off.

Daisy sighed, dropping her iPhone to the desk with a thud. "Do we have to?" she whined.

Before I had to invent something diplomatic to say, Faith spoke up. "Sweetheart, your birthday's in three months. If you want Holly to have the book finished in time, you're going to have to help her."

"But I'm tired and I've got three scenes left to shoot," Daisy fired back, pouting. "Can't you work with her today?"

Honestly, it wasn't a bad idea. I did have pages full of notes and questions for Faith, and I hoped I could get more thorough information from her than from her daughter.

"Does that mean you'll go and finish your work on set?" Faith replied.

At this, Daisy sighed dramatically. "All right, Mama." She stood up and stretched, then yawned. "But then I only have one more day this week, right?"

"That's right." Faith smiled. "Now you go on and apologize to the crew for being a touch late. Tell them I have a coffee cart coming at four o'clock."

"'Kay, Mama," Daisy said happily, almost skipping out of the office. If I hadn't been there to see an eighteen-year-old skipping, I wouldn't have believed it. "See ya later, Holly!"

As soon as Daisy was gone, Faith clucked under her breath. "That child . . . she works so hard."

I wondered where Faith got her work ethic. And how many coffee and sweet treat trucks it took to keep the crew from stringing Daisy up with the lights.

"I don't know how much help I can be"—Faith shrugged—"but I'll tell you anything I know."

"Then let's get started," I answered as brightly as I could manage.

The amount of information Faith was able to provide over the next three hours was nothing short of staggering. Everything I'd tried to poke and prod out of Daisy (and with no success, I might add) came freely flowing out of her mother. She also turned out to be a very sweet, if somewhat dim-witted and trusting, person. By the close of our afternoon, I realized that Faith really did think Daisy was hardworking and well intentioned. I worried for her.

At a little after four, we walked by Stage 3 so Faith could check that the coffee cart had arrived. A line of crew members wound from the truck window all the way back onto the stage. We'd been standing there for about three seconds when a very young guy with a CIA-looking earpiece rushed over and deposited drinks in both of our hands. I looked up at Faith in surprise, especially since mine was clearly an ice-blended mocha (the only kind of coffee I like has been bludgeoned to death by chocolate and whipped cream—but how could she know that?).

"How did you do that?" I asked, not sure if I was impressed or disturbed.

Faith shrugged. "You seem like the type of person who's into dairy and chocolate."

I stared at her for a second, recognizing the insult but not quite understanding it. "Um . . . you mean, human?" I took a long sip from the mocha; it was obscenely good.

As we drifted back toward the stage entrance, Faith gave me a sweet smile and laughed. "We haven't had dairy in years. You know, the human body wasn't designed for cow's milk."

I couldn't help but survey Faith's slight frame. In my opinion, she needed about a month's worth of dairy and a couple hundred pounds of steak. But I couldn't exactly say that to my employer. "Speak for yourself, Faith. If I gave up milk and chocolate, I'd lose the will to live inside a week."

From the look on Faith's face, I recognized that she was about to carry this over into a food indoctrination, and I knew that would lead to nothing good. I needed to change the subject. Luckily, just then I caught sight of Daisy's "living room." The one that matched the Dixsons' almost exactly.

"I have a question: Is there a reason you have so much of the same furniture as on the set?"

Faith glanced through to the fake living room and laughed. "Oh, that? It's because Benji's an interior design genius. I swear, that man should be an interior decorator to the stars. My girlfriends keep trying to hire him to redo their houses, but he claims he's happy with his job."

"And what is his job?" I asked. I knew the names of about five crew positions, and most of those were courtesy of close friends who have those very jobs.

"He's the show's production designer," she told me, as though it explained exactly what he did. It didn't. I still had little idea of this man's job description other than furniture buyer. I also wondered why she referred to a grown man as Benji.

Just as I was about to ask, Faith's phone rang. She glanced down and saw it was Jamie, then rolled her eyes and pressed ignore. Suddenly my questions about their affair were ignited. "You aren't going to answer that?" I asked.

"If he needs something, he can leave a message," Faith replied, her tone curt. She steered us back toward the offices.

I shouldn't ask. I knew it wasn't my place. But damn if I wasn't curious. "Is it true you were . . . *involved* with him?"

"It's not that much of a secret," she said, shrugging.

I lived in a culture where it didn't need to be a secret that a married, publicly Christian woman cheated on her husband. "Can I ask . . . why him? You meet handsome, talented men every day. . . . Pick one of those dumb, shirtless guys from that HBO show."

"Jamie was always just so sweet to me," she said. "I swear, no one has ever treated me so well before."

That poor woman, I thought. "Really?" I couldn't help asking. "He always seems so . . . brusque."

Faith looked up at me in confusion. It took me a moment to realize that she didn't know what the word meant.

"Umm, abrupt. He's always so abrupt with everything."

"Oh," Faith drawled. "That's just his way. He's a very busy man. But he has a good heart."

It's funny, I'd drawn the conclusion that Jamie was lacking that organ entirely. "Then why did your relationship end?" We were really off the topic of the book at this point, but Faith's life was far more interesting than Daisy's. At least, the parts of Daisy's life I was allowed to talk about. Plus, it was nice to connect with Faith on another level. It made me feel a little less like any old paid employee.

Faith looked away from me, and I thought she was about to cry. But she just shook her head and shrugged, her eyes dry. "I don't remember exactly. One day we were crazy in love and the next. . . . Well, you know how these things go."

I scanned my brain for a similar experience in my own life, but I couldn't find one. I'm not sure I'd ever been "crazy in love" in my entire twenty-five years. "Of course," I lied, too embarrassed to tell her the truth.

"I wish I was as strong as you," Faith said. "Or as smart. You've got that amazing brain, people see it as soon as they meet you. Pretty's all I've ever been, and I'm getting right up on my expiration date. At least Daisy has all that talent. I've got nothing but my face."

I'd seen Daisy's show; she didn't have *that* much talent. Apparently Faith had never learned the power of her beauty, and she was right about one thing—she was approaching an age where that revelation was moot. But if she really was as hard a worker as Vaughn claimed, surely she could see the value in that? I was ashamed of whatever person/people were responsible for her belief that her self-worth began with her face and ended in her silicone double-Ds.

We finally reached the offices and found Daisy was out front talking to a couple of other kids her age. As they were all smeared with ridiculous amounts of unnecessary makeup, I figured they must be her fellow actors. If you can call what they were doing acting. Faith and I were going to continue on when Daisy reached out and yanked me into her little group.

"Oh my God, this is Holly, the writer I've been telling you about," she gushed, hugging me tightly. I still didn't understand what about our limited relationship caused her to think we were in any way close, but I wasn't going to argue with something that made my job easier. "It is so awesome writing an autobiography."

Faith grinned at me, offering a reassuring thumbs-up.

"Hi," I said meekly, waving to the gaggle of teenagers who were clearly in Daisy's thrall.

"I'm telling you, if you work really hard, one day maybe you'll get to write your own autobiography," she said. "I mean, probably not, but why not reach for the stars!"

I told myself that when I got home that night, I would finally start writing. Given the limited brainpower of my subject, I figured it couldn't be altogether difficult to channel her folksy/ignorant persona. But as the minutes (and then hours) ticked away, I found myself listening to the same stretch of digital tape over and over again, with no idea what to put on the page. I had no starting point, no beginning to my story. I had only fragments of a teenager's warped life, most of which I couldn't even use. This was supposed to be a book about America's Sweetheart, but that persona was completely an act. If I was supposed to channel the fake Daisy, I hadn't seen enough of her to know the voice. I was writing about someone I had never met.

The sky outside my window was already starting to lighten when I finally gave up. I had been hunched over my laptop on my ancient couch with only two of its original springs, and when I straightened up, I heard (and felt) a number of muscles attempt to snap back into place. A lot of writers have aspirations like Oscars and Pulitzers; at this point, I was bucking for an IKEA desk and an apartment big enough to hold it.

It wasn't until I was brushing my teeth that I realized I hadn't seen Jamie at all. Which meant I hadn't gotten paid. And if someone demanded to see pages between now and the next check, I was screwed. As for my current money situation, I was pretty sure I still had enough to pay my rent the following Monday, but it would be tight. And forget about any trips to the grocery store until the Dixsons' check cleared. They now owed me $16,500 and I was worried about $80 worth of groceries. I wasn't scheduled to see Daisy that day, but I knew I'd have to do something. I couldn't wait indefinitely for that check.

But I had to get it without ever letting them know just how dire the situation was. I figured it was unwise to tell my bread-and-butter (and only) client that I'd starve without their business. Then they'd have me over a barrel. Well, *even more* over a barrel.

Jamie didn't answer his cell phone all day. I called three times, leaving two messages. I wanted to spend all day hitting redial on my cell, but I also didn't want him to call the police and accuse me of stalking. His ego was enough out of whack that I was sure he'd believe just that.

It then occurred to me to call Faith, but I didn't have her number. In fact, I didn't have anyone's number but Jamie's. This struck me as odd, considering that I'd just spent a week practically living with these people, but I guess privacy is paramount in this industry. God knows how many little girls would die to have Daisy's cell phone number.

By the afternoon, I remembered that I did have one more, very important, number—Vaughn's. I immediately called him and, after assuring him I wasn't canceling our plans (little did he know I would've found a way to get there with a broken back), was given Faith's contact info. Which turned out to be no help at all.

"Ohhhh," she drawled. "Well, shucks, I don't know anything about payments, Holly."

First of all, who says *shucks*? Last I'd checked, the calendar had progressed well beyond 1955. And not even real 1955, but the parallel universe years chronicled in *Father Knows Best*. Second, how could Faith not know anything about their money? I know every detail about every damn cent in my checking account and, usually, in my change bucket. I couldn't fathom getting to a point where I didn't have a clue how much money was going in or out.

"Do you happen to know where Jamie is, then?" I asked, forcing a polite tone I definitely didn't feel.

"Hmmmm . . ." she mused, taking a maddeningly long pause to think about it. "He and Deacon might be golfing with Jeff today."

Never mind that I didn't have a clue who Jeff might be. What the hell was Jamie doing golfing with his ex-lover's husband? I had already given up trying to understand this family dynamic, but it really got weirder by the day.

"Jeff?" I asked, not really caring but figuring that Faith wanted me to guess.

"Jeff King, the head of Idol Pictures. He's a longtime family friend."

Okay . . . I had never heard of either the man or the company. But then, every actor and writer has their own "production company" (also known as a scam to get more money on the back end), so it wasn't that surprising.

"He wants to fund the movie De Niro has in mind for Daisy," Faith said. "So far he's not willing to go over forty mil, but I think Jamie and Deacon can talk him to seventy. We want to keep it small, after all. The Academy loves low-budget movies."

For $70 million, I could start my own country and declare myself the lord and unquestioned master of my subjects. And I could afford to pay those subjects in gold bullion. Jamie was off making a $70 million deal and he couldn't pay me the several thousand he owed me?

"Do you know when he'll be back?" I asked. Using Camille's logic, I decided to bluff. "My, um . . . agent will be really upset if he doesn't get his check this week."

"No idea, sweetheart," she told me. "But I'm sure he'll call you back soon."

"Thanks," I replied, disappointed. I didn't believe he'd call me back soon. In fact, I was fairly certain I would only hear from him when he needed something from me.

"Hey, listen," Faith added quickly. "We're having a dinner with some of the ladies from the Universal movie Daisy was in last year. Would you like to come over and join us? I'm sure they'd love to talk about Daisy."

Crap.

In my initial research, I'd done a complete filmography for Daisy, and had even Netflixed the movie in question. Daisy had a tiny part, but she had been one of ten women from an ensemble cast filled out with some of the most powerful, successful actresses in Hollywood. And they were all having dinner together—tonight. The same night I was supposed to go hang out with Vaughn.

I knew what I needed to do, of course. This was just a movie (and a free one), and I hoped the opportunity would present itself again. As a responsible, hardworking adult, I knew the right answer was to respectfully bow out of the movie and spend the night listening to other disgustingly rich superstars talk about how wonderful my disgustingly rich client was. It would all be lies and platitudes, of course, but their quotes would help sell the book. A book I got half the revenue from.

Luckily, Faith's next words made my decision much easier. "You can't use any of what they tell you, of course."

It was one of the most ridiculous things I'd ever heard Faith say, which was pretty telling. "And why is that?"

"Oh, honey-bunch. These are very private women, even more famous than our Daisy, if you can believe it. Now, we can't have them feeling taken advantage of. Or worse, that we're trying to eclipse their fame."

What I couldn't believe was that a group of grown women might be threatened by a teenage pop star writing the world's tamest memoir. That there were people, however few, with higher star power than Daisy Mae—that was no great stretch. "Well, then . . ." I said, stalling for the proper way to word my refusal. "I would very much love to be a part of this, but I worry that if these women give me great information about Daisy, I might really want to use it. I don't know what's to be gained with conversations I have to pretend didn't happen."

"Oh, you are so right," Faith agreed. "I hadn't even thought of that. And I know you need to work with Daisy some more, but the show's filming in Rome next week . . ."

I needed to work with Daisy a *lot* more. This book was supposed to be about three hundred pages and I still hadn't found a way to start the first chapter. I desperately hoped that with more conversations with Daisy, a little bit of her public persona would shine through and onto the page. And Rome, *really*? I was twenty-five and had never even been to Canada. I was totally in the wrong business.

"That is a problem," I couldn't stop myself from saying. I wanted to be accommodating, but on Monday, I would have been on the project for a full four weeks. At this rate, the book would be done in seven to eight months, if ever.

"Hmmm . . ." Faith said again.

She paused for another interminable length of time, as though waiting for me to make some kind of suggestion. I wasn't about to do that. They hired me, let them figure out the logistics of the job.

"Do you have a passport?"

The prospect of an impromptu Italian vacation absolutely thrilled me—for about four and a half seconds. Then I remembered being left in Miami with an obscene hotel bill and no flight home. Not to mention, based on my current financial situation, I couldn't afford to eat in Rome.

But I did have a passport. I had gotten it two years earlier while reading *The Secret*. The book said that to attract things to your life, you just needed to plan on them appearing. So I got a passport, anticipating a whirlwind jaunt around the globe. But I hadn't gotten my European adventure and there still wasn't a single stamp in the little booklet. Maybe *The Secret* had brought me that trip to a run-down Newark Radisson for my cousin Marie's fourth wedding, but I refused to count that as a vacation. My uncle was mugged in the hotel parking lot and I got a case of food poisoning from a local Mexican restaurant during the rehearsal dinner.

"Yes," I replied. Again, I wanted to accommodate their needs—and I sure as hell wanted my own Roman holiday—but I wasn't going to stupidly walk into a repeat performance of Miami. If I fell for that again, it wouldn't be the Dixsons' fault, it would be mine. "And I'd love to come with you, but I do have a few concerns."

"Of course, Holly. What do you need from us?"

I was beginning to think I'd been addressing my problems to the wrong people all this time. "Honestly, I'll need a round-trip ticket, and my hotel room will have to be paid for up front."

"Of course," she said again, sounding surprised. "I wouldn't expect you to pay for yourself while you're working. I'll tell Jamie you need a per diem as well."

My opinion of Faith shifted faster than the weather. One minute, she sounded like an idiot, and the next, she was the most reasonable boss I'd ever had. I was starting to get whiplash.

"All right, then," I said, hoping I wouldn't regret my decision. "I'll go wherever you need me."

"Daisy will be very happy to hear that," Faith told me. "And by the way, Vaughn Royce is coming, too."

I swear, the thought hadn't even occurred to me. But now that it was there. . . . "Oh."

"He actually asked me yesterday if we were bringing you along," she added.

My throat felt stuffed with dry cotton balls. "Oh," I croaked again.

"Anyway, I'll make sure your travel arrangements get squared away," Faith continued. "And I just know Jamie will call you back real soon."

"And you're going to Italy, too?" I asked. I would feel infinitely more comfortable with the trip if I knew Faith would be there to rein in her monster offspring.

"Are you kidding?" She laughed. "You think I'm passing up a trip to Rome?"

CHAPTER 11

I spend a lot of time in airports, which sounds annoying, but they're among my favorite places. Of course I could take private jets, but then I wouldn't get to see and meet my fans from all over the world. During concerts and on press tours, it's so hard to find time to connect with the folks who've kept me on TV all these years. Running around the big airports of the world, there's a weird sense of intimacy. There's nothing greater than when a little girl stops me on her way to her seat and asks for my autograph. It's a request I can never say no to.

I parked at the Fox lot at ten after six, one of the only people pulling into the parking structure at that hour. I was thirty minutes early, but that's inevitable in Los Angeles. Traffic is so unpredictable that the same trip can take seven minutes one day and forty the next. So I always err on the side of congestion; this was one of the few times I was wrong.

Security gave me a map, my first indication that the Fox lot was bigger than the one I'd visited the day before. There was a studio store and commissary, a medical department, and even a child development center. As I wound through the streets, I saw that most of the soundstages were occupied and running. A few network TV stars milled around while crew people moved lights and a frantic woman ran down the street with an armful of suits that were taller than she was. I felt very small and insignificant, but not in a bad way. This studio lot had all the magic I'd been waiting to witness with Daisy.

I made my way to the correct theater (there were apparently several) and found I was still quite early. As I pulled out my phone, Camille called. This was not a moment of serendipity, as you might think. Camille doesn't like to leave messages, so she calls again and again until you answer. This was just the first time I noticed, as my ringer broke about six months ago.

"Are you there? Is he there? What did you wear?"

"Why are you so excited?" I asked. "I don't even know if this is a date."

"It is. Of course it is." I love how decisive Camille can be, but I don't find it particularly reassuring, because she's frequently wrong. Though she is always the first to admit when she's wrong. "The guy came to your hotel room at ten P.M. And he brought dinner. The last time Donnie brought home dinner it was a Whopper and it was because he was too full to eat it himself."

Donnie, the prince among men. But I was sober, so I kept my mouth shut. "He didn't kiss me."

"He kissed your cheek. That's way better."

"He didn't offer to drive me here." We argued like this all the time. My mother loved Camille and often said that we were like Statler and Waldorf from the Muppets.

"Phhht. The man has a job. You don't think he left work just to come see this movie with you?"

I hadn't considered that. Looking back down the street, I again noticed how the lot was in full swing pretty close to 7:00 P.M. No one was showing any sign of packing up for the night. "I bet you're right, actually."

"Of course I'm right. Just don't mess this up. You get this weird, malfunctioning robot thing when you get nervous."

If I wasn't worried before, I was now. "I am not a robot."

"Not a well-functioning one. You're like one of those robots with loose wires that shocks people all the time."

I saw Vaughn turn a corner and wave to me. "I have to go, Vaughn's here."

"Ooh, what's he wearing?" Camille also doesn't know when to quit. Which is probably why she's still with Donnie.

I couldn't have answered her even if I wanted to, as Vaughn was now right in front of me. I really wanted to get off the phone before he accidentally overheard Camille barking questions or, worse, advice. "Gotta go," I said again.

"Call me later!" I heard these words as I pulled the phone away from my ear and shut it.

"Hi," Vaughn said, smiling. I couldn't remember the last time anyone looked so happy to see me—and that included my cat. "Glad you made it. Any trouble finding the studio?"

"Not at all," I told him, standing up.

He leaned in for a hug and I was momentarily caught off guard. I must not hug that many people. As he pulled me close, I caught a whiff of what was either aftershave or a very appealing natural musk. I could feel myself getting nervous again, perhaps owing to how few dates I'd been on in the last several years.

"Let's get inside before all the good seats are taken!" Much to my surprise, Vaughn grabbed my hand and lightly pulled me into the building. Maybe it was a date, after all.

The movie was only two hours, but it took so long to check in everyone's cell phones and tablets (the movie had just opened to the public that day), it was nearly ten o'clock before we finally escaped back into the open air.

"Are you hungry?" Vaughn asked me.

"You didn't see me gnawing on my arm during the twenty-minute balcony fight sequence?"

Vaughn laughed out loud. "How about dinner?"

About twenty-five minutes later, I was having an X-rated love affair with the pulled pork at SmithHouse on Santa Monica Boulevard. I'd been there a couple of times before, and it was a great restaurant with fairly good food and a small price tag given its tony Century City address. I was no less terribly nervous and fluttery with Vaughn, but when I'm hungry, I'll step over grandmothers and adorable little children to get to my meal. Camille still thinks I'm making this up, but I swear that when my stomach is empty, my hearing is dulled considerably. It wasn't until I'd wolfed down several bites of barbecue that I finally noticed Vaughn was jabbering away about something.

"I've never really understood that fixation. I mean, I like his movies, but I don't get the hype. You know?" He looked at me inquisitively, waiting for my opinion.

I had no idea how long he'd been talking, but I'd missed everything. I thought about lying my way out of this, but that's not my style. Instead, I shrugged and offered him a sheepish smile. "Ummm . . . I'm sorry, who are you talking about? I was a little busy making eyes at my food."

I thought he might be upset or at least offended, but Vaughn laughed. "I didn't want to say anything, but I wondered if I should leave you two alone. I felt a little voyeuristic."

"Oh, it's fine," I assured him. "It's an open relationship."

"Speaking of relationships . . ." he said, trailing off.

My head snapped up so fast I think it almost detached from my neck.

"You're not . . . you know . . ." Vaughn looked at me expectantly. "Pregnant, are you?"

Of course. "Not unless I've been abducted and impregnated by aliens. Or really rude fertility specialists." I should have known he'd heard the rumor. Not only did he work closely with the Dixsons, but if part of his job was controlling Daisy's image with the public, he must have been aware of all of their press releases.

"I didn't think so," he said. I may have misinterpreted the expression, but it looked like relief to me. "Though why Jamie didn't come up with a simpler explanation, like you're diabetic and had low blood sugar, I don't know. He's always making things needlessly complicated."

"Wow, that is a better explanation," I agreed. "And closer to the truth. We just hadn't eaten all day and they strapped me into a dress that was way too small."

"Did Jamie make you wear one of Daisy's dresses?" Vaughn asked.

I stared at him for a few seconds, wondering if he was kidding or just really clueless about weight and clothing. I'm five-ten and wear a size 8; Daisy is five feet even and swims in a size 0. I was starting to think she shopped in the children's section or appropriated doll clothes into her wardrobe. I'm pretty sure adult human beings aren't supposed to be that size, and I had trouble believing Vaughn couldn't see that.

"I think I could maybe fit my arm into one of Daisy's pant legs," I finally answered, a little dumbfounded. "She's like a sluttier version of Tinker Bell."

"She is way too skinny," Vaughn agreed. "I hate that little girls watch our show and think that's how they're supposed to look. It's not normal."

"To be fair, that idea didn't come from actresses, it came from producers. If you look back at the seventies and eighties, women on TV weren't nearly as skeletal as they are now," I pointed out. "So some of the fault lies with your job, not hers."

Vaughn speared a piece of brisket and held it up proudly. "Do you really think I advocate eating nothing but tomatoes and onions? I think frozen pizza is its own food group."

"Oh, how I wish that were true," I replied. "After a particularly bad breakup, I decided that only frozen burritos and Klondike bars would heal my pain. I gained ten pounds, but I was never more excited to eat dinner."

Vaughn laughed out loud and nearly choked on his brisket. "Then you know the miracle of food. So don't even tell me that you're going to let Daisy warp you into not experiencing the best Italian cuisine in the world next week," he continued, playfully staring me down. "I won't have it. I'll stuff you full of lasagna and tiramisu myself if I have to."

I'd had that conversation with Faith maybe five hours ago. How did Vaughn already know about my decision? "So you know I'm going to Rome," I said.

"Faith called me as soon as she hung up with you. She said she needed my approval to have you along during filming."

I didn't believe *that* for a second. Faith said that Vaughn had been asking *her* all week if I was accompanying Daisy overseas. So I doubted that she suddenly felt the need to ask his permission. Not to mention that the Dixsons weren't the type of people who sought approval for any one of their harebrained decisions. But if Vaughn didn't want to admit to pestering Faith about me, I would be nice and not call him on it. Though it was difficult.

"Thank you for letting me tag along, then. I'm sure it will be an interesting week."

"Have you ever been there?" Vaughn asked.

I raised an eyebrow and shook my head. "I've never been *anywhere*."

"But you do have a passport, right? If not, it's probably a little too late to get one."

"I do. I've just never had to use it before."

Vaughn studied me thoughtfully. "For someone about to take their first trip to Europe—and an unexpected, first-class trip at that—you don't look too excited."

"Miami didn't end so well," I said. "And Jamie still hasn't paid me back for the hotel or the car."

"Shocker," Vaughn replied. "We have a ten percent overage written into the budget for all of the 'expenses' Jamie never gets around to covering."

Suddenly, shoveling all of that pulled pork into my mouth didn't seem like such a good idea. I hoped I wasn't about to vomit all over Vaughn's dinner. "He doesn't pay his bills?"

Vaughn's expression went sour, and I knew he regretted his words. "Listen, I'm sure he'll pay you." He paused, probably trying to choose words that would soothe my mind without having to tell a lie. "You just need to keep on him about it. If I were you, I wouldn't do any more work for them until the check clears."

I appreciated that he was trying to make me feel better, but that was a stupid thing to say. It's easier said than done to simply refuse to do work; it was essentially a strike or work stoppage, and it would very likely result in my immediate dismissal. Not to mention, I was about to fly six thousand miles to a foreign country with these people. Nothing like being stranded in a strange land and pissing off the people who feed and house you.

Then I realized Faith hadn't called me back with any details of the trip, and the last thing I wanted was another 6:00 A.M. wake-up call. My heart had had enough shocks in these last few weeks.

"I'll get the money out of him, don't worry," I said, feigning confidence. I was practicing for my direct dealings with Jamie. "Do you know when we're leaving? Faith said she'd make the arrangements but didn't get back to me with specifics." It was an increasing wonder to me that these people ever ended up where they were supposed to be at any given time.

Vaughn's eyes widened in surprise. "You're kidding me, right? The travel office didn't call you?"

There's a travel office?

"No one has told me anything."

Vaughn shook his head, still seeming remarkably astonished for someone who had worked with the Dixsons for so long. "To-morrow night." He laughed. "We've had the show's tickets booked for months. Actually, when you called to ask for Faith's number, I thought you were going to back out of tonight so you could pack." He turned a little red and added, "I was really glad when you didn't."

I'm sure my own face went red. I liked the thought that he was a little nervous around me, too. It made me feel better about being a malfunctioning robot with exposed wires. A large part of me was now thrilled with the thought of spending a week in Italy alongside Vaughn, but the worrywart part of my brain said that I should stay home writing and watching HGTV on my couch. Voluntarily putting myself in the hands of the Dixsons was an invitation for all sorts of disasters.

"You have access to all of the travel details, right?" I asked, choosing to leave my neurosis inside my head.

"Everything." He nodded. "I get e-mail updates with all new info, including yours. I knew five minutes after the travel office booked your ticket."

"Then can you forward me what I need to know?" I asked. "And I probably should get home. I've got to pack, find someone to watch my cat, and manage to pay my rent before tomorrow night."

"You never told me your cat's name," Vaughn said as he pulled out his phone and started scrolling through e-mails. "I feel like I should know it, since I've heard all about him and his hatred of gardeners and mail carriers."

"Smitty." I nodded. "He is kind of an asshole. But I think that's what I like about him."

"Smitty?" Vaughn laughed, briefly glancing up from his phone. "Where'd you get that name?"

I was a little embarrassed to admit this, especially to a man. "Um . . . well, I've never really liked cats, but when I found Smitty, he was just a few days old and curled up outside my building, practically starving to death. I only meant to take care of him for a couple of weeks and then find him a home, but by then I was smitten."

Vaughn had stopped playing with his phone and was eyeing me strangely. He looked a little disturbed by my story, though for the life of me, I couldn't figure out why. He remained silent for far longer than I was comfortable with before quietly saying, "He's the smitten kitten?"

"No," I replied, shaking my head. "*I'm* the smitten kitten."

Vaughn continued to watch me with that disconcerted expression for another second or two before he snapped back to reality and resumed reading through his e-mail. He typed a few things, then nodded toward me.

"You should have everything on your phone in just a minute," he told me, his voice huskier than normal.

"Oh, my phone doesn't get e-mail. It barely makes calls, and texts sometimes take a whole day to show up."

"We need to work on that," Vaughn said. "You work for teen royalty, you have to be available twenty-four hours a day. In the meantime, all of the info should be in your e-mail. Let me know if it's not."

"How do you know my e-mail address?" I asked.

"I have my ways."

I wondered if it had been given to him by Faith or someone else on staff or if he'd deliberately sought out that information. But I didn't ask.

"You just know everything, don't you?"

"No," he replied. "Sometimes I think I know surprisingly little."

We had driven over from the Fox lot separately, so I didn't expect much to happen on the walk out of the restaurant. Vaughn headed for the valet stand.

"I'm parked on the street," I said. What I didn't tell him was *why* I was parked out on the street. I get a lot of strange looks from parking attendants when they see my car, as though it might contaminate the nicer cars in the garage.

"I'm sorry, I should have mentioned the valet."

This wasn't my first time at SmithHouse; I was perfectly aware of the valet. But I didn't say that. "It's fine. I'm right around the corner."

"Okay, then," Vaughn said, leaning in and hugging me again. "Good night. I'll see you at the airport?"

I don't know that I expected a kiss, necessarily, but I did at least think he'd offer to walk me to my car. I had the whole scenario worked out in my head; he'd offer and I'd politely refuse—twice. I wasn't sure what to do when no offer was made. I was even more unsettled when he simply waved and walked away from me after the hug.

I waited a few more seconds—for what, I don't know—and then turned and headed down the street toward my car. I still wasn't sure if this was a date or not.

Since my last trip had been sprung on me with three hours' notice, a full day seemed luxurious and decadent. I was able to pack thoughtfully, and Camille offered to watch Smitty and take me to the airport. The only truly nerve-racking part was that when I wrote my rent check and slipped it under the manager's door, I was acutely aware that I was heading to Europe with exactly three hundred dollars to my name. It was less money than I'd had when Jamie first called. Considering that the euro was worth so much more than the U.S. dollar, I figured I could buy a few meals and maybe a souvenir bag of pasta. Anything more than that and I'd return to Los Angeles to find my Goodwill couch on the front lawn, the new hangout spot for the neighborhood's feral animals.

Camille begged me to take a few hundred from her, but I just couldn't. I hate being in debt to anyone, and I also hate starting out any paycheck already in the hole. If I had to buy a giant pepperoni and slowly eat it over the course of the next eight days, so be it.

The length of the trip was also a revelation to me. I was surprised a kids' show was spending so much time and money on a two-part episode, but Camille claimed it wasn't that unusual. She even thought they must have been shooting some of the script back in the studio, because eight days of travel time wasn't nearly enough to film two episodes. I was starting to think the film industry was just a constant bloodletting of cash.

"I can't believe you're going without that check." She'd threatened to lock me in her bathroom when I told her I still hadn't been paid.

"I'll get it," I exclaimed, again trying to show more confidence than I felt. "I just haven't seen Jamie in the last couple of days. But he'll be in Italy with the rest of us. He can't avoid me there."

"At which time he'll give you a check you can't possibly cash until you get back."

I hadn't really thought of that. Apparently, I did not have a head for business. I suppose that's why I still lived on Diablorado Street.

"Your mother's really worried about you. We talked for an hour this morning."

"Does it strike you as odd that you talk to my mother more than I do?" I didn't really mind. In fact, I found the whole thing amusing.

Camille didn't answer my question. "You didn't even call and tell her about the trip to Italy."

This was true. And entirely my fault. I tried to talk to my mother once a week, but things had just been moving so fast lately that I'd forgotten to check in with her. "I'm sure you'll talk to her tomorrow, so tell her I'll call her from Rome."

"You'd better. I don't want to hear it if you don't." Camille turned in to the LAX departure queue, which crawled along at a snail's pace. The airport is always a bit of a nightmare, but it never bothers me; I can understand why everyone is so desperate to get out of Los Angeles. I'm just fine waiting patiently for my turn.

"And at least I'll get the check, even if I can't cash it right away," I pointed out. We were both quiet for a bit until we reached the individual terminals. "Tom Bradley," I told her, referring to the legendary international terminal that looks more like a stock trading floor than an airport. It's a wondrous hangar-like building packed twenty-four hours a day with people shouting in a hundred different languages. I like to think of it as the terminal of Babel. "Right past number three."

"Got it," she said, clearly still not pleased with my decision making.

"Come on, don't be like this," I groaned. "I don't want to spend this entire trip thinking you're mad at me."

"I'm not mad. I'm just worried about you."

"And that's very sweet," I told her. "But I'll be fine."

As we pulled up to the Bradley Terminal, Camille gave me a look that said she didn't believe me. But her attention was quickly diverted to Vaughn, who (along with Derek, the apparently still-employed producer) was corralling an enormous group of people.

"Make sure you nail him before you leave European soil," Camille said as she popped the trunk and started to step out of the car.

"He hasn't kissed me," I hissed as quietly as I could. "He didn't even walk me to my car. It wasn't a date."

"Even if it wasn't officially a date, he wanted it to be a date," Camille replied, walking around to the back of the car and yanking out my suitcase. "Make a play and he's yours."

Because it's *my* life and it often plays like an Abbott and Costello sketch, Vaughn looked up and spotted us exactly at that moment. I don't know if he'd heard Camille, but she wasn't speaking particularly softly. I wanted to punch her in the head.

"Hey, Holly. Hey, Holly's friend," Vaughn called out.

Rather than simply wave and get back in the car like a reasonable human being, Camille made a beeline for Vaughn. She shook his hand with what looked like enough force to break his fingers.

"Camille," she said brightly. "Glad to finally meet you. I've heard great things."

"So have I," he replied. "I'm Vaughn."

Camille threw a mischievous look back over her shoulder at me. "Oh, I know what your name is, Vaughn. Do me a favor and take good care of our little Holly, all right?"

"You have my word," Vaughn said with mock seriousness.

I wanted to melt into a puddle and die.

"*Little* Holly?" I heard the question followed by an amused giggle from somewhere in the pack of crew members. I recognized Daisy's voice immediately, but it took me a second to spot her Thumbelina frame amid the crowd. "More like 'Attack of the Fifty-Foot Woman.'"

We hadn't even gotten inside the terminal and already this was like some high school field trip, and I was the audiovisual geek. I quickly gave Camille a hug, trying to force her on her way. I could have sworn she reached into my jacket pocket, but I figured it was just my imagination, so I ignored it.

It actually wasn't until twenty minutes later when I was disrobing in the security line that I realized what she had done. And several minutes too late.

Vaughn was a person ahead of me in line, and he cleared the metal detector just as the first of my belongings disappeared into the X-ray machine. I had just pushed in my carry-on when the TSA agent stopped the line and pulled out my jacket.

Figuring he'd want to talk to me, I hurried through the detector and made my way toward Vaughn, who was putting his shoes back on. I never even got a chance to speak to the TSA agent before he pulled a handful of bright gold metallic condom packages from the pocket of my jacket. From the corner of my eye, I could see that Vaughn's mouth was just as agape as my own.

The TSA agent chuckled a bit to himself, then put the condoms back into my pocket, patting it. "For future reference, sweetheart, those should probably go in your carry-on."

I nodded, grabbing my things swiftly from the conveyor belt. I was so mortified I couldn't even look at Vaughn as I forced a laugh and said, "That Camille, she has a real sense of humor." I had to say something to stem the tide of my terror.

Much to my relief, Vaughn burst out laughing. He laughed so hard he had to stop tying his shoes and double over for a minute. "Wow," he said, straightening up and wiping his eyes, "Camille is a real jerk."

"She's not," I replied. I don't know why I was defending her just then, but it seemed like the right thing to do.

Vaughn finally stopped laughing and put a hand on my shoulder. "Not an actual jerk. I meant the lovable kind that tortures you in ways no one else can."

"Oh." That was certainly true enough. "Then yes, she's a jerk."

Vaughn put an arm around my shoulder. "Come on, let's get to our gate."

I'd flown first-class to Miami (and coach on the return), but the experience was nothing compared to transatlantic first class. The aisles were wider, the seats cushier, and I was shocked to discover that they reclined flat. I was still raising and lowering my seat when Vaughn put away his luggage and sat down next to me.

"It's a long flight. Pace yourself. Save some of the amusement for hour nine when you want to bang your head against the window."

The chairs were more comfortable than my bed, and I had a TV in front of me. How could I possibly get bored? "You don't like flying?"

Vaughn shrugged, settling back into his seat. Now that most of first class was on board, the rest of the crew was streaming on. I was again struck by just how many people were coming with us. "I don't mind it. But I have to go to New York a lot so I'm kind of over it."

I zoomed my seat up and down one last time. "I don't think I could ever get tired of this."

He put his hand on mine and patted it. "Trust me. By the end of your time with Daisy, you'll be over it."

Speaking of Daisy . . . I looked around the cabin and didn't see her. There were still two empty seats at the back of the first-class cabin. "Where is she, anyway? She was at the curb with us."

"She'll be here," he told me. Vaughn leaned into my ear, his breath ticklish. I had to fight the urge to giggle like a little girl. "I guarantee she's hiding out in the first-class lounge until everyone else has boarded. That way she doesn't have to say hello to everyone and pretend she cares."

Of that statement, only one part stood out to me. "There's a first-class lounge? What did we miss?"

Vaughn laughed, squeezing my hand. I was starting to feel like this trip wasn't the worst idea after all.

CHAPTER 12

When you hear about a film set, it seems like the only folks fans want to talk about are the actors and directors. But it takes so much more than just little old me to say a few lines and smile. We have talented writers who make up my words, hair and makeup people to help me look my best, a camera department to capture it all, and world-class editors to cover up any mistakes I make! These are the real heroes of my show, and I hope they know just how much they mean to me.

I enjoyed the first couple hours of the flight, but as the night wore on, it did get pretty dull. Vaughn fell asleep around 10:00 P.M., joining most of the rest of the cabin in their weirdly synchronous snoring. I was more than a little jealous, as I stayed awake despite my ever-growing exhaustion. No matter how heavy my eyelids felt, I couldn't fall asleep. I did flip through the movies but couldn't pay attention to more than thirty minutes at a time. I was also upset to discover that Jamie wasn't on the flight with the rest of us; I'd been hoping to badger him for my check while he had no way to escape.

Vaughn woke up just as we started to descend into Frankfurt, our layover airport. The late-afternoon sun streamed through the windows, stinging my overtired eyes.

"Not a bed, but not terrible, either," he said, stretching.

"Couldn't sleep," I told him. I was rapidly approaching a toddler-like level of grumpy.

"Walk around the Frankfurt terminal while the sun sets. It'll help your body get used to the time change. Then you can at least grab a nap on the next flight."

"Where will you be?" I asked.

"While I'd rather explore the German version of American fast food with you, I have to powwow with the other producers."

"Boo," I told him.

I did as Vaughn instructed, spending time in the waning daylight, but it didn't help. Nearly everyone passed out again on the Frankfurt-Rome flight, but I stayed wide awake, glaring out the window at my second sunset in twelve hours.

As we deplaned and went through customs, my body was thoroughly confused. I've taken plenty of cross-country flights home for Christmas and other visits, but I've never experienced the jet-lag hell that is crossing an ocean. When we landed, it was nine-thirty at night, the exact same time as when we left Los Angeles. I was both hungry and a little nauseous, and plain worn out. I don't recall ever being that tired in my entire life. I wanted to pay attention to every detail of one of the oldest cities in the world, but everything seemed shimmery and a little out of focus. I felt like I was in some crazy dream.

I was also a little dazed by the reorganization that took place at the Fiumicino airport. Though most of the crew had been in economy class, we were still—all 150 of us—together in some sense of the word. This changed immediately once we collected our bags.

I was literally pushed into a group with Daisy, Faith, and Derek (and about ten others I didn't know), while the rest of the crew and Vaughn headed out toward a bus at the curb.

"I'll catch up with you later," he told me, waving.

"Where are they going?" I finally asked. At that moment, I wasn't really worried about where Vaughn was disappearing to, I was just too addled to make sense of what was happening.

"The crew has their own hotel," Faith told me, her tone intimating that I should have already figured that part out for myself.

"Isn't Vaughn a producer?" Maybe he was one of those bosses who tries to pretend he's one of the little guys. They always think it boosts morale, but in the end, it appears condescending.

"Do you think those monkeys can check themselves in?" Daisy snorted. "John'll be back at our hotel in a couple of hours. He needs to get the grunts settled and pay out their per diems."

There was that term again. *Per diem.* I took Latin in high school, mostly because I had airs and wanted to be different than the rest of the French- and Spanish-taking students, so I knew that it translated to "per day." But I didn't understand what it meant in the work sense. I was just too embarrassed to ask. I was also irritated by Daisy's disdain for her crew. It wasn't like she was about to be poached by the Jet Propulsion Laboratory herself.

"You don't call them monkeys at work, do you?" I asked. It was perhaps an unwise question, but I wasn't firing on all cylinders.

"Daisy has a lot of respect for her crew," Faith piped in with what I assumed to be a stock answer. "Don't you, baby?"

"Yes, Mama," Daisy replied automatically, and with zero sincerity.

I thought about pointing out that her crew was filled with people far more skilled than she, and that the last person I would want to piss off was someone like a focus puller, but I kept my mouth shut. If she wanted to make fun of some poor grip and then risk having a stand "accidentally" fall on her head, that wasn't my problem. It also hadn't escaped my attention that Axel and Sharla, who seemed to be the closest to Daisy save her mother, were relegated to the monkey hotel. So much for loyalty. I wondered if that meant Faith would be sleeping next to her darling daughter.

A small van pulled up and the producers and execs began loading themselves into the back. I started to move toward it, but Daisy quickly grabbed my arm and made a clucking noise.

"You're kidding me, right?" she exclaimed.

I didn't bother responding, I just turned and waited for Daisy to explain her objection. Maybe she was supposed to get in before me, maybe we were being helicoptered to our hotel, I didn't really care.

"Our car will be here in a minute. We don't ride with the producers."

"They like to talk shop in the car," Faith added, trying to make Daisy's words sound less offensive. I wondered if Daisy had any idea just what the rest of us thought of her. Or if she even cared. As soon as the execs had all loaded in and pulled away, Faith leaned in to my ear and said quietly, "You know, your friend Vaughn worked pretty hard to get that seat next to you on the plane. There was no room left in first class—he had to bribe one of the other producers to move back to coach."

I didn't answer her. I was so tired and weary that I couldn't even make sense of what she'd just said. We waited for another two to three minutes (with the silent, unnamed bodyguards, of course) before a large Mercedes SUV pulled up and we were finally allowed to get the hell out of the airport. I was still excited about seeing Rome, but the only thing I really wanted to see at that moment was a bed. I didn't care if it was the hotel for the haves or the one for the have-nots. As long as bugs didn't crawl all over me and there was a reasonably clean blanket, I would be just fine.

I noticed very little about my room upon check-in. I dropped my suitcase in the doorway, used the bathroom, and then fell almost facefirst onto the bed. It was after 11:00 by the time I fell asleep, and so I was completely chagrined when I woke up with a start at 3:00 A.M. My body felt like I'd just gone seven rounds, but my mind snapped back on the instant I opened my eyes and I knew that trying to return to sleep was futile.

I was also ravenously hungry. We had been served a meal on the first flight, but after crossing a zillion time zones, I didn't know what time I'd last eaten. I also had no idea if there was any restaurant or store open, but I thought I might as well give it a shot.

Before I left the room, I decided to shower, lest I offend anyone with my day-old outfit and inevitable airplane stink. Now more awake than when I checked in, I noticed the peculiarity of the Italian bathroom for the first time. The toilet seat was almost non-existent and there was a strange metal cord hanging down in the shower. I tugged on it and played with it for a few minutes, but I couldn't figure out what it was supposed to do. I felt like I'd fallen through the looking glass and everything had minute and subtle differences from the United States. Part of me almost expected the shower to shoot Prosecco instead of water. In my present state, I wouldn't have minded.

By the time I made it out of my room, it was nearing four o'clock. I didn't try to call anyone, lest I accidentally wake up some lucky soul who was able to sleep, so my only real option was to head down to the front desk and talk to a hotel clerk. I had only just turned the corner from my own little stretch of hallway when I heard voices.

A few seconds later, I walked by a room with the door propped open. I didn't mean to glance inside, but I'm nosy and couldn't help myself. The room had been appropriated by Daisy's show, and there wasn't a bed in sight. Instead, there were a number of desks in two rows facing each other, and then a couple of couches. Several men and a woman were arguing about the date of the fall of the Roman Empire.

I smiled to myself and tried to tiptoe by to avoid disturbing them, but I hadn't even cleared the door when I heard, "Hey, you're the ghostwriter, aren't you?"

Surprised, I looked up to find that all the eyes in the room were on me. "Yeah," I answered, suddenly feeling shy. "Hi." Per the end-less reminders that I had signed a nondisclosure agreement, I wasn't sure what I could say or how much they knew. The people in the room had a definite advantage over me.

An enormously tall man with slate black hair and eerily gray eyes stood up and crossed to me, shaking my hand. He was so handsome it was almost intimidating. "I'm Ben. Welcome to the writers' room."

I surveyed the group, a little wide-eyed at the thought of gainful writing employment. I'd never envisioned a writing career that in-cluded a steady, living-wage paycheck. "I'm Holly," I replied, waving to the rest of the group. "You're all writers for the show?" There had to be eight of them, which was blowing my mind. It took eight people to create Daisy's bubble-gum dialogue? Considering their highbrow topic of conversation when I entered the room, I was will-ing to bet several of these people had Ivy League educations. The fact that they'd ended up here made me terrified for my own prospects.

"The rest of these no-accounts, yes," Ben replied, smiling. "I'm the production designer."

I suddenly realized I was standing in front of Benji, interior designer extraordinaire. I couldn't believe Faith had left out of her description how incredibly hot he was. No wonder all of her girl-friends wanted to hire him. "I've seen your work . . . on the stage and in the Dixson living room," I said. "Faith is a huge fan of yours. What are you guys working on?"

Ben laughed, blushing and looking away. So the hot guy was also humble. "The writers and I are trying to work around some of the location challenges."

"And why are you doing that in the middle of the night?" I asked.

One of the men sprawled on a couch spoke up. "Because the cheap-ass producers only gave us a day to make changes. Tuesday's the first day of shooting." Until that moment, I had forgotten that we lost Sunday completely in the transatlantic voyage.

A pretzel magically flew across the room and hit the man in the face. I realized it had come from the woman writer when she hissed, "And you shouldn't talk like that in front of Daisy's lackey. Keep running your mouth and we'll all get fired."

"Oh, no," I said. "Believe me, I'm not a tattletale."

"Right," the woman said, heaving herself out of a chair. "Listen, Benji, you can flirt with the production puppet, but we've got to get some sleep. Pages are due by two P.M."

Grumbling, the writers all began to stand and file out of the room. Not one of them made eye contact or spoke to me as they left.

Ben patted me on the shoulder. "I wouldn't worry about them. They're just jealous that you work fewer hours and probably get paid a lot more."

Maybe I could befriend them by admitting that so far, I wasn't getting paid at all. "Please, you don't have to stay up on my account. Feel free to go to bed."

By way of an answer, Ben stepped back and gestured for me to enter. He crossed to one of the recently vacated couches. "I wish I could. I can't sleep more than three hours with this jet lag."

"I didn't know that was a thing until tonight," I said, taking a seat on the opposite couch. I didn't remember him from the plane, but then, there were only a handful of people in first class with Daisy. There must have been dozens of crew members I hadn't seen yet. "I'm hoping it'll wear off by tomorrow night."

"I wouldn't hold your breath. I've been here for almost a week and I'm still a perpetual zombie."

"They sent you to Rome a week early?" I suddenly wanted to be a production designer.

Ben grinned, reading my envy. "I was *working,* but I'm not going to lie and say it's been terrible."

"Since you've had a chance to explore the area, are there any restaurants or grocery stores open now? I'm about to start eating the stuffing out of the couch."

"Sorry. Rome isn't a late-night town. But the hotel starts serving breakfast at six."

"Where's that flying pretzel?" I asked, seriously looking around for it.

"Don't eat a pretzel from a hotel floor. Even a five-star hotel." Ben stood up and crossed to a small cupboard, opening it. He dug around for a minute, emerging with a handful of small packages. "Pringles, Kit Kat, something called a torrone bar, or honey-mustard pretzels?"

"Yes, please." I stood up and walked over to him, taking the entire pile off his hands. "And we all have those minibar drinks, right?"

Ben stared at me, dumbfounded. "You're going to eat all of that. At four A.M." It wasn't phrased as a question, and I chose to take it as a directive.

"Probably." Figuring he would be too polite to kick me out, I started walking toward the door. The guy clearly had work to do and I had a sugar rush to get under way. "Thanks for the snacks."

"You're welcome," he said, still eyeing my haul. "Will I see you tomorrow?"

"I'm sure you will," I said, making a beeline back to my room.

Note to self: the writers have all the good junk food.

I spent the next several hours stuffing myself full of craptastic food and watching European MTV. There were only two channels in English, and one of them was BBC News. I was far too tired to pay attention to world affairs, so I chose MTV. And it did not disappoint.

We all know that in the United States, MTV is a bastion of reality shows, but in Europe, it seems they actually play music videos. And while it was nice to hear some words I recognized, I was also fascinated by the Italian version of rap—twenty-something, pasty white boys trying desperately to emulate Eminem and Jay-Z. The best part was that the music itself was absolutely dreadful.

I was entranced by what sounded like a French pop star when there was a knock at the door. I glanced at the clock and was surprised to discover that it was now eight o'clock in the morning.

I opened the door to find a gum-chewing, wiry little guy on the other side. He was weighed down by stacks of papers and a box of envelopes and looked like he'd rather be anywhere but here. I couldn't imagine how jaded the guy must be to be irritated by a trip to Rome.

He shoved a packet of papers and an envelope at me. "Production meeting at the Siena in thirty minutes." Sighing like I'd just spit in his face, the kid turned around to leave.

"I'm sorry, what?" I asked, not sure what I was supposed to do with the things I was now holding.

"Pro-*duc*-tion *mee*-ting," he repeated, as though I was either deaf or profoundly stupid. I was pretty sure his attitude was far worse than his pay grade allowed.

"Yes, I heard you," I replied. "But I don't know what that is, how it involves me, or what these papers are."

The guy blinked back at me for a few seconds before sighing again, louder this time. When he spoke, his words came out infuriatingly slow, in case I had trouble following along. "The producers want everyone over at the crew hotel at eight-thirty. It's when we all talk about what's going to happen over the next week. I just gave you the schedule, a map, a contact list, and your per diem."

So I'd finally get to find out what a per diem was. Awesome. "Oh" was all I said, feeling like a moron. "Thanks."

Rolling his eyes, the guy smacked his gum so loud it could have broken the sound barrier and then shuffled off down the hall.

I went back inside my room and glanced over the pages. There were a lot of schedules that meant almost nothing to me and a map of Rome that would probably come in handy. Then I opened the envelope and had heart palpitations. If I was worried about spending my last three hundred dollars in Italy, I needn't have been. Inside that little white envelope—in brightly colored cash—was more than a thousand euros. Given the ever-fluctuating exchange rate, that totaled somewhere near eighteen hundred dollars. I felt a little dizzy and had the sudden desire for a really expensive glass of wine. Then I remembered that it was very early in the morning and that I was about to go to work. Viva Roma.

The crew was staying nearby at the Hotel Siena, which was cute but far less posh than our own InterContinental. As I made my way to the production meeting I was certain I had no business attending, I took my time and watched Roman life unfold all around me. The buildings were beautiful, but crammed together the way a child might construct a Lego city—haphazard and dysfunctional. The street was narrow and jutted out at odd angles, and there were Vespas as far as the eye could see. I found myself smiling at businesspeople, men clad in suits and women all dolled up in dresses, straddling the backs of their shiny bikes and whizzing through traffic.

It was so lovely outside I had a difficult time forcing myself back into a cramped hotel. And it didn't help that the production meeting turned out to be three hours of every department discussing what they needed and reviewing script details and changes. Maybe I should have paid attention and learned more about the way a film crew works, but thirty minutes in, my mind wandered completely out of the room. I like to think I was astrally projecting to someplace more interesting. Like a dental checkup.

At close to noon, an angry-looking older producer I hadn't met ended the meeting and told the crew the call time for the following morning. He barked out something named a "precall" that brought some departments in at three-forty-five in the morning. I didn't understand what a precall was, but it sounded like hell on earth. Then the producer told the assembled crew to prepare for lunch and a tech scout, another term I didn't understand. I noticed that Ben headed off with the barking white-haired producer, but not before waving to me. I waved back, his presence making me think about those delicious Kit Kat bars.

Vaughn walked over just as I stood up and stretched.

"Sorry I couldn't connect with you last night," he said. "I got caught up with the crew until after midnight and then I didn't want to wake you up."

"That's okay. I figured as much. But you wouldn't have been disturbing my sleep. I got all of about four hours."

"I wish I'd known that." Vaughn glanced over at the crew members making their way through the door. He looked uncomfortable. "How do you know Benji?"

"Met him at four A.M.," I explained. "Hustled some junk food off him. Nice guy."

"That's . . . cool. You know, if you need anything, I can have a PA go get it for you."

I stared at him, realizing with astonishment that his tone was laced with jealousy. Given how attractive Ben was, I wondered if Vaughn and the other guys on set saw him as competition. I thought the jealousy was sweet, but I wasn't going to play into any macho hang-ups. "Thanks, but I think I can go in search of my own sustenance. I should have plenty of free time while Daisy's shooting her scenes."

"Right," he said, still looking troubled. "Do you want to come with us on the tech scout? I thought you might find it fun. We can be bus buddies." He cast one more fairly worried glance at Ben.

So that was why he'd invited me to this meeting. "I'm sorry, I can't," I said. "This is likely the only completely free day Daisy has. I'll probably get less than no information out of her, but I at least have to try. I need to come up with material for this book somehow."

Vaughn nodded for what seemed like forever, shoving his hands in his pockets. I swear to God, he looked like a dashboard bobblehead. There was an unbearably long silence before he finally said, "Yeah, of course. So . . . I'll see you later?"

"Sure. Have fun."

"Oh, that's pretty much impossible," he said, waving and heading for the door.

I waited until Vaughn was well out of the room before I headed toward the exit. If I'd had any lingering doubt about his interest in me before this encounter, it was completely erased now. Jealousy over a man I've just met isn't normal "friend" behavior. The only real question now was what he planned to do about it. Because so far, he hadn't made any move to transition our relationship to something bigger. Rather than worry about it, I decided to get back to work and let things play out.

I heard the commotion in Daisy's room before I saw it. I was barely off the elevator when I heard an inhuman screeching that made sense only if it came from a two-year-old or a goose being skinned alive. This girl could have a career in horror movies if she wanted.

"I fucking hate you people," she screamed. "You did this to me on purpose! I know you did!"

I could hear Faith trying to calm her down, but the mother's tone was so much lower I couldn't make out any of the words. I turned back around and tried to grab the elevator, but the doors slid closed and dinged. I backed myself up against the wall and pressed the down button like a jackhammer.

"You are a stupid fucking whore and I *hate you*!" At this point, Daisy began sobbing at the top of her lungs. I was again astonished by the force and intensity of her crying; I've had some bad things happen to me before, but I've never sobbed with that kind of vehemence.

Before the elevator made it back to my floor, Jamie stepped into the hallway and spotted me. "Oh, thank Christ," he said.

Damn. He eyed me like a vulture eyes a rat with a lame leg, and I knew I wasn't getting away from this. "I'm sorry, I shouldn't be here."

Jamie stepped over and grabbed me by the arm, pulling me back toward the room. His fingers dug into my flesh and I somehow knew they were leaving bruises. Aside from his roguish, too-tan good looks, what did women see in this scumbag?

"You absolutely should."

He was strong enough that his one-armed yank propelled me a few feet into the room. My sudden presence caused Daisy to stop, mid-sob, and launch herself at me. Before I could properly react, she was sniffling and crying all over me.

"I—I—I h-hate them," she stammered. I was reminded of a little kid I once babysat who could cry so hard she would momentarily pass out. I was always afraid to upset her and inadvertently cause brain damage. I think I once gave that little girl cotton candy and Jolt for dinner, just to avoid a crying fit.

"Now, I told you it was an accident," Faith cooed. She sounded calm and Julie Andrews–like, but I noticed she stayed on the other side of the room.

Daisy's head snapped up from my chest and she glared at her mother, nostrils flaring. "You're a liar. A dirty, cocksucking *liar*." If I had ever called my mother a name, she would have backhanded me into Kingdom Come. But then, unlike Daisy, I wasn't possessed by the fame demon. She turned to look up at me, putting on her best poor-me expression. I didn't buy it for a second, but I feigned a little sympathy. "I have a suitcase with all of my medications, and they *purposely* didn't bring it."

"Sugar dumpling," Faith said, "we took it with us to the airport. We must have just missed it at baggage claim. The airline will find it and send it over real soon, I just know they will."

"Oh, *Jesus*," Jamie said under his breath. He was being a big help, I could tell.

She needed an entire suitcase for medications? A list of possible prescriptions floated through my mind. Lithium, antibiotics (she *was* apparently a tramp, after all), human growth hormone. I thought about asking why they didn't find a local doctor if these prescriptions were so important, but I was pretty sure I didn't want any detailed information from Daisy's medical history.

"I don't believe you," Daisy shot back, her chin jutting out and knocking me in the chest. I was waiting for her to let go of me, but it didn't seem like that was in the cards. "You want me to suffer because you're jealous. You're all jealous."

There were only three of us in that room with her, and I was reasonably certain none of us were jealous of Daisy.

"That's it," Jamie said, taking a wad of cash out of his pocket. "Hols, head down to the liquor store and pick up some vodka."

"I've already had a drink," Daisy pouted. "It didn't help."

"Then have more," he shot back. "Enough vodka and you won't be able to feel your face, let alone worry about your damn medicine."

I gingerly detached myself from Daisy and took the enormous pile of bills Jamie slapped into my palm. I didn't want to spend my afternoon searching for an Italian liquor store, but it was better than being stuck inside this room. Jamie then put a forceful hand to my back and pushed me out of the room, again causing physical pain and a growing sense of rage.

As soon as we were in the hallway, I jumped out of the way of Jamie's grasp. "I have asked you not to touch me like that," I warned him.

"What?" he asked, like I was speaking a foreign language.

"In Miami," I replied, trying to maintain my composure. My fuse is shorter than Bruce Banner's, and once I blow, I turn into the Hulk and stampede through small cities. I was trying desperately to keep myself in check, as I didn't want to get fired in a strange country and with little money to get home. "You slapped me on the ass and I asked you not to touch me like that. I don't appreciate it."

"Sure, whatever," Jamie replied, rolling his eyes. "Just go get the vodka, will you?"

"Why can't you go?"

"Because the press will take pictures and say that I'm buying it for the brat," he said, almost shouting the last word so that she could hear it inside the room.

"Which you are. Besides, they've already gotten pictures of me, if you recall."

Jamie shrugged. "And Perez Hilton thinks you're a knocked-up alcoholic. It's perfect."

Perfect was just about the last word I'd use. I was in a feisty enough mood to say, "I'll go, but I want my check when I get back."

There was a clueless, blank hole where Jamie's expression should have been. "What are you talking about?"

"My check," I repeated. "You owe me almost seventeen thousand dollars. And that's just as of last week. In three weeks, you owe me another ten. I want the check written out and in my hand before I give Daisy a drop of liquor."

"Women are such pains in the ass," he muttered. Jamie looked like he was trying to slyly talk to an imaginary person behind him, but we were—of course—the only people in the hallway. Maybe Daisy wasn't the only one who could benefit from lithium. "Fine. Just get the damn vodka."

I hit the down button hard enough that it hurt my palm. Fortunately, Jamie turned and went back into the room, so I wasn't forced to endure another uncomfortable silence. Just as the elevator opened, my stomach rumbled and I realized it was lunchtime. *Screw Daisy,* I thought. *She'll get her precious vodka, but I'm eating lunch first.*

I still didn't know what press Jamie was talking about. By the time I dropped the bottles of booze and ran, I had been back and forth from the hotel twice and there wasn't a single reporter nosing around the entrance. Unlike in Miami, no one here seemed to care who Daisy was, further upping my estimation of Italians.

When I got back to the InterContinental, the desk clerk said that I had a package. He handed me a medium-size manila envelope; the only writing on the front was my name. Given my work with Daisy, I was momentarily concerned that it might contain a bomb. But it didn't tick and not many people would know my name, anyway, so I decided not to worry about it.

I was in the elevator when I tore open the envelope and saw that there was an iPhone box on the inside, along with a note. "Courtesy of production. Use it on us while you're here and then I'll switch the contract to you when we get back to L.A. Vaughn."

My mouth just about fell open. Vaughn bought me a phone? Or he got the show to buy me a phone? I hadn't even bothered to bring my ancient cell, knowing I couldn't use it here. As soon as I got back up to my room, I got to work exploring this tiny little device I'd lusted after for so long. Despite my Playskool first phone, I wasn't tech-stupid, I was just too poor to be tech-savvy.

Excited, I pulled out my address book and called my mom. I could kill two birds with one stone.

She didn't answer on my first try. Figuring she didn't recognize the number, I called back a second time. "Who is this?" she demanded.

"It's me, Mom. I just wanted to call you from Rome. Say hi and see how you're doing."

"Oh, I'm fine. Won big at bridge last night. Debbie Paul lost her shirt."

My mother's ongoing rivalry with Debbie Paul was one for the ages. It was like the Hatfields and the McCoys of suburban quilting clubs. "I'm glad to hear it. She plays dirty, anyway."

"She does," my mother agreed. "What's this number you're calling from?"

"The show gave me a new cell phone," I told her. "I thought you should be my first call."

"For free?" My mother's voice turned shrill. I should have realized—my mom doesn't believe anything is free. When I was a kid, we were poor enough to get weekly shipments of government cheese, but she would never let me eat it. Despite the slim pickings on our own dinner table, my mother dutifully donated every bar of cheese to people needier than we were. "Holly, you know nothing is free."

"It's not exactly free, Mom." I fought my growing irritation. She didn't understand this world, which made me wonder why I bothered telling her about it at all. Why didn't I just say I used my paycheck to buy my own phone? "It's part of my fee." That wasn't exactly true, but she wouldn't know the difference.

"But Camille said they hadn't paid you yet."

Dammit, Camille. First the condoms, now this. "They have," I said, lying by omission. "They just owe me a lot more."

"Okay, dear," my mother said, sighing into the phone. "Make sure you keep after them. No one protects you but you."

"I love you, Mom," I told her. "I'll talk to you when I get back to L.A."

I hung up the phone much less excited than when I had opened the package. But I wasn't going to let my mother's worry ruin this moment—for the first time in my adult life, I had a phone that didn't look like I'd found it at a pawnshop.

The room phone rang at 6:00 P.M., waking me from a long nap. I could see the shadows cast by the already dimming light outside. I'd slept through the entire afternoon.

"Hello?"

"Holly," came the nasal whining from the other end of the phone. "Where *are* you?"

I was actually a little impressed Daisy knew how to use a telephone to call from room to room. Then I noticed that she had asked where I was when she had clearly called my hotel room, and was decidedly less impressed. "You know where I am. What do you need?"

"You're coming to dinner, right?" Her voice was strained, and I couldn't tell if she was deliberately trying to sound upset or if she was just drunk and slurring her words. The latter thought greatly concerned me because up until now, she'd managed to handle all the vodka in that enormous Mountain Dew cup with nary a wobble. If she really was drunk, she must have plowed her way through several of the bottles I'd bought.

"Dinner?" I asked.

"Heinz Beck is hosting us at La Pergola tonight. I made sure your name was on the list."

"Thank you," I replied, a little confused. I wasn't stupid enough to think Daisy had done it out of the kindness of her heart. Whatever the reason, I would find out eventually.

"I invited your boyfriend, too. Mom said you'd want someone to talk to."

My boyfriend. So people were already talking about me and Vaughn. I didn't know if that was a bad thing in this business—or if no one cared. I also thought about correcting the boyfriend label, but I knew any more on the topic would only bore and annoy Daisy. "That's very nice of you. What is the attire?"

"Huh?"

"The dress code, Daisy. What type of clothes should I wear?"

This earned a giggle from her end. "Nothing you own, that's for sure."

Daisy said this like my entire wardrobe was composed of potato sacks and pleather pants. "What I'm asking," I continued tersely, "is if I should be wearing a dress."

"Oh," Daisy managed to squeeze out in between bursts of laughter. The question of her sobriety was quickly settling itself. "Yeah. Yeah, totally."

The car ride to La Pergola was my first real glimpse of the city. The sun was low on the horizon, the dying rays glittering off windowpanes, and the warm yellow of the streetlamps just beginning to glow. For the first time, I noticed that Rome looked like a city in the process of excavating itself. Relatively new buildings stood alongside ancient columns missing their tops, and every few blocks we passed a site populated with scaffolding and giant sheets of plastic. The workers had all gone home for the day, but it still looked like the world's largest archaeological dig. Each time we paused for a stoplight, I had an urge to jump out of the car and go exploring on my own.

But I was a good girl and stayed put, listening to Daisy chatter on about how she'd just gotten a Facebook message from this hot actor on ABC's new science-fiction show. I heard all about his ass and how she'd slipped her phone number into the back pocket of his jeans during a charity ball. He hadn't called yet, but the message totally meant she was in play. I thought about asking why he wore jeans to a charity ball, but I don't understand the rules of celebrity fashion. Maybe the jeans were handwoven from organic cotton and cost five grand.

I nodded politely, even adding a few oohs and aahs for effect, but I knew I couldn't use a single word of this gibberish. It had nothing to do with the story of her life, and I knew her handlers didn't want me even hinting that she was a total . . . let's just be nice and say "player." Besides, even if she did hook up with Mr. ABC Sci-Fi, he'd be gone before the book got to a publisher. So I pretended I cared, but what actually intrigued me was not the content of her words but her tone.

Outwardly, I maintained the picture of the happy, well-adjusted employee, but internally, I was truly questioning Daisy's mental health. Earlier today she'd been in a white-hot rage and now she was just one bright, sunshiny day. I'd seen this transformation twice and wondered if she was bipolar. Everyone has mood swings, but this was nothing short of a roller-coaster track. Maybe her "medication suitcase" really did have lithium in it and her idiot handlers had replaced the missing prescription with vodka. Never mind that alcohol worsens natural chemical imbalances. I was no doctor, but it seemed to me like a catastrophe waiting to happen.

We crossed over the Tiber River and I could see the dome of St. Peter's Basilica gleaming in the distance. Daisy continued to yammer, never even glancing out the window. I noticed with much sadness that I seemed to be the only person in the car with any interest in what lay outside.

"Where's Jamie?" I asked at one point. First, he was MIA on the flight over, and now he was skipping a staff dinner? Wasn't he supposed to be Daisy's business-savvy shadow?

"Making a deal with Cinecittà," Faith replied absently while texting on her cell phone. I'd never heard of Cinecittà, but I was too embarrassed to say so.

"You're so *bo*-ring, Mom. No one cares. . . . Oh, I almost forgot. I have something for you, Holly Bear." Daisy reached into a hidden pocket of her dress and pulled out something on a chain.

She tossed the chain at me, and I caught it in surprise. It then took me a full thirty seconds to untangle the metal to realize there was a clear stone at the center of the necklace—and it was *big*. "What is this?" I asked.

Daisy shrugged and yawned. "Italy gave it to me for working here or something. It's supposed to be like a really colorless diamond."

"It *is* a colorless diamond," Faith corrected her gently. "And it's from the Italian government."

I turned it over in my palm, perplexed. Daisy was just giving me a diamond necklace? "This is beautiful, but . . . don't you want it?" I've never been one for jewelry. I have pierced ears, but I haven't worn earrings in so long I don't even know if I could.

The look she gave me was one of utter exasperation. "Um . . . I'm supposed to wear a two-carat diamond? Everyone will think I'm poor." Daisy yawned.

Maybe I should have been offended by the implication that *I* was poor, but she was right. So I simply tucked the necklace in my purse. "Thank you, Daisy," I said. "That's very nice of you."

She looked startled that I had expressed gratitude. "Oh, sure. It's no big deal. I've got a boatload of Prada in my room if you want some of that stuff."

Faith leaned across the seat and spoke quietly into my ear. "Just don't try to sell that, okay? Diamonds are laser-engraved by their designers and we don't want people knowing Daisy just gave away a hundred-and-fifty-thousand-dollar diamond."

I almost choked hearing the dollar amount but managed to suppress the urge. It's no wonder rich people stayed that way; people were willing to give everything to them for free.

When we got to La Pergola, I was surprised to discover that it was in a hotel. And a Hilton, at that. As the car slowed to a stop, Vaughn was waiting at the curb. He opened the door for us before the driver could even turn off the engine.

He was dressed to the nines in a pin-striped suit and tie, his hair slicked back. He reminded me of a younger version of Batman's butler, Alfred. "You look beautiful."

"Ugh, *shut your face*," Daisy groaned, climbing out of the car after me. She pushed Vaughn aside and marched toward the restaurant. "Holly Bear, tell John his voice gets on my nerves."

"Sorry," Vaughn called after her. He turned back to me, winked, and then whispered, "I'm not sorry."

He held out his arm, and I stared at it for a few seconds before realizing he was asking for mine. No man had ever walked me on his arm. I was also hyperaware of the change in his behavior since this morning. He no longer seemed nervous or uncertain around me; in fact, this version of Vaughn was uberconfident. I still couldn't get a real sense of him. But I took his arm and followed him into the restaurant, smiling to myself when he reached across and lightly squeezed my captive hand.

"I never get to go to these things," he told me.

This statement surprised me. Vaughn had had an expensive suite in Miami, and I was sure he had one in Rome, too. He was a producer with enough power to have someone buy me a five-hundred-dollar cell phone and he didn't get invited to these kinds of events? If he wasn't one of the cool kids, who was?

The restaurant itself was beautifully appointed and the view was heart-stopping. That moving-target vista of St. Peter's I'd gotten from the car was nothing compared to the full-on Vatican City panorama I was treated to once inside. And beyond it, the entirety of Rome was laid out like a living treasure map. When we all took our seats, I purposely situated myself so that I was facing the window. That way, when the dinner conversation made me want to swallow jagged pieces of glass, I'd at least have something to divert my attention.

Vaughn took the seat next to me. The rest of the long table was populated with the show's executive producers and director, Daisy, and Faith, a few actors I recognized but couldn't quite place, and a teenage boy and his parents. Before I even had to ask, Vaughn leaned over and whispered that this was Colby, the boy who played Daisy's younger brother on the show.

Noticeably absent from the table were Jamie, the bodyguards, and, once again, Axel and Sharla. Apparently, a fancy meal couldn't be wasted on the underlings. Not that I should be surprised, given that Vaughn wasn't supposed to be on the list, either. I also took note of the fact that we were the only guests in the entire restaurant. It wasn't an enormous dining room and I knew Italians ate later than Americans, but I would have figured there'd be other diners by eight-fifteen.

"Where is everyone else?" I said quietly to Vaughn.

"La Pergola is closed on Mondays," he whispered back. "The executive chef is hosting a special meal for Daisy."

"Let me get this straight. Daisy, who eats nothing but tomatoes and onions, wanted to come to this gourmet Italian restaurant? Is she planning on eating marinara sauce out of a soup bowl?" I couldn't think of any other menu item that could possibly fit into her anorexic diet.

"Let me start by saying that this is not just a 'gourmet' restaurant." Vaughn laughed, slipping into a condescending tone I'd not yet heard him use. I didn't like it. "La Pergola is a three-Michelin-star restaurant, the only one in Rome. And I'm not here because I care if Daisy's forced to eat nothing but her napkin, I want to try Heinz Beck's rabbit with sweet pepper cream."

I stared at Vaughn for a moment, perplexed. "Are you a judge on *Top Chef* or something?" The most expensive restaurant I'd ever eaten in was probably Benihana.

"I'm just educated on high-end cuisine," he said primly.

"You're a snob," I replied. I was mostly joking, but there was a little bit of truth to it.

He winked at me again. "I'm a foodie."

A ludicrous number of waiters swarmed the table and began filling everyone's glasses with about twelve drops of white wine. When a waiter reached me, I asked if I could also have a glass of water, which earned me a look of utter contempt. "Still or bubbles?" he said, speaking English and looking like he loathed every syllable.

I'd felt out of place with these people (Daisy and the glitterati, not Italians) from the very beginning, but this question made me feel like a chimney sweep trying to dine with the Queen of England. I always request water in restaurants, and never once has anyone asked me if I wanted it with bubbles in it.

"Still?" I guessed. Tap water is fairly still, isn't it?

At Daisy's end of the table, an argument was brewing, but I kept my eyes down and eavesdropped, lest I be dragged into it.

"It's legal here, Axel told me so," Daisy snarled at her mother. The nice version of the teenager had again disappeared. A terrified-looking waiter glanced back and forth between the mother and the daughter, not sure who to take orders from.

"*I don't care,*" Faith hissed, the sheen on her sweet southern persona wearing off. "We need pictures of you holding a wineglass like I need more holes in my head."

"She is correct," the waiter said hesitantly. It was difficult to tell if his halting speech was a result of limited knowledge of English or because he was afraid to say the wrong thing. "In Italy, it is acceptable to buy alcohol at sixteen."

Faith threw the waiter a venomous look, but Daisy beamed. "See?" our resident Pop-Tart gloated. "I told you so."

With the crook of a finger, Faith and the waiter put their heads together and for a few seconds I couldn't hear what was being said. Then he straightened up, nodded, and snapped his fingers for the other servers.

Like a military unit, all of the waiters vanished from the table in a synchronous move, reappearing two minutes later with plates of some sort of fish. One of the plates magically materialized in front of me, though I hadn't ordered anything or even seen a menu yet. I was staring down at the dish in front of me when everyone else (including Daisy) began to eat. I also noticed that a brightly colored child's sippy cup was placed in front of her. I was pretty sure there wasn't milk inside.

"What's wrong?" Vaughn asked, speaking out of the corner of his mouth. Though the rest of the table was just a few bites in, Vaughn's plate was completely empty. In fact, it was so clean it looked like there hadn't been food on it to begin with. I still hadn't even picked up my fork.

"I don't eat fish," I said quietly. It's true—unless it's a tuna fish sandwich covered in mayo, I have no interest. I've tried everything from lobster to orange roughy, and it's all about as appetizing as a sewer drain.

"You *have* to," he said, his Dad voice creeping in again. "There is a lot of seafood on this tasting menu, and you can't send back full plates. Not in a place like this."

I had only seen tasting menus on television shows, but I knew it meant we didn't have a choice in the dinner selections. The chef would send out what he felt were his best dishes, and we were expected to smother him with praise. I tried to take a bite of the first course, but I just couldn't. I could see Vaughn eyeing me with disappointment, but I didn't care—and I didn't appreciate the attitude. When I thought no one was looking, I slid the piece of fish onto his plate, and he fortunately remained silent and ate it.

For the next two and a half hours, food came out of the kitchen at regular intervals, most of it some variety of fish. I did manage to consume most of the two courses containing shrimp, and Vaughn was right about the rabbit. It was the best piece of meat I'd ever eaten. The food just kept coming, and I started to feel drugged and lethargic. Though I paid little attention to Daisy after her outburst, I did notice that she ate everything that was put in front of her. I couldn't figure it out. Was it not "so 2004" to eat rabbit? Of all animals, I could see her freaking out about people cooking adorable little bunnies.

By the time we got to dessert, I was close to bursting. But when a plate packed with mini confections appeared in front of me and Vaughn leaned over and whispered, "I'm happy to take those off your hands," I almost speared him with my fork.

"You touch my chocolate cake and you'll lose that hand," I replied, pulling the plate away from him. I'm very protective of my desserts.

I glanced across the table and saw that Daisy was plowing through the plate like her life depended on it. I couldn't help but stare as she took down a smallish block of tiramisu in one bite. Maybe she thought calories didn't count in foreign countries?

I was even more astonished when she asked for more of the hand-made chocolates, which she called the "little candies." The waiters quickly returned with a sealed package of them, which she promptly tore open and began devouring. I tried not to stare at Daisy like she was an animal in a zoo, but I couldn't stop myself.

As I watched Daisy out of the corner of my eye, a man walked down to our end of the table and leaned in to Vaughn's ear. "Since you're here, you don't mind taking care of the check, do you? I left the production cards in my room."

Vaughn's face showed his annoyance. "Sure. Which card do you want me to use?"

"Go with the platinum." The man straightened up and patted Vaughn on the back. "Good boy."

I'd wondered about Vaughn's youth compared to the other producers, and this exchange answered a whole host of my concerns. I had seen him as some big fish in this odd little aquarium, but apparently he was just one of runts. And he didn't look particularly happy about that.

As the other producer walked away, he conferred with a waiter and nodded in Vaughn's direction. A moment later, the waiter approached us and handed Vaughn the check, quickly skirting away. I didn't mean to look but accidentally caught sight of the total. For our endless dinner and the roughly fifteen bottles of wine consumed at the table, the show was paying seven thousand euros, or about twelve thousand *dollars*. Vaughn tucked the platinum card into the billfold and set it upright. He looked irritated, but I knew that wasn't about the total.

Then he turned to me and said, "What are your plans tomorrow?"

"Um . . . I don't know, why?" In my short association with the Addams Family, I'd learned not to make any plans. Doing so was only an invitation for the Dixsons to destroy them.

"I might have time for lunch tomorrow," he said, like it was an enormous windfall that he be allowed to stop to refuel his body. "I have to make sure we get going in the morning, but I'll be free by one o'clock. And Daisy has to be on set all day."

This is one of the many, many things I hate about men. A woman would have said, "I have time tomorrow, would you like to go to lunch?" rather than lobbing the information out there and hoping you'll pick it up and run with it. We hadn't known each other all that long and I was already tired of the undecided nature of our relationship. Were we friends? Were we something else?

"That sounds great," I replied.

"Just come by the set. I'm sure Axel and Sharla would love to see you."

It was true, I hadn't seen either of them once since we left L.A. I hoped they were out at some Roman nightclub, getting into all sorts of strange situations and making out with random Italian guys. I was far too boring to do (or enjoy) any of those things, but it was fun hearing about them.

Everyone began standing and moving toward the elevator. I threw a glance toward Daisy and Faith, dreading the car ride back. I wasn't ready to be alone with Hurricane Daisy so soon. Vaughn must have seen my look because he leaned in very close to my ear and said, "Do you need a ride?" His breath was tantalizingly warm, and just before he pulled back, his lips accidentally grazed my skin.

"Holly Bear, *come on*," Daisy whined from the elevator. "I don't want to ride by myself with *the witch*." Faith clenched her teeth and looked away.

The things we do for our jobs. "I really should go with them," I said quickly. "But I'll see you tomorrow."

Vaughn cast a dubious glance toward Daisy, but she just kept gnawing on a fingernail. "Really?" Seriously, how did she always manage to miss the nasty and chagrined looks that were constantly being leveled at her?

"Yes," I said.

"Okay," he said, holding up his hands.

When the elevator doors opened, Daisy stepped inside and yanked me in with her. Vaughn took a few steps to follow us, but she swiftly shook her head. "You can take the next one, John." The door closed. "I like John, but you can do *so* much better," Daisy said to me.

Faith looked away and giggled. "Oh, Daise. That's mean."

I had no idea if Faith was insulting me or Vaughn. For my own sanity, I chose not to ask.

CHAPTER 13

I love to travel. There's nothing so wonderful as waking up in a different city and knowing there's a whole new culture to explore right below my window. I've been lucky enough to go every-where from Tokyo to South Africa to Venezuela and so many places in between. I like to collect souvenirs from every city I visit, though my mom is starting to think I'm a hoarder. She's always saying, "Daisy, do you really need another snow globe from Russia?" I do! Though at this point, I don't think I can fit any more shelves in my room, but I keep trying!

I managed to get a relatively normal night's sleep, but it ended all too abruptly at five-thirty, when a dull roar started somewhere below my balcony. I tried to ignore it, but about twenty minutes in, the sound exploded into a sea of cheers, and I realized that the noise was actually hundreds of little girls chanting for Daisy.

I walked out to the balcony and watched in shock as the crowd pressed in on all sides to get a glimpse of the actress, who had just emerged from the hotel. Though Daisy was flanked by her body-guards, she walked right up to her fans, shaking hands and signing autographs. She honestly looked gracious and sweet, just like the teenager I'd first met. God, how I wished the public persona was the real Daisy. It would make my job (not to mention, my life) so much easier.

Once I had shaken off the last bits of sleep, a thought occurred to me. Yesterday, there hadn't been a single fan outside the hotel, and today, it was a madhouse. Where were these girls when we'd first checked in, and how did they find out we were here? I also noticed that Daisy stayed outside until quarter after six, signing posters and taking pictures with fans for more than half an hour. While this looked cute and respectful from the outside, I knew she was supposed to be on set at 6:00 A.M. And judging from the time it took the line of cars to maneuver past the rampant screaming teens, I guessed she would end up being about an hour late. Daisy was again making it perfectly clear that in her world, her time was more important than anyone else's.

If I expected the crowd to dissipate after their idol had left for set, I was wrong. They just sat down in the middle of the street and started singing her songs in adorably accented English. I wondered if they had any idea what those words meant. It was clear I wasn't going back to sleep, which meant that I should actually try to do my job. I couldn't believe I'd been putting it off for an entire month. Or that I hadn't been fired by now. I'd set up my laptop the day before, but hadn't gone near it since. I paced back and forth in front of my little hotel desk, worried that sitting down and attempting to write would only result in further proof that I was utterly unqualified. It took over an hour before I could summon the courage to pull back the chair and toss away the random pieces of clothing that covered my laptop. It may have been further than the day before, but that was still my limit.

I left my poor, lonely laptop and went to find breakfast.

At just before noon, I went off in search of Vaughn and the filming location. I knew I had reached Piazza Navona when I saw the throngs of girls packed together like underage sardines on one side of a police barrier. The officials had penned them in, and the kids were surprisingly quiet, watching the activity of the crew with silent reverence.

The police momentarily pegged me as an overgrown fan and tried to herd me behind the barrier, but I took out the schedule and managed to get Vaughn's name out before they dumped me off altogether. When they finally realized I worked with the show, I was dragged to a row of a trailers by an officer, probably the only unattractive man I'd yet seen in Italy.

Inside the trailer, there were three women knee-deep in a mountain of paperwork. The officer pushed me up the stairs, then said to them, "*Ospite di* Vaughn Royce."

One of the women, clad in ratty overalls and a bandanna, looked me up and down before pulling out her walkie-talkie and saying, "Diana for Vaughn. What's your twenty?" She didn't bother addressing me and the other two didn't look up.

"South side of the piazza, with Colby and Daisy," came the staticky reply.

Diana looked up and stared at me humorlessly. "Can you find that?"

"I think so," I answered, a little intimidated by her demeanor.

"Good. Stay out of the shot." She turned and resumed her work, as though I'd already left the trailer. To avoid any problems, I hauled ass and did just that.

It wasn't that difficult to stay out of the shot because it didn't looking like *anything* was being shot. The cameras and lights were all set up in the plaza, but there were no actors, and most of the crew seemed to be chatting or hanging around by the snack table. I made my way around to the south side and found Vaughn and another man talking to a very tense Daisy and the young boy from dinner the night before.

"I need you to focus, Daise," the man told her, trying to get her to make eye contact with him. He attempted to chase her gaze, but Daisy didn't look like she was all there. She was biting her nails and anxiously shifting her weight from foot to foot.

"Yeah," she answered. Even her voice was spacey. "Yeah . . ."

"This is a disaster," whispered a voice behind me.

I turned to find an exhausted-looking Sharla. I smiled and gave her a quick hug. She seemed like she needed it. "What's going on?"

"I was up to put makeup on her at four-thirty," Sharla said with a shrug, yawning. "But I'm not a miracle worker. There's only so much I can hide."

I was standing ten feet from Daisy, and she looked amazingly beautiful to me. She also seemed strung out, but that impression had nothing to do with her face. And though I hadn't been able to see her up close during her parade through the fans that morning, she had been downright chipper then. I wasn't sure why she all of a sudden looked like an escapee from *Trainspotting*.

"What are you hiding?" I asked. "She looks fantastic."

"She's out of her gourd," Sharla answered. "When I got to her this morning, she hadn't gone to sleep yet and was trying to cut her own hair with kitchen shears."

At this point, I was starting to believe that there were really two Daisys, and Jamie was able to use whichever one suited his purpose at that particular moment. Though I couldn't imagine why he'd ever choose the crazy nymphomaniac.

"I saw her this morning with the fans, and she seemed fine."

"She can be anyone she wants," Sharla said, yawning again. "At least for a few minutes." If that was true, Daisy was a better actress than I gave her credit for. "Listen, I'm going to nap in my trailer. Catch you later?"

I nodded and waved good-bye, realizing there probably wouldn't be a lunch. At about the same second, Vaughn spotted me and offered an apologetic smile. *Sorry*, he mouthed.

"Don't worry about it," I replied quietly. "I'll talk to you later."

I had just turned to walk away when Daisy finally spoke. "I don't want her here," she said coldly.

"Who?" Vaughn asked. It was a logical question; there were hundreds of people in the piazza at that moment.

"The makeup girl," she replied, her tone vicious. "I want her gone from here *now*."

Surprised, I looked over my shoulder at exactly the same time Sharla did. She was ten steps closer to the trailers, but well within earshot. The poor girl couldn't do anything but gape.

"Come on now, you love Sharla," the unnamed man cooed, trying to pet Daisy on the arm.

Daisy heaved the man's hands off her, her gaze never leaving Sharla. She honestly looked like she wanted the makeup artist dead. It was one of the scariest faces I've ever seen. "Fuck her," she replied. "Keep her away from me."

Several people hastened over to Sharla, but she moved away faster. I caught up with her just before she got to the makeup trailer. She tried to hide her face, but I could see that she was crying.

"Are you okay?" I asked, horrified. When she nodded, I put my hand lightly on her shoulder. "What was that about?"

This time, Sharla shrugged. "She's like this sometimes. She'll get mad at you, too," she told me. "You get used to it." Despite her words, Sharla sure didn't seem used to it.

She stepped up into the trailer and quietly closed the door. Bewildered, I skirted back around the piazza and was almost to the street when I—literally—ran smack into Ben. Given his enormous stature, I bounced off him and fell backward. In a very Fred Astaire move, he reached one tree trunk of an arm out and caught me before I could hit the ground.

"I can see why you're not named Grace," he said, smiling.

"I happen to be very resilient," I replied, still a little too shaken to smile back. "And I drank a ton of milk as a kid, so I have bones of steel."

"I have a feeling you need them," he mused. "Are you here working with Daisy?"

"I was actually going to have lunch with Vaughn, but there's a . . . situation. He can't get away." I didn't know how much I could say. The last thing I wanted to do was crank up the rumor mill on set. I would have been surprised if the crew wasn't at least partially aware of what was going on, but it wasn't really any of my business.

"I was about to head over to Maccheroni, if you'd like to join me. I could use the company."

I had no idea what Maccheroni was, aside from the pasta, but I was hungry and I didn't have the foggiest idea where to find a good meal. I'd already noticed that every other restaurant had a sign proclaiming the "tourist menu," which made me think those eateries were the T.G.I. Friday's of Italy. I'd come all this way—I wanted to experience the best food the city had to offer. I was also eager to put the weirdness of the last few minutes behind me.

"Lead on," I told him.

Compared to La Pergola, Maccheroni was much more my speed. A small, homey restaurant with simple decor and a menu with dishes I understood. I had a rigatoni carbonara that very nearly made me weep with joy and a can of Diet Coke I'd been craving since we landed (the Italians call it Coke Light). And while conversation with Ben didn't have the same acerbic, sarcastic edge as with Vaughn, it was delightfully direct and *easy*. It was refreshing.

"How's the writing going?" Ben asked me partway through the meal.

I glanced up in surprise, realizing instantly that not a single other person had yet asked me that question. Not Vaughn, not Faith, not even the damn manager who'd hired me. I briefly considered making up something noncommittal and cutesy, but I went with the truth. Ben seemed like a just-the-facts kind of guy.

"Honestly, it's not," I said, almost relieved to be voicing my worry for the first time. "I just can't get inside her head, I guess. I'm supposed to be writing this 'behind the curtain' look at a pop star's magical life, but the girl the world knows so well doesn't really exist."

Ben nodded thoughtfully and then shrugged. "That's part of Hollywood life, though. We're selling a celluloid dream, not reality. People don't want reality."

I considered his words for a moment before responding, "Doesn't that ever make you sad? Knowing that it's all just a front . . . that's there's no real magic?"

Ben's face softened into a smile that somehow made him seem even sexier. "Oh, magic does exist." He sounded so confident about this fact that I immediately believed him. "But it can't be planned or replicated; it comes and goes so fleetingly. So we movie and TV types just try to give people a reasonable facsimile thereof, some close approximation to help them remember their own magical moments."

I'm the writer, and I could have never crafted that sentiment in a million years. It was beautiful—but it also didn't help me do my job. "So how do I create a facsimile of a facsimile?"

This earned a hearty laugh from Ben as he wound his pasta around his fork. "You stop thinking about it so much."

"What does that mean?"

"You're trying to think this all through, be analytical and precise . . . but that's not who Daisy is." Ben shrugged again, still grinning. "I'm pretty sure she doesn't think about one syllable that comes out of her mouth. So pick the logical starting place and just *write*. Write like you're making fun of her voice. Just let it all come out and edit later."

I stared at Ben for a couple of seconds, wondering if he was a genius or an idiot. It couldn't be that simple. Could it?

After lunch, we walked down to the Pantheon, which was packed from one side to the other with tourists. For all the talk of the recession crippling tourism, European holidays sure looked alive and well here in Rome.

"Pantheon means 'to the gods,'" Ben told me. "Marcus Agrippa designed this as a central temple where people could worship as many gods as they chose. As long as the god's statue was in the building."

"How do you know that?" I asked.

"I have a master's in architecture," he replied, like it was just some Eagle Scout badge he'd earned. "I've always found Roman construction fascinating. We can't build an apartment complex that can withstand a nine-point-oh earthquake, but they have buildings that have stood for thousands of years."

I have a lot of hobbies and weird, geeky interests, but they all suddenly seemed petty. I felt like I should take up French literature or computer programming before I had the right to talk to Ben again.

"Have you been to the Forum yet?" he asked.

"I haven't really been anywhere," I admitted, embarrassed. "I was a little preoccupied with Daisy and napping yesterday, and last night we all went to La Pergola for the never-ending dinner."

"I'm playing hooky tomorrow, if you'd like a personal tour guide."

"You're playing hooky?" This was an unexpected revelation; most movie people act like their jobs cure cancer and no one else in the world could possibly handle the pressure but them. It's why they have no lives and endless streams of exes. I thought back to Vaughn saying he didn't have any hobbies because work was the only place he really wanted to be.

The corners of Ben's mouth curled up in amusement. "I've been working for nine days in a row; I think I deserve a few hours off. Besides, it's just a TV show. If they need something, they'll call me. And until they do, there are plenty of places I'd like to see."

"Like what?"

He hesitated, blushing a bit. It's so rare to see men turn red. "The Vatican," he said. "Wednesday is the papal audience."

I was raised a lapsed Catholic and I'd never heard anyone excited about seeing the Pope. My mother used his name as a curse word or a threat. When she'd caught me kissing a boy in the garage, she'd shouted that once the Pope found out, I'd be excommunicated and banned from heaven. Even then I didn't think the Pope cared what I did in the garage as long as it didn't involve genocide. But it was sweet that Ben wanted to go see Il Papa.

"It sounds like fun," I said. "Count me in."

"Since I'm disappearing tomorrow, I should probably go back to work today. Although . . ." He paused, smiling at me again. "I'd rather not."

"It is a beautiful day," I agreed. "It's almost a crime to be stuck at work on a gorgeous Roman afternoon."

"That's true, but I'm enjoying the company, too."

"Me, too," I replied. "But you won't like me very much if I get you fired. So scat."

"Will you be at the hotel later?"

The question seemed unnecessary to me. At least for the next week, I lived at that hotel. Of course I'd be there later. "Yup."

"Maybe I'll see you," he said, offering a wave as he turned and walked away.

I spent the rest of the afternoon wandering up and down the streets of Rome, finally sightseeing the way I'd been dreaming about for days. I stopped for gelato at Giolitti and ate until I thought I might have given myself diabetes. I made myself order only the flavors I didn't know, working my way through chestnut and a strange coconut until I got to a cream variety that made my eyes roll back up into my head. Then with my change, I walked to the Trevi Fountain and made so many wishes the magic fountain fairies probably tuned me out.

It was a busy, hot afternoon, and the fountain was crowded. I knew I should make my wishes, force some poor stranger to take my picture, then vacate my spot for another anxious tourist, but I couldn't do it. Right at that moment, sitting on the stone ledge, I felt intoxicated by the city. Even a bulldozer driven by a hot Italian man couldn't have moved me from that seat.

I watched nuns in full habits eat ice cream and priests with expensive briefcases chatter away on their cell phones. There was something surreal and hazy about this place, despite the graffiti on nearly every block. For the first time in a very, very long while, I wasn't worried about anything. And as I threw coin after coin in the fountain, I wished for things I didn't even know I wanted. A book deal, the love of my life, to lose twenty pounds, and to finally make my mother proud of me. I know the popular wisdom is that voicing your wishes cancels them out, but I don't believe that. I think that all too often, we don't get what we want because we're too afraid to put it out there. And on my perfect Roman afternoon, I wasn't afraid of anything.

I realized that for the last eighteen months, I'd lived in a limbo of my own creation. Doing the work required of me, but never an ounce more. And it wasn't because I had a poor work ethic, I was just too terrified to hope for anything more. All the dreams of a successful writing career had been shoved as far back in my head as I could manage, and I'd purposely focused only on the step right in front of me. If I only worried about my next paycheck, I couldn't obsess about how this or that article would further my career. Or wouldn't.

And in the last month, my concern had been if I *could* do the job, not whether I actually wanted to. The song "Take the Money and Run" had been playing on loop in my brain and I wasn't even worried about finishing the autobiography, only about doing enough to get the next check.

But those silly coins, all ten of them, signaled a new era in my life, and I knew it the instant they left my hand. Not only *could* I do this job, I could be good at it. I knew I could. Though I wasn't allowed to talk about my work, I was fairly sure the ghostwriting community was small and the right people would know what I'd done. Above and beyond that, if I could pry the rest of the checks out of Jamie's greedy little fingers, that money would give me the freedom to do what I wanted for at least a year (much more if the book sold well).

As my last coin dropped into the fountain, I knew that I was done with the status quo. This isn't to say that I had any idea what was going to happen next. On the contrary, I was acutely aware that choosing this job had thrust me into a perfectly uncertain world, and not just for the duration of my work with Daisy. But I had a strange feeling that no matter what happened, it would all work out for the best.

The sun was setting before I finally began heading back to the hotel. I was enthralled with this place, though a little confused by not having heard a single word I understood since lunchtime. As I walked, I watched the endless adoring couples heading out for dinner, hand in hand. I couldn't remember the last time I had experienced that feeling, or if I ever really had.

I'd had boyfriends, to be sure, but none of them had really knocked my socks off. This isn't to say they weren't lovely human beings (my taste runs toward the monogamous, vanilla guys), but no one had ever made me breathless and dizzy. And I didn't count Vaughn's effect on me because it wasn't real. Or at least, I didn't know if it was real. Anyone can make you swoon. It's when that first flush of attraction has passed and their touch still makes you weak that it counts for something.

Maybe I was naïve and searching for some ideal that didn't exist. It wouldn't be the first time. But I'll wager I wasn't the first woman filled with promise and hope by a simple stroll through the Eternal City. Or the last.

When I got back to the hotel, I had a message from Vaughn. Rather than call him back, I just walked up to his room, which turned out to be exactly one floor above mine. The door was open as I approached, and I could see that he was talking on both the room phone and his cell at the same time.

"We'll be wrapped by ten tomorrow night, just like we promised," he said into his cell phone. Then, into the room phone, "Make sure you don't send any knives up with that. Seriously, no knives. I'll find out if you forget."

I knocked softly and he waved me in. Vaughn patted the bed, gesturing for me to sit down next to him, but I chose to take a seat over by the balcony. I wasn't yet comfortable enough for the bed.

After a few minutes, he said, "All right, take care," and hung up both phones. I still don't know if those last words were to one of the callers or both. "Hey, you," he said, finally looking up at me.

"Hey, yourself."

"Sorry about lunch today. It got a little weird on set." Vaughn wiped a hand across his eyes and I could see how worn out he was.

"No problem," I said. I almost asked about the knives, but everyone was obviously trying to keep sharp objects away from Daisy. "I know you were busy. Ben ended up taking me to lunch."

Vaughn's eyebrows went up. "You had lunch with Benji?"

I had to ask Ben why everyone called him that. He was this somber, intelligent guy and the crew had given him a dog's nickname. It didn't make any sense to me. "Yeah, we went to Maccheroni. It was amazing, you would have loved it."

"I had dry, tasteless macaroni and cheese for lunch," he said. Then he looked truly pained, and I had to hope he wasn't so in love with food that a bad mac-and-cheese meal could inspire such a reaction. Then again, I'm really one to talk. I'd almost stabbed Vaughn just for eyeing my dessert. "We flew six thousand miles to get the same catering we could have had in L.A."

"I was about to go get something to eat. You hungry?"

"God, yes," he said, almost leaping to his feet. "I hear there's this place down by the Spanish Steps—" And then his cell phone rang. Vaughn looked at the screen and groaned. "Ah, damn."

"It's no big deal," I promised. "We'll talk later."

"No, really. Just let me take care of this and then we'll go."

I was dubious, but I decided to give Vaughn the benefit of the doubt, so I remained where I was.

"What is it, Jamie? I was about to go out for dinner." From the tone of his voice, Vaughn didn't think much of Daisy's manager, either. Then he clenched his teeth and his face lost most of its color. "You're kidding me . . ." Vaughn listened for a few more sentences, growing wearier by the second. "What exactly did she break?"

At this point, I stood up, knowing that dinner was out of the question. Vaughn looked up at me with that apologetic expression I'd now seen twice that day. "Like I said," I whispered. "No big deal."

I patted Vaughn on the shoulder as I walked by, and he grabbed my hand and held me there for a second. "Will you . . ." he whispered, pulling the receiver away from his mouth a bit, "go to dinner with Benji instead?"

Vaughn sounded awfully territorial for someone who hadn't even staked a claim. I was certainly attracted to him, but I was already getting tired of his noncommittal behavior. "I'll probably order room service and work. It's what I should have done, anyway."

"Oh. Cool." Despite his obvious exhaustion, Vaughn smiled a little. Then he remembered he was on the phone with Jamie, who had apparently continued to yammer in his absence. "Yeah, yeah, calm down. I'll go talk to someone at the front desk and write a check. No, we will not get thrown out of the hotel."

Good night, I mouthed, heading out of the room.

Vaughn waved to me but didn't turn around. For someone who'd seemed so concerned about me just a moment ago, he appeared to have already moved on to other matters.

Though it took every ounce of my willpower, I did exactly as I had promised, returning to my room and my long-standing stalemate with my laptop. With Ben's words ringing in my ears, I finally sat down at the desk and booted up my computer. I had just been overthinking things. I could do this.

As soon as the blank page popped up, I prepared for the rush of terror and indecision, but I forced my brain back to our first working session in Miami, when I had asked Daisy about school. I couldn't write "My mom's got all that crap," so instead, I typed—

> Everyone always asks me how I got started in this business, but it all happened so quickly, I don't really remember. One day I was just a regular kid in my school's talent show and the next, people were handing me scripts and taking my picture.

Once the first paragraph was done, I just kept going. By eleven, I was up to thirty-three pages and gaining confidence by the minute. I wrote until my wrists ached and then slumped into bed, happy and relieved. Ben had been right—this wasn't rocket science after all. In my own little way, I had conquered Daisy Mae Dixson.

I was again awoken by the little girls singing "Date Night," but on this morning, I didn't mind nearly so much. If I did have a complaint, it was that they could at least have switched to one of Daisy's other songs. I was starting to hear "Date Night" in my sleep.

Ben and I met in the lobby at eight and snuck out of the hotel like we were two teenagers on our way to elope.

"I don't know why we're being so secretive," he said, laughing.

"Because these vultures will hook you with their claws and devour you if they find out you're on your way to have fun," I replied. "You're working, Ben, you have to be miserable." I checked to make sure the coast was clear, then grabbed his elbow and pulled him through the lobby. "Now come on, we have a date with the Pope."

In the last twenty-four hours, I'd grown quite accustomed to coming and going in front of the hormonal hordes. Once they saw it wasn't Daisy, they went back to their songs or stories or braiding each other's hair. But on this morning, one teenager (who was at least two years too old to be a Daisy Dixson fan) gasped at the sight of me. At first I thought I was imagining things, but then the girl tried to grab my arm and yelled, *"Cugina, cugina!"* It sounded like a dirty word, even in Italian, and I was relieved when Ben removed the girl's hand and swiftly guided me through the crowd.

I was still shaken up as we rode the subway to Vatican City. "What in the hell do you think that means? *Cugina?*"

"Cousin," Ben answered. "*Cugina* means cousin."

If he spoke fluent Italian, I was going to kill myself. I couldn't even bring myself to ask the question. "Oh." I nodded. "Perez Hilton thinks I'm Daisy's pregnant, alcoholic cousin."

Ben gave me a look, trying to figure out how much—if any—of it was true. I knew the look because I'd seen it twice now, with both Vaughn and Camille. "I assure you, I am not pregnant, an alcoholic, or related to Daisy in any way."

"That's pretty weird."

"I know." It was nice to be around someone who recognized the insanity of everything instead of just acting like it was completely normal. The people in Daisy's life spent all of their time trying to pretend a straitjacket was really a ball gown. The scary part was that there were moments I was starting to believe it.

"I can't say I'm terribly surprised." Ben laughed. "They all do whatever they want and the rest of us have to deal with the consequences. Last season, Jonathan Adler lent us a lamp for one of the main sets, and Daisy just decided to take it home. It was a seven-hundred-dollar lamp that wasn't even available for sale to the public yet, not to mention that we didn't own it, either. But she liked it, so your little friend Vaughn got out his magic checkbook and made the problem go away."

"I think she broke hotel furniture or something last night," I told him. "I was supposed to have dinner with Vaughn, but he had to smooth over some trouble with the hotel staff."

Ben listened to what I had to say, but waited a few seconds before speaking again. "You know what? We are two thoughtful, reasonably intelligent human beings. Just for today, let's pretend we're any other tourists in Rome. We'll turn off our phones and pretend we've never heard the name Daisy Dixson."

"Can we be spies?" I asked. "And give ourselves spy names?"

Ben stared at me, trying to decide if I was serious. "You are an interesting woman" was all he said.

I wasn't really kidding about the spy names (hey, why not?), but when it became clear that Ben wasn't receptive to the idea, I just reveled in being Holly for the day. Not someone's employee or lackey, just me.

We spent the entire morning at the Vatican, even kissing the Pope's ring. I bought my mother a blessed rosary, hoping it would make up for my recent lack of phone calls, and along with Ben, marveled at the strange grandeur of the world's only religious city-state. If St. Peter's Basilica is any indication, God is a really big fan of gold leaf. We have that in common.

Though I wanted to keep my emotions in check in front of this man I barely knew, I found myself overwhelmed a number of times that day. First by Michelangelo's Pietà, depicting the Virgin Mary holding the dead Jesus in her arms, and then again when we finally reached the Sistine Chapel. I say "finally" because the museum around it is a labyrinth of signs and stairs that seem to go on for miles. I had almost given up when I set one foot inside the chapel and inhaled so deeply I almost passed out. The masterpiece was like nothing I'd ever seen before, nor would I even trust myself to describe it with any measure of accuracy. It was, quite simply, breathtaking.

By 1:00 P.M., I was light-headed and overwhelmed, and I was grateful that Ben recognized this without having to be told. We found a small restaurant for lunch, stuffed ourselves with pasta, and then found some more gelato. I was already full up to my ears, but the thought of just passing by the ice cream shop was unacceptable, so I shoved down more food and hoped I wouldn't have to vomit into a nearby trash can.

In the afternoon, we explored Castel Sant'Angelo and the residential neighborhood of Trastevere. Rome is such a tourist attraction, I never really thought about the people who call the city home. We sat in a park and talked as school let out for the afternoon, flooding the swing sets and benches with giggling children. The mothers stood by chatting, sometimes offering a snack or doctoring a small wound. It was unlike anything I'd seen in the United States. I know that we have a million parks, but there's such a cliquey atmosphere to our neighborhood interactions. I grew up in a small town and knew the names of maybe ten percent of the people on my block, and I certainly never would have thought to strike up conversations with most of those folks. Here it was like every mother was a sort of parent to every child, regardless of how well she knew him or her. The sense of community in this tiny Roman enclave made me never want to leave. Three times, one of the mothers walked by and nodded to us, each time with a "hello." I couldn't figure out how they knew we were American, but we were highly amused by it.

I'd love to say I recall every detail of that day, but I don't. Ben and I walked and walked, and talked and talked, for twelve full hours. And try as we might, we couldn't see everything in one day. We both wanted to visit the Colosseum, but by the time we made it back to that part of town, the tours had shut down for the day. It was after eight when we realized that our legs were numb and our stomachs were empty.

We stumbled back toward Piazza Navona and stopped for pizza at Montecarlo, a boisterous place brimming with college students and locals. We took seats in the back and worked our way through the greatest margherita pizza I've ever tasted. By this point, the waistband of my jeans was cutting off the circulation to my legs, but I didn't care. If I gained twenty pounds in Rome, it would be worth it.

When the waiter approached with the check, I asked to see the dessert menu.

"Oh, dear God," Ben moaned, laughing. "You cannot be serious. If we eat anything else, we'll need to have our stomachs pumped."

"We're in one of the greatest cities in the world. I think it's actually illegal here to skip dessert."

Before he could talk me out of it, I ordered a piece of ricotta cheesecake and chocolate mousse. This earned a fresh round of groaning, but Ben didn't stop me.

"So . . ." he asked the instant the waiter was out of earshot, "is it true you're dating Vaughn Royce?"

I glanced up from my coffee, unsure how to answer that question. "Where did you hear that?"

"Sharla. She said the two of you had been hanging out since Miami."

There really was no such thing as a secret on a film set. "*Hanging out* is a good way to put it."

He watched my face for a few moments, though I'm not sure what he was looking for. "But you want to date him."

Ben was more direct than anyone I'd ever met, including my mother. It felt especially odd because there also didn't appear to be any judgment in his questioning. "I don't know," I told him. I almost left it there, until I realized Ben could be a good sounding board. Unlike Camille, he didn't have any preconceived notions about me—and he knew Vaughn fairly well. "I think he's interested in me. We've spent a good deal of time together. But he's never told me how he feels, one way or the other."

"And you're not sure how you feel about him?"

"I'm not." I paused, considering the question. Despite my attraction and the emotions swirling around in my head, I'd tried not to focus too much on Vaughn. Not in the middle of a job that had the potential to change my whole world. "I like him. I think he's a lot of fun, and we definitely have things in common. But I don't like uncertainty. And for someone who puts so much effort into what he does and says, he can randomly be pretty thoughtless."

The desserts arrived and neither of us made a move to eat them. Ben ignored the waitress, instead continuing to focus on me. In my limited time with him, I'd already noticed that you could almost see the gears turning in his brain when he was mulling something over. It was like opening the front of a working clock and peering inside.

"I'm not going to tell you what to do," Ben said. He paused, still constructing his thought. "Vaughn can be a lot of fun and I can see why the two of you get along. But be careful around him."

I was taken aback by the warning. I waited to see if there were more specifics, but Ben appeared to be done. "Okay." I didn't know what else to say. Thanks? I will? You have nothing to worry about?

Ben seemed satisfied with my response, and even dug into the desserts. After engaging me in conversation all day, he was surprisingly quiet for the last part of the meal and the beginning of our walk back to the hotel. The behavior didn't immediately raise any red flags, as I'd already noticed Ben didn't make idle conversation. When he spoke, there was always a purpose to his words. So when he stayed quiet, I assumed he simply had nothing left to say.

Boy, was I wrong.

A few blocks from the hotel, Ben reached out and lightly grasped my hand. I was so astonished I came to a screeching halt, causing an older woman to run into me. She cursed me with an Italian word

I didn't know, then veered around me. I still hadn't moved. It was a miracle I hadn't instinctively yanked my hand away. I think the whole event was so unexpected my mind couldn't process what was happening.

Ben must have seen the look on my face. "I'm sorry, I probably shouldn't have done that." He did not, however, let go of my hand. Maybe he was afraid I might run away once untethered.

I had no idea what was going on. "I'm just surprised. Especially given our earlier conversation."

"Really?" Ben's expression said that he didn't believe me. "Because I like to think of myself as a fairly transparent person. I thought I was making myself pretty clear all day."

Not clear enough, apparently. "I'm sorry. I really didn't notice. And you said to be careful with Vaughn, but you didn't say not to date him."

"I'd never tell you what to do," he said. "But I also wouldn't leave you doubting how I felt about you. You're great. You deserve someone who treats you that way."

The implication being, Vaughn wouldn't. More than anything, I couldn't wrap my head around the fact that Ben was attracted to me. I could see how I fit with a man like Vaughn; he was handsome, but in a quirky, tortured intellectual way. We were two peas in a geek pod. But Ben, he was different. He looked like he could pose for a Calvin Klein ad in the morning, spend his afternoon working on the design of a new Trump skyscraper, then go home and grill a porterhouse to perfection. He was direct, almost statesmanlike, and I hadn't yet noticed a quirky bone in his body. I don't know exactly who I would have paired him with, but it definitely wasn't me.

I mulled over these concerns so long that Ben took my silence the wrong way and released my hand. "Look, it's fine. We're both adults, I'll get over it."

"What?" I cried. Usually, I screw things up by opening my mouth. This time I'd done it without a single word. "No, my reaction isn't what you think. Honestly, I don't know what my reaction is. I'm a little slow sometimes."

"But it's probably not a great sign that you're this shocked," he said, rubbing his jaw thoughtfully.

I had to make a split-second decision, and I didn't quite know how. While I would have preferred a few days to think about the possibilities with Ben, I knew I didn't have that kind of time. Men like him claim they recover from romantic defeats, but they really don't. Any chance I had with him started and ended right at that moment. But how could I choose when I hadn't even considered him in that way?

And then there was the issue of Vaughn. I was attracted to him and I thought he was attracted to me, but he'd yet to make a move. And here I had another—pretty fantastic—man that I could just pluck right off the vine. I momentarily felt like a cheater until I realized I had no real responsibility to Vaughn. If he was truly jealous about me going out with Ben, he could tell me himself.

In the end, I used a method that has yet to fail me. I opened my mouth and just waited to see what came out.

"Can I be blunt?" I asked.

"Better than just about anyone I've ever met," Ben replied. "But yes, please say what you need to."

Partly because I need to move to think and partly because we were holding up the sidewalk traffic, I started walking again. Putting one foot in front of the other in a measured, methodical way made it easier to pace my thoughts. "I know that a lot of women eye every man like a piece of meat, but my brain doesn't work that way. And this isn't some game. . . . I don't even bother playing games, it's too exhausting."

"I didn't think you did," he said.

"What I'm trying to say is that I'm an idiot." When Ben opened his mouth to protest, I quickly added, "Socially, anyway." I paused, trying to find the right words, and fast enough that this didn't dissolve into an awkward silence. "I like you, I really do."

"But not in that way . . ." Ben finished.

"I didn't say that." Those four words were the first I hadn't actively constructed, so I suddenly knew what I wanted. Sometimes I even surprise myself. "I just needed a minute or two to think about it."

There are some moments in life when it feels like the physical atmosphere around you changes in a blink of an eye. In one instant, I was nervous and confused, and in the next, I felt a static charge in the air.

Ben gave me his cute little smirk. "And?"

I launched myself up on my toes and kissed him. He was unprepared for the kiss, but it took only a second or two before he relaxed into me. Vaughn could be noncommittal all he wanted, but that wasn't the way I operated.

Like I said, sometimes I even surprise myself.

Our fingers were still intertwined when we approached the InterContinental. In fact, we were both so dazed from the recent revelation that we failed to notice the melee outside the hotel until we were less than a block away.

Though how I could have missed it, even from the end of the street, I don't know. The fans had been pushed to one side of the block, and paparazzi now swarmed the entrance, illuminating the façade of the building with rapid camera flashes. And in the space directly in front of the door, two police cars were parked haphazardly, the officers being ushered inside by Vaughn.

"Oh, God," I said under my breath. Ben was too stunned to say anything at all.

We approached the security line and were shouted at for a few seconds before Daisy's big, silent bodyguards saw me and walked over, moving the sawhorse aside for me and Ben to enter. We hustled inside the hotel, and I didn't even realize I was still clutching Ben until Vaughn caught sight of me, shooting an angry and pained look at our hands.

Vaughn recovered well, turning and crossing to us. I think it helped that he had bigger things to worry about.

"What's going on?" I asked, filled with dread. Whatever was happening, I knew it couldn't be good.

Vaughn took a moment to answer, a panicked expression on his face. When he spoke, his voice was hoarse, terrified. "Daisy's missing."

CHAPTER 14

For someone so young, I do have a lot of responsibilities, which can feel a little heavy at times. I can't be late for work or to a meeting. Not only is it rude and bad business, since I'm the star, but very little can happen without me. If I'm late or don't show up where I'm supposed to, it costs people money. And if there's one thing my mama taught me, it's the value of a dollar.

But it gets hard sometimes when thirty people always have to know where you are. I can't disappear for an afternoon at the movies or a quiet lunch by myself. In my world, there's no such thing as quiet.

Ten minutes later, we were piling into Daisy's suite with the Italian police leading the charge. At the door, Vaughn stopped me, his eyes carefully trained on Ben.

"It's not appropriate for your friend to be here."

In the haze of the last few minutes, I'd almost forgotten about Ben's presence. Well, not his presence so much as the strangeness of it. There was so much strange to go around, my newfound crush got lost in the mix. But Vaughn was absolutely right; Ben shouldn't be anywhere near this debacle. And to be honest, I wasn't sure I should be, either. It wasn't like I could write about any of it.

"It's not a problem," Ben said quietly. "I'll talk to you later." He squeezed my hand and backed away, but not before exchanging a death stare with Vaughn.

"I don't know why she's even here," Jamie yelled in my general direction. His face was red and puffy, and he looked like he was about to have an aneurysm. I'm sure he was just adding up the financial losses incurred with every passing hour. I wasn't sentimental enough to believe that he actually cared about Daisy's welfare.

"I asked her to come up," Faith replied tearfully. She had been sobbing for most of the last few minutes, and there was a trail of makeup and snot running down her face. She didn't seem to notice. "Holly's one of Daisy's best friends."

I was what now?

"Fine," Jamie barked. "But get inside and close the fucking door. The last thing we need is the rest of the hotel hearing about this."

"The rest of the *world* knows about this," Vaughn shot back, being far more insubordinate than I'd yet seen him. "How the hell did that happen?"

It took two of his monster strides for Jamie to cross the room and get right in Vaughn's face. Though Vaughn was about the same height, Jamie had a good forty pounds on him—there was little doubt in my mind who would go down in a fight. I also suspected Jamie wasn't above fighting dirty.

"Listen to me, you pissant piece of shit," Jamie hissed. "The little bitch hopped on the back of the motorcycle in plain view of the paparazzi. They all have pictures of it. What was I supposed to do?"

"Keep her under control," Vaughn shot back coolly. "How about that?"

I had yet to hear the story in its entirety, but I had gleaned the basic outline of events. As I had seen myself the previous day, Daisy was increasingly bizarre and spacey, though no one could say exactly why (or what she was on). After throwing a tantrum over the lunch truck being late—which I couldn't understand at all, given her weird diet predilections—she'd started screaming at the fans. Right in front of the sea of photographers and videographers.

When Jamie had tried to calm her down and forcibly pull her away from the crowd, Daisy had apparently bitten him and then run out into the street, whereupon she jumped on a Vespa that was stopped at a light. Why the cyclist hadn't thrown her off the bike, I'll never know, but he continued on with Daisy on the back, disappearing from sight before the police and security could respond. By the time of the frantic meeting, Daisy had been missing for three hours and hadn't contacted anyone.

"I'm sure she's fine." Faith sniffled softly. "She's a very resourceful girl."

The eyes of everyone in the room moved to Faith as if to say, *Really?*

"I don't care how she is," Jamie hissed. "The little whore fucking bit me. Has everyone forgotten that?" He held up a haphazardly bandaged hand that was bloody on one side.

"You should probably go to the hospital for that," I said, cringing. "Human bites almost always get infected."

My random, esoteric knowledge was met with a look that said Jamie was hoping my face melted off. "Was I talking to you?"

Fine, I thought. *Let the wound fester and you can die from Daisy's insanity.*

The police began speaking in rapid-fire Italian, which prompted nothing but looks of confusion from the occupants of the room. I caught a few words that sounded familiar, but that may have been due to their similarity to English words I already knew.

"I don't know what you're saying," Jamie boomed, using the flawless, age-old logic that if someone doesn't speak the same language, you should yell louder. "We need to find Daisy. *Now*."

"We are many of us out looking," one of the men replied haltingly, taking long moments to formulate his words.

"Really? 'Cause all I see are assholes standing around, staring at their own feet," Jamie roared in the cop's face.

From the withering look Jamie received in return, it was clear that the officer didn't exactly understand what was said, but he didn't like the tone being leveled at him. The cop turned and started a new line of conversation with his fellow officers—not that we understood a word of it.

"I should call Deacon," Faith said. "I can't believe I forgot to call Deacon. I'm sure he's already seen the press and is out of his mind. He'll want to know what's going on."

Jamie glared down at Faith like she was the lowest form of slimy, disease-ridden insect. "If Deacon gave a flying fuck, you'd have already heard from him."

His tone was so cruel, Faith burst into a fresh round of sobs and ran off to the bedroom. Vaughn sighed and rubbed his eyes. Everyone in the room seemed stuck, unable to think of anything to do or say.

The silence must have been unbearable for Jamie as well, because he unleashed another expletive-laden barrage on the police. The officers continued to try to communicate, but they knew only a few words of English, and it wasn't long before the room was a cacophony of two clashing languages.

Vaughn, who had thus far ignored me, leaned over and said quietly, "I need to hire a translator before Jamie decks one of these guys and we get tossed out of the country."

Now, an idea had been floating around in my mind for the last several minutes, but I knew it was a bad one. Or at the very least, ill-advised. But as the tension continued to escalate, I began to think that any option was worth consideration. So I opened my mouth and hoped that I wouldn't regret my words.

"Um . . . there is someone who might be able to help."

"Who?" Vaughn cried. "I'm desperate, I'll take anybody."

I had a feeling he might change his mind in the next few hours. "I think Ben speaks a little Italian. I'm not positive, but he managed to communicate pretty well today." In fact, in the entire fourteen hours we were together, he'd never hesitated with a single order or even hello on the street. And I suppose he could have been bluffing, but he looked like he understood every comment or question lobbed at him.

Vaughn's gaze immediately went blank. I've never met anyone whose main reaction is having no reaction at all. "Huh" was all he said at first.

From across the room, I heard Jamie grunt. "Who's the damn president of this godforsaken country? I want him in this hotel room in twenty minutes!"

Finally, Vaughn sighed. Without looking at me, he said, "Find Ben."

By 1:00 A.M., the room had taken on a deathly pall. We were all still there, sitting silently in the living area, but people rarely spoke. And though Ben had claimed his Italian was rudimentary, he had no problem conversing with the police officers. Which, as the night wore on, became less and less of a necessity as the tips and sightings dried up. I remained in the center of the couch, sandwiched between Ben and Vaughn. I kept waiting for one of them to move, but neither budged.

At about midnight, someone had given Faith a Valium, and so she was now relaxed and a little loopy, wandering around the room like a drunken fairy. She stayed largely quiet, but every once in a while felt the need to remind us that Daisy was an excellent judge of character and never got into any real trouble. We all just nodded, barely listening.

I spent the night trying to formulate an opinion on the current crisis. I'd love to tell you that I felt empathy for Daisy, but I was oddly apathetic. I know it sounds terrible, but she was the architect of her own destruction and part of me truly felt like she needed to hit some kind of bottom if she had any hope of developing into a decent human being. As long as the people in her life insisted on bailing her out of every scrape, they were only reinforcing the belief that the rules didn't apply to her. And even if she was above the general law now, I knew that most starlets in her position didn't have the happiest endings. Once Hollywood was done with her—and that happened to all of them sooner or later—she'd be nothing but a relatively unskilled has-been with no ability to live within her means.

At one-thirty, just after Faith fell asleep on the floor, the phone rang. She was so drugged, she didn't even roll over. Vaughn was quicker than Jamie, deliberately grabbing the receiver before the manager could reach it.

"Hello?" There was foreign chattering on the other end of the line, and after a few seconds, Vaughn thrust the phone at Ben without making eye contact. "Here."

"*Ciao,*" Ben answered. "*Qualche notizie?*"

Out of the corner of my eye, I could see Vaughn mimic the words. Jamie stared at Ben from a few feet away, waiting for a facial expression that might betray the tone of the conversation, but every piece of information Ben received was met with only a thoughtful furrowed brow.

"*Sì, ho capito. . . . Dove?*" He listened quietly, nodding to himself a few times. "*Grazie. . . . Arrivederla.*" Ben carefully replaced the phone, then seemed to consider what he'd just heard.

"Jesus, Benji," Jamie exclaimed. "Just tell us what's going on."

Ben threw me a nervous look, and I knew he didn't relish having to share whatever piece of information he'd just learned. *Oh, God*, I thought. *What if she's dead?*

The truth was far less disturbing, but in the grand scheme of things, just as salacious. "Um . . ." Ben hesitated. "Well . . . they found Daisy."

"Where?" Vaughn demanded, just as angry with Ben as if he'd been responsible for kidnapping Daisy and holding her for ransom.

"She's in jail."

CHAPTER 15

I don't remember life before Hollywood, and that can be scary sometimes. Because literally all I know in this world is what it means to be famous, both the good parts and the bad. I don't really understand what people do in offices all day or how hard it is to be a construction worker. If my career suddenly ended tomorrow—and I know it could—I wouldn't have the first idea what to do next. The way people disappear from this business, I don't even know if there is a next.

It was 7:00 A.M. before anyone was permitted to have contact with Daisy. By then, Ben and I had gone back to our respective rooms, and while I can't speak for him, I was fast asleep. So I was nothing short of livid when my phone rang just before 8:00.

"Sorry to wake you," Vaughn said, not sounding sorry.

"What do you want?" I groaned, burying my head in my pillow. I was already perfectly aware that the Rome episode was probably dead, and that meant we would all likely be sent back to L.A. in the next twenty-four hours. I desperately needed sleep if I was going to endure another daylong journey around the world.

"Can you come to the police station in Porta Maggiore?" he asked, sounding exhausted. "You have every right to say no, but I could really use your help right now."

If they thought I was dragging another ten bottles of vodka down to a police station, these nutbags had another thing coming. "And why would I do that, Vaughn?"

"Because Daisy says she won't talk to anyone but you. And the officials won't let us see her without her permission."

Daisy didn't really think I was one of her best friends, did she? Because that made less than no sense. We had only been working together for a month, and in that period, we'd spoken maybe a dozen times. I was an acquaintance, to be sure, but nothing more than that.

"Seriously? Why does she want to talk to me?"

"I don't know, Holly. All I do know is that I have to finish shooting this episode and I only have two days' worth of scenes without Daisy."

"You're going to finish?"

"We don't have a choice. We've spent four million dollars on this two-parter. If we come back without enough footage to air, we're all canned."

I flopped on my back, wishing like hell that I'd never called Jamie Lloyd in the first place. Smitty and I would be destitute and living in Griffith Park, but that seemed preferable to this ridiculous circus. "Fine. Let me throw on some clothes and I'll be there as soon as I can."

"God, I love you," Vaughn replied.

It took all my energy not to tell him to shut the hell up.

Daisy was a tiny little girl, but curled up on the jail cell's cot, she looked like a doll. A damaged, strung out doll. When they announced my presence, she didn't even look up, nodding into her folded-up knees and murmuring "okay" in a childlike voice.

I crept into the cell with trepidation, still not sure what I was doing here. For Daisy's sake, I hoped she was unaware of the insanity taking place outside the police station, even though I could faintly hear the shouting from inside. Word of Daisy's arrest had quickly leaked to the press, and now everyone was out for blood. Including the police themselves. They had refused to release her for forty-eight hours, despite Jamie's protestation that she had so much work left to do, she wasn't the slightest flight risk.

"Hi, Holly Bear," Daisy said quietly, still with her head buried against her knees.

There wasn't anywhere else to sit inside the tiny cell, so I found a place on the cot, situating myself as far away from her as I could. I didn't have the first clue what I was supposed to say.

"How are you doing, Daisy?"

Her shoulders moved up and down in a shrug, but she didn't answer or look up. This was going to be even more difficult than I had anticipated.

"Vaughn said you wanted to see me?"

There was a long pause before she finally replied, "I'm in trouble."

"I know." The police had caught Daisy outside a local hotel, snorting cocaine with a group of local teenagers. To make matters worse, she had enough in her purse that she could be charged with intent to sell. Jamie was still trying to work out how these matters were dealt with in Italy, but it wasn't looking good.

There was another drawn-out silence before Daisy picked up her head and gave me a wounded look. With the lines of anxiety creasing her face (not to mention the substances in her body), she appeared to be older than her mother. The change was nothing short of shocking.

"They all know, right?"

I nodded. "Jamie, Vaughn, and your mother are all here. I'm sure the other producers will know soon, too, if they don't already."

Daisy shook her head, then cocked it toward the little window above the bed. "I meant the people outside. You know, *everybody*."

I almost wondered if I should lie to her, just to get her through however long she had to be in this room. Also, I was concerned about her reaction, as I didn't particularly want to get punched in the face, especially not on my measly three hours' sleep. But despite her many, many flaws, she deserved better than all the lies she was constantly being fed.

"It's all over the news," I admitted. "And it's just about prime time in L.A., so I'm sure they've heard about it over there, too."

Daisy considered this information, nodding. She unfurled her body a little and leaned back against the wall. I could tell just by her facial expression that a sea change had occurred overnight. Gone was the bratty little teenager; before me sat the seasoned Hollywood veteran. "There's no such thing as prime-time news anymore. I'm sure one of the gossip sites had it up within fifteen minutes of my arrest. Besides, it's not like my fans watch the news." She paused, then laughed humorlessly. "Not that I'll have many fans left after this."

"Why did you do it?" It was a question I knew I shouldn't ask, but I couldn't stop myself. If she understood the ramifications of her actions, I wanted to understand why she was willing to throw everything away.

Daisy's gaze was nothing short of chilling. When she stared back at me, her eyes looked dead, soulless. I didn't know where the bright, bubbly adolescent had gone, but I wanted her back. I would even take the screaming, cussing demon-child over the still, hollow shell of a person. This version of Daisy was terrifying.

"I told them what I needed and they didn't listen. Jamie's been giving me pills since I was thirteen. You can't just take those things away from me and think I'll still be Pollyanna."

I was surprised Daisy knew who Pollyanna was. "What sorts of pills?"

Daisy shrugged. "I have hundreds of them with hundreds of different names. Amphetamines, painkillers, muscle relaxers, barbiturates, benzodiazepines. For a while I was even taking ketamine just so that I could sleep."

"Isn't ketamine used in animal anesthesia?" I asked, horrified.

I wouldn't even know where to get a drug like that. And I'd never heard of benzodiazepines.

"Yeah, but they use it on people with serious spinal injuries and stuff. I looked it up once."

I wanted to point out (but didn't) that there's a big difference between spinal damage and a bout with insomnia. This girl was so warped I wasn't even sure she would understand my objection. For about the millionth time since I'd started this job, I was overwhelmed with a rush of loathing for Jamie. I was also pretty angry at Faith, but I was inclined to believe she just didn't know any better.

"I know they didn't bring that suitcase on purpose," Daisy continued, sighing. "When we were packing, Jamie tried to convince me to hide all the pills inside clothes pockets and shoes. When we flew back from Nice, a customs guy wanted to know who they were all for, and Jamie made some excuse about how Axel was our 'medic' and he wanted to hold on to everyone's prescriptions to avoid ODs. We got away with it, but Jamie's been nuts about that ever since."

"Didn't all the bottles have your name on them?"

Daisy gave me a sympathetic smile that reminded me of all the condescending little looks I'd given her in the last month. "Of course not. No one doctor would be stupid enough to write me four scripts for Adderall. You go to a bunch of doctors and give them all fake names. I've got tons of 'em, from Lulu St. James to Nancy Bennett."

I suddenly found all of that sympathy I hadn't been able to summon for Daisy over the long, tense night. All this time, I had assumed she was gaming the system in every way imaginable, but I was too naïve to realize that she was the one being used and abused. And even though she didn't possess an ounce of book smarts, she was savvy enough to recognize that she meant nothing more to these people than a paycheck.

"What can I do for you?" I couldn't think of a single way I could help her out of this mess, but I was willing to try. I was certain I'd hate her guts again just a few minutes after she was freed from jail, but for the moment, I felt a certain camaraderie.

"Nothing. You're the only one who doesn't want something from me. I wanted to talk to one real person before I have to put on my weepy face and pretend I'm sorry."

"What do you mean I don't want anything from you? I'm getting paid to be here." If I hadn't been hired to be nice to Daisy, I doubt I would have exchanged two pleasant words with her.

Daisy rubbed her eyes with the heels of her hands. "Oh, Holly, you don't have a clue how to use people. It wouldn't even occur to you."

She was right, but that didn't make it any less shocking that she knew it. Up until this conversation, I didn't think Daisy paid any attention to the people around her. I didn't validate her answer only because I knew I didn't need to.

"What do you think will happen?" I couldn't imagine winding up in a prison in a foreign country.

"It'll be fine, I swear. Jamie will get them to 'lose' the evidence and I'll get a slap on the wrist. We'll finish the dumb episode and Nick will air the rest of this season before they cancel me because I'm 'considering college' or a movie career. They'll really want me dead, but won't want to admit that their star is a coke fiend. Then Jamie and my dad will bleed me dry for ten years until I'm old enough to sell jewelry on QVC."

Nothing about that sounded fine. I also couldn't believe Daisy had thought about any of these things and that she was probably spot-on.

"You can send the rest of the idiots in here," she said, closing her eyes. "I'm ready to get back into character."

"Sure." I stood up and crossed to the door, where a guard was waiting to let me out. Before I got into the hallway, Daisy called after me.

"I know this is gonna sound retarded, and I totally have bigger things to think about, but I don't understand why you don't just nail Vaughn already. You totally want to."

I turned and looked back at her in astonishment, unable to hide a smile. "Because if someone wants me, he shouldn't toy around with me. It's all or nothing."

"Cool," she said, smiling back.

"You've known his name was Vaughn all along, haven't you?"

Daisy laughed. And not her cutesy little giggle; it was an honest, genuine laugh. "Yeah," she admitted. "I just like that it drives him bananas."

"Cool," I said.

At ten o'clock that morning, I was seated next to Vaughn in a tiny street café. A glut of pastries was spread out before us, but neither of us had yet touched anything but the coffee. And we'd already had plenty of that.

We'd done all we could for Daisy, which was remarkably little. She had begged for a chocolate donut, so I'd found her the closest approximation the neighborhood had to offer. As I'd passed the small bag through the bars, I also suddenly understood her radical change of heart about food. As long as she was on the amphetamines, she had no appetite at all, and the steady diet of tomatoes and onions was more of a habit than a desire; once off those medications, she was starving twenty-four hours a day.

We left Jamie and Faith to plead for her release or quick judgment, and Vaughn wanted to find food before the delayed start of their filming day finally began. Daisy wouldn't be there, but Vaughn said he had to shoot something, even if it was only birds landing on lampposts. As for me, I just wanted to get out of that police station. After hearing what had been done to Daisy for the last eight years, I felt like I needed a *Silkwood* radiation shower.

"I need to look for a new job," Vaughn said, poking a custard-filled pastry until the filling oozed out the side.

"Or you could pursue directing," I suggested. "I'm willing to bet that after six years, you have a little money stashed away."

He turned and stared at me, but it didn't really seem like he was looking *at* me so much as in my general direction. "Honestly, even after all of my time in the industry, I don't know how people become directors. I'm not the least bit qualified."

"I think you're searching for an excuse," I told him. I knew from experience that it was much easier to simply not try than to try and fail.

But Vaughn shook his head vehemently, as deep in denial as I had been for the last couple of years. "I'm not like you. I can't just take it on faith that if I shoot something, an audience will magically appear."

"And that's your loss," I said, trying to keep my tone firm but not harsh. "If you want to spend the rest of your life as a glorified babysitter, I'm sure you can get another job exactly like this one."

"They're talking about giving Colby his own spin-off." He said this like the network was thinking about going into the dogfighting business.

I certainly did feel bad for Vaughn and the entire crew, knowing that their fountain of riches was likely about to run dry. But for them, there would be other jobs. I wasn't quite so confident Daisy would come out of this unscathed.

"What about you?" Vaughn asked. "I mean, it's not like this autobiography is going to be the tween sensation Jamie had hoped. What's going to happen to your job?"

Though I hadn't vocalized my concern, I'd been worried about losing my job ever since we'd discovered Daisy had been arrested. There probably wasn't much of a market for the book now, and I didn't exactly feel great about the fact that I still couldn't cash that enormous check. Part of me wanted to FedEx it home to Camille along with my bank card and have her deposit it before Jamie could change his mind and cancel it.

"I don't know," I said. "But we're being really selfish here. Our jobs may be in jeopardy, but we can get new ones. Daisy may not be so lucky."

"How can you possibly feel sorry for her?"

"Because she's eighteen years old with an unlimited bank account and no one to teach her right from wrong," I replied.

Vaughn shook his head and began tearing up little pieces of pastry and dropping them back on the plate. He wasn't interested in Daisy's problems right now, only that he'd have to be the one to clean them up. Or at least, try. This debacle had very likely already gone past the point of no return.

"What a town without pity can do . . ." I needed to go back to sleep. The world was starting to take on a hazy, unreal quality, and I knew that no decision I made under these circumstances would be the right one. "I'm going to head back to the hotel to take a nap. And you should take a shower before work, you smell like sweaty boy."

I've personally never minded that odor, but I figured the rest of the crew might. Not to mention, it was probably unprofessional to show up to work unkempt. Then again, Vaughn appeared to be right—a film set really is a lot like a monkey house. . . . This one seemed to be a place where pretty much anything went.

Vaughn turned and stared at me for a few seconds, with that strange, blank expression I still hadn't figured out. He was so social and, well, talkative that I couldn't imagine what was going on inside his head that couldn't be readily translated into words. This was one of his main differences from Ben; Vaughn talked constantly but often said little, while Ben used words sparingly and to much greater effect. It was like Vaughn lacked the ability to be straightforward. It was maddening. "You're right," he said finally.

He took out a wad of euros and threw a few down on the table without counting, then stood up. I followed along behind him and noticed that Vaughn didn't say another word, even out on the street.

We still hadn't addressed the elephant in the room—my new "association" (or whatever it was) with Ben. I'd seen the look on Vaughn's face when he saw the two of us holding hands, and I'd been waiting for him to say something. Anything. He had every right to, given our time together over the last couple of weeks. As we walked back toward the InterContinental, I thought perhaps this would be the moment it would all come out.

As usual, I was completely wrong.

"I think I still owe you lunch," he said finally. "And since we're a dead show walking, I don't think anyone will care if I just walk off set for a little while."

The fact that he still hadn't brought up Ben made me crazy. "Wouldn't that be dinner?" I asked. The call time for the crew had been pushed to 11:00 A.M., and meals always happened six hours later. Five P.M. was hardly lunchtime.

Vaughn groaned. "You're right. And it's a terrible time for dinner, too." He made a face, thinking this over. "How about tomorrow, then? We don't really have that much to shoot today; we should be back to normal by tomorrow morning." He paused, breaking into a wry little grin. "Well, not normal. You know what I mean."

"Tomorrow," I agreed. "I may be asleep until then, anyway."

"Listen, tell Ben I'm sorry for calling and waking you guys up this morning."

I may be dense, but I saw this comment for exactly what it was—fishing. Vaughn wasn't really apologizing, nor would he have cared if he'd woken Ben up with a punch to the face. He was asking if Ben had been there with me this morning when he called. Ben wasn't, of course, but I considered lying. I wasn't sure if the impulse was because I wanted to make Vaughn jealous or simply because I didn't want him to think a negative answer implied doubts about Ben. But as I said, I'm a terrible liar, so I usually end up telling the truth.

"Don't worry, I was the only one in that room for you to wake up and annoy," I said. He didn't respond.

After that, we walked largely in silence, probably because we were both too tired to think. I'd at least gotten a catnap—Vaughn had been up since yesterday morning. As we approached the InterContinental, I noticed that the police barricades were still set up and the little girls (now accompanied by quite a few mothers) were sobbing and holding up signs. Among those I had Ben translate for me later were "vai a casa" (or "go home"), "traditore" ("traitor"), and "Daisy é una butana" ("Daisy is a whore"). I felt that the last one, though true, was unnecessarily harsh considering she'd been caught doing drugs, not participating in a sex club orgy or giving a blow job on a street corner.

And I knew that school didn't start for another several weeks, giving these girls a plethora of free time, but if they suddenly hated her so much, why bother wasting their precious summer vacation on an idol they felt had betrayed them? There was no doubt in my mind that most of these girls were the same ones who had been cheering for Daisy so intensely just twenty-four hours before—I recognized a number of them. I'm sure they were shocked by her arrest, but to take this all so personally—fame really is a fickle bitch.

When we had finally navigated the melee and were safe inside the hotel, Vaughn deliberately stopped at the front desk and gave me a hug. It was sweet, but much too long. I tried to ignore the fact that I really do love sweaty boy smell. Especially his particular vintage. I may have broken off the hug a little too quickly before dashing to the elevator. I still felt guilty about kissing Ben, even if I wasn't sure whether I'd done anything to feel guilty for.

Vaughn wasn't my boyfriend. If he wanted to be, then he needed to step up and say something. If not, there was a lovely and sweet man somewhere in this very hotel who appeared to want the job. I'm not a player—I never have been. But I was also starting to see that in the past, I didn't take enough care of myself. My job or my heart. Those days were over.

I did sleep most of the day, my dreams interrupted at one point by a strange ripple of noise from below my balcony. I registered the noise, decided it was probably ex-fans booing Daisy and I didn't care, and slipped back into unconsciousness.

I finally woke up around seven, when there was a light knock at my door. It was so faint, in fact, that I still can't believe I heard it. I practically tripped over the covers trying to get out of bed, and then hip-checked myself on the wardrobe just before I reached the door.

My side was aching from what would soon be a spectacular bruise, but I promptly forgot about that when I found Faith on the other side of my door. "Hi," I said in surprise. I waited for her to speak, but she just glanced at her feet, then cast a nervous look down the hall. "Um . . . do you want to come in?"

Faith shook her head slightly. "Could you come up to our suite?" she asked. "I'd really like to talk to you about something."

"Of course." I glanced down at myself, realizing that I was wearing pajamas. I didn't want to be fired while wearing Care Bears shorts, as it would only serve to increase my humiliation. I really needed to start sleeping in my work clothes, the way people kept barging into my hotel rooms. "I should change first."

"Oh, I don't care what you have on," Faith drawled. "Could you come up now?"

"Is there a reason you don't want to talk in my room?" I asked. My room wasn't the penthouse, to be sure, but it was a suite at a five-star hotel. If she had an objection, I wanted to know what it was.

"It's not a good idea," she whispered, peeking into my room like there might be photographers behind the bed. "Please? Can you come upstairs?"

"Sure." I was irritated, but I figured it would be more trouble to argue than just to go and get this over with. "Just give me one second." I put on the hotel slippers and grabbed my room key and a sweater. At least I had fallen asleep with my bra on.

No sooner had we walked to the bank of elevators than Ben emerged from one, surprised to see me. Partly, I'm certain, because of my attire. He looked down at Funshine Bear in astonishment, then back up to my face.

"I was just coming to find you," he said.

"I'll be right back," I told him. "I'll call your room when I'm done."

Like the respectful man he is, Ben just nodded and allowed Faith and me to enter the elevator alone, even though he probably needed to use it to get back to his own room. If I were him, I wouldn't have wanted to be in that elevator, either. Hell, *I* didn't even want to be there.

Faith didn't say another word until we reached the suite, ushering me in ahead of her. Jamie and Daisy were sitting on couches opposite each other, Daisy curled up and biting her nails. If I had to guess, I'd have said she was coming down from all the drugs. She somehow looked even more tired than that morning, sallow and peaked. Though for the first time, I noticed that she'd put on a few pounds just in the short time we'd been in Italy. I wondered how much you had to eat to gain weight in three days.

"I'm sorry we couldn't talk in your room, but the police found three recording devices in our suite this afternoon," Faith told me. "This is the only room we can be completely sure is safe."

Call me crazy, but if they already found three microphones in the room, wouldn't it stand to reason that any *other* room would be safer than their own? And who the hell was recording them, anyway?

"Deacon, our publicist, and our lawyer will be here by tomorrow morning. We tried to hire a private jet, but there were customs issues." Faith took a seat next to Daisy, then gestured me toward Jamie's couch. I desperately looked around the room for another open seat, determined not to sit next to the degenerate most responsible for this crisis. I finally dragged a chair over from the little dining table and placed it between the sofas. I knew it was conspicuous, but I didn't care.

The room fell silent, and I waited for someone to tell me why I was here. I thought I knew, but I wasn't going to fire myself. If they wanted to get rid of me, they were damn well going to have to do it themselves.

It was quiet for at least two more minutes, which felt like an eternity. Everyone seemed to be staring at the ceiling or playing with their hair. I found myself getting angry. All three of them were cowards, and no one wanted to be the first to talk. Finally, it was Daisy—the last one I would have thought—who spoke up. "Just tell Holly what we want already."

Jamie glared across the room at Daisy. "I told you, as far as the world is concerned, you've gone fucking deaf and dumb. Keep your mouth *shut*."

To her credit, sweet little Daisy Mae Dixson glared right back at Jamie, her nostrils even flaring a bit. She looked like a horse ready to trample a crowd. "I'm done listening to you. Fuck off."

Rather than respond, Jamie just flipped her off, turning his head away like he couldn't bear to look at her. I'm sure every glimpse of her face was just another reminder of how much money they were losing by the hour. As sad as it was, that's probably what most people were thinking.

"Well, as Daisy said, we were hoping you could help us," Faith asked meekly, staring at me through lowered and nervously fluttering lashes.

My mind instantly went blank. What could these people possibly want from me? I thought back over the club debacle and my public humiliation at the hands of Perez Hilton, and wondered if they were about to ask me to try something ridiculous to pull attention away from Daisy's arrest. How I could possibly compete with one of the world's biggest celebrities snorting her future up her nose with a bunch of teenage miscreants on a public corner, I had no idea. And I really didn't want to find out. One more appearance on the news and my mother would send me to rehab. And not one of the good rehabs; all we could afford were those places with scratchy hospital sheets and a lot of people handcuffed to their beds.

"In what way?" I kept my voice cool and nonchalant, even though it was exactly the opposite of how I felt. I knew that the second I showed weakness in front of these people, they would pounce on it.

"The tone of the book will obviously have to change now," Faith replied.

The tone of the book? They didn't even know what the tone was. In the last month, no one had asked to read a single word of what I'd written. For all they knew, I was writing a tell-all detailing Daisy's sexual escapades. In fact, the further I'd gotten, the more I was convinced that this entire project was just a useless exercise that no one had any intention of getting published. Jamie hadn't mentioned a Random House or a Simon & Schuster, and there was no one checking up on my progress. If I'd spent their money and wasted the rest of my time gallivanting around town, they had no way of knowing.

"Mama means that we need to use the book as damage control," Daisy explained, yawning.

"Stupidest fucking idea I've ever heard. . . ." Jamie mumbled.

"Do you have a better idea?" I couldn't believe my own brazenness. But considering the direction this was all headed, none of us had a lot left to lose. And Jamie was the manager, after all. It was his job to handle her career and public persona. I couldn't believe that he was trying to wash his hands of the disaster he'd created.

Jamie stood up, towering over all of us like a really tan, really vicious dinosaur. "It's too goddamn late," he roared, causing Faith to flinch. "Our prized show dog went and got herself knocked up by a mutt. She's dirty—nobody wants her anymore."

"I have never gotten knocked up."

"Good for you! It's a fucking metaphor," he shot back. Jamie began pacing back and forth in front of the couch. He still wouldn't look at Daisy. "We all just need to admit that we're circling the drain here. We ride out the rest of the TV season and then give it up. Let's be honest with ourselves."

On the opposite couch, Faith began to sob. Daisy reassuringly reached out and smoothed back her mother's hair, but Jamie just sighed loudly and dramatically.

"Aw, Jesus. Here we go again. . . ." He walked into the small kitchen and opened a cupboard, pulling out a bottle of whiskey.

"I am so sick of you," Faith said haltingly, hyperventilating after each word. I'd never heard her say anything mean to or even about Jamie. "This is my child, I'm not just going to give up on her."

"Mama, it's okay," Daisy said.

"Just wait for Deacon to get here," Jamie replied, downing an overflowing shot glass. "He agrees with me. We pack her off to rehab and then see if we can get her on that D-list sober-living show."

"Maybe I should go to college," Daisy suggested. "And study like, gorillas or something. Be like that Sigourney Goodall lady who lives in the woods. I totally love animals."

This earned a derisive sneer from Jamie, but he didn't speak again until he'd taken a hearty swig right from the whiskey bottle. "Sweetheart, we had to bribe your studio teacher to pass you just so that you could get a high school diploma. You have a fourth-grade reading level. The only college that would ever take you is DeVry University, and you'd flunk out in a week."

So no one had noticed the Sigourney Goodall thing but me? I didn't bring it up. This conversation was quickly devolving, and I was still sitting there in my Care Bears best, wondering what the hell I was doing in that room in the first place. If they wanted me to change the tone of the book, I would have loved if someone told me what I was changing it *to*. Although the good news seemed to be that I was keeping my job, at least for now. Though it didn't seem like Jamie particularly wanted to pay me or anyone else at the moment. As for the comments about Daisy's intelligence level and education, Jamie was probably right, but he didn't need to be such a prick about it.

"If you paid to get me out of high school, why can't you pay to get me into college?" Daisy replied snottily. I knew she wasn't really serious, but it was a good point. Idiot legacy children buy their way into Ivy Leagues all the time.

"With what money?" Jamie asked, throwing up his hands. I wondered how much he'd had to drink before I'd even walked in the room. "In about three months, the only marketable skill you'll have left is your ass. And I don't think *Hustler* wages will buy Yale a new library."

"Stop it, just stop it," Faith screeched, covering her face with her hands. She stood up, rocking dangerously on her heels. Her mascara and eyeliner, usually so perfect, were melting in great raccoon-like circles around her bloodshot eyes. Faith was starting to look like a meth addict's mug shot. "I want you out of this room. *Now.*"

From the kitchen area, Jamie rolled his eyes and tucked the bottle under one arm. "My pleasure. You three can whine and cry over each other all night. I'll be at the nearest bar." He stalked to the door and slammed it behind him.

"He's right, you know," Daisy said.

Faith stopped crying and turned to her daughter, sniffling loudly. "No, he's not. He's not right about everything. He just thinks he is."

Daisy looked at me. "What do you think, Holly?"

Six weeks ago, I was writing reviews of low-end spas and movies everybody had already seen. Now I was sitting in the penthouse suite of a five-star hotel in Rome, counseling one of the biggest celebrities in the world. She may have just gone from famous to notorious, but that didn't lessen her importance in the grand scheme of things. I wasn't in any position to offer her advice, and I knew it.

I could barely get my own life in order, let alone find a way to pull Daisy off the edge of this precipice.

"I don't know about these things," I said.

"Oh, I know that," Daisy replied, a touch of mockery in her voice. "But you're like one of those boring, regular people who watch my show and buy my albums."

No, sweetheart, I thought. *You're wrong about that. But glad to know your ego is intact.*

"What I wanna know is, what would make you like me again?"

In that moment, it finally struck me as odd that Daisy was still facing jail time for drug use, possession, and possible sale, and the only thing we were talking about was resurrecting her career. Either they had already bought off someone in the Italian government and had no fear of harsh prosecution or every one of them had seriously screwed-up priorities.

As for trying to make Daisy likable again, my views were too tied up with my personal opinions to be a valid tool. But I had to say something. "Truthfully, I am really tired of famous people claiming they did nothing wrong and complaining about the consequences of their actions. I would love to see someone admit that they made a mistake and be truly committed to making amends. If anyone came out and said, 'Yes, I have a drug problem and I'm working on it,' I think my opinion of them would go up. Look at Robert Downey, Jr."

"But she doesn't have a problem," Faith protested. I would have argued with her assertion—since it was so clearly wrong—but it can't be easy looking at a child you raised and admitting that you've screwed her up twelve ways from Sunday. I didn't expect an entirely self-aware assessment of the situation from Faith.

"That's not what Holly's saying, Mama," Daisy said.

Actually, it was exactly what I was saying. How anyone could think it was perfectly normal to take "hundreds of pills" (by Daisy's own admission) was beyond me. In my entire life, I hadn't cumulatively taken hundreds of pills.

"She's saying I just pretend I'm sorry and people will feel bad for me." Her eyes were round and anime-like. Suddenly, Daisy didn't look so worn and defeated and I could see little sparks of the idealistic ingenue back in her. Her renewed hope and optimism greatly lessened my sympathy. I had a feeling that any minute, the same old spoiled, prattling little pop star would burst forth and I'd want to strangle her.

Faith shot me a look of concern. "Our publicist said we should issue a statement saying that Daisy thought it was baby powder. She thinks we shouldn't admit guilt."

Baby powder, really? Who would intentionally snort baby powder? What was she going to claim, that her nose had that "not-so-fresh" feeling? "No one believes those statements" was all I said.

"But Nelly repped those video game girls who got caught stealing from the Bulgari event. She's really expensive."

Because expensive always equals good. I remembered Camille telling me the story about the Bulgari theft, and it was ridiculous. Two hosts from a cable video-gamer show went to a private event at the jewelry store and tried to shove necklaces and bracelets down their dresses. When they got caught, they claimed the jewelry was theirs and that they always stuffed their bras with precious metals. Even after being convicted and sent to jail for a six-month sentence (which, due to overcrowding, got shortened to five weeks), the gamer girls refused to admit guilt. To this day, they still cry foul over Bulgari taking away their "personal property" and "insulting their character."

"Certainly you know the entertainment industry better than I, but you asked for my personal opinion. And if memory serves, those girls lost their show."

Faith frowned. "I think you're right. . . . Maybe we should fire Nelly; she is awfully expensive. But we did just pay to fly her over here."

"I'm not saying you have to fire her," I replied, chagrined. These people were like lemmings, unable to formulate an opinion unless it was given to them. It was no wonder that Jamie was able to get away with so much. The Dixson ladies really were just looking for someone to tell them what to do. "But she does work for you. If there's something you don't agree with, tell her. She can't do anything you don't want her to."

This earned looks of astonishment from both Daisy and Faith. It was like no one had ever imparted this wisdom to them before. "But then . . . how do we know the right thing to do?" Daisy asked.

I wanted to say "Try thinking for yourself," but I figured that would come off as too harsh. If my chief complaint about Jamie was his condescension, I couldn't very well start channeling the same spirit. "It's true, we don't always know what to do," I admitted. "And we pay advisers and consultants to give us the benefit of their expertise. But in the end, we have to listen to that advice and do what feels like the best fit for us."

Faith finally stopped sniffling. "Well, Deacon and Jamie want Daisy to go to rehab and Nelly wants us to say Daisy's never seen drugs in her life."

"What do you think, Daisy?" I asked.

"You're the only one who ever asks what I think," Daisy said quietly, biting her nails again.

"What? Everyone asks you what you want. We're all here for *you*."

A glimmer of the world-weary professional peeked out as Daisy glared at her mother. But it was just a peek; even as she spoke, the cutesy teenager was back. In fact, the shift happened so fast I wondered if I'd imagined it. "You ask what I want to drink, where I want to shop. No one asks me what I think."

"What you *think*?" Faith parroted, perplexed.

"You're eighteen. Almost nineteen," I pointed out. "It's time people stopped making decisions for you."

Daisy looked away and resumed biting her nails. Having made

decisions for myself my entire life, I couldn't imagine what it must be like to try to work through your first major choice at eighteen. "I want to hear what Nelly has to say," she replied. "But I'm tired of Daddy and Jamie telling me what to do. They mess things up more than they help." She turned to her mother. "Remember during my last contract negotiation when we nearly lost the record deal because Dad thought we should get seventy percent of the profits? He doesn't know what he's doing—he's just greedy."

"Okay, then," Faith said. "We'll all go to sleep early tonight and decide what to do in the morning. And thank you for your help, Holly."

Faith and Daisy both got up and began moving around the suite, attending to tasks. I was clearly being dismissed, though my purpose in this room still hadn't been defined. I had no idea what I was supposed to be writing about, if anything at all.

Much to my astonishment, Faith walked over and kissed me on the head. "Have a good night's sleep, Holly."

The move startled me into action, and I got up and walked to the door. It was only seven-thirty and I'd only just woken up, but that didn't lessen the impact of the kiss. In my entire twenty-five years, even my mother had never made such a sweet gesture. I knew how much she cared, but she was always a little aloof. If I hugged her for too long, she'd grunt and say, "Yeah, yeah, you love me. I get it. I love you, too."

I walked into the hallway, unsteady on my feet. I wasn't sure what was real anymore. Or what I wanted. So I wandered through the hotel in my pajamas and slippers, finding myself at Ben's door without even planning it.

"Hey. I guess you haven't had a chance to change yet."

"Oh, I've changed plenty," I replied. "Listen, are you hungry?"

"Starving. I have to help my crew strike the set later tonight, but I have some time until then. Do you want to go out for dinner?"

"No. How do you feel about room service?"

CHAPTER 16

It seems like everyone always wants something from me. Sometimes it's money, sometimes it's power, and sometimes it's sex. The problem is, in show business, these things are all tied up together and I can never tell which it is. I always want to believe that a person is interested in me for me, but I don't even know if that's happened yet. I'm starting to think it never will.

By the time Ben had to leave for the set, it was ten o'clock and my lips were nearly raw. I didn't have sex with him or anything—though I'm not exactly a prude, I've never really believed in casual sex—but I will say that the eating portion of our hotel room date took up only about twenty minutes of our time.

When he left the hotel, I walked back up to my room and was surprised to find Vaughn sitting outside my door, texting on his phone. When he saw me, he looked up, eyeing my shorts and laughing.

"I was always a big fan of Cheer Bear."

I unlocked my door, kicking him lightly with my slipper. "Are you the one who should be making fun?" I asked, staring down at him. "I'm not the Mr. Stalker Man waiting outside some poor, innocent girl's hotel room."

Vaughn heaved himself off the floor and followed me into the room without asking. "You are neither poor nor innocent."

I threw the key onto the wardrobe and kicked off my slippers. "If my check from Jamie doesn't clear, I will be very poor indeed."

Vaughn walked over and flopped on my bed. There was something in the familiarity of the move that greatly unsettled me. I don't know if I was still angry about his indecisiveness with me or weirded out because I'd just been rolling around on Ben's bed a few floors down. Beyond that, my own bedsheets were still haphazard from my nap and it made the entire scene feel a little . . . dirty. "You should get dressed."

"It's ten P.M. Why would I get dressed?" I caught sight of myself in the mirror, realizing I looked like a refugee from a horror film slumber party.

"Because I need food. And a very large glass of wine." Vaughn scrunched up his face in thought and then added, "Or a bottle. A large *bottle* of wine."

I folded my arms across my chest with mock consternation. "And just how do you know I don't already have plans?"

"Because your new little *boyfriend* had to go back to work to break down the outdoor set," Vaughn replied. "I heard the Art Department call for him."

I hated this. If he wanted to say something, why couldn't he just come out with it already? And going out with Vaughn right now was a terrible idea. If I had been mentally and emotionally confused a few hours ago, the three glasses of Prosecco I'd imbibed myself since then wouldn't help matters much. But being cooped up inside a hotel in Rome, when I might never be back here again, seemed wasteful and ludicrous. All I had to do was keep my wits about me and watch my mouth.

"Fine, one drink. Come back here in ten minutes."

Vaughn yawned, making no move to get off my bed. "Throw on some clothes in your bathroom. It'll take me more time to get up to my room and back than it will for you to change."

"You're infuriating," I told him, grabbing a pair of jeans and a top from the wardrobe.

226 * RACHEL STUHLER

"It's part of my charm," he replied, grinning.

I went into the bathroom and shut the door firmly, hoping it seemed like I slammed the door in his face.

The concierge recommended Gusto, which took us near the river-side neighborhood of Spagna and a bustling restaurant and wine bar. As was turning out to be the case with most Roman eateries, the quietest place was not outside on the patio but in the very back, away from the university students looking for a hookup. And though I'd just eaten dinner, I still somehow found room for more pizza.

"God, I hope that check clears when we get back to L.A.," I said, lifting yet another piece of greasy, cheesy pizza from the plate. "Because I am going to need a whole new wardrobe. By the end of this week, I'll have gained at least fifteen pounds."

"Try to tell me this food isn't worth a few weeks of elastic-waist pants." Vaughn had a piece of pizza in one hand and bruschetta in the other. We'd imbibed two bottles of wine between us (I had a surprising new fondness for white wines), as well as a few glasses of Prosecco sent by some Roman man who seemed determined to ignore Vaughn's presence at our table.

I have a general rule about how much I'll drink on any given day, and it involves stopping when I can no longer make sense of my wristwatch. But by this point, I'd been unable to tell time for quite a while and it didn't seem to be slowing me down. I choose to believe my decision was based on the influence of Italy and not on my present company.

"Please tell me you've worn pants with an elastic waistband and that there are pictures." I began giggling uncontrollably, the alcohol making everything seem funnier than it really was.

"I was the sweatpants kid for a year of middle school. I got really fat and refused to let my mom buy the 'husky boy' jeans."

This sent me into a fit of laughter that doubled me over and almost sent me to the floor. I was still clutching the upholstery of the booth when a waiter started weaving through the room shouting, *"Conto, conto!"* My face was flat against the slick booth, and the sideways legs rushing through the restaurant made my head spin.

"What does that mean?" Vaughn hissed, leaning over and ducking his head under the table to look at me.

"The check," I replied, having looked it up after the first time I had to resort to mimicry to get my bill from a waiter. "He's handing out people's checks. I think it's last call."

"But . . ." Vaughn sat up, leaning his head back on the seat. "It's not even one. I don't want to go to sleep."

It was past time to go home, and I didn't just mean back to the hotel. It was somehow only Thursday, and though we were here until Monday, I was ready for my Roman holiday to come to an end. This whole Dixson fiasco had greatly complicated my life, and though there hadn't been much there to begin with, it was an existence I was familiar with. I didn't know if this was the new normal, or if these weeks were just an anomaly never to return.

"You know what the song says," I said, wagging an unsteady finger at Vaughn. "You don't have to go home, but you can't stay here."

He stared at me without a trace of joking and shrugged. "I'm happy to go anywhere you're going."

I flagged down the waiter and paid the check, suddenly desperate to get out of the restaurant. I was in dangerous territory and I knew it. The worst part was that I knew exactly how to stop it but I wasn't sure I was willing. My constitution was weak and I hated myself for that.

I gave the waiter an obscene tip, which is considered pretty offensive in Italy, since the servers earn a living wage covered by a service charge written into the bill. It's a lot like telling the restaurateur that you don't trust he's taking care of his employees. But I almost felt like I was paying him for my escape rather than my meal and drinks. As I executed the transaction and waved away my change, I noticed that Vaughn was too close to me for comfort. He lurked right at my back, invading my personal space and further clouding my already questionable judgment. As soon as he ever-so-casually put a hand to the small of my back, I bolted out the front door.

Once outside, I started to look around for a cab, but he grabbed my hand and dragged me down the street to the tree-lined Tiber river walk.

"We have to go back to the hotel," I said and pulled back, making very little real effort to disentangle myself from his fingers. His hand was smooth and soft, and cool to the touch. I tried to remember what Ben's hands felt like, but couldn't. I told myself that it was because of my current state of inebriation. I also couldn't figure out why everyone suddenly wanted to hold my hand.

"Why?" Vaughn asked, tugging me toward the river, which glittered from the lights reflecting off its surface. "This is Rome, for God's sake! It's the most romantic city in the world."

"Isn't Paris supposed to be the most romantic city?" I asked, stumbling along after my hand. I was having this encounter with the wrong man, my brain screamed. If the word *romantic* was going to figure in a conversation with Vaughn, it should have happened before now. What was I doing and why wasn't I running down the street away from him?

"I've never been to Paris," he replied.

We reached the river's edge and I ran my free hand against the cold stone of the wall, needing something calm and steady to hold me up. Abruptly, he spun me around and pressed me up against the wall, his body just centimeters from mine. Vaughn finally let go of me, but then used his now free hand to reach up and graze the outline of my chin. I felt frozen, ashamed of what I was allowing to happen, but so desperate to let it all play out the way I'd wanted it to.

"What are you doing?" I asked in something between a whisper and a moan.

Vaughn leaned very close to my face, his lips so close to mine that

I could feel his ragged exhalations. The sensation rippled across my skin, making me dizzy. "I don't know," he replied, his tone sincere.

I thought he was going to kiss me, but Vaughn only touched his forehead to mine. In that moment, it felt just as intimate.

"I don't want you to date Ben." He sighed.

"Why?" I knew the answer to that question, but I had to ask.

Before he answered, Vaughn dragged his nose lightly across the tip of my own. Even now, he was still toying with me. It was maddening, but I felt powerless to stop it. "You know why."

I jerked my head back, just out of his reach. I was already making this too easy for him. "No, I don't. Tell me."

He reached up and threaded his fingers into my hair, grasping gently but with just enough force that it momentarily stopped my breath in my throat. "You shouldn't be with him."

There was so much left unsaid at the end of that sentence. I felt like I was losing my mind. I couldn't possibly be misinterpreting his meaning; why couldn't he just make the words come out of his mouth like a normal person?

I could feel my lower lip jutting out in a decided pout. The alarm bells were going off in my brain, and I knew that if I wasn't careful, the alcohol would shortly turn me into an annoying, sobbing mess. I could already feel the pressure of the moisture creeping out from the corners of my eyes.

"Then say it. We're not teenagers. I'm tired of playing games with you."

Instead of answering, he kissed me. His lips were hard, forceful—almost biting. His hands wrapped around the sides of my face, pulling me deeper into his orbit. I'd thought about this a million times since our odd little dinner on the balcony in Miami. There were so many moments I'd hoped for this, even prepared myself for it, and now. . . . It felt wrong. Not because I didn't like the kiss. But in light of his strange behavior and my increasing attraction to Ben, I couldn't enjoy it.

I was the one to finally pull away, but it probably took me far too long to do it. "I have to go," I said. I pushed away and tried to walk back toward the street, the alcohol in my system making the pavement feel uneven.

"Then let's go," he said. "Come back to the hotel with me."

"We're staying in the same hotel."

"That's not what I meant." He chased after me, trying to grab my hands. I yanked them out of reach.

"I know what you meant." I kept moving toward the street, which seemed impossibly far away. I didn't turn back to look at Vaughn because I was afraid if he tried to kiss me again, I wouldn't resist. "And you know why I can't."

"Because of Benji?" Vaughn's tone was derisive, mocking.

"Benji is a dog's name." I hadn't asked Ben how he felt about the nickname, but I had a sneaking suspicion he didn't love it.

Vaughn increased his speed, coming up right behind me and lightly putting his hands on my hips. "I'm better than that guy."

I whirled around, pushing away his hands. "What makes you think that? You had a million chances to make a move on me before tonight and you didn't take them. And then as soon as someone else expresses interest I'm suddenly worth the effort?"

"Are you mad at me or you?" If I didn't appreciate Vaughn's condescending "Dad" voice, I really didn't like his mocking tone, either. There was something aggressive about it that made me nervous.

"Sometimes I think I've got a handle on you," I said. I started moving again, backing away from him slowly. "Then you become this other person. The truth is, I don't know who you are or what you want."

"I want everything," he blurted out.

I didn't understand what that meant, but I got the sense it was the truest thing he'd said to me since the moment we met. "Then it's too bad that's not the way the world works."

I finally reached the street and started to head for the piazza on the opposite side. Even though we'd only been outside for about twenty minutes, the neighborhood had fallen fast asleep. There wasn't a taxi or moving vehicle anywhere in my range of sight. And owing to the endlessly flowing Roman vino, I couldn't remember how to get back to the InterContinental.

I could hear him following along behind me, though his gait had slowed. "Holly, please. Let's talk about this. We can get some coffee and—"

I didn't turn around, but I did hold out my hand for Vaughn to remain where he was. "Just stay away from me, at least for right now. We'll talk tomorrow. "

This time, he didn't try to follow.

It took me a few attempts, but I managed to find my way back to the hotel without help. It was only a five or so minute walk, but I still found the street signs a little fuzzy, making the trip far longer than that.

My mood worsened as I walked into the lobby and saw Vaughn was already there, hanging out with several male crew members. The guys were all talking and laughing, and Vaughn looked like he didn't have a care in the world. As I crossed to the elevator, I heard him say, "It's early, there must be an open bar around here somewhere." He didn't even look at me as I passed.

When I got back to my room, I realized with horror that I had a message from Ben. The light on the phone blinked so innocently I almost didn't have the strength to play back the recording and listen to that man's sweet, adoring tone. Especially when he said he hoped I "was fast asleep and having wonderful dreams." He thought I hadn't answered because I'd already gone to bed.

I'd just accused Vaughn of toying with me, but I was no better. I'd been so furious with him for playing the same game I was. I

232 * RACHEL STUHLER

threw myself on the bed and cried until I fell asleep. Things would be better tomorrow, I told myself. They had to be.

Someone was banging on my door. I managed to force one eye open long enough to catch a glimpse of the clock. It was just after three-thirty, which meant that I'd been asleep for a little over two hours. Judging from the way the numbers swam in front of my gaze, I was still mostly drunk.

And the banging just kept up, vibrating through the entire surface of the door. Or maybe the alcohol just made it seem that way. I wondered if Vaughn had continued drinking and was now doing his best *Streetcar* Stanley impression, and would soon start yelling my name from the hallway.

As if on cue, I heard a booming, "Holly!" Much to my surprise, it wasn't Vaughn, or any voice I could recall having heard before. "Holly Gracin," the voice repeated loudly. "Please answer the door."

I scrambled off the bed, now a little scared. I had no idea who was on the other side of that door and I certainly didn't want to open it to a complete stranger. I thought about calling Ben or the front desk, but then I remembered I had a peephole and figured I should at least see if I recognized the person before calling in the cavalry.

I crept to the door quietly, just in case I decided I wanted to pretend I wasn't there. I instantly felt foolish when I peered out and realized that the man in the hallway was one of Daisy's nameless bodyguards. Apparently, I'd never heard him speak before. I pulled off the chain and opened the door, wondering why the hell he was waking me up in the middle of the night.

"Yes?" If I'd looked like a character out of a horror film before going out, I couldn't imagine what my current appearance was.

"I need you to get dressed and get your things ready," he told me.

I racked my addled brain for any photo shoot, interview, or even helicopter tour of the city that Faith had warned me about, but there was nothing. I hadn't a clue where I was supposed to be right now or why.

"For what?" I asked, feeling foolish. "It's three-thirty."

"I know that, Ms. Gracin, and I'm sorry," the bodyguard said apologetically. "But I need to have you at the airport in an hour. If you can't get everything packed, one of the PAs can finish and have the rest sent to you in Los Angeles. Just get everything you need to get back home—money, toiletries, passport. Make sure you have your passport."

I stared at him in shock, certain I must have heard incorrectly. "I thought we weren't leaving until Monday night." I wondered if maybe I'd slept through the entire weekend and not noticed. That was physically impossible, right?

"There's been a change of plans. Mrs. Dixson will explain everything in the car. But please, it's very important that we go *now*. You need to be at the service entrance by four."

The bodyguards were always fairly humorless, but this guy looked like he was trying to prevent a bloody coup. I wanted to argue with him, tell him that I was going back to bed and that I wasn't leaving this country without seeing the Colosseum, but his terrifying enforcer stare told me that something pretty bad had happened or was about to happen.

"Okay." I nodded. "Do I need to check out? I don't know where the service entrance is."

"We'll take care of the hotel paperwork." The bodyguard pointed down the hall in the opposite direction from the main elevator bank. "Take the freight elevator at the back of building all the way to the basement level and it will let you out in the kitchen. Mrs. and Miss Dixson will be waiting for you there."

So we were all leaving. Something really was very wrong. I almost didn't want to know what it was. "Thank you," I stammered, unsure what else to say.

Sensing my fear, the bodyguard reached out and touched my

arm. "Everything will be fine. We will get you out of here and back home."

Before I could give myself an opportunity to become paralyzed with terror, I closed the door and got to work rounding up my belongings. It seemed like this happened all too often around Daisy and her menagerie.

The scene in the kitchen was chaos. The bodyguards and several members of the hotel staff were there, herding me, Daisy, and Faith toward a loading area at the rear of the hotel. We were practically shoved into one of the crew passenger vans, and without having to be told, all of the occupants (except for the driver) sank down in their seats, out of sight of the windows.

I still hadn't had a chance to ask what was going on, but there was such an urgency to everyone's movements that I knew better than to open my mouth. As we pulled out onto the street, I saw Daisy lean in to her mother, clutching Faith's wrist tightly. She whispered "Mama" before burying her head in Faith's shoulder.

As we navigated past the front of the hotel, part of me expected to see the fans protesting with lit torches or screaming obscenities, but it was relatively quiet. There was nothing to indicate that all hell had broken loose.

My first real clue as to the nature of the emergency came at the airport check-in. When the person at the luggage desk asked for Daisy's passport, she passed it over the counter but grasped Faith with her free hand. The teenager's grip was so strong that her knuckles were white. The mother and daughter exchanged silent looks of worry as the airline attendant entered the information into the computer and I realized Daisy thought she was going to be stopped by the authorities.

But after about a minute, the man handed the ID back to Daisy. "Have a safe flight, Miss Dixson," he told her in accented English.

Faith, the bodyguards, and I similarly got through check-in and security without incident, and there was no waiting at all when we arrived at the gate. Our two burly protectors went right to the desk and the entire group was escorted on even before they announced boarding. Up to this point, neither of the ladies had so much as said "good morning" to me.

It wasn't until we had taken off that Faith leaned into the aisle to tell me quietly, "I'm sorry for all the craziness."

"What happened?"

Faith threw a questioning look back at Daisy, who was skulking in the window seat with a baseball cap hiding her long, blond hair. I didn't think the look made her any less conspicuous, but if it made her feel better, that was all that mattered. "Go ahead and tell her," Daisy said. "She's going to find out when we land, anyway."

Faith nodded and then hopped the aisle to take the empty seat next to me. "We're in a little bit of legal trouble."

First of all, how was that news? I was discombobulated from the sudden and unexpected traveling and lack of sleep (not to mention the amount of alcohol that probably still coursed through my veins), but I knew that it was Friday morning. Which meant Daisy had been arrested more than two days ago, giving us all plenty of time to adjust to the shock. And second, I wasn't sure what the penalty would be for cocaine possession and possible sale, but I didn't think there was anything "little" about this run-in with the law.

"Isn't that what your lawyer was flying in to take care of?" I'd just realized that we had taken off three hours before the damage control squad was due to land. Deacon and his minions probably had no idea that they had just flown across the world for nothing.

"Things are more complicated than we thought," Faith said. "Just after eleven last night, a tabloid found Sharla's phone number and called her for comment on the Italian government revoking Daisy's bail. Of course, the little darlin' came right over to the hotel and told us."

"Sharla?" I couldn't believe a tabloid had gotten her phone number. I wondered if someone had sold it. Then I selfishly wondered if someone would sell mine. "If the press is hounding her, why isn't she on our flight?" I would have thought Faith would want the makeup artist as far away from the debacle as possible to prevent any further leaks.

Faith's gaze flicked nervously over to Daisy, who was deliberately staring out the window. But when the momager turned back to me, her usual smile was plastered to her face. "Well, Sharla had a long night with us, I just thought she could use a little rest. She'll be along shortly with the rest of the crew."

"I didn't want her here," Daisy announced loudly, her face still turned away.

I'd given my petulant teenage client more leeway than the rest, but I was too tired and irritated to indulge her just then. "And why is that? What exactly did Sharla do to make you so mad? You've been treating her like dirt all week."

"It was just a tiny squabble," Faith told me, patting my hand.

"She always wants to be around me, it's so annoying," Daisy continued. "I'm sick to death of her." During this entire exchange, she kept her eyes trained out the window. "And she yelled at me for trying to cut my hair. . . . She yelled—at *me*."

I remembered the lunchtime freak-out in Piazza Navona. At the time, I hadn't considered why Daisy was so mad at Sharla, or even if there was a reason other than the weather or the day of the week. "She was trying to be your friend," I replied.

"They're freaking extensions. So what if I cut them, Axel can just put in some more."

It can take all day to put in individual extensions, and I'm told it's remarkably tedious work for hairstylists. Sharla was just trying to prevent more work for Axel. "Be as sick of her as you want, but she just saved your ass."

"And we are *so* grateful for that," Faith said. Maybe her "we" was meant in the royal sense because clearly Daisy wasn't grateful for shit.

"Why is Italy revoking Daisy's bail? Is that even legal?"

"I don't really understand it myself, Holly," Faith said, finally putting away her fake, beauty pageant expression. "After Sharla came to see us, it took a few more calls to figure out what was really going on. I guess the government decided they wanted to make an example of Daisy and revoked her bail so that they could rearrest her and hold her until the trial."

"What?" About fifty percent of my brain had been asleep since we'd first taken our seats on the plane, but this shook me wide awake. "When would they hold the trial?"

Faith hesitated for a moment, and I could tell she was fighting tears. "They could delay it from six months up to a year. We're actually pretty lucky. The police knew our lawyer would be landing around nine; they were going to arrest Daisy at eight, right when the courts opened for the day. If the tabloid reporter hadn't tipped off Sharla, we wouldn't have been able to get away."

Usually I'm of the opinion that Hollywood types are given a free pass for their indiscretions, but this level of vengeance didn't seem normal. It felt more like persecution than prosecution. I'm not an expert on drug offenses, but I didn't think the sentence would extend to a year, let alone the time just waiting for trial. Although, perhaps that was the point. The government wanted to send a message but knew that Daisy would likely get a slap on the wrist. This could be a back-door way to publicly flog her. Still, we had just fled the country. I didn't imagine that would help Daisy much, either legally or with public perception.

"Won't she just be arrested when we land in Los Angeles?"

"No, there are extradition laws. They would have to petition the U.S. government and prove that their case is strong and worthy of all the trouble. Since the case is pretty weak, they'll probably just drop it. But Daisy will be banned from Italy."

With every passing day, I was increasingly happy that I wasn't famous. I might never be able to afford to go back to Italy, but at least I wasn't legally prohibited from doing so. A few unanswered questions lingered in my mind. "How did the reporter find out about the arrest, anyway?"

Faith gave me the same warm, yet slightly condescending smile that I'd given her many times. It was the oh-sweetie-you're-cute-but-so-stupid look. Now that I was on the receiving end of that expression, I realized just how irritating and obvious it was. Not to mention, a little bit arrogant. I'd have to restrain myself in the future. It also finally made me realize that Faith wasn't as dim-witted as she seemed. Maybe she was sweet and cute like a fox.

"Reporters are creative, Holly," she said. "If they managed to bug our hotel room, don't you think they probably have an inside source at the police station?"

I'd completely forgotten about the recording devices. Well, in all honesty, even at the time I'd thought Faith was being paranoid. I had convinced myself that the tiny little "microphones" were probably just pieces of metal or foam feet for lamps or vases. Now I wasn't so sure. I thought back to all of the people who had traipsed in and out of that suite in the last couple of days. All of them were co-workers, police, or service people. It depressed me to think that a cop might have bugged a pop star's room to make a few extra bucks.

I didn't respond to Faith's comment. I couldn't think of anything to say. This wasn't my reality and I had no right to offer my ill-informed opinions. Instead, I merely shrugged and shook my head. It seemed as good an answer as any.

"I've contacted the doctor from *Rehabilication*," Faith continued, casting a forlorn glance across the aisle at Daisy, who had either fallen asleep or passed out. "He's made an offer to help us through this. I think we should take it."

Rehabilication, the popular reality show where D-list methed-up celebrities went to dry out and try to make a little more money before they became completely unemployable. I was pretty sure that was the show Jamie and Deacon wanted Daisy to join, but Faith had seemed so against the possibility just twelve hours ago. Apparently, things had changed. And so much the better—the girl definitely needed rehab.

"That's good," I said, trying to be supportive. Dr. Chace (his first name, not his last) seemed like a pompous douche, but he was known for getting results.

"He says we should have the book ready for a publisher within a week of Daisy getting out of his facility."

Faith phrased this as a statement rather than a question, which confused me greatly. "Um . . . when would that be?" I asked, wondering how it wasn't an obvious question.

"Daisy would like to spend a few days at home first, but I'm thinking we should take her down there as soon as we land. It'll look better in the press."

Still didn't answer my question. I'd never even smoked a cigarette, let alone done illegal drugs, so I had no clue how long rehab lasted. "So when does the book have to be finished, exactly?"

"Oh, of course, dear." Faith laughed. "Four weeks."

I'm not sure if it was terror or my ever-worsening hangover, but I threw up a little in my mouth. I barely made it to the bathroom before my two dinners and endless parade of alcoholic beverages streamed out of me and into the gross airplane chemical toilet. I had to be done in four weeks. Of course I did.

CHAPTER 17

Life as a celeb is like living in a box made of one-way glass, and I'm the one on the inside. Everyone can see my every move, but I can't tell who's watching. I'm not allowed to have privacy. I'm expected to tweet and Instagram everything I do to millions of people I don't know, and this makes them think they have every right to judge my decisions.

I've had people come up to me and say that my last boyfriend is too good for me, or not good enough. They've said that they hated/loved/went out and bought the shorts I was wearing at lunch two weeks ago. Most of the people who criticize me claim that they're not even my fans. My question to them is: if you don't like me, why are you still reading about me?

Fifteen hours later, we touched down in Los Angeles. By this point, I was exhausted and fighting tears of confusion and fear. My life felt like a mess and I didn't know what to do to fix it. I had kissed Vaughn and left Rome without a single word to Ben. I also somehow had to write three quarters of a book in four weeks, a feat that seemed impossible, given that I'd already used every last bit of information Daisy and her family had offered and I highly doubted I would suddenly have more access to her once she was under lock and key in rehab.

I wanted to go home and cry until my body lost the ability to produce moisture. But before I could take out my cell phone to call Camille, a limo driver appeared in baggage claim and Faith grasped my hand tightly. When we landed, I was tired but fairly relieved that it was still only 1:00 P.M. Pacific time; now I realized that I was going nowhere near Diablorado Street in the foreseeable future.

Making things worse, someone had tipped off the paparazzi. Since the flight had literally been booked three hours before departure and you can't use cell phones while in the air, I was floored that a secret this big could have been leaked to the press. But I suppose fifteen hours is a long time in a world that's so connected. All it might have taken was one asshole in coach using the plane's Wi-Fi to brag on Facebook about passing Daisy on the way to the bathroom.

Inside the baggage claim area, there were one or two photographers doing a terrible job of trying to stay incognito. They bobbed and weaved through the crowd, ducking behind passengers as though we wouldn't notice their enormous lenses. But just outside the automatic doors . . . there were so many people packed so tightly together—all with those same humongous cameras—that I couldn't even see the taxi stand. The most surreal part was that the paparazzi were completely silent. I was used to hearing them shout inane questions at Daisy, idiotic queries like "Is it true you sleep in Louboutins?" and "What do you say to the rumor that you can't read?" Seeing them now, quiet and ready to pounce like a pack of Saharan predators, was even more strange and unsettling.

Just as I'd predicted, the baseball cap did nothing to hide Daisy's identity. Even before we reached the crowd of vultures, a few plucky little girls ran up and asked for selfies. The weirdest part was that Daisy obliged, even offering the girls one of her phony smiles. The sky was falling and Daisy was taking goofy pictures.

At the same time the bodyguards began rounding up our luggage, what looked to be an entire precinct shift of police officers appeared and surrounded us. I hadn't seen anyone call them, and not a word was exchanged with Daisy, Faith, or the bodyguards,

242 ★ RACHEL STUHLER

but the cops immediately fell into a well-spaced circle and moved us toward the door. So this is where all of my tax dollars go?

And then, just as soon as Daisy's foot crossed the threshold of the terminal, the world exploded. There's no other word for it. One second, we were moving in an orderly fashion while silent photographers snapped pictures, and then the next, it was sheer pandemonium. In my time with Daisy, I'd seen plenty of interactions with the paparazzi, but I'd never witnessed anything like this. I hadn't thought it possible, but the shoving was harder, the shouting was louder, and absolutely no one was concerned about hurting her. It took me only about a minute to realize what had changed—Daisy was no longer America's Sweetheart. They wanted to see her break, even if they had to make it happen.

Questions were yelled over and over again, but it was nearly impossible to make out any of them because of the noise level. We hadn't even made it to the curb when Daisy began to sob hysterically, her sunglasses hiding very little of her emotional outburst. As the tears dripped untouched down her face, I knew that it would be only minutes before that close-up appeared on every gossip site in the universe. And no one would feel sorry for her, despite the fact that this was likely the first true emotion Daisy had felt in years. People would click on the picture again and again and laugh because this is what passes for entertainment.

It also struck me that even as Daisy's net worth went down in her own career, her capital had just skyrocketed in other ways. All of those tabloids who'd tried desperately to dig up dirt on her for years had just been handed a golden goose that would lay eggs for months, if not years to come. My suspicions were confirmed when my new cell phone rang less than thirty minutes into our limo ride.

"Hi," I said, trying to preempt whatever Camille was no doubt about to yell. "How did you"—I didn't want to say "get this number," because I knew it would sound highly suspect—"know how to get a hold of me right now? I just got off the plane."

"Your mom gave me your new number," Camille said. "I just saw you on the news!"

I inconspicuously turned down the speaker volume and tried to figure out how to have this conversation without upsetting Daisy further. "Oh, really . . ." I replied stupidly, at a total loss for words. "Um . . . what are you watching?"

"Are you deaf?" Camille yelled. "I just told you, the news."

From the other side of the limo, Daisy groaned and said, "Stop talking."

"I'll just be a sec, it's my . . ." Think fast, think fast. My gynecologist? No, too gross. My financial planner? I don't even know what you say to those guys. "Agent." They didn't know Gerry was semifictitious and the most I'd seen of him lately was his signature on my checks.

"Huh? Oh, right. . . . You're still with them, aren't you?"

"I'm not sure when I'll be free," I said.

"Okay, then I can be your agent for a few minutes. Pay me ten grand and do the chicken dance," Camille said, whistling loudly. I knew the sound had to carry into the limo. "This Daisy thing is insane. It's everywhere. I'm at work and I just flipped on the KTLA news at one, and there you were! Daisy's the top story!"

"I'm not really sure I'm okay with that *deal.*" I don't always think well under pressure.

"Hol-*ly,* shut the eff *up,*" Daisy said, pulling the baseball down over her eyes. "Your voice makes me wanna vom."

"Oh my God, I can hear her," Camille whispered, giggling. "Were you there when she had her meltdown? I can't *believe* you didn't call to tell me about this."

I glanced up at Daisy before I spoke again, my voice decidedly softer this time. "We can discuss the particulars later."

"Oh, yeah. I figured. In the meantime, you need some rest, or a facial or something. You look like you were kicked in the face by a horse."

"Thank you," I replied. Couldn't just one person lie and tell me I looked gorgeous? "I may need a ride back from that meeting. If you wouldn't mind."

"Sure thing, where from?"

That was the sixty-four-thousand-dollar question. We'd gotten on the 405 south from the airport and hadn't stopped since. It was especially strange since Los Angeles technically ends just a few miles below LAX, so I didn't know where we were going. "Um. I'll have to get back to you on that."

Before Camille could answer, Daisy leaned over and snatched the phone out of my hand, ending the call. She made a face at the cell and then tossed it back to me. "Your agent can wait." Then she balled herself up on the seat and either fell asleep or feigned it.

I was almost afraid to speak again, but Camille had brought up a good point. I had no idea where we were headed. I glanced out the window and saw some sort of bizarre, Blade Runner–looking structure made out of steel and white lights. "Where are we?"

Faith followed my gaze and stared at the odd little construction that was surprisingly close to the beach. "I think it's the Naval Weapons Station in Seal Beach."

I'd never been to Seal Beach, but I knew it was somewhere in Orange County. And we were in the far left lane of the freeway, so I was fairly certain the driver wasn't getting off anytime soon. "Where are we going?"

"To Dr. Chace's facility in Dana Point."

All I wanted to do was take off my shoes, maybe puke a few more times, and then go to sleep for at least a week. I'd brushed my teeth on the plane, but my mouth tasted like a small woodland creature had died in the back of my throat. Not to mention that my sunglasses were packed in my still-missing luggage and the blinding California sun was doing nothing to help the raging hangover headache that was blossoming at the base of my skull. I was being kidnapped.

"And how far away is that?" I asked, hoping the desperation in my voice wasn't obvious.

"We should be there in another hour, as long as traffic isn't too bad."

By 4:00 P.M., I was sitting in the lobby of what looked like a really ritzy country club. It was supposed to be a top-notch rehab facility, but there was a golf course out back and a fancy little café with umbrellas and a coffee bar. I suppose if you're going to charge someone seventy thousand dollars for a month of care, you'd better make it worth the money.

No one had spoken to me in almost two hours, and I'd long since read through all the pamphlets, including "Put Down That Crack Pipe—For Good!" and "Nymphomania—The Silent, Sexy Shame." I'd spent the last forty minutes destroying the human race in Plague Inc. on my new cell, but even that wasn't holding my attention anymore.

Both Vaughn and Ben had called me, but I hadn't answered either time. I was feeling really guilty about my own actions, but also increasingly suspicious about why I was here.

The more I thought about it, the less sense it all made. When I'd been pulled out of bed at three-thirty, I'd assumed that the bodyguards' actions were simply to protect me. But the truth was, they wouldn't have cared if I'd leapt out of the plane at thirty-five thousand feet, so long as Daisy was safe. Which begged the question—why was *I* removed from Italy with the two women? No one else, even Jamie, had been along on the flight. I could have just as easily been booked on a flight later that day or the next, as Sharla apparently was. No, there had to be some ulterior motive at work here. I just wasn't sure what it was. And I definitely didn't like being a pawn in someone else's game.

"Excuse me?" A stunningly pretty brunette bent down and smiled at me. "Can I get you anything? A Pellegrino? An espresso?"

246 ★ RACHEL STUHLER

I wanted to ask her for a bed, a bath, and an industrial-size bottle of aspirin. "Flat water would be amazing, actually. I'm a little dehydrated from the flight." As this was a rehab facility, I decided to refrain from detailing the several bottles of wine I'd ingested in the last day or so.

"Of course," the brunette said sweetly. "Mrs. Dixson said you just came from Rome. And I know Dr. Chace is sorry he can't see you until six-thirty. He's in the city doing an interview with CNN."

Up until that moment, I'd thought I was just waiting for Faith or a ride home. I had no idea I was there to meet with the media-whore addiction specialist himself. I momentarily worried that someone was about to try to commit me to treatment for some imagined vice, but then I remembered that I was no one special and didn't have any money. I was useless to Dr. Chace.

I glanced at the time on my cell phone and nearly burst into tears. "I wasn't aware he wanted to see me. I was just waiting for someone to take me home."

"Dr. Chace was very insistent about meeting with you." I stared at her flawless eyeliner and perfect curling-iron waves and wondered if she was an aspiring actress. Or, given the good doctor's career, a talk show host. "Why don't you have a snack in the café? Our chef makes an award-winning crème brûlée."

Despite the fact that I hadn't eaten since the night before, I had no interest in five-star rehab cuisine. "Listen, I don't even have any money. We left so unexpectedly that all I have are euros."

"We accept all major credit cards," she replied.

"I don't want a snack," I said, a little louder than I intended. I was officially angry. "I want to go home. With the exception of a two-hour nap, I've been awake for two days and I stink like airplane seats. I just want to go home. I am happy to come back tomorrow— or whenever's convenient—to meet with Dr. Chace."

The brunette stared at me blankly, apparently unsure how to handle my outburst. I would have thought a rehab employee would be used to unruly behavior, but this chick looked like I'd just thrown a banana cream pie in her face.

"We can comp the snack," she said uncertainly. "I'm sure no one will mind."

I was beginning to think the collective IQ of the entertainment industry was fifty-eight. I wasn't going to be able to argue my way out of this. "Whatever you want."

"Give me your impression of Daisy's world. And be honest." Dr. Chace leaned his chin onto his hand and stared at me pensively.

I couldn't stop staring at the guy's eyebrows. They were overly plucked and then drawn on again. It was bizarre, like looking at a drag queen Liza Minnelli impersonator. I'd been with this guy for ten minutes and I'd already realized he was as vacuous as a hot-air balloon. I desperately wanted to know what clown college he'd gotten his medical degree from.

"Well . . ." I started, not sure if I was even legally allowed to be honest, "it's certainly hectic."

"Mm-hmm . . ." he said, nodding. The expression was so contrived and phony that I glanced around to make sure we weren't being filmed. When I realized that we were, in fact, alone, I decided that Chace spent so much time in front of a camera his affectations must just come naturally now. "*Hectic.* Interesting word. Expand on that."

"So you need to know this for her therapy?"

"In a manner of speaking, yes. I leave the substance counseling to my staff. My concern is making sure that when Daisy is ready to step back into her life again, there's still a life worth living." He didn't say it, but I was sure he meant that a "life worth living" had to be a profitable one. Chace paused, returning to his best evening news stare. "Now, let's go back to 'hectic.' Walk me through what you mean."

Was this guy for real? "Hectic," I repeated, fighting the urge to let my voice drip with sarcasm. "As in, very busy, very turbulent. There are always a ton of people around her." I wanted to add that Daisy seemed afraid to be alone, but I knew that would be crossing the line. In some circles, it might even be considered slander. If I understood my contract right, I wasn't allowed to tell anyone I knew Daisy even if she was standing right next to me.

"Busy, busy." The doctor was proving himself to be a highly photogenic parrot, always speaking in perfect little sound bites. No wonder the talk shows loved him so much. "Turbulent, yes. Continue."

"Um . . ." This dude was knocking me off my game. I didn't know what he was looking for. I thought I was here to help with her drug treatment, but Dr. Rehab himself didn't seem at all interested in that. "You know, maybe I just think there are too many cooks in the kitchen. Daisy's an adult, I think it's time everyone stepped back and let her take control of her own life." Now I was insulting not Daisy but Dr. Chace. I wanted him to know that I didn't think he had the Dixsons' best interests at heart.

"Too many cooks. So true, so true. What you're saying is, I need to take a look at Daisy's circle and weed out a few of the unnecessary elements."

He wasn't kidding. He really didn't get that *he* was an unnecessary element. I wasn't sure if I wanted to start laughing or crying. "What is it you need from me, Dr. Chace? Your assistant said you very much wanted to speak with me. I'm happy to help in any way I can, but I'm not going to lie, I'm very tired."

He leaned forward in his chair, crossing his legs like a scientist contemplating the deepest mysteries of the universe. "Life is a very tiring endeavor, indeed." The doctor paused for a moment, staring off into space. After a few seconds, he continued, "I think you're very important to Daisy's recovery. She thinks very highly of you, not to mention that through your work together, you've come to know her better than just about anyone else."

None of that was even remotely true. "You still haven't told me what you need."

"I would like you to start coming down here every day to work with Daisy. I think the conversations would be a form of therapy for her, and then we can also make sure our little project stays on track."

I didn't miss his use of the word *our*. "So you'll be involved from here on out," I said.

Chace nodded, his brow crinkling. More like folding. I could only assume that he was Botoxed into oblivion. It made him look simultaneously twenty-five and eighty. "I think that's best for everyone," he replied. "You see, I *want* my patients to succeed. I *want* them to prosper. Just not at the expense of their health and well-being. If I'm part of this awesome team, then I can ensure that Daisy continues to grow in her professional life as well as in her psyche."

I would never find out for sure, but in that moment, I was convinced that Dr. Chace must have signed some sort of management contract with Faith. I know I'm a cynical person, but what was the likelihood that the media-darling doctor was really just being selfless? I wondered if every project Daisy secured from here on out would be "produced" by Dr. Chace. Nice work if you can get it, I suppose.

"I'm happy to come back whenever you want," I told him, before quickly adding, "Although I'd like tomorrow to myself to get over my jet lag and run a few errands."

"The day after tomorrow, then?" Dr. Chace asked, standing up and shaking my hand.

"Absolutely." I followed him out of his office and down a hallway toward the lobby. "Can I ask you a question? Why do you call yourself Dr. Chace? That's your first name, right?"

The doctor laughed, slapping me on the back. "Chace is my first name, yes. But my last name is too long and complicated for TV."

"What is it?"

"Connelly," he replied.

"But that's a really common name," I blurted out. "And it's only three syllables."

"Trust me," Chace replied, winking down at me. "Two is the maximum, but one is better." As we reached the reception desk, Chace patted me on the back again. "I'll see you in a couple of days."

He turned and headed back down the hall, leaving me with pretty brunette receptionist 2.0. This girl was slightly more exotic-looking than the first and had sandy, muted green eyes, but from ten feet back, I wouldn't have been able to tell them apart.

"Hi," I said to her. "Could you tell Mrs. Dixson that I'm ready to go home now?"

The green-eyed vixen gave me the same blank stare as her day-shift counterpart. "Um . . . Mrs. Dixson left to check into her hotel two hours ago. And her instructions were very clear about not calling to disturb her until tomorrow—she was very tired."

I pulled out my cell phone, trying to hide my frustration. One of my earlier activities had been downloading endless new apps and games over the rehab center's free Wi-Fi. Among them was Uber. I pulled up the app and asked for a fare quote back to my apartment, thinking this would be the easiest way home. Until I saw that the ride would cost $150. Even if I could charge it, I couldn't waste that on a one-way trip.

Camille was going to kill me. "I'm going to need to wait in the lobby for a couple of hours until someone can come pick me up."

"Our café is open until ten," Green Eyes said brightly. "You should try our award-winning crème brûlée."

If I thought my night was going to get any better after I left the Dana Point rehab center, I was wrong. Camille was, indeed, pissed when she finally got down to Orange County, but the grumpy ride home got even worse when she dropped me off at my apartment.

I knew something was wrong the instant I walked up to the

second-floor landing. There were clothes and shoes strewn all over the concrete, and I nearly dropped poor little Smitty—locked in a cage under my arm—when I realized that the mess was the remains of my luggage. Whatever idiot was responsible for our baggage being retrieved from the airport had apparently decided it was perfectly acceptable to leave my suitcase outside and unprotected. My building had a security gate, but as usual, someone had propped it open. The words BITCH and WHORE (spelled HORE) were written on my door with lipstick, and scratched underneath in the peeling paint was the suggestion GET BETTER SHIT. I agree, nameless thief.

Luckily, all of my important documents were in my carry-on, so I wasn't worried about someone selling my passport or driver's license, but my souvenirs were gone, including my peace offering to my mother, the blessed Vatican rosary. The irony of someone having stolen a rosary was not lost on me, and I only hoped the recipient of said religious artifact would appreciate it. Mostly, I was just annoyed that I had to spend twenty minutes outside in the dark, rounding up my unmentionables.

But the hits just kept on coming. By the time I got to settle properly into my apartment, it was after midnight, and I stupidly decided to listen to my messages before scarfing down stale cereal and going to bed. I should have done so at Rehabilication, but I have a remarkable ability to ignore anything that makes me uncomfortable. I almost let the messages go until tomorrow, but I forced myself to hit play.

There was the embarrassed, mostly silent message from Vaughn that basically said, "Ummm . . . yeah, I'm sorry, let's talk tomorrow"; the confused, slightly hurt message from Ben wondering what had happened; one from my mother asking if I'd landed all right (*dammit*, Camille); and finally, a message from Jamie that nearly stopped my heart.

"Heyyyyyy, Hols . . ." it began. Even before the third word, I knew that Jamie had been drunk when he left the message. "Listen, about that check . . . er . . . We're havin' some problems with the budgeting and stuff and . . . yeah . . . You don't want to cash that thing just yet. I'll get back at ya soon."

I sank onto my aging, sagging couch and Smitty sauntered over and settled into my lap. If I stayed on this job for another month, I'd probably be homeless.

Not surprisingly, Jamie didn't return my calls the next day. I did go to the bank my paycheck was written from, only to discover that less than several hundred dollars remained in the account—nowhere near enough to cover my salary. I exchanged my euros and was thankful not to have spent that much in Rome. At least I had five hundred dollars in cash and a tiny bit of room left on my credit card until I could resolve this money debacle.

I tried to reach Faith, but her phone was off all day, going directly to voice mail. I figured I would see her the next day at Rehabilication, but unless I reached her today, I wasn't sure how I was supposed to get there. My car has a ninety-minute time limit, and driving down to Dana Point from my apartment would far exceed that. I was willing to bet my engine would explode somewhere around Long Beach, leaving me nearly an hour from my destination, not to mention without a way to get back home. I knew I could always ask Camille for help, but I didn't think that was fair, nor was I in the mood to see her. She'd warned me about not getting that check before Italy, and the last thing I needed right now was an "I told you so."

So that left me with renting a car, but I was dangerously close to maxing out my credit card. I'd never charged more than three hundred dollars at any one time, and now I was inching ever closer to the seven-thousand-dollar limit. The minimum payment was low enough, but I still needed my paycheck if I had any hope of putting a dent into that bill.

I knew I needed to be frugal, but staying cooped up in the house all day would only make it that much easier to obsess. I made the executive decision to find a cheap place for lunch and then "splurge" on a matinee movie. I was midway through my BBQ chicken pizza when a bartender switched one of the overhead TVs to the E! Network, which was right in the middle of *E! News*. I was sliding off my chair to request a channel change when the screen cut to a shot of Jamie, playfully squeezing a beautiful and familiar looking Hispanic teenager.

"Can you turn that up?" I found myself asking the bartender.

"Sure," he replied.

On TV, Jamie and the unnamed girl were beaming at each other like old pals. I had a bad feeling about this.

"So tell me, what prompted this switch?" the perfectly coiffed interviewer asked, shoving a microphone in Jamie's face.

"It was a mutual decision. Daisy has been looking to take her career in a new direction, and while I wish her nothing but the best of luck, pop music is really my home. I'm excited about working with Ariceli and securing her future in the music world."

I knew I'd heard the name before. I didn't know the whole story, but I remembered hearing that Ariceli was discovered from a YouTube video of her singing at her high school dance. She'd gotten more than a million views in the first week, and now every record label was tripping over themselves to get to her. As for Jamie, apparently the years he'd spent molding Daisy's career had meant nothing more to him than a paycheck. At the first sign of trouble, he'd bolted to the next moneymaking warm body that entered the room.

This was exactly what I'd been trying to point out to Dr. Chace. The only people in Daisy's life who truly seemed to care about her were a makeup artist and a hairstylist who didn't rate a dinner at La Pergola or a room in the fancy hotel. Everyone wanted a piece of her, but only so long as that piece paid constant dividends. Daisy had a ten-year, wildly successful career that had benefited hundreds of people. I had wanted to believe that those around her would continue to rearrange deck chairs until the *Titanic* sank out of sight, but they'd fled as soon as her ship sprung a leak. Aside from her mother and the opportunistic doctor, no one was even trying to plug the hole.

The worst part of this realization about Jamie was that it reminded me of Vaughn. As soon as Daisy was arrested, Vaughn had been concerned about his next job. He'd moved on before she was even released from jail. I didn't understand him, and I was increasingly confused as to why I had been attracted to him, or if I still was.

I'd tuned out the television for a few seconds, but just as I drifted back, I heard the anchor say, ". . . doubt that we're getting the full story from Daisy's camp or Jamie Lloyd. *E! News* has confirmed that Nickelodeon has canceled Daisy's show and recalled the crew from their Rome location shoot. At this point, rumors that Daisy escaped Italy only hours before her bail was revoked remain just that. In other TV news, NBC's fall lineup . . ."

The anchor kept talking, but I stopped listening. I wasn't particularly upset, I was just sad for Daisy. She was being hung out to dry. I suppose the only consolation was that for the next several weeks, she was probably shielded from all the bad news. At least, I hoped she was. I didn't imagine this kind of media pressure was conducive to recovery.

I spent the rest of the day wandering around town with no particular direction. I went to see a mildly funny movie about an old man, his ne'er-do-well grandson, and a mischievous dog, bought a new book, then hit up a grocery store for supplies. I played blind and dumb in the checkout line as two teenagers giggled over the horrible tabloid photos of Daisy. The girl's so gorgeous, I couldn't figure out how they'd gotten such terrible pictures of her. The whole time I was silently counting the ever-shrinking amount of cash in my wallet. I knew I should've stayed home and spent the day working through a box of frozen veggie burgers, but after all of this drama, I had to believe everything would work out. I had to believe I would get paid.

I was watching a fantastically terrible, yet addicting, TV movie at ten that night when my cell phone rang. Even before I knew who was calling me, I didn't want to answer. The list of people I didn't want to talk to was growing ever longer. But I saw that it was Ben and I couldn't ignore a second call.

"Are you all right?" he said, altogether bypassing hello. "By the time I got up yesterday, everything had gone to hell. I tried to call you as soon as I found out you were gone."

"It's a long story," I replied, not sure what to say to him. I wouldn't have put it past Vaughn to have told Ben that we'd kissed, to spite me or to make him crazy. Even if he didn't know already, I'd have to be an adult and tell him myself. I just didn't think it was appropriate to have that conversation over the phone. "But I'm fine. Are you back in L.A.?"

"No, I'm actually at the Fiumicino airport with the rest of the crew. They gave us a full day to pack up."

"Wow, fancy. I got about fifteen minutes. And that's fifteen minutes' notice coming out of a dead sleep."

"I'll be back home tomorrow," Ben said hopefully. "I'd like to see you."

I wasn't sure whether I wanted to see him or not. I felt like I did, like we had a real connection that might lead to something bigger. But I also knew I had just screwed things up, perhaps beyond fixing. And that made me want to avoid the situation until that became its own solution. Maybe I was a malfunctioning robot after all.

"Gee, I'd like to see you, too, but I'll be down in Dana Point, working with Daisy. I probably won't get home until late. And I'm sure you'll need to sleep after trekking around the globe for half a day."

There was a pause on the other end of the line, and I knew Ben wasn't pleased with my response.

"You're right," he said finally. "But I want to see you soon."

"Of course. Just travel safe and I'll see you in L.A."

There was another pause before he added, "I miss you, Holly."

I put my head in my hands and sighed deeply, away from the handset. "See you soon, Ben."

As I hung up the phone, I couldn't decide if I was going to hell for my actions or if I was already there.

Ultimately, I did have to rent a car the next day, and I chose a Dodge Charger because it was only four dollars more expensive and wouldn't make me look like a pauper in front of the rich folks. Because of the traffic on the ever-nightmarish 405, it took me almost three hours to get to the rehab center, and I had to stop four times along the way to pee. It was, however, truly thrilling to drive a vehicle that smelled nice and had a working air conditioner.

Ten minutes inside the door, I was even more dubious about Dr. Chace's methods. One of the brunette fem-bots settled me into a table in the "Zen Garden" just before Daisy ran out of the building, and directly toward me, at full speed.

"Holleeeeee," she squealed, extending the last vowel far longer than anyone over the age of twelve ever should. "Oh, my freaking God! I have been missing you like crazy, crazy, *crazy*!" Daisy spoke so rapidly that she didn't even pause to take a breath until after the third *crazy*.

"Hey, you," I replied as she squeezed me into yet another extremely awkward hug. "You look . . . happy."

Happy wasn't the word for what I was witnessing. Though Daisy was fortunately wearing a shirt that covered up her enormous breasts, she was still wearing far fewer clothes than I would have thought proper in a place like this. She actually looked pretty cute—that is, if she was about to head off to a high school gym class. Her jersey shorts were an inch below her ass, and her obscenely tight Rainbow Brite T-shirt showed off the bottom of her midriff.

And her behavior just seemed odd. I'd now seen Daisy in both the thrall of her medicine cabinet and the crash of narcotic withdrawal, and this didn't look like a girl who was coming down off a serious addiction (or forty). In fact, she seemed just as high as ever. As soon as Daisy pulled away from the hug, she started bouncing up and down on the balls of her feet like she couldn't stand still, even for a few seconds.

"Are we gonna talk today?" she said, bouncing harder. I didn't get to answer before she rushed on. "Because I have learned so, *so* much in therapy and I can't wait to talk all about it." I started to reply, but again, motormouth outpaced me. "Holly Bear, I know now that God wants me to help kids all over the world with addiction. That's my calling and I need to listen to Him."

Never mind that Daisy had only been in rehab for about forty-two hours now and couldn't have possibly had more than two therapy sessions. Never mind that she was *clearly* on some form of chemical substance. What I wanted to know was when, in the last two days, little Miss Nymphomania had found religion.

"Okay . . ." I said, blindsided by this somehow shinier version of Daisy. "Then let's sit back down and get to it."

"Do you like iced tea?" she asked, making no move to take a seat. "Because I didn't think I liked iced tea, but then I came here and they try to get you to lower your sugar intake—I think to help detox your body or whatever. And the first time I tried it I was like, yeah, whatever. But then the second time I was like, whoa, this is de-*lish*."

I stared at Daisy, thinking that if I had to endure this manic behavior for the next several hours I might use the award-winning crème brûlée torch to light myself on fire. "I do like iced tea very much."

"Then we should totally get them to bring a pitcher of it out here," Daisy replied. "But first Mama says you gotta go talk to her and Dr. Chace about boring business stuff. I've gotta go do meditation for a little while and then we can work and you can meet my new boyfriend!"

I had no idea how Daisy could possibly make it through a meditation session without vibrating her way out of the room. I was also more than a little astonished by her comment about the new "boyfriend." Ben was my first real date in two years and Daisy had a boyfriend after a day and a half? And who in their right mind would want to date a fellow drug addict?

I left Daisy to her meditation and headed back to the lobby to see if I could find Faith and, I hoped, get paid. Or have a conversation that didn't move at the speed of light.

"That can't be," she said, shocked. I also noticed that she threw an embarrassed glance toward Dr. Chace. I hadn't wanted to bring this up in front of the doctor, but Faith insisted that Chace needed to hear "everything" that was going on, good or bad. "That's the incidentals account, we always keep half a million in there. You know, for emergencies."

I abhor those must-be-nice people, but in this case, it really *must* be nice. My emergency fund was two twenty-dollar bills stuffed into an old sardine can in one of my kitchen cabinets. "I'm sorry, Faith, but I went to the bank myself. There was only a few hundred dollars left."

"And Jamie called and left you that message?" Faith started pacing the room, biting her nails. "What do you think he meant by that?"

"I don't know. But I can tell you, he was pretty drunk."

"Well, that's unacceptable. I'll make sure he takes care of this today. How much have we paid you so far?"

This was not a conversation I was hoping to have with her directly. One of the reasons people have agents and managers is so that they don't have to make these deals for themselves. The closer your relationships to your clients, the less effective you are in negotiating with them. But Faith had asked me a direct question and it wasn't like I could just ignore her.

"Based on the first payment and the Miami expenses that were never reimbursed, I've cleared about three thousand dollars," I said, trying to remain strong. I really didn't want to upset Faith, but I wasn't going to relegate myself to the poorhouse to make her feel better.

"Three thousand? Out of how much?" An expression of horror was beginning to dawn on her face.

"Fifty," I replied, looking down at my feet.

Faith didn't speak for another few seconds. She anxiously walked the length of the room several times, then went over to her purse and pulled out her cell phone. "I'm so sorry, Holly. I'll get this settled right now."

Faith's cell was off, and as she booted it up, I came to a mortifying realization—she didn't know about Jamie representing Ariceli. I didn't know what to do, if I should say something or keep my mouth shut. It wasn't my place to deliver that kind of news, but she deserved to know, didn't she? How could Faith or Daisy begin to rebuild a career without all the information? Dammit, I hated that man.

"Jamie's got a new client," I blurted out.

Faith and Dr. Chace shared a look, and I was instantly sorry I'd opened my mouth. I was also irritated that these two were already bosom buddies considering they'd never met each other until two days ago. Again, I couldn't shake the feeling that membership in the fame club comes with a decoder ring and a secret handshake.

"Daisy has been Jamie's only client since she was ten," Faith replied, offering me a patronizing smile. She glanced back to Dr. Chace for support, but this time, he look troubled. Well, as troubled as he could look with the limited movement of his facial muscles.

"We haven't seen him here yet," Chace pointed out. "Jamie did say he'd come down as soon as he landed . . ."

260 * RACHEL STUHLER

"You don't know how these things work. He's just busy. Whenever we're putting together a new deal, I don't see him for days. And with this mess . . ." Faith's smile faded from patronizing to pained, but she managed to keep it for at least a few more seconds. "He knows we're fine and he doesn't have a spare minute to drive all the way down here."

"I saw him interviewed on *E! News*," I said, keeping my tone quiet but firm. "He said he'd just signed that YouTube girl, Ariceli." I had to stop Faith; I couldn't keep watching her rationalize Jamie's betrayal.

Her façade crumbled. As she spoke, I could see her lower lip quaver. "The one who sang that ballad version of 'Pour Some Sugar on Me'?" Faith whispered, crushed.

So *that's* the song Ariceli sang at her talent show. Of course every man over the age of five had logged on to YouTube to watch a sixteen-year-old cutie croon about being "hot, sticky, sweet." "I think so," I said.

Faith slowly walked over and sat down, burying her face in her hands. She was still holding her phone, and just as she hid her face, I saw the screen light up. It dinged, signaling that she had voice mails, but Faith ignored the sound.

Dr. Botox crossed over and put a hand on her back. "Now, Faith. We discussed the possibility that Daisy's age might pose a problem. She's not fifteen anymore, there are a lot of people who won't be as interested in her."

First of all, gross. Second of all, how was that the issue at hand? Faith just found out there was no one steering the ship and that the last captain had made off with at least half a million dollars. I couldn't see how calling an eighteen-year-old a used-up has-been was part of a constructive dialogue.

"Forget about that," I said, unable to stop myself. "The more important thing is cutting off Jamie from your bank accounts. Right now."

Faith waved me away without looking up. "I'll get you paid, Holly. I really will."

I didn't want to say this, but I had to be honest. "I'm not as concerned with fifty thousand dollars as I am with the millions that Jamie has unfettered access to. You need to shut him down as soon as possible." As the words came out of my mouth, I knew I'd pretty much just suggested that Faith hold on to her cash for as long as she wanted. I wondered if the melted Hershey's miniatures on Camille and Donnie's couch would stain my clothes if I was forced to take up residence on it.

"You're right," Faith replied, standing up. "I need to call Deacon and our lawyer."

"Where is Deacon? Shouldn't he be back by now?" We'd flown back two days ago; he could have turned right around and arrived just a few hours later.

"Oh, he'll be in Europe for a little while longer," Faith said, scrolling through her phone. "Fashion Week is coming up, and Milan's not that far from Rome."

Seriously? What is wrong with these people? "In that case, you can't wait for Deacon," I pressed. "You need to take care of this yourself."

"How?" I couldn't tell if Faith's tone was defensive or just bewildered. "Jamie set up those accounts."

With this kind of oversight, I was sure Jamie had been stealing from the Dixsons for years. "Your name is on all of them, right?"

Faith shrugged, throwing another look up at Dr. Chace. "Sure . . . I mean, my name and Daisy's name are on all of the checks and credit cards."

I glanced at my watch, trying to add up how many working hours were left in the day. "Okay," I said, wondering how this had suddenly become my responsibility. "Change of plans. Faith, you and I are going to the bank. I'll work with Daisy this afternoon."

"Maybe I should go, too," Dr. Chace said.

I hope he knew from my expression that I wanted to stab him

in the neck. "That won't be necessary. It's time only Faith and Daisy were in charge of the money."

"Okay," Faith said, putting a shaky hand against the wall to steady herself. "But we're going all the way back to Beverly Hills?"

I almost asked why we would do that, but then I realized what she meant. It scared me that the Dixson thought process now came so easily to me. "No, Faith. Every bank has branches all over the area. We'll find the closest one."

Chace started to follow us out of the room. "Really, maybe it's better if I—"

I held out my hand, preventing him from touching Faith. "You've done enough," I said. "I'll handle things from here."

CHAPTER 18

When dealing with the paparazzi, it's better to pretend they're not really people. Because if you acknowledge that the guys and girls chasing you down the street are someone's husband, father, sister, daughter, you have to question everything you think about humanity. I'd never cause a traffic accident and risk the lives of other people just to get a picture of a teenage actress eating an ice cream cone—would you?

It took two hours, but by 1:00 P.M., only the Dixsons had access to the Dixson money. Although if I hadn't been there, Faith probably would have signed over power of attorney to the personal banker who helped us. Jamie had indeed stolen the half million from them (he was nice enough to leave $219), which posed big problems for Faith and Daisy in the short term. While they technically had millions of dollars to their name, only $500,000 was liquid at any given time. This made sense to me, as a checking account earns little to no interest, but it baffled Faith. She couldn't grasp the rules and regulations of CDs and mutual funds and why she couldn't just pull the money out right then. The immediate solution was for the ladies to live off their black American Express cards for the next month, which, incredibly, had no limit. In front of the nice, middle-class banker, Mr. Roach, Faith told an adorable little anecdote about once buying an Aston Martin with that card. I don't think he was amused.

As we left, I caught Faith eyeing me with something resembling admiration. I don't know that anyone's ever looked at me that way before.

"How do you know all of this money stuff?" she asked, incredulous. "I didn't understand half of what he was talking about . . . CDs and mutual funds and interest penalties."

"Um, I don't know." How could she not know "this money stuff"? The woman was nearing forty.

As we got back into the car, Faith whistled. "All I can say is, I hope Daisy grows up to have as good a head on her shoulders as you do."

The comment disturbed me, though I couldn't figure out just why.

After I returned with her to Rehabilication, Faith ran off to speak with the family lawyer and I finally found time to work with Daisy. Though I didn't exactly get a lot of work done. I more or less sat in silence while she and her new boyfriend made out for three hours. One of Daisy's only contributions to the afternoon was giggling, "Isn't he just so smart?" As "he" never spoke to me, I wouldn't know.

The boyfriend was an actor (shocking, I know); a hulking, high-lighted-blond Adonis who starred on a CW show about sexy super-heroes. The producers had written him out of the first few episodes so that he could get a "sobriety tune-up." Because blond actor superhero just happened to be a not-so-recovered heroin addict.

"It's totally fine," Daisy whispered to me when Lee stepped away to take a phone call. "He only snorts the heroin. He's completely terrified of needles. So there's nothing to worry about."

I can't even tell you why I stayed the entire three hours, especially since it meant my end time placed me smack in the middle of afternoon traffic. But I was desperate to get any information that might help me finish this so-called book by my rapidly approaching deadline. Though why I was continuing to work without getting paid, I also can't tell you.

I couldn't return the car until the next morning, so I drove back toward my apartment, excited that my only roommate was incapable of speech. Meowing is so much easier to interact with sometimes.

But as I turned onto my street, I saw a bunch of guys hanging out in front of my building and I was immediately nervous. It was dark enough that I couldn't see exactly what they were doing. And while I don't live in the worst neighborhood in L.A., the sight of ten loitering men on my street at near 8:00 P.M. definitely gave me pause.

I had already decided to keep driving past and turn on the first available street when I finally realized what was going on. The men in front of my building weren't the usual neighborhood suspects— they were photographers. And that could only mean someone had finally discovered my name. The only question left was whether they knew my actual job title or if they still thought I was the pregnant, alcoholic cousin.

I'd passed through the throngs of paparazzi a number of times now, but they'd never been interested in me before. It was bad enough being along for the ride as Daisy was interrogated by shouting and flashbulbs; I didn't think I could handle the questions being directed at me. So I kept going, turned onto the next block, and pulled over at the curb. I put in a call to Faith, who didn't answer immediately. I had to call back a second and then a third time in quick succession before she finally picked up.

"Sweetheart, is everything all right?" Faith asked. I could sense slight annoyance, but she kept it under control, apparently giving me the benefit of the doubt.

"No," I told her, more upset than I'd even realized. "There are paparazzi in front of my house. I don't know if they really know who I am or if they're just trying to get more dirt on Daisy."

"Oh, no, did you say anything?"

The Dixsons clearly do not hang out with the right people.

"Nothing," I insisted, a little hurt that she'd think otherwise, "I didn't even stop. I drove around the corner and called you."

There was silence on the other end of the line. "I don't suppose you have an overnight bag with you?"

"I don't."

Faith sighed, sounding tired. "Okay, sweetie, I want you to drive to our house. Do you remember where it is?"

I didn't like this plan one bit. "I remember, Faith, but I can't just run away. I have a cat. If I'm not there to feed him in the next couple of hours, he'll start eating the couch."

"Well, you can't say anything to those bloodsuckers," she shot back, momentarily abandoning her southern politeness. "You have a nondisclosure agreement. We're paying you for your discretion."

"You're not paying me at all," I couldn't stop myself from saying. "And I wouldn't give them a word, not a single word, with or without that contract. I'm just not used to being hunted down by parasites with cameras."

"You can't stay there, Holly. Those people don't go away."

"I don't know what to do," I admitted, my voice a little weepy.

"I'll take care of everything. Do you think you can handle them just this once?"

I didn't want to but I also didn't really have a choice. "I guess so."

"Okay, you run in there and grab your clothes and your kitty cat and head on over to the house. I'm staying down here in Dana Point, but I'll call over and talk to our security. They'll get you all settled in."

"All right."

"It's gonna be fine. And I promise you, Holly, I'll get you paid just as soon as I can. Now you go to the house and get some sleep, sugar, and we'll see you down here tomorrow."

I hung up and threw my phone on the seat before shifting into reverse. I reluctantly made a three-point turn, heading back toward the inevitable confrontation with the paparazzi. I managed to get out of the car with little fanfare, but as soon as I stepped into the streetlight on the corner, the yelling commenced. Someone must have had a picture of me already, because a number of the paps recognized me immediately. It only took me a second to realize that being photographed with Daisy at LAX—my second time in public with her in just a few weeks—must have made me a target. My only moment of amusement came when they all took off running toward me, trying to meet me at the street corner. As though I wasn't going to walk directly toward them on my way to my front door.

My good humor died when the first asshole bumped into me, almost knocking me to the ground. I had to force my way down the block as more and more of the photographers made physical contact with me. If I didn't know better, I'd have thought a couple of them were attempting to pickpocket me. When one of them grabbed the back of my shirt, I very nearly pushed him away, but before I did I had the presence of mind to consider that they might be trying to bait me. I hadn't seen them do this with Daisy (maybe because until recently, she was still a teenage media darling), but Camille once told me that the more ruthless freelance photographers will sometimes try to get the subject to hit them. It makes for great drama and there's always the possibility the photog can sue and earn some extra cash.

I just trained my eyes on the ground and kept moving; with the constant flashbulbs, I couldn't see any farther ahead, anyway. My phone rang again and I automatically answered, thinking it was Faith calling back.

"I'm hurrying, I swear," I said, trying not to get all shaky in front of the photogs. I knew that everything I said was being recorded and would be analyzed by a million ears.

But it wasn't Faith. "Holly, are you okay?" I heard.

With the crazy noise and questions and flashes going off in my face, it took me a moment to place the voice. I even glanced down at my caller ID to make sure I was right. It was my old boss from

Kragen Publishing, Susan. "Susan, this isn't the best time," I said, turning sideways to avoid a collision with a cameraman.

"I know that, honey. That's actually why I called. Why don't you come on down and tell us your story—as an unnamed source, of course. If you're going to be followed like this, at least you should make money on the deal. Am I right?"

I could just make out the front door of my building beyond the sea of bodies, and I was relieved to see that it was locked for once. But I didn't know what to do about Susan; I hadn't a clue what she was talking about and I didn't have the time to figure it out. "I'm sorry, what? Why would I do that?"

On the other end of the line, Susan laughed. Or I think she did, I could barely hear. "I'm with Radar these days, Holly. I thought you knew that. When I saw those pics of you in Miami, I just knew I had the perfect source tucked up my sleeve."

I hastily unlocked the gate and slid through, slamming it shut behind me. Hands and cameras were thrust through the bars like it was some kind of weird prison-break attempt. As I turned to flee up to my apartment, I suddenly knew what she meant. It was no accident that the vultures had descended upon me; Susan had leaked my name.

As soon as I turned a corner out of sight of the cameras, I pressed the phone to my mouth and said, "You did this to me."

"Oh, come on, Holly," she replied. "You would have killed for a scoop like this at *Westside*. And that wasn't even the big leagues."

At *Westside Weekly*, I'd written unnecessary movie reviews and talked about who looked terrible at the Oscars. It was a far cry from siccing money-thirsty wannabes with loose morals on every assistant and acquaintance with an easily accessible address. It would have never occurred to me to flash a few hundred (or grand, I don't know) at anyone who could divulge celebrity dirt.

"You're going to have to get your scoops from someone else. I'm not going to sell out my boss."

Susan laughed again. "Hon, until a few days ago, it was your boss who called us."

Still shaky from my encounter outside, I dropped my keys into the long-dead hedge to the side of my front door. "What?"

"Radar's had a deal with Daisy for years. She or one of her people calls to say she'll be at the Ivy or shopping at Saks and we send a photog out."

"I don't believe you." Actually, I didn't know what to believe anymore. Just because Susan had plenty of reason to lie to me didn't necessarily mean she was. And Daisy and Faith had done some pretty bizarre things; I wouldn't put it past them to have paps on retainer.

I finally located my keys, but my unsteady hands still had trouble maneuvering them into the lock.

"Ask her," Susan said. "We even have a system. If she doesn't want to be photographed, she wears the same clothes two or more days in a row. We don't take any more pics because it looks like they were all taken on the same day."

That was one of the most fucked up things I'd ever heard. "Then call her people and ask for information."

"No one's talking. I think you know that. And after everything that we've done for her."

Yeah, I felt terrible for Susan and her paparazzi brigade. "Do me a favor and lose my number, okay?"

"Holly—" was all she managed to say before I hung up the phone. I was so furious, I nearly threw the phone at the door. The Holly of a few years ago would have, but I've learned the hard way that when you throw breakable things against a hard surface, you have to replace them and get down on your hands and knees to pick up the pieces. I really liked my new phone. Instead, I flung open the door and let it bang against the wall.

Smitty meowed at me and my phone rang again. For the third time. The caller ID read JAMIE LLOYD. I knew this would be good.

"What?" I asked. He wasn't worthy of pleasantries.

"Hols, so glad you answered."

"What's up, Jamie?"

"I was kind of hoping you could help me out." He instantly slipped into his charming mode, which had long since failed to move me. "I'm in a little bit of a pickle."

I swear I don't take pleasure in the misfortune of others, but I smiled to myself. "Is that a fact?"

"Yes, well . . ." Jamie paused, I'm sure waiting for me to ask, all a-flutter and panicked, what was wrong. Fat chance. "I don't know what your plans are tonight."

"Very busy right now," I said as I struggled to get Smitty into the cat carrier.

"Oh . . . So I suppose you couldn't take a few spare minutes and ride out to Temecula?"

I hesitated, still unable to figure out what sort of game Jamie was playing. I'd never been to Temecula, but I was aware that it was an area south of L.A. known for vineyards and bed-and-breakfasts. I also knew it was roughly two hours away, and I'd already spent five hours in the car today. I was curious to see what favor Jamie wanted, but not that curious.

"That's not a few spare minutes, Jamie," I replied. "What is it exactly you need?" Smitty leapt out of the carrier before I could latch it. I saw him shoot through the air and under my sagging couch. I'm sure he thought I was about to pack him off to Camille's again.

For at least ten seconds, there was dead silence from the other end of the line. Either it was killing Jamie to have to ask me for help, or he'd dropped the phone. I knew which was more likely. Finally, he sighed and said, "I need some money, and I need it tonight."

"What? Where are you?" Had he gotten drunk and impulsively bought a vineyard?

"I'm at the casino." Then he repeated, "I need some money."

And then I knew where the Dixsons' half-million-dollar "incidentals" fund had gone and my paycheck along with it. This stupid prick treated his golden goose like his own personal piggybank, robbed her blind, and then expected everyone to rush to his aid. "How much is 'some'?"

"Fifty grand."

"You have *got* to fucking be kidding me."

"Hols, listen to me. I know that—"

"Shut your mouth," I said, throwing my hands up. I knew he couldn't see my hand gestures, but they made me feel better. I'd reached my limit. "You've stiffed me on thousands of dollars and now you think I'll just clear out my bank account to help you?"

"It's not that much money. You're overreacting. You've been spending too much time with Daisy and Faith."

"Did you gamble away the five hundred thousand you stole from them?" I couldn't resist asking. "Here's a news flash, jerk-off, they're going to have you arrested."

Jamie whispered, "I didn't lose all the money at the casino. There's an underground poker scene in the area. High-stakes, you know."

No, I don't know. I haven't a clue what high-stakes anything means because I've never made it above the poverty line in my entire life. I couldn't believe that Mr. Hotshot Hollywood Agent was daring to ask me, once the recipient of government cheese, to loan him fifty Gs.

"You have a lot of nerve calling me."

"Who else was I going to call?" Jamie asked. "Faith and Daisy hate me, and Deacon said he can't help me from Milan."

The latter was almost certainly bullshit. Deacon could rectify this situation with a single phone call, so either he'd said no or he'd refused to take Jamie's call. "What about your new pretty princess, Ariceli?"

"She's a high school student with no record deal. How is she supposed to help me?"

"And thanks to you, I'm basically an unpaid intern." Great. This was one more unpleasant bit of information I had to give to Faith. "You're on your own, Jamie."

"They'll kill me, you do know that."

Everything with these people was so overblown and dramatic. "They're not going to kill you over fifty grand," I said. "If you died, how would they ever get paid? The worst that will happen is they'll . . . I don't know, break your legs or something."

"Thanks for nothing, Holly."

"The feeling is entirely mutual, Jamie."

"I know how you feel about me, but don't get lulled into their world," he warned me self-righteously. "They act like they care about you, but they don't. They'll use you and just throw you away. They do it to everyone."

"I think you're talking about yourself. Go to hell, Jamie." And before he could do it, I hung up on him. I immediately tried to dial Faith, but the phone went straight to voice mail.

I knew I should go pry Smitty out from under the couch, but I couldn't seem to move. I was staring around my wreck of an apartment, unable to think of a single thing I should take with me to the Dixsons'. Sure, I needed a few changes of clothes, but aside from Smitty, no one missed me when I was gone. I rarely got mail that wasn't a utility bill or addressed to Resident. And I knew, without looking, that my cupboards contained four plates, two chipped bowls, and no utensils that weren't plastic. I had no assets, save a gifted diamond albatross that I couldn't even sell.

Faith had said that she hoped Daisy grew up to be like me, but how much had I really grown up at all? I was twenty-five years old and I didn't own an iron or a fork. I was living in some state of arrested development, and only when everything started to shift under my feet did I finally see my life for what it was. It was depressing as hell.

"Come on, Smitty," I said, plodding toward my Goodwill couch. "We're going for a ride."

It was after midnight by the time I made it to the Dixson house. The guard was very sweet, even taking my bags out of the car. From inside the carrier, Smitty hissed at him, clearly not as big a fan.

"Mrs. Dixson says you can choose between the guest wing and the guesthouse," he told me. "She had Anna get both of them ready. All new sheets, food in the fridges, everything you'll need."

It was really the only right way to end such an insane day . . . by stepping further through the looking glass. I stared up at the mono- lithic house, which despite being vacant of every full-time occupant was completely ablaze with light. I didn't know if I could handle sleep- ing in that enormous palace by myself, so I said, "Guesthouse, please."

Little did I know that the guesthouse was larger than the home I grew up in. It was two stories all on its own, with three separate bedrooms, two baths, and a full kitchen. It was also tucked so far behind the pool and tennis court that I couldn't see the main house. I stood in the doorway, mouth open, for a good ten seconds.

"Are you all set?" the guard asked. "I have to get back to the gate."

"Oh . . . of course. Thanks." I was still so startled I hadn't moved past the front door.

The guard must have seen the look on my face because he smiled and patted me on the back. "It's crazy the way these people live, right?"

"It sure is," I said, finally working up the courage to set Smitty down in the living room. "Have a good night."

"You, too, Ms. Gracin." He turned and headed back toward the house, leaving me alone.

I moved around the guesthouse, checking things out. It was spotless in here and, even more disturbing, completely quiet. Es- pecially in the last month, I had slept in a number of places, all of them noisy. My apartment building is always a little bit like a techno rave, and even the hotels had been boisterously loud at times. But here it was like a tomb.

Smitty adapts far better than I. Before I had picked which bedroom to sleep in, he had jumped up onto an open windowsill and fallen asleep. In the still silence of Holmby Hills's mansion row, it took me far longer to close my eyes.

At 9:00 A.M., just as I stepped out of the shower, I heard a voice echo through the guesthouse. "Ms. Gracin, I have a package for you at the guard station."

I momentarily froze, wondering if someone had just walked in. But the voice sounded too canned, too tinny to be in the same room with me. Then I spotted the intercom on the wall. I walked over, intending to respond, but there were no fewer than thirty buttons and only a handful of them were labeled. The rest were color-coded in some way that probably required a manual to figure out. In the end, I had to throw on some clothes and make the five-minute hike to the front gate. Seriously, it took me five whole minutes.

The guard on today's shift was less talkative than the one from the night before. He handed me an envelope and then turned back to his book. It made me feel even lonelier. I was halfway back to the guesthouse when I opened the envelope and found a small, black plastic credit card. It was one of the unlimited Amex cards, and *it had my name on it*. I halted next to the pool, staring at the card in disbelief. Then I saw that there was a small note inside the envelope, which read, "Use this for whatever you need."

And if I thought the weirdness for the day was over, I was wrong. When I walked back inside the little house (I use the word *little* only in comparison to the main house), my phone was ringing.

"Hello?" I said, out of breath, having sprinted the last few yards to get to it.

"Good morning, Ms. Gracin," came a different voice. This one was female. "I saw you were up and around. Do you need anything?"

I pulled the phone away from my ear and stared at it, confirming that I had no idea whose number was calling. As far as I knew, I'd never heard that voice before. "I'm sorry, who is this?"

"Anna. I am the Dixsons' house manager. Do you require anything this morning?"

"Um . . . I don't think so." When the guard had said the name Anna, I'd just assumed she was a maid. I've never met anyone with a house manager. I wasn't even sure what that job entailed, aside from the obvious. Did she live in the house full-time? Or was she just on call twenty-four hours a day like everyone else seemed to be?

"If you do, please call me at this number or press seven-two-nine on the intercom," she told me. "And when you're ready to head down to see Mrs. Faith, you can pick up the keys from the guard station."

"What?" I had left the keys to the rental car on the front hall table, figuring I'd need it for the foreseeable future. I definitely wasn't going to stay at the Dixsons' and let them see my rotting heap of metal. But as I turned to glance at the table, I saw only my purse. I had left the keys out, hadn't I?

Reading my mind, Anna replied, "Mrs. Faith had me return your car to the rental facility this morning. She says you can take one of theirs for as long as you need it."

So someone *had* just walked into the house without asking me. I didn't know if that was normal in rich-people land, but it was disturbing. What if I'd been walking around naked? Didn't they have a sense of personal space? "Uh, okay," I said.

"If you tell me which car you'd prefer, I can have Mike bring it around for you."

I didn't know who Mike was or how many cars the Dixsons owned. "Why don't you choose?" I suggested. "I don't know much about cars."

"Of course, Ms. Gracin. It will be out front for you in ten minutes."

As I hung up, I wondered if I'd found a monkey's paw or Aladdin's lamp and just forgotten about it. Really, people lived like this every day of their lives?

Even before I had my things gathered for the day, my phone rang again. I swear, I'd never been so popular in all my life. And it was another phone number I didn't recognize.

"Hello?"

"Heya." It was Axel. "Sorry to call so early."

I didn't mind that Axel was calling me, but where had everyone gotten this new number? I hadn't even learned it yet. "No problem, I'm awake. What's up?"

"I was wondering if you could do me a favor?" His tone was different than I was used to. There was no trace of the bubbly guy I'd come to really enjoy. Today, he actually sounded sad.

"Sure. Tell me what you need." A lot of people had been asking me for favors lately, and the hairstylist was one of the few I was happy to oblige.

"I went and bought some of Daisy Mae's favorite green-tea Kit Kats and I was hoping you could take them to her. It'll cheer her up."

"Green tea?" Weren't Kit Kats chocolate and cookie wafers?

"They're Japanese," he said. "She did a mini tour through Asia a couple of years ago and she fell in love with them. When she's feeling sick or upset, they always make her smile."

"Why don't you take them down yourself?" I didn't mind being the errand girl, but I figured Daisy might appreciate having one more friend to talk to.

"Faith said she couldn't have visitors." I could tell by his tone of voice that he didn't believe her. And he was right to have doubts. While a lot of rehabs do restrict visitors for the first few weeks, Dr. Chace had specifically asked to meet with Daisy's friends. I knew they'd requested that a number of actors and actresses come down to Dana Point, but so far, no one had shown up or even responded. Maybe Axel wasn't famous enough to be a "friend."

"Then I'm happy to. I'll text you later and we can meet up."

"Thanks, bitch. I owe you one."

Despite Faith's suggestion that I be at Rehabilitation by 9:00 A.M., I'd already learned enough about Daisy's therapy schedule to know that on Mondays she wouldn't be free until almost two. So rather than wait around all day, I decided to have an early lunch with Camille after running by Axel's apartment and grabbing the very cool looking green-tea Kit Kats. I needed to reconnect with reality before I completely lost my mind. I just forgot to warn her about my new photographer entourage. She showed up in sweats, no makeup, and a baseball cap, and immediately wanted to hurt me.

She wanted to go back home and change, but there was a free table at A Votre Sante, which almost never happens on a weekday during the lunch rush. I told her to put her back to the window and deal with it.

"What do they want? You're no one."

"Thanks," I replied, sticking out my tongue. "And they know that. I'm guessing it's because they can't get a good sight line on Daisy."

"How's the book coming?" she asked.

"What book?" I laughed. "Daisy doesn't remember anything and Faith tells stories like she's reading them from a ship's log. I now have five chapters and I've already used every word they gave me, except for the *um*s and *uh*s. Somehow I don't think the information I have will be very appealing to their target audience."

"I heard about that Ariceli girl. Holy shit." Apparently forgetting she was mad at me, Camille started to giggle.

It was so nice to talk to someone with the right perspective on this situation. She was one of the few people I knew in L.A. who realized that this faux-reality was nothing more than a façade. I love the girl, even if she can't get away from her loser, fungus-like growth of a boyfriend.

"Oh my God, I forgot to tell you! I was the one who had to break the news. Faith had no idea."

"No," Cam said, leaning so far over, her pigtails fell into her salad.

"I swear. And Jamie stole at least a half mil from them before he left. Faith doesn't know for sure because she has no idea how much money they have."

Just as Camille officially burst out into a fit of snarky laughter, I saw movement outside the little restaurant and realized I wasn't going to get to finish my tuna salad sandwich. "Damn it," I muttered, watching as Ben struggled to get past the paparazzi.

Camille stopped laughing and glanced over her shoulder to see what I was looking at. Instead of commiserating, she whistled. "Please tell me you know that gorgeous creature." Until that moment, I didn't realize I'd left out a big part of the Rome experience. Not that you can blame me—there was so much story to tell.

"I think I'm dating him."

"What?" she practically shouted.

Before I could answer, Ben lumbered over to the table and stared down at me, smiling sheepishly. "Hi."

"Hello there," Camille said.

"Um . . . hi."

"I swear to you, I'm not stalking you," he said. "But there's video of you on the Internet and I recognized A Votre Sante. And I live about four blocks away."

I looked back and forth between Camille and Ben, stunned. "There's what, now? We've been here for a half an hour."

Camille gave him a knowing smirk. "And what were you doing trolling the gossip blogs?"

Ben shrugged, still towering over the table like a giant. "Honestly, they're the only way the crew has been able to get info on our show. We didn't get any official word it had been canceled, that all came from the Internet."

Camille pulled a chair over from a neighboring table, not bothering to ask the occupants if they needed it. "Please, have a seat. I'm Camille."

Ben glanced at the chair but didn't sit down. "I'm Ben," he replied, shooting a look toward me instead of Camille.

"Ben, really, have a seat. Don't worry about the deer-in-headlights look you're getting from Holly. She doesn't handle surprises very well." She leaned over and whispered loudly (as though I wouldn't still hear her), "I think she's a little autistic."

I hate when she tells people that. It's made me so paranoid in the past that I actually went for testing, and just so we're clear, I am *not* autistic. "Stop saying that."

"Then start acting like a normal human being."

"I have to drive to Dana Point after lunch," I blurted out automatically.

"Oh . . . okay," Ben replied, turning a little red. He glanced back at the door. "I'm sorry to interrupt your lunch. I guess I'll see you around."

Just like in Rome, I realized that if I let him walk out the door, I would never hear from him again. Part of me felt relief at the possibility of that outcome, but I had to concede that the relief could just be my cowardly laziness. As Ben turned to walk away, Camille smacked me—hard—on the back of the head. I also hate when she does that.

"I can be back for a late dinner," I said. "If you're free, that is. Eight o'clock, maybe. Or seven-thirty if we meet somewhere further south, like Santa Monica or Venice."

"You don't have to," was his answer.

"I want to. Don't think this has anything to do with you." I nodded toward the maggot photographers waiting right outside the door. They were a great scapegoat for my cowardice and indecision. "Have you noticed the swirling shitstorm that is my life right now?"

Ben cast a dubious glance back toward the paparazzi. "I imagine that is pretty crazy." He paused, a thought seeming to just occur to him. "Um . . . do they follow you everywhere?"

"This is a fairly new thing. But so far, yes. I'm actually staying at the Dixsons' because of it."

"Then why don't you come over and I'll make you dinner?"

Camille raised an eyebrow at my lumberjack would-be boyfriend. "You cook?"

Ben nodded. "After college, I spent two years at Le Cordon Bleu." Of course he did.

"Why don't you just text me your address and I'll come over as soon as I can."

"Okay. Nice to meet you, Camille." Ben waved and headed back out to the feeding frenzy on the sidewalk.

"You, too," Camille called after him. She watched as he disappeared, then snapped her head back toward me. "What in the hell is the matter with you? Marry that man."

"A few weeks ago, you said Vaughn was delicious," I retorted, sulking.

Camille rolled her eyes. "Look, I don't know what happened in Italy, but you came home with that gorgeous piece of ass as a boyfriend, so Vaughn is dog meat as far as I'm concerned. Or did you manage to screw things up even worse than I think you did?"

"Vaughn kissed me. After I kissed Ben. And I don't think Ben knows about it yet."

"Not the end of the world. You two have only started dating. If you want to fix things, then tell him the truth before someone else does and ruins everything. As for Vaughn, if you've had Ben's tongue down your throat and enjoyed it, it's time to move on." She paused for a second, then exclaimed, "And why the eff didn't you tell me you were living at Dixson Central? When did *that* happen?"

"Eat your salad," I replied. "I have to get to work."

My afternoon with Daisy was surprisingly productive. Heroin-addict Lee was busy with a visit from his sister, Dr. Chace was doing yet another guest spot on CNN, and Faith was off trying to reassert her dominance over Daisy's career. With no distractions (and seemingly, far fewer mood-altering drugs), Daisy was compliant and—dare I say—even a little bit fun. I gave her the green-tea Kit Kats, and she happily munched on them throughout our session, sharing fun little stories about Axel and Sharla and their tour adventures across the world.

Now that the tone of the book was changing and her battle with prescriptions was known to the world, it actually gave us something to talk about. And judging by the way Daisy was quick to blast Jamie for getting her hooked on pills as a child, she had already heard about his defection. I knew she and Jamie had had their moments of friction, but I didn't realize just how much she hated him. I wondered if she knew about his affair with Faith, but we had such a great rapport, I was terrified to bring it up.

The saddest moment of my afternoon came when Daisy sighed and said, "I can't sleep in here. Every night, I'm lucky if I get an hour or two."

"Why?" I asked.

"I don't like being alone. That's why I always have my friends sleep over. When I'm alone, I think too much. I think about what an awful person I am and how much I hate myself. But Dr. Chace doesn't let me have people in my room after ten. So I sit there by myself all night."

I wasn't equipped to respond to that admission. More than anyone I'd ever met, Daisy really did need therapy. I just hoped to God that Rehabilication was able to help her. Given my interactions with Chace (and that stupid name), I was a little dubious of his competence. And to tell the truth, that wasn't my job. I was there to talk Daisy through her life and reorganize it in some sort of coherent, PG-13 way. So I largely kept my mouth shut, listened, and kept my pen to the page.

I never did see Faith that day. I left Rehabilication around six-thirty and climbed back in the Dixsons' enormous Lincoln Navigator. When I told Daisy which car I was driving, she referred to it as the "grocery store ride" or "Mom car." This was my second experience driving it and I was still unsettled by the car asking "Where would you like to go today?" every time I started it up. I hadn't figured out how to park the monstrosity yet, and I was pretty sure valet stands didn't take my magical black Amex.

I also tried not to overthink my dinner with Ben. Because I assume every situation will end in a gloomy disaster, I didn't expect too much. A big part of me was actually hoping he would decide he didn't really like me and end things himself. Yeah, I'm that much of a wimp.

When I reached Ben's apartment in Brentwood, I could smell the meal from the front porch. Ever the traitor, my stomach growled loudly. I was also immediately uncomfortable by how much nicer his neighborhood was than mine. His building had a French Provincial feel to it, and he even had window boxes overflowing with blooming flowers. If I was lucky, maybe I'd started dating a gay guy.

Ben must have been waiting for me because he answered the door about three seconds after I knocked. I smiled at him, but I'm not sure if I came off as shy or creepy.

"I wasn't sure if you'd actually come," he said.

"I wasn't, either," I replied.

We had a nice, if slightly strained, dinner, but we'd no sooner settled onto the couch with a glass of wine than I suddenly knew the inner workings of my brain were far less clandestine than I imagined.

"You can tell me you're in love with Vaughn. It's okay. It's what I thought initially, anyway. I feel stupid for discounting my intuition."

I stared back at Ben, the only thought in my head, *Why does he have to be so pretty and perfect?* "What?" was all I could muster.

Ben gave me his adorable smirk and looked away. Even his eye-lashes curled up in an impossibly unnatural way. I was definitely physically attracted to him, but I still didn't know about the rest. Hell, I didn't know *him*. The Roman fling had happened so fast it bred a false sense of familiarity. Back in the light of day, I still had to figure out how much of it was real. "Holly, be honest with me. I deserve that much."

I hesitated for a second, thinking about how angry Camille would be if she discovered I'd blown this relationship to smithereens. I briefly considered pulling out the dumb, flirty persona that works on most men, but I am neither of those things. And it's exhausting to pretend to be someone you're not. Not to mention, it's rude and disrespectful to play games with another person's emotions.

"I don't know what I'm doing," I said. "And I don't know what I want. But I'm not in love in Vaughn. I'm not sure how I feel about him, exactly, but it's not love."

"Fair enough."

"But there is a reason I've been avoiding you and it isn't that I don't like you. I do." I paused, trying to come up with the right words instead of the swirling, confusing mess of thoughts and syllables that I'd thus far been unable to untangle even in my own brain. "I was honest with you about Vaughn. But the last night in Rome, something happened."

"Okay." Ben didn't move or show any sign of upset. He really was one of the most reasonable people I'd ever met. I almost didn't know how to deal with that.

"He and I got into an argument and he kissed me. I didn't ask for it but I probably took a little too long to stop it." I forced myself to add the last part. I thought it would be disingenuous to just say that Vaughn kissed me. It wasn't like I slapped him or immediately shoved him away.

Ben took a sip of wine, considering what I'd said. "I knew he'd try. Vaughn doesn't like to lose." I had been prepared for anger; I wasn't sure what to make of this reaction. "I really do like you. I want you to have whatever makes you happy."

"About that," I said before I could stop myself. "*Why* do you like me? I mean, you're insanely good-looking, ridiculously smart, and I'm pretty sure you could build a house with your bare hands if you wanted. You're like the Marlboro Man without the cancer."

Ben laughed, and instantly that strange tension that had hung in the air all night shattered into a million pieces. I swear, it was even easier to breathe. "That's the dumbest thing anyone has ever said to me."

"No, it's not. I get why Vaughn likes me, but you. . . ."

"You're beautiful. And talented, and witty . . . What's not to like?"

"I'm not Daisy. I don't get guys like you."

He paused for a moment, watching my face with a precision that made me nervous. "By which you mean you don't deserve a guy like me."

I didn't know what to say to that. "If the shoe fits, I guess. . . ."

Ben shook his head. "If it's just that you're more attracted to Vaughn than you are to me, then I won't say anything to try and stop you. But if you're attracted to him because he's what you feel you deserve, then I'm not just going to stand aside. You deserve a hell of a lot better than someone who keeps dangling the possibility of relationship over you."

In all of my hours of tossing and turning over this issue, I'd never been able to pinpoint the problem as easily and succinctly as Ben just had. It was also becoming clear just how much he disliked Vaughn. "I thought you'd be mad."

"We're adults, Holly. You and I spent a very little bit of time around each other and not that much happened between us. I'm not furious that you hadn't yet made up your mind about me."

"I've been terrible to you."

"A little bit, yes," he agreed quickly. "And to make it up to me, you need to give me a month. Just one month. And if Rome was just a showmance, then fine. But you owe it to me to find out for sure. Then if you still want Vaughn instead of me, I won't argue."

"A showmance?" I laughed.

"Yes. A showmance, a locationship, everybody on a film crew has one once in a while." Ben winked at me. "But I'm a keeper."

Unless he was a secret wife beater or member of the Ku Klux Klan, he was right. "A month, huh?" When he nodded, I smiled and shrugged. "I think I can do that."

CHAPTER 19

This town makes it very difficult to have real friends. I've talked about how hard it is to know if someone cares about you or if they just think you can get them a job, but there's more to it than that. You lose the ability to trust people, and that's the most dangerous thing of all. You start to see ulterior motives, liars, and cheaters everywhere, even when they're not there. And the moment you question a true friend, the moment you start to wonder if that person called the tabs or took a picture of you at your worst, that friendship is doomed. Not because you can't trust them, but because they can't trust you.

Ben turned out to be right—despite their seedy intrusiveness, the gossip blogs were absolutely the best place to get information about Daisy's career. Those bastards at TMZ knew more about her life than she did. They gave me a heads-up as to what questions would be hurled at me the next time I stepped outside. No one managed to get close to Daisy's house, but once I reached Sunset Boulevard, I was fair game. The blogs also gave all of us a pretty clear view of Jamie's political maneuverings. According to Perez Hilton, Jamie had used every one of Daisy's studio connections to get Ariceli's demo recorded, and now he was going after Nickelodeon to secure her a TV show. It was like watching the circle of life in a piranha tank.

I spent the next week working with Daisy every day in Dana Point, driving back and forth in Faith's Navigator. Most nights, I drove back and had dinner with Ben at his apartment. We tried to go out to a restaurant a few times, but it was difficult to eat with all of the flashes going off in our faces. I very deliberately kept him away from the Dixson compound, mostly because I didn't feel comfortable having guests over without permission. I knew I wasn't some babysitter sneaking in her boyfriend after hours, but it still felt wrong. It wasn't my house, so it wasn't my place to entertain any-one but my invited cat. So we huddled up in his French Provincial apartment, and most nights Ben read through my day's work with Daisy, giving me notes. It was also nice to know that someone—anyone—cared what I was writing.

My nights with Ben were sweet and calm, but I still felt like my relationship with him was lacking a certain fire. And it wasn't about sexual chemistry, I totally wanted to rip his clothes off. It's just that I never experienced that static shock when seeing him walk into a room. Maybe that was nothing more than a childish fantasy. I couldn't help but think that if I hadn't experienced that intensity with Vaughn, I would have been happy as a clam with Ben.

And in that entire week, I didn't hear a single word from Vaughn. I tried to call him back in response to the mumbling apology he'd left on my voice mail, but he didn't answer. Each time my phone rang, it was someone else. Now that Daisy's show had been shut down, I didn't even know where I could find him. I wondered if maybe it was better this way.

My life moved forward at an anxious, steady pace until the fol-lowing Wednesday. I'd taken to checking the blogs before I left for work every morning, but that particular day, I saw something that made me spit hot coffee all over my laptop. There was a story about Jamie stealing the half million dollars and Daisy considering a "baby powder" defense for her cocaine bust . . . and I was credited as the source.

I was so upset that I didn't even notice as my laptop began to sizzle. I heard it in some corner of my mind, but my heart was thumping so loudly that it drowned out the dying wail of my computer. It had to have been Camille—or Donnie—who had ratted me out. It *had* to. I hadn't said those things to anyone but my best friend. Furious, I pulled out my cell phone and called her.

"Heya, mama," she answered.

"What the fuck is wrong with you?" I shouted into the speaker.

There was a momentary stunned silence on the other end of the line before Camille regrouped and said, "Please don't speak to me like that."

"I'll talk to you any way I damn well please! How could you sell things to TMZ behind my back?"

"I have no idea what you're talking about, Holly."

I started to cry. "I asked you not to tell Donnie anything. That fat, slimy bastard will do anything for a buck. I *begged* you and you did it anyway. He sold me out, Camille. It's all over the Internet."

"Wow," she said. "I can't believe you'd accuse me of that. And thanks for calling my boyfriend a slimy bastard."

"What else am I supposed to say about him? He sits on your couch all day and spends your hard-earned money, but thinks it's beneath him to marry you. The guy's a loser," I said. "How do you get a hold of the people at these blogs? Do they have a tip line? Hell, do they even pay that well? I hope it was a damn lot of money because I'm going to lose my job over this."

There was silence on the other end of the line. "I didn't repeat any of that to Donnie. Not a word. You asked me not to."

"Oh, really?" I cried in disbelief. "Then how am I quoted as saying that Daisy was going to tell the Italian government she thought the cocaine was baby powder?"

"I would assume they got it from you."

"I'm not a goddamn idiot, I haven't talked to the paparazzi," I practically screamed. In all the years I'd known her, I'd never been this upset with her before.

"No, but you've sure as hell talked in *front* of them," Camille replied. "Do you really think those scumbags are above coming into a restaurant and eavesdropping on other people's conversations? You weren't exactly quiet."

I thought back to everything I'd been "quoted" as saying. Had I really been dumb enough to talk about all of those things in public? I racked my brain and quickly realized that Camille had to be right. I'd sat right there in A Votre Sante and a couple of days later in a Peet's Coffee and told her everything that had happened in the last few weeks. I could have leaked it to the paps myself, or one of the patrons could have smelled an easy payday. I was the asshole.

"Oh my God. I'm so sorry."

"Apology not accepted," Camille replied. "You can't just accuse me of all of this shit and think a simple sorry will cut it. You really believed it was me. And again, you called my boyfriend a slimy bastard. You can't take that back."

"But I am sorry." I started crying again, but this was an entirely new moment of terror. I was going to lose my job *and* my best friend in the same morning. "I didn't mean it."

"Yes, you did," Camille answered. She let out a deep sigh and then added, "I can't talk to you right now."

"But—" I didn't get to say anything else because the line abruptly disconnected. It was just as well, as I had no real follow-up to my *but*. Camille was right, I did think Donnie was a waste of DNA. There was no coming back from my assessment of him.

Figuring I might as well take all of the bad news at once, I called Faith. She answered on the second ring, and I instantly felt guilty when she said, "Are you all right, sugar? I saw TMZ this morning."

Was *I* all right? Maybe Faith was functionally illiterate. "I didn't know they were listening," I blurted out, bursting into a fresh round of tears. "I was having lunch with my best friend and I think they were listening in at one of the nearby tables. I'm so sorry, I understand if you want to fire me. I can be out of your guesthouse in an hour."

My weepy, terror-filled apology was met with a cutesy little laugh. "Oh, sweet pea, don't you even worry about it," Faith said. "It happens to all of us sooner or later. I once made the mistake of filling a prescription for the dogs over the phone, and twelve hours later, X17 was reporting that Deacon had cheated and given me herpes."

I was so dumfounded by her reaction that I couldn't think of anything to say but "What?"

"You didn't say anything terrible." Faith laughed. "You didn't say that we worship Satan or that Daisy votes Democrat. It's fine—really."

"Um . . . okay. But I am sorry. I'll be more careful from now on."

"I'm sure you will, Holly. Now, I've got to get back to work with Dr. Chace. I'll see you down here later?"

I nodded even though she couldn't see me. "Yes, Faith. See you soon."

I hung up the phone and slumped onto the nearest kitchen barstool. It was only then that I turned my head and noticed that my laptop was soaked and the screen black. Stunned, I tapped a few keys and then tried to boot it up, but to no avail. My computer was dead and I was the one who'd killed it. All because of those evil spies at TMZ. Luckily, as a result of owning a refurbished, five-year-old laptop that often died for no reason, I e-mailed myself my work as soon as I finished it, but now I was without a way to finish the book. And no money to buy a new laptop. I wondered how my financial situation could possibly get any worse.

Daisy had a clear schedule on Wednesday mornings, so I worked with her until lunch and then came clean with Faith about what had happened with the computer. As always, Mama Bear Dixson was cool as a cucumber, mildly assuring me that we'd "figure something out." While I was shaken and weepy over the morning's events, I felt better just knowing I had such a big supporter on my side. Faith bought my meal and told me stories about growing up in the South.

"I didn't know you were a preacher's daughter," I told her. It made sense. While it was true their actions could be decidedly unwholesome, who among us doesn't make a bad decision once in a while?

"Oh, yes," Faith said, laughing. "My papa was as fire-and-brimstone as they come. You so much as touch a drop of liquor and you've earned yourself a front-row seat to Satan's ten o'clock show."

"Was? When did he pass?"

Faith's expression turned cloudy and she took a long sip of her Diet Coke. Looking down at the table, she said, "Well, he hasn't exactly passed on. At least, I don't think he has." There was another deliberate pause before she added, "We haven't spoken in a little while."

Judging from the look on her face, I guessed that the "while" wasn't so little. I almost asked for a specific number, but then I thought better of it. "So he doesn't approve of your Hollywood lifestyle?"

"That's a big part of it, yes. But Papa Hanson is also really opposed to making more money than you need to feed the ten children the Lord intends you to have." There was no mistaking the bitter edge that came with the words *ten children*. Faith shook her head, getting the same snarl I usually get whenever my mother calls. "After Daisy was signed to her first TV show at ten years old, my father tried to cure her of the 'demons' that must surely have taken over his grandchild. That was the last time I spoke to him."

"My mother's worried I'm going too Hollywood," I told her. "Ever since the press release saying I'm pregnant, she seems to think I'm too impressionable and stupid to take care of myself with all of the Tinseltown sharks swimming around me."

I expected a cooing apology for starting that rumor or at least commiseration for our overly zealous parents, but Faith just threw me an irritated look. "So?" she said.

"I'm sorry?" I asked, startled.

"Well, we weren't talking about you, Holly. Yeesh." I'm pretty sure my mouth fell open, but I didn't say a word. I was still staring at her when she started speaking again like the interruption never happened. "Of course, I always wanted to be an actress when I was little, but Papa Hanson wouldn't hear of it."

I am not important—message received.

I thought maybe Faith actually was mad at me and was just too passive-aggressive to tell me directly, but when I left for the day, a new MacBook Pro was waiting for me at the front desk. Faith hadn't said a word to me about it or left the building, so she'd clearly sent someone to buy me a new computer while I was working with Daisy. All I can say is, being rich strikes me as damn cool.

I drove back toward Ben's, excited to show off my new toy. I also hoped that computers were in his wheelhouse of endless knowledge, as I don't know how to do much beyond boot one up, type, and surf the Internet. I was surprised to find that someone was waiting for me outside of Ben's apartment building, and even more surprised that it was neither Ben nor a member of the paparazzi. It was Jamie.

"I don't have time," I said, walking right past him.

"Just give me five minutes. That's all I ask," he said, jogging after me.

I stopped, mostly out of curiosity. And now that I could really see him, Jamie looked like garbage. His eyes were bloodshot and he hadn't shaved in days. It wasn't even the five o'clock shadow that makes some men look rugged and sexy; this was an unkempt man under some serious stress. "Well, they didn't break your legs."

"I took care of that," Jamie said.

"Then why are you here?"

"I need your help. I've been trying to talk to Faith for days but she won't even answer my phone calls." He looked like he was about to cry.

"Oh, go to hell." I actually wanted to spit on him, but I have better manners than that. "You screwed yourself out of a job. I'm not helping to get you back in with them."

Jamie shook his head, wiping a tired hand across his mouth. He shifted his weight back and forth and strangely turned completely around in a circle. Either he was high or he really didn't know what to do with himself. "You can't blame me for this."

"Are you *kidding*? You're really trying to tell me this whole disaster isn't your fault? You get Daisy hooked on drugs to control her, then just take them away because you're worried about getting caught. Of course there'd be no consequences to a drug addict going cold turkey! Of course you can just wipe out a client's bank account, get yourself indebted to underworld gamblers, and expect the rest of us to bail you out!" I took a step forward, sticking my finger right in his face. "You are the most despicable piece of shit I've ever met, and I don't have an ounce of sympathy for whatever hole you've just tripped and fallen facefirst into."

"I was a good guy!" This time, I think Jamie really was hiding tears. He turned his head away, swatting ineffectually at his eyes. "When I met them, I was just a baby agent at CAA, desperate to keep my job. Everyone loved sweet, talented, perfect little Daisy. And Faith . . ."

"Yeah," I shouted back. "I know all about you and Faith. Did she get a wrinkle or a gray hair and you just decided you needed to move on to some college freshman?"

"What?" Jamie looked genuinely confused. "I didn't leave Faith. She left me. I wanted her to leave Deacon, marry me. . . . But she said it was just a 'business relationship' and that if I wanted more I had to go somewhere else. She didn't even care about me. Two years and she didn't give a crap about anything but sex."

That was the first red flag. But I still wasn't convinced. "You'd say anything to get my help. But Faith's a sweet person, she'd never intentionally hurt someone. I'm sure she cared about you. I know it."

Jamie stared at me in disbelief. It was that are-you-really-this-stupid look again. "You think *I'm* the wizard behind the curtain?" He laughed, a loud, booming, staccato sound. "Hols, I gave you more credit than that. Faith doesn't care about you or me or anybody else. I'm not even sure she really loves Daisy. What she loves—what she *craves*—is the money and power. Do you really think a ten-year-old Daisy was just dying to leave her friends and move halfway across the country to work twelve hours a day? That was Faith's dream, and she hasn't let anyone stand in her way."

I thought back to our conversation earlier, when Faith hadn't wanted to hear a single thing about my own life. I'd thought we were becoming friends, but I'd been firmly put in my place. A large rupture formed in my confidence and trust in Faith. But I wasn't about to believe that Jamie was just some poor, innocent Hollywood lamb unwillingly led to the slaughter. "You're all disgusting."

"Fine. I'll take some of your disgust as long as you acknowledge that a lot of it goes back to the evil queen."

At that moment, Ben opened the door and stepped out onto the stoop. "I saw your car pull up a few minutes ago. Is everything okay?" I saw him throw a warning look at Jamie.

"I was just going, Benji," Jamie said just loud enough to be heard. Then to me he added, "You know what, you don't have to advocate for me. Maybe the biggest help is keeping me away from all of those bloodsuckers."

"I'm sorry things turned out this way." I was astonished to realize that I meant it.

Jamie nodded and started to back toward his car. "Just don't trust them, Hols. If they have to—hell, even if they just get bored one day—they'll hang you out to dry, too. They do it to everyone eventually."

I was so upset I didn't even watch Jamie leave. Instead, I just ran up the stairs and disappeared into Ben's apartment. Unfortunately, it wasn't twenty minutes later that another large crack formed in my camaraderie with Faith; as Ben and I opened up the computer, attached to the invoice was a note that read, "Don't worry, we'll just take this out of your check."

To which Ben replied, "Did you ask for a five-thousand-dollar computer?"

I tried to give Faith time to figure out her financial situation, but by Friday of the next week, I was down to twenty-six dollars in cash. Yes, I had the credit card, but I didn't think it was appropriate to just go around charging my personal life to the Dixsons. I also had the feeling my purchases were now being tallied and would be deducted from my total fee. So I only used the card for gas and related work expenses and all too quickly burned through my leftover per diem. My patience officially ran out at 10:00 A.M. on Friday, when she pulled up in front of the rehab center in a brand-new Bentley Mulsanne.

"Isn't it gorgeous? And the dealer gave it to me for six grand a month, can you believe it?" I stood there, dumbfounded, as she swatted me playfully on the arm. "After everything that's happened, I thought I deserved a toy. Do you think I should get Daisy one as a reward when she finishes rehab? Or do you think she'd like the Azure more?"

"I have less than thirty dollars to my name and you just bought a *Bentley*?"

Faith blinked up at me innocently. "Well, thirty thousand isn't a lot, but it should be enough for you to get by until I can free up some money."

All of Jamie's words came rushing back. In the last two months, I'd had lots of reasons to hate these people. But never before had

I been so furious that I felt like I might black out at any moment. They'd left me in Miami, nearly convinced my mother (and the rest of the world) that I was a slutty alcoholic, wasted endless hours of my time, and had now left me with two tens, a five, and a one-dollar bill. I'd managed to convince myself that it was out of necessity, that Faith ultimately had my best interest at heart. But now, with the black metallic Bentley gleaming in the California sunshine, I realized that Jamie was right—I meant nothing to them. It took every ounce of my strength not to burst into tears. The Dixsons had basically turned my life inside out.

"I don't have thirty thousand dollars, I have thirty *dollars*. And a nearly seven-thousand-dollar credit card bill that is entirely expenses from this work I'm doing for you. I'm scrimping and saving every last cent so that you can go out and blow hundreds of thousands of dollars on a hunk of metal that you'll think is out of style in eight months."

"I think you're just a little tired and so you're overreacting," Faith said in her best mom voice. "No one can live on thirty dollars, Holly."

"You're right, they can't!" I said, barely holding back the flood of tears. "How much do you think I make a year? You're my employer and you haven't paid me in two months! How much do you think I have left after that?"

"I hadn't thought about it." Her tone was shifting, the sweet veneer beginning to wear away and the true Faith reemerging.

I'd only just arrived, but I pulled out the keys to the Navigator. "I'm done working until you pay me."

Faith seemed too surprised to move. She stood there and watched me walk back to the Lincoln, not speaking until I'd already un-locked the driver door. "Holly? Holly, sweetheart . . ." She quickly switched back to her mom tone, but it was too late.

I paused for just a second, looking at Faith over the roof of the car. I couldn't walk back toward her because I didn't trust myself not to punch my boss in the face. "Yes?"

"Um, would it help if I bought you lunch? We can sit down and talk it all out. You know the café here—"

"Good-bye, Faith," I yelled, climbing into the car.

I made it exactly two exits on the 405 before I started sobbing hysterically. Traffic was heavy enough that my emotional waterfall didn't inhibit my driving too much, but I did get a number of very strange looks from the occupants of nearby cars. As though no one's ever had a breakdown during rush hour before.

I'd just reached L.A. County when my phone rang. Thinking it was probably Faith, ready to apologize, I plugged in my headset and answered without looking at the caller ID. The car apparently had Bluetooth, but I hadn't figured out how to link my phone.

"Hello?" I said, sniffling. I quickly wiped my nose on my sleeve so that she'd be less likely to notice I'd been crying.

"Holly? Baby?" The universe really did hate me. The only person I wanted to talk to less than Faith was my mother. "Are you all right?"

"I'm fine, Mom," I lied. "But it's not the best time."

"You're not fine. You've been crying. Holly Ann, you may have moved to the other side of the country, but I still know you better than anyone else."

Do you? I wanted to ask. "I'm having a bad day."

"No matter what it is, you can tell me. Even if you really are pregnant, I'll understand. I promise."

I was prepared for nagging or judgment, but I wasn't prepared for that. I burst into tears, my sobs loud and ugly. My mother didn't speak, she remained silent and let me finish. "I'm not pregnant, Mom. I would have told you. It's these people I'm working for."

I had just given her another huge opening for judgment, but to my surprise, she didn't take it. "Camille doesn't like them much. We've both been worried about you. Is there anything I can do? I think Great-Aunt Linda is married to an attorney."

Hearing this, I started to laugh. It was part laugh, part cry, and

I'm sure I sounded like a crazy person. "I've never needed a lawyer before." My mother's words were so uncharacteristically sweet, I didn't want to point out that a New York lawyer probably hadn't passed the bar in California.

"You have to protect yourself," she said, repeating her earlier warning to me. "I know you always want to see the good in people—it's one of your best qualities—but most people are only looking out for themselves."

"They're awful. Every one of them. I've made such a mess of things and I don't know how to fix it."

"Tell me all about it," my mother said. "I don't know much about these things, but I'm here to listen and give whatever advice I can."

This made me cry even harder. I couldn't speak for almost a minute. "I can't, Mom. I have a contract that says I could be sued if I even told you who I was working with. You only know because it's been all over the television. They think of everything."

My mother may not be well educated, but she does have a set of smarts all her own. "But if it's as bad as you say, wouldn't they already have broken that contract? I don't think you have to listen to them anymore."

I thought back to that contract I'd spent an hour reading. At the time, I'd only done it out of excitement. I hadn't considered that we'd even get this far in the process, let alone that one of the clauses might have to be executed. I remembered the fee schedule and agreement that I would incur no expenses of my own. The Dixsons had breached the contract almost from the very beginning. My problem now was that I didn't know what to do about it. I tried to think about Great-Aunt Linda's new husband, but I remembered quickly that he was an actuary, not an attorney. So I didn't even have anyone to call for a recommendation.

"It seems to me they're in more trouble than you," my mother continued. "I don't think that little girl can handle much more bad press."

I wondered if that was true. Daisy looked so bad already I couldn't imagine that a contract dispute would add that much fuel to the fire. "I don't want to go to the press. I couldn't do that. I just want to finish this job and get the money I'm owed."

"Sometimes in life, we have to do things that are against our character," my mom told me. "We do our best to be good, moral people, but there's only so much a good person can take."

Not that anyone would ever write a biography of me, but if they did, my current working title was "Only So Much a Good Person Can Take." "Thanks, Mom," I said, and I meant it. I felt considerably better than at the beginning of our phone call, and that wasn't something I often said after talking with my mother. "I really thought you were going to say 'I told you so.'"

"I know you think I'm hard on you, Holly. But I only want the best for you. No matter what that is."

That got me choked up again. "I'd better go," I said, trying to keep my endless tears at bay. My mother can handle a lot of things, but sentimentality is not one of them. "I'll call you over the weekend and let you know how things are going."

"All right, Holly. Bye bye."

My mother didn't say "I love you," but I didn't need her to just then. I understood, perhaps for the first time in my life, that she didn't need to say it to feel it. It was a sharp contrast to Faith, who was always so effusive but probably meant little of it. I thought back to Jamie questioning if Faith even loved Daisy and considered that he might be right.

By this point, I hadn't moved so much as an inch in the last two minutes. The weight of the last few days overwhelmed me and I started to sob again. I didn't realize how loud I was—with the windows down—until a Kleenex was handed to me from a neighboring car. Surprised, I looked up to see a teenage girl smiling at me sympathetically.

"What did your mom do?" she asked.

I gratefully took the tissue and blew my nose. "She was right." At least there are some decent people left in this world.

"Ugh," the girl said, shaking her head. "That's the worst."

Without intending to, I ended up at Ben's front door. I was still taking our relationship one day at a time, but I can honestly say my first thought when leaving Dana Point was that I really wanted to give him a hug. That had to be a good sign. I couldn't remember if he was working today, so I was relieved when he answered after just a couple of knocks.

"I thought you were working with Daisy today," he said, smiling down at me warmly.

It was a powerful thing, knowing someone was always so genuinely glad to see me. I reached up and put my arms around his neck, gently pushing him back into the apartment.

"I didn't come here to talk."

I closed the door with my foot, wondering if the picture would make it onto any of those gossip sites for Vaughn to see. I almost hoped it did.

A lady never kisses and tells, but I will say that I never made it back home that night. And lest you think I'm an animal abuser, I'd already fed Smitty that day and the Dixsons' house manager promised to look in on him. Because I couldn't take any more bad news, I'd turned my phone off just before walking up to Ben's, so I missed the apologetic message from Faith that came in just after 5:00 P.M. She said she still couldn't cover my total salary, but that she'd put enough in my bank account to cover "certain expenses."

The next morning, I was momentarily stymied by the message until I remembered that my bank account information was listed on the contract I'd signed with Jamie, in case they decided to wire the money over. I was half-asleep and clad only in one of Ben's gargantuan football T-shirts when I called the automated bank number to hear my balance.

I gasped loudly as the tinny, mechanical voice told me I had eighty-five hundred dollars. Maybe I wouldn't need a lawyer after all.

Ben stepped out of the bedroom, holding a pile of clothes. "You're a slob, you do know that, right? I swear, you leave a trail of dirty clothes behind you everywhere you go." He stopped short, seeing the look on my face. "Is everything all right?"

I turned around and looked at his beefy, shirtless form and sighed. "I think I have to go to work today." Seeing Ben in his half-naked Adonis glory, I was actually a little disappointed that I'd just gotten paid.

"Did they give you the rest of the money?" he asked.

"Well, no . . . but they gave me some of it," I said. "At least I'm not destitute."

"How much of the total?"

For the first time I could remember, I was truly irritated with Ben. "Eighty-five hundred."

"Out of fifty." It was a statement, and an annoyed one at that. Ben looked away and shook his head.

"Yes, out of fifty. But it's something . . . Faith listened to me yesterday."

"Come on, Holly," he said, giving me a hard look. "You don't think that, do you? She wasn't listening to anything but the sound of you driving away. She could have gotten you the whole fifty if she really cared. Your mother was right about these people. Faith's just worried about getting sued."

My mind went immediately to the Bentley. Ben was probably right, but I'm as stubborn as they come. I wasn't about to admit that I was being naïve. Especially not when he was speaking to me in that tone of voice. "If I don't finish my job, I don't deserve the rest of the money."

Ben stared at me for a long few seconds. "So that's it. . . . You're just going to go back there and continue to let them treat you like some grinder monkey?"

"I don't even know what that means."

"It means that they wind you up and you just go, no questions asked." Ben's voice was heated, raised. I'd never really seen him get upset before. I couldn't decide if I found it scary or really hot.

"This is my job," I answered. "What am I supposed to do?"

"What you're supposed to do is show these people that you're worth more than being treated like shit." I'd also never heard Ben swear before. He threw up his hands. "Go ahead if you're really going to go. But I don't want to listen to one more anecdote about being left behind or unfed or used as a drug mule. If you go back to that job, you know exactly what to expect."

I nodded, stung. "Fine. But I'm not a slob," I muttered, more for myself than for him. "You're a neat freak with OCD." It was true; everything in his apartment was arranged symmetrically, and when something moved out of place, he spent ten minutes measuring it back into position. I'd also noticed that he touched every doorknob or handle exactly three times. Until now, I'd been too nice to say anything. "Now, can I have my clothes? There are like a billion people with cameras outside."

I reached out for the pile Ben was holding, but he pulled it back. "These are your clothes from Tuesday. Your Monday dress is crumpled in the corner of the bathroom, and your outfit from yesterday is hanging on the chair in the dining room. Which would you prefer?"

I snatched my Tuesday clothes out of his hand and moved toward the bathroom. "Smart-ass." If I was going to lose this argument, at least I could have the last word.

CHAPTER 20

When things go wrong, it's easy to run away and hide, pretend it's not happening or claim there's nothing to be done. But we always have a choice. We can sit down and let the walls crumble or we can find a way to build a new, stronger wall. The first step in doing that is admitting that the only person who can really help you, is you. I'm not saying it's not important to have family and friends by your side. It is, but they can only do so much. In the end, you're the one who needs to make the changes. You're the one who has to say, "I deserve to be happy. I deserve to succeed."

I agreed to return to work, but not without talking to Faith first. I needed her to know that the games of the last couple of months could not continue. It would have been an uncomfortable conversation no matter what, but the fact that I currently lived in her guesthouse made it that much worse. Luckily, she hadn't been home since our return to L.A.

I sat across from her at a table in the Rehabilication café, thinking neutral ground would be best. I tried to channel Ben, the sanest person I knew. "I appreciate the money, but you will pay me the rest. And that includes every expense I've incurred since starting this job. I understand you're still sorting out your finances, but I will not turn over a finished manuscript until we're current on payments."

"Okay. Anything else?" Faith sounded annoyed, but I didn't care.

"Two things." I reached into my bag and pulled out a large plastic-bound folio and pushed it across to her. I'd had it printed up the night before. "First, I need you to read the work I'm doing. We're a team here; I can write down the words, but I need your feedback."

Faith opened the cover and flipped through the pages. "I can do that. The other thing?"

"Let Axel and Sharla come visit Daisy." This was the part of the conversation I was less certain about. I knew it was dicey, challenging Daisy's mother over her personal affairs, but I felt strongly about this. "You've invited so many people to see and talk to Daisy and they never come. I know a makeup artist and hairstylist aren't the A-list visitors you were hoping for, but they love her. And they've stuck with her, which is a hell of a lot more than you can say about the rest of those assholes."

She didn't answer right away. Faith continued to flip through the pages of the book, reading a passage here or there. When she finally looked up, she said, "I suppose. She does love them, too."

My business with her finished, I stood up. "That's everything. Let's get back to work."

Faith reached up and grabbed one of my hands. "I am sorry, you know. You've been just wonderful through this whole ordeal. I don't know what we'd do without you."

"Thanks," I said. I didn't believe a word of it.

I worked with Daisy nearly every day over the next two weeks, and if I didn't know better, I'd say she matured years in those fourteen short days. She was still having insane, rabbit sex in every available corner of the rehab facility, but when she wasn't talking about Lee's physical prowess, we actually had some pretty interesting conversations.

Deacon never made it back to California to visit his daughter. He stayed in Europe for the duration of Fashion Week, then made a pit stop in Barbados for, as he told Faith in an e-mail, a "much-needed vacation." What he was vacationing from, I'll never know. During that time, Daisy only had two regular visitors aside from her mother and me. Twice a week, Axel and Sharla carpooled down and spent the afternoon, sometimes joining in on our sessions and often doing Daisy's hair and makeup to keep up her spirits. I couldn't help but think back to Rome, where Axel and Sharla weren't considered important enough to ride in the nice car, stay at the fancy hotel, or eat in the five-star restaurant. I thought it odd that none of those who had "made the cut" so much as bothered to send flowers or call to check in, no matter how many times Faith pestered them to. I hoped Daisy realized now who her true friends were, though I didn't waste my breath asking.

On one of their first "glam" afternoons, I sat out front with Axel while he smoked. Technically, he could've had a cigarette in the courtyard, but he said Daisy had quit when she was sixteen and he didn't want to tempt her.

"I know it was you," he told me. "Daisy Mae wouldn't question her momma about something like visitors."

I shrugged, unwilling to take credit for something any decent person would have done. It was unfortunate that I was one of the few decent people in this situation. "She needed you. And I think you needed her, too."

"She can be a wicked little bitch, but we're besties."

"I have a question. Daisy doesn't call paparazzi, does she? Radar tried to get me to rat her out—I didn't, of course—but they said until rehab, Daisy was the one behind most of the stories about her. But that's nuts, right?"

Axel took a long drag of his cigarette and stared at me. It was all the answer I needed, but after he exhaled, he said, "Nobody's gonna tell your story but you."

Even after all this time, I still wasn't sure pictures of Daisy on the elliptical were her "story." "So she'd just call them up?"

"Daisy Mae is a proper diva, she doesn't need to do her own dirty work." He pulled his phone from his pocket and brought up the contacts with one hand. The other stayed on his cigarette. He held up the phone for me to see "Radar" listed in the contacts. "I've got 'em all, even the little ones."

"Wow."

"And you know, she always lets me keep the money, too."

I'm embarrassed to admit that it wasn't until Axel and Sharla's third visit that I realized I was no better than Daisy, at least not when it came to Camille. My friend had done everything in the world for me, from giving advice to babysitting my ornery cat, and I'd repaid her with mistrust. And maybe Donnie wasn't the greatest guy in the world, but if the last few weeks with Ben had taught me anything, it was that adult relationships are not easy. I had been single for so long that I'd forgotten.

I was searching for a way to make amends when I remembered the diamond necklace Daisy had given me in Italy. It was still crumpled up in my purse, signaling my level of interest in jewelry. But I thought I might know of a way to put it to good use.

On a Thursday afternoon, I was sent home just after one because Chace needed a special "media coaching" session with Daisy. I drove back up to L.A. and right to Camille's apartment. I knew she was at a casting session in Dallas, but I also guessed that Donnie had stayed home to ride the couch, which was confirmed when he opened the door after my first knock.

I was prepared with a speech, but I was momentarily stymied when I noticed how good Donnie looked. He'd lost about twenty pounds and wasn't wearing his usual holey sweats. Instead of a greeting, I blurted out, "Are you on your way to a job interview?" That probably wasn't the best the way to start.

"No," Donnie replied, crossing his arms. "I'm home working on a rewrite."

Here it comes, I thought. The big project pitch—also known as why I should spend six months working for free on a movie that would never get made. But the pitch never came.

"I'm really busy, did you need something? I assume you came to apologize, but Camille's in Texas."

"I know that. I actually came to see you." I reached into my purse and pulled out the necklace. It really was a gorgeous diamond, if you were into that sort of thing. The light caught the stone just right and momentarily made me see pink. "I know that you always tell Camille you guys can't get married until you can afford a ring, so I wanted to help out. Here." I held the necklace out for him.

"That's a necklace, not a ring."

"Yes, but it's a two-carat solitaire. It's a colorless diamond, which I hear is a good thing. All you'd have to do is get it reset as a ring." I thought my plan was genius; I might be able to give Camille what she so desperately wanted, but it was also a test. If Donnie had the diamond in his hand and still wouldn't propose, then he'd leave no doubt of his douchebaggery.

Donnie didn't even touch the necklace. His arms stayed firmly crossed in front of him. "I don't need your diamond."

I knew it. I just *knew* that he'd been making excuses all this time. The only question was how I could make Camille see it. "It's not charity, I swear. It came from Daisy Dixson. I figured since she caused this whole mess, she should pay to fix it."

Donnie stared at me for a long moment. "You're a piece of work, you know that? I don't need your damn necklace because I already bought Camille a diamond."

"What? You did?"

"*Yes,* I did. I've been saving up for it for two years. I thought it would take me another year, but I signed a deal with Screen Gems last month."

If my eyes were wide before, they were saucers now. I really need to work on my poker face. "Oh" was all I could think to say. "That's fantastic."

Donnie nodded, offering me a tight grin. "Yeah, I asked you for a year if you wanted to work on this idea with me. I finally gave up and wrote it myself."

Camille had been right from the beginning. Until utter desperation led me to take the Dixson job, I'd never committed to anything. It was just easier to make fun of Donnie than to put in work on a project that might be rejected. I was the commitment-phobe, not Donnie.

"I am so sorry, Donnie," I said, tears welling up in my eyes. "I pretend I know everything and . . . I'm just feeling around in a dark room, hoping I find the door . . . but I really am sorry."

"Aw, geez, Hol. Don't cry." Again proving himself the better person, Donnie reached out and put a hand on my shoulder. "I could use your help planning the proposal."

"Done," I said, launching into a hug that probably crushed him.

"And please, just call Camille. She misses you like crazy."

"Also done," I said, my hand already reaching for the phone.

On the day before Daisy was to be released from rehab, I got called into a meeting in Dr. Chace's office and was introduced to a man from Fairgate Publishing. He stayed quiet as Chace counseled us on the stresses of the newly free addict superstar, but as soon as Chace and Faith stepped away to talk to Daisy, the Fairgate man zeroed in on me.

"I'm Stephen Scott," he said, shaking my hand. "And I'm a big fan of your work."

"Really?" I didn't mean to sound so astonished, but up until that moment, I had no idea any publisher was interested in this project.

Faith hadn't told me she was passing along my pages to anyone, not that she owed me that information. "I mean, great."

"How close are you to finishing the book?" he asked. "Daisy will be on *The View* Monday to talk about her time in rehab, and we'd like her to announce it then."

It would require an all-nighter over the weekend, but with the relative calm of the last two weeks, I'd made remarkable progress. In that time, the book had shifted from being an autobiography of a pop princess to a cautionary tale of excess and growing up too fast. This was partly out of necessity, since neither Daisy nor Faith really cared about their lives before fame. Faith kept telling me she just couldn't remember much, but I increasingly felt like that period was deliberately forgotten.

"I can make that deadline. But to be honest . . ." I didn't know if it was appropriate to question this guy, but I knew my idiot agent wasn't going to look out for me. I had to be strong and determined if I ever wanted to be taken seriously. "I don't feel comfortable turning over any material until I've been paid. And so far I've basically only gotten expenses."

I instinctively took a step back, expecting some sort of outrage, but Stephen just nodded calmly. "Of course. We'll set up a meeting on Monday and exchange the draft for a check. We need to have you sign a new contract, anyway."

"Why's that?" I knew I sounded suspicious, but I didn't try to hide it. After having been used and abused by these people, I was more than a little nervous that they were now trying to write me out of any royalties.

"Because Fairgate Publishing is assuming control of the book," Stephen explained. "We'll pay you directly." He broke into a knowing smile. "And our checks always clear."

"I get fifty percent of the royalty share," I added quickly. I figured I was about to be handed a contract that was a mile long and largely inscrutable, so I wanted to be explicit about that point up front.

"I've read your original agreement. And if you don't mind my saying, after having met these people, you deserve more than that."

I couldn't help but laugh. "I like you," I said. "I really do."

Stephen pulled out an iPhone and began clicking away on an e-mail. "And your information is all in the contract, yes?"

"It should be. Why do you ask?"

"Your ticket to New York has to be in your legal name or they won't let you on the plane."

I hadn't realized the contract signing was going to take place in New York. Though it was the Mecca of the publishing universe, so I should have expected that. I tried not to let my excitement show too much. Despite the fact that I never want to live there, I love Manhattan. And I hadn't been able to afford to visit since graduating from college.

"Holly Ann Gracin, just like it says on the contract," I said.

"Since you're so close with Daisy and Faith, why don't I put you all on the same flight Sunday morning? And is there someone you'd like to bring—on us? I don't want you to be stuck in the city for days by yourself."

I was definitely feeling like I could get used to this kind of treatment.

Later that night, Camille and I were waiting in line at Diddy Riese again. Celebration or commiseration, there was nothing like fresh ice cream sandwiches. The only difference was that this time, our respective men were with us. I had profusely apologized to Camille both in person and on the phone, but she was already past it. And I knew that in a couple of weeks, when she and Donnie got engaged, it would slip her mind completely. But I wouldn't forget. I knew I needed to be a better friend.

"Listen, I have to go to New York next week for the book. Do you want to come with me?"

Camille smiled, but instead of answering, she glanced back at Ben and Donnie, who were getting along like a house on fire. We caught the sentence "He didn't even use an elevated batten system, can you believe it?" It was Greek to me, but the men laughed like it was grade A comedy.

Turning back to me, Camille winked. "Take your man. We'll take a spa weekend after you get back."

I'd already considered taking Ben, but that was a whole new relationship step. The first trip together. Was I even ready?

Reading my mind, Camille leaned in and whispered, "You've come so far. Don't punk out on me now, Gracin."

As you might expect, Daisy's release from Rehabilication was nothing short of a media explosion. Despite the jurisdictional problems, a cavalcade from the LAPD came down to Orange County to escort her back home. I wasn't there for the madness, but I saw it all play out on the news. It may sound strange that a starlet being released from rehab is worthy of live coverage in the middle of the day, but in Los Angeles, the local news is kind of a joke. There's very little mention of politics or the rest of the world, but if there's a car chase or a celebrity showing up for court, every local channel carries a live feed.

But if any of those paparazzi media outlets thought Daisy would waste her biggest bargaining chip by talking to them, they were sorely mistaken. She quietly moved into the waiting vehicle and didn't get out again until the car disappeared into her gated estate. The only person who had a seemingly endless stream of things to say was Dr. Chace, who found his way onto CNN just five hours after Daisy's release.

"I feel good, knowing that I've saved a lovely and talented young performer. And I thank God every day that I'm here to share my gifts with the world." Beware the man who can turn any situation into a story about him.

The added benefit of Daisy being sprung from the facility was that the photographers no longer had any interest in me. I walked into the local grocery store just a couple of hours later and was pleased to discover that my shadow was my only companion. By that night, I was able to move out of the Dixsons' guesthouse and back into my dark, dank little hovel. It wasn't nearly as swanky as the places I had stayed in the last two months, but it was home—for now.

I was proud of Daisy; the vultures weren't able to get a single picture of her from the Wednesday of her release until we met at the airport early Sunday morning.

"I feel really weird about this," Ben said as we lugged our suitcases toward the terminal.

"Why?" I momentarily worried that I shouldn't have asked him to come with me. Maybe it was too soon? But he'd said yes so quickly and had certainly seemed excited about the trip.

"I've never spent time with the Dixsons like this," he replied. "I'm below the line."

A couple of months ago, I wouldn't have understood that comment. As Camille explained it, there are two types of crew members, above and below the line. Those "above the line" are considered master craftsmen or artists and have the ability to negotiate their wages, while those below fall into a standardized salary range. An easier way to explain it is to call them the haves and the have-nots. Nowhere else in the world would Renaissance Man Ben be considered a have-not, but Hollywood is one strange little burg.

"Who cares? Do you really think these people are better than you?"

It didn't help my point that at exactly that instant, the noise level rose tenfold and we knew Daisy had arrived. The paparazzi, who'd been relaxing and chatting among themselves when we walked up, were now chasing Daisy's town car to the terminal entrance. Without uttering a single syllable, she and Faith moved slowly toward the door, keeping their gaze down at the ground.

"No," he replied, shaking his head. "I like being below the line." I waited for the sarcasm and realized he was being honest. Ben had no interest in the Hollywood life, at least not the kind those photogs were interested in. The more I got to know him, the more there was to like about Ben.

Luckily, there were police officers and TSA employees waiting to shepherd us through ticketing and security, so with a few hundred more flashes and questions, the photographers blessedly disappeared. Only then did Daisy give me a hug and seem to notice Ben by my side.

"Huh," she said, staring almost directly up at him with her seablue gaze. "I knew you were nailing someone, Holly Bear, but I thought it was Vaughn. Don't worry, I've done plenty of grips and electricians in my time." Maybe I'd given her too much credit for her heightened maturity level. Then again, maturity doesn't necessarily make you smarter.

Ben turned white and shifted his eyes toward me, remaining silent.

"Ben's a production designer," I replied.

"Oh, so you're like a carpenter?"

Ben shot me another look, clearly not sure how to respond. "I run the art department." He paused, then added, "I picked out that furniture in your house."

"Cool," Daisy replied, slapping him on the arm. "You guys will love the W Hotel. The beds are awesome for sex."

Before I had to invent an adequate response for that, an airline employee walked up and offered to get us settled into our seats. As we walked the Jetway, Ben cast a longing glance over his shoulder like a man about to be led to the gallows.

Though we weren't permitted to personally accompany Daisy to *The View* (from here on out, the publisher didn't want to give the media any opportunity to connect me to her book), Ben and I had VIP tickets to the show. I'd never seen a live show taped before, and it moved at an alarmingly efficient pace. But the most unexpected moment of that morning came when Daisy entered the studio with not only her mother but a smarmy, terribly unattractive man.

"Who do you think that is?" I whispered loudly to Ben.

He gave me a strange look in return. "That's her father."

In more than two months, I'd seen neither hide nor hair of this man. He'd purposefully avoided every second of his daughter's melt-down and recovery, only to reappear once there was more money to be made.

My assessment was confirmed as soon as the show returned from commercial break and Daisy began her talk with the ladies of *The View*. The conversation started out much like any celebrity inter-view, except that Daisy introduced her parents to the hosts and the people at home. But it quickly moved on from being upbeat and fun; the show landing Daisy's first televised interview post-rehab was a major get, and the hosts didn't waste any time zeroing in on the controversy.

Over the hour-long show, Daisy talked about the evils of the Hollywood fame machine and how it was now her duty to help struggling young people everywhere exorcise the demons of ad-diction. God had called her to write a book, and who was she to question God? She was beautiful, poised, articulate, and managed to sniffle at just the right moment to elicit emotion. I knew it was utter bullshit and I was on the edge of my seat.

But the performance of the morning went to Deacon, who kept one arm around his long-suffering wife and tightly gripped his daugh-ter's hand throughout the interview. With anguish in his voice, Deacon told Whoopi Goldberg how guilty he felt, trusting that the producers and managers had Daisy's best interests in mind. "She thought she was making me proud," he said, choking up. "And I thought I was making her happy." The sick bastard came off like father of the year.

After the taping, Ben and I walked the fifteen blocks to Fairgate Publishing, enjoying the early fall day. The best part was that it was business as usual in New York; none of these people knew who I was, nor did they care. It was the most liberated I'd felt in weeks.

Due to the nondisclosure issues, Ben wasn't allowed in the room with me when I signed my new contract for the book. Stephen Scott apologized profusely, but I didn't really mind. I just wanted this entire affair over. I use the word *over* loosely—I knew perfectly well that there would be rewrites to the book, but right now that felt like child's play compared to what I'd already endured. And given my ongoing difficulties getting paid, I'd already plotted the directions to the nearest branch of my bank. That check would be cashed before lunchtime.

My next shock of the day came when Stephen handed me the payment envelope. I knew it was uncouth of me, but I couldn't help but peek under the flap. After everything, I wasn't going to be careless now. But the check didn't read fifty thousand dollars (or forty-two, which was the remaining balance); printed very clearly on the amount line was "one hundred thousand dollars." I glanced up at Stephen, sure it was an error.

He must have anticipated my reaction because he smiled and said, "The rest came from Daisy's advance. She thought you should have it."

For a few seconds, I was worried I might pass out. The world suddenly got very quiet and I could no longer hear Stephen speaking or the midday Manhattan traffic outside. I waited for the onslaught of dizziness, but it never came. Instead, I merely shook the publisher's hand and thanked him. After all of the times I overreacted to the most ridiculous, minuscule things, someone had just handed me a check for a hundred grand and I was fine. Perfectly fine.

"I know this must have been a traumatic experience for you," Stephen said, laughing. "But they're not all this bad."

"Well, even if that's true, it's not like I can go around advertising my services. That contract you had me sign says that I can never tell anyone what I've just done."

"That's true, but we can certainly call you again. Half of our business is celebrity memoirs. That is, if you're interested."

"Call anytime" was all I said. I wasn't sure I really meant it, but I said it anyway.

When I deposited the check, the bank teller gave me a suspicious look, glancing back and forth between my face and the readout of my account. "This is quite a bit of money," he said.

"I'm very famous in Japan," I said. From behind me, Ben swatted my arm.

Feeling rich in so many ways, I spent the rest of the morning convinced I'd finally banished whatever cloud had been hovering over me. Daisy was off on some print interview and Ben and I had the afternoon to wander around the city until we were all supposed to meet up for dinner at Daniel on the Upper East Side. As we popped back into the hotel for a quick change, I was practically blissful.

That is, until I noticed Ben staring past me to the front desk. I didn't even have time to turn all the way around when I heard, "Oh, hey there."

And there was Vaughn, standing at the check-in desk, luggage at his feet. I couldn't imagine what he was doing in New York, and at the very same hotel, no less. He had nothing to do with the book.

"Hi, Vaughn," Ben said.

He took a step forward, but I didn't immediately join him. It wasn't until Ben prodded me with a hand to the small of my back that I was able to move. My legs practically creaked from their unwillingness to walk across the room. But once I got there, I did give Vaughn a (somewhat stiff) hug, and Ben politely shook his hand.

"Things going well with the book?" Vaughn asked.

I hoped Ben would answer that question for me, but he's not the kind of guy to do that. The two men stood there, waiting for me to answer. "Great. New contract signed and everything."

"I saw *The View*. Daisy came off like a real pro. I was proud of her."

He was proud? A month ago he wanted to run screaming from her to any producing job that would have him. And now that she was back on the right track, he was proud of her?

"Listen, I was just headed out to grab lunch. Are you guys hungry?" he asked.

"Sorry, we've already eaten," I said.

"That's too bad. But I'll see you at Daniel tonight?"

I was again annoyed by Vaughn's presence. Why was he invited to Daniel? Why did he have to reappear in my life just when I'd managed to put him out of my head? "I'm sure you will."

I headed for the elevator, Ben following close behind me. After I stabbed the elevator button, he put an arm around my shoulder. "We haven't had lunch."

"I know."

"You have to talk to him sometime," he said, kissing me on the forehead.

"I beg to differ."

At the same moment, the elevator dinged and so did my phone. I pulled it out of my pocket and saw that it was a message from Vaughn. It read: *Can we talk? Alone?* I held it up for Ben to see. "Is this asshole serious? Like I wasn't going to show you?"

"That's only a statement on what he would do in this situation, not on you." I liked Ben more every day, and I valued his intelligence, but sometimes his fortune cookie wisdom felt a little preachy. "You should go."

"No way."

We stepped into the elevator. Ben reached out and threaded

318 ★ RACHEL STUHLER

his fingers through mine. "Do you know why you're so upset right now?"

I held up my phone with my free hand. "Yeah, I'm pretty clear on that."

Ben shook his head. "It's because you never got closure on what happened in Rome. So you should go, hear what he has to say."

I couldn't believe Ben was saying this. I know that he's no immature, lovestruck teenage boy, but I wanted him to be at least a little bit jealous. The way Vaughn had been jealous of him. It was completely irrational, but that didn't change how I felt.

"I don't care what he has to say." But that was a lie. I wanted to know. I was firmly infatuated with Ben, but that didn't make me any less confused about what had happened with Vaughn. But the guy hadn't been able to give me a straight answer a month ago, I couldn't imagine anything had changed in the weeks since.

Ben's gaze was carefully trained on the numbers of the elevator as we ascended. I could tell he didn't really want to look at me, which made me very nervous. "You do care. If you didn't, you wouldn't be upset."

He had me there. "I'll go if it'll make you happy."

"Don't do it for me," he said. "Do it for you."

It took a few text exchanges, but I met Vaughn out front of the hotel an hour later. Ben said he was going to Union Square to meet up with a few college buddies and would catch up with me before dinner. I hated watching him go, but not nearly as much as I hated seeing Vaughn step out of the hotel.

"Where do you want to go?" he asked.

I threw him a look. "If I have to talk to you, cupcakes are required."

He smiled at his shoes. I was mildly glad that he was embarrassed, too. "That excited about this conversation, huh?"

"I'm only here because Ben insisted," I said. As we turned the corner onto East Fiftieth, my feet began moving faster. Part of me needed buttercream frosting and the other part just wanted to make sure there were witnesses.

"I've thought about calling you a million times," he said, edging closer to me. "I picked up the phone every day and thought, *I want to talk to Holly today.*"

"But you didn't call." After the first couple of days, I hadn't really wanted him to call, anyway. But I did want to know why he didn't.

"What was I going to say?"

"That you're a jerk, that you led me on." When Vaughn didn't immediately respond, I glanced up at him and was surprised to discover how irritated he looked. Really, *he* was annoyed with *me*? I felt inside out and exposed, unable to get my bearings. And I was seriously angry with Vaughn for ruining my perfect day. "Why did you even want to talk to me today? Why couldn't you just leave me alone?"

Before Vaughn spoke, he put his hand on the small of my back. That touch brought me right back to that last unfortunate night in Rome, and I felt my internal temperature rise. I knew it was meant to be a sweet, soft gesture, but it felt inappropriate. I quickly stepped out of his reach, and his annoyed expression returned.

"We should have had this talk a while ago," Vaughn started, speaking quietly. He glanced at me for some sort of agreement or reassurance, but I kept my expression as neutral as I could manage. It was taking all of my effort not to shake uncontrollably under his hand. "I am sorry that you felt like I led you on."

"Don't say that like it's all in my head." Some men have a way of making women feel their concerns are crazy. It took me a long time to realize that, more often than not, this is just a deflection of responsibility. And a weak one at that. "You may not have kissed me until Rome, but you sure made me think you wanted to."

"Because I did," he said. "I like you, we have fun together."

"Then why did it take you so long?"

"Seeing you with Ben . . . I thought my head would split open." Vaughn pursed his lips, which was much the same expression Ben got when talking about him. "I knew I was in trouble the second he first mentioned you."

"*I* told you about Ben," I said, confused. "After that endless meeting in Rome."

Vaughn's face looked momentarily startled, but he quickly recovered. "Right . . . What I meant to say was, when I saw the way he looked at you at the production meeting." I was about to ask a follow-up question when he quickly added, "I should've done something then, it was stupid of me not to . . ." He reached up and brushed his hand against my face. This time, I couldn't stop myself—I flinched.

There was still a disconnect in this conversation. I wanted to know why he'd waited until Ben expressed interest before he made a move; Vaughn not only wasn't answering, he was just parroting what I'd already said. Even if I could let that go, I had other problems with him. "And why didn't you return my call once we got back to L.A.?"

"I was embarrassed," he told me. "Things didn't exactly turn out the way I'd hoped."

I watched his face as he admitted his "embarrassment." Prior to working with Daisy, I'd never been particularly good at knowing when people were lying to me. I must have been getting better, because I knew, right then, that Vaughn was flat-out lying.

"But now we're both here and we can fix it," he said, reaching out to touch my back again. This time, he didn't even make contact before I jerked away.

"Fix what?"

Again, he seemed stymied by my response. "Well . . . now we tell Ben. You're the only one I want, Holly. And I know how you feel about me, I've always known."

I didn't know how I felt about him, how could he possibly know? How could he think things would be so easily resolved? If he had said any of this to me weeks ago, nothing would have played out the way it had. I was just beginning to see how arrogant and self-serving he was.

"There's nothing to fix. I'm dating Ben."

"For real, Holly? You want to date a production designer?"

I'm not one for physical violence, but I came very close to slapping him across the face. "What's wrong with that?"

"Do you really think someone from the art department is going to get you into the right parties? Introduce you to the right people that will get you those big jobs?" He stared at me like I was the batty one, like he was trying to save me from myself.

"I don't care about those things." Until that moment, I didn't realize just how bad a judge of character I must be. Daisy and Faith, Donnie, even my mother—I was wrong about everyone. Vaughn had seemed like a sweet, charming guy who only wanted to get to know me better, and it turned out he was one of the worst.

"Everyone cares about those things."

Watching his irritation grow, I suddenly knew why he'd kissed me in Rome. And why he hadn't returned my phone call in Los Angeles. "Oh my God. The dinner at La Pergola. 'I don't get invited to these things.' You wanted to date me because it got you closer to Daisy's inner circle."

My mind flashed through the last couple of months, every word, every gesture. Maybe Vaughn did like hanging out with me, but I was of no use to him as a girlfriend until I could have ingratiated him with Daisy. "And you stopped calling when your show got canceled. Because you thought I couldn't help you anymore."

We reached the bakery and I stopped outside. I didn't want his sliminess to sully perfectly good cupcakes. Because I'd need a few to cleanse my palate of this conversation.

"You're being stupid," he said. "If that were true, why would I be standing here with you right now?"

"I assume because the whole world is looking at Daisy again and not just as some teenage screw-up." I still wasn't sure how these things worked, but I may have even been more valuable to him now.

"Say that it would be beneficial for us to date. What's so wrong with that?"

I wished he'd started our conversation with that very sentence. It would have made everything after unnecessary. I opened the door to the bakery. "I'm going to go eat cupcakes. You're going to go to hell."

"You're behaving like a child," he told me. "And you're making a huge mistake."

"The mistake would be if you took a single step to follow me." I didn't allow him any rebuttal. I pulled the door closed behind me and didn't bother looking back.

I was on the edge of tears when I ran into Daisy in the lobby. I wasn't mourning the loss of Vaughn (I'm not that weak), but I was a little overwhelmed by his deceit. She had just come back from her print interview and was in high spirits. I expected her to take one look at me and tell me that crying made her want to vomit, but she was strangely considerate.

"Holly Bear, what's wrong?" Daisy asked.

I sniffled desperately, trying to regain my composure. But in the end, I didn't have that much self-control. "I don't know what to think," I admitted, rubbing my eyes and accidentally smearing my black eyeliner. I'm sure I looked like Miss America.

Daisy put her arm around me and led me to the lounge area. "Is this about Ben and Vaughn?"

"No. Yes. There's no choice there, I'm crazy about Ben."

"Oh, thank God." Daisy leaned in and touched her head to mine. It was the sweetest gesture I'd ever seen her make. "I was hoping you'd realize that. Vaughn's a tool."

"He is. I just don't understand it. All of that effort so he could have a girlfriend who might get him into a few parties?" I shook my head, pulling away from Daisy a bit so that I could actually see her face. "I wish he hadn't kissed me in Italy. Vaughn gave me some bullshit about how when Ben first saw me in Rome, he knew he had to make his move, like he was hurt or jealous. I should have listened to Ben to begin with; he always said it was about winning. That Vaughn just didn't like to lose. "

Daisy suddenly looked confused. "In Rome?" She shook her head. "That's not right."

"What?" I remembered my own life quite well, thank you. "Yes, it is. I met Ben in the middle of the first night. I told Vaughn about it at the production meeting and he got all weird and jealous. Not that that part of it matters in the grand scheme of things."

Daisy made a face and then shrugged. "Well, I guess that's sort of how it happened. But Vaughn was weird and jealous days before we left for Italy."

"Jealous of who?"

"*Ben!*"

"Daisy, what are you talking about?"

It was the first time I considered that she might actually like me. "The very first time Ben saw you, he asked like everybody who you were. Even my mom."

"But I told him who I was." I thought back to that night in the writers' room; I had clearly identified myself. But Ben somehow already knew I was Daisy's ghostwriter. I hadn't put that together before now.

"Not in Rome, on set in L.A.," Daisy said, rolling her eyes at me. "That day with the coffee truck. I guess you said something all funny and cute and then he asked like a trillion people who you were."

The day with the coffee cart. I hadn't known what Ben looked like. He could have been ten feet in front of me and I wouldn't have recognized him. "He never told me that."

"Yeah, it's pretty cute, right?"

Several threads of this story were starting to bother me. "But at the airport you didn't even know Ben's crew position."

Daisy made a face. "There are like two hundred crew members, I don't really care what they do. But I do know their names—Mom drills it into me. She thinks it's rude to say, 'Hey, guy behind the camera.'"

And yet, she had no problem deliberately calling Vaughn "John" for six years. "Huh."

Daisy put a hand on my arm. "Let Vaughn go, he's not worth your time. Ben seems pretty great. And damn if he isn't hot."

I laughed out loud. I really needed that. "He is, right?" I wasn't sure it was appropriate, but I gave Daisy a hug. "Thanks for listening."

She gave me one of her perfect little grins. "No probs, Holly Bear."

When I walked back into the hotel room, Ben was seated by the window, staring out at the Manhattan skyline. "My friends said I could stay with them. So you don't have to worry about me."

I was immediately confused. He looked so sad, so resigned to losing me to Vaughn. I couldn't understand it. "Why would you go anywhere? You're here with me."

"I just thought . . . I may not have been there, but I know what Vaughn said to you."

"Who cares what Vaughn had to say?" I asked. "Most of the time, he's only speaking to hear himself talk."

Ben finally turned to look at me, his surprise apparent. It was the only thing he'd ever done that hurt my feelings.

"You didn't really think I'd fall for his bullshit, did you?" I was offended that this man I'd grown so close to, who seemed to understand me better than I understood myself, thought I was stupid enough to choose Vaughn over him.

"Guys like him, they always win. Even if they have to lie."

"I knew it was a lie."

I crossed the room and sat down on the bed, reaching my hand out to touch Ben's knee. It was a simple gesture, but I needed it. I just needed to touch him. "And you're so sure I want him?"

He stared at me with his wounded gray eyes and I instantly knew that I had miscalculated a lot of things. I'd assumed he wasn't jealous, even made the leap that I couldn't be that important to him. But Ben was mature, not uncaring. And for the first time, my stomach fluttered. Not in the infatuated, adolescent way it had when I met Vaughn, but something deeper, stronger.

"I was worried," he said, his voice cracking. "I don't want to lose you."

I leaned forward and placed my hand against the side of Ben's face. "I'm not going anywhere."

When I kissed him, it felt like the rest of the world fell away.

Daisy's dinner was held in Daniel's Bellecour Room. As Ben and I walked to the restaurant, I expected to feel mounting dread over encountering Vaughn yet again. I wanted him to crawl back into the sewer drain he'd emerged from a little more than two months ago. But when Ben wrapped his giant, warm hand around mine, I realized I didn't care about Vaughn at all.

Not that I had any doubts about my decision, but two seconds inside the door, Vaughn reinforced it. He was standing with a willowy brunette in some assemblage of flossy fabric that may have been a dress. Or it might have been tissue paper.

I had no intention of even addressing him, but as Ben and I passed on the way to the bar, he touched Ben's elbow. "Benji, Holly. Have you met my date, Michelle Fairgate?"

Ben and I exchanged a look of barely disguised amusement. It took every ounce of my willpower not to burst out laughing.

"Nice to meet you," Ben said, shaking the woman's hand. "If you'll excuse us."

As soon as we were clear, we both started to giggle. "Well, I can't compete with a publishing heiress," I said. "So I guess you're stuck with me."

Ben leaned down and kissed me. "There's no one I'd rather be stuck with." He nodded toward the bar. "Can I get you a drink?"

"Whiskey sour."

He walked to the bar, and I was standing alone for just a moment before Daisy approached me, a glass of champagne in her hand. Since it had been such a traumatic day, this didn't automatically strike me as odd.

"I really think things are going to work out with Benji the carpenter," she said. "I can feel it."

"It's going pretty well so far," I told her. And then I finally asked the question that had piqued my curiosity more than a month ago. "Hey, do you know why people call him Benji?"

Daisy nodded. "Yeah, Vaughn gave him that nickname. He claims it's because Ben always does what production needs, but I think it's because Ben makes him feel insecure. But then, Vaughn always seems kinda insecure." It was a remarkably astute observation from the Teen Queen.

As we talked about them, we both glanced toward the bar in time to see that Ben and Vaughn were standing next to each other. Ben leaned over to say something to Vaughn, and though we certainly couldn't hear their conversation, the look on Ben's face was nothing short of venomous. I found it irresistibly sexy. Next to me, Daisy giggled.

Suddenly, I remembered how odd it was that Vaughn was in New York in the first place. I'd thought about it earlier but had quickly been distracted. What *did* he have to do with the book?

"Wait, why is Vaughn even here?"

Daisy's grin grew wider. "I'm the one who asked him to come.

I'm meeting with De Niro and his people on Wednesday and I told them I wanted to bring Vaughn on as a producer."

This was an extra piece of the puzzle. No wonder he'd wanted me as his girlfriend; I may not have been a Fairgate, but he thought I'd gotten him a film producer job. "But you know he's a terrible person, right?"

"Oh, definitely," she said. "But you live in L.A. Everyone's a terrible person. At least Vaughn is good at his job."

"But why is he here tonight? These are all your book people."

Daisy lightly tapped me on my cheek, smiling. "I did it for you. Axel and Sharla told me what happened in Rome. They were afraid you still liked him. And Vaughn can be charming, but not for very long. I thought you should have the opportunity to finish things. Or whatever that's called."

I couldn't believe she went through all of this trouble just for me. "Closure."

"Right, closure." Daisy and I watched as Vaughn went back to the heiress. "You really dodged a bullet. He's also pretty awful in bed."

I shouldn't have been surprised. Not after everything I'd seen and heard in the last couple of months. But I was. I chose not to acknowledge her words.

"So you're officially signed on to do 'Back Alley'?" I asked, changing the subject.

"Yep," she said. "After a page-one rewrite from the author of the book." Daisy looked up at me and winked. So she had actually been listening to me.

A very handsome man in his late forties walked into the room and waved at Daisy. "Who's that?" I asked, fearing that he might be her latest romantic conquest.

"Oh, that's my new manager, Cy," she replied, raising her champagne glass. "I've been trying to get him for years, but he's always been a little out of my league."

I could have sworn I'd just heard Dr. Chace telling the reporters at CNN that he would be representing Daisy. But he had talked continuously for ten minutes, so it was possible that I'd mixed things up. "What about Dr. Chace?"

Daisy laughed out loud like it was the funniest thing she'd ever heard. "That moron?"

"That moron claims he just saved your life," I said. It was only then that I noticed the glass of champagne in her hand. "And speaking of rehab, is it really a good idea to be drinking? Not only are you underage, but you're an addict."

In response, Daisy drained the last drops of liquid from the glass. She glanced around to make sure we were out of earshot before leaning in and saying, "Do you really think I went to rehab because I'm an addict?"

I did, in fact. I'd been privy to all of her recent manic highs and lows, and there were only two explanations that made sense—either she was a drug addict or she had serious mental issues. Or both. "Come on, Daisy. The pills? The cocaine on the Roman street corner? You have to know that's not normal behavior."

"Do you want to know a secret?" There was something different in her voice. It took me a moment to realize it was the same persona she'd affected in the jail cell. The one I'd found so frightening and soulless.

"Sure," I replied. Actually, I didn't want to know any of her secrets, but I was a little afraid to say no.

Cool as a cucumber, Daisy shrugged and winked at me. "I've never used cocaine in my life."

If she was about to use that bullshit baby powder excuse on me, I was ready to walk right out the door. "I'm sorry?"

She shrugged again, staring across the room at her mother and the new manager. "I've wanted to get rid of Jamie for more than a year now," Daisy began, sounding like a forty-five-year-old cocktail waitress rather than a teenybopper starlet. "I'm tired of recording these crap songs and working on my mindless show. But every time

I brought him a script I liked, he said it wasn't time yet. Jamie was never very good at seeing the big picture, he's only ever been concerned about the money coming in right now."

"Then why didn't you fire him?"

Her jaw set in a tight, determined line. "My parents signed a ten-year contract with him that didn't expire until I was almost twenty-one. I couldn't take two more years of his lying and mismanagement. Not to mention, I had three years left with Nickelodeon."

I instinctively took a protective step back from Daisy; she was truly scaring me. "So you, what, faked a drug arrest?"

"All of it. I purposely left the medication suitcase in the back of our car on the way to the airport, I made everyone think I was losing my mind, and then I paid those kids to get cocaine all over me. I figured if the cops caught me red-handed, they wouldn't bother testing my blood."

"But you said Jamie made you take all those pills . . ." I couldn't make sense of what was happening here. This was turning out to be the strangest day of my life. And considering the last couple of months, that said a *lot*.

"He did, but they're pills. I'm not worried about taking ketamine or Demerol. They're prescriptions."

Okay, so Daisy wasn't exactly the diabolical mastermind she imagined. "How did you get drugs into Rehabilication?" I had to ask. "That first day I saw you, you were high as a kite."

Daisy patted me on the back patronizingly and laughed. "Oh, Holly Bear, there's no easier place to score drugs than a rehab center. You just need to have money or to be okay with giving blow jobs. And I've got both covered."

I was in shock. Everything I'd known about my last few months was a lie, a fabrication, or a misunderstanding. I just couldn't believe that the Italian fiasco had been engineered entirely by a teenage pop star. "Wait a minute—when you asked to have your memoirs written . . ."

"*Please,* bitch," she said, waving me away. "You knew the first day I wasn't interested in talking about my stupid-ass TV show. I just had to keep things going until you really had something to write about."

Holy Mother of God. This girl was positively Machiavellian. "I wish you'd told me that two months ago." In spite of myself, I laughed. "This would have been a lot less stressful."

"I am sorry," she replied, actually seeming sincere. "But I couldn't take the chance that you'd rat me out."

"What'll you do now?"

Daisy turned to me and smiled, her bright white veneers almost gleaming under the overhead lights. "I'm going to live, however I want. But first, I'm going to kick my mother and father the hell out of my house."

"Oh," I said, just remembering something. "Thank you for the bonus. I didn't expect it."

Daisy laced one of her arms around my back and leaned in to me. Without high heels on, she was so much shorter her head barely came to the top of my bra line. "Holly, you were the only thing that got me through this. You deserve every penny."

From across the room, Ben caught my eye and smiled.

EPILOGUE

When I was a kid, I thought one bad day was the end of the world. If Logan P. called me a name and everyone laughed, I thought that would be my name forever and people would forget to call me Daisy. It sounds silly now, but I think we do the same thing a lot more than we'd like to admit. When a guy breaks up with us, we say, "I'll never love anyone again." But we do. When we don't get the job we want, we say, "My career is over." But it's not.

Tomorrow is not today. And anything can happen tomorrow.

The day the book was released just happened to be my twenty-sixth birthday. I woke up that morning in my new apartment near the beach and wondered if anyone would buy it. Given that I was owed fifty percent of the royalties, this was no small consideration.

In the six months since I'd finished writing the book, a lot had changed. Daisy had guest-starred on an acclaimed HBO show as a junkie politician's daughter and was practically a shoo-in for an Emmy nomination, and she'd just finished shooting that gritty drama with Robert De Niro. Less than a month after her appearance on *The View,* Deacon came out of the closet and announced that he was leaving his wife for a cabana boy he'd met in Acapulco nine years ago. Faith turned back to her faith and began selling religious-themed jewelry on QVC. They were lovely pieces, and I'd even bought a few of them myself, mostly as a thank-you to my mother and a reassurance that I was no longer destitute. And Donnie and Camille are planning their wedding, which will include me in a lime green dress. I think she knows it's hideous, but for her, I'll wear it proudly.

About a month before the book's release, Jamie was arrested for statutory rape. According to court documents obtained by CNN, Ariceli's mother caught the two of them having sex in her hot tub. Jamie went to jail and Ariceli never did record an album. She tried out for one of those television singing competitions, but one of the judges felt she had a "skanky vibe" and she never made it through the first round. One good thing did come out of the arrest, though; as the reviews for the book started to pour in, Jamie's actions lent a lot of credibility to "Daisy's" words.

As for me . . . As I said, I no longer live in that hellhole on Diablorado Street. I have a two-bedroom apartment in Santa Monica, and on days when the smog isn't too thick, I can actually see the ocean. Smitty spends most of his afternoons perched in the open windows, enjoying the sun and salty air. And in case you were wondering, I didn't bother painting over Jamie's cell phone number when I moved out. I figured he deserved a prank call or two.

Which brings me back to my birthday. I awoke to a wonderful breakfast of pancakes, bacon, and chocolate milk, prepared by my fantastic boyfriend. I'd like to say I enjoyed it, but I was really just counting the minutes until the bookstore opened.

"Do you think anyone will show up?" I asked. Daisy was going to sign copies at the store right down the street at 10:00 A.M.

"I'm sure they will," Ben said, kissing the top of my head.

We got coffee (or my mocha-ice blended version of coffee, covered in whipped cream) and walked the six blocks to the store. Just before we reached the plaza, I stopped short and buried my face in his shoulder.

"Oh God, what if no one comes? What if the book sells ten copies?"

He kissed my forehead sweetly. "If the book sells ten copies, we'll take that thirty dollars and have a moderately priced lunch. It won't make any difference."

Ben put an arm around my shoulder and resumed walking, giving me no choice but to follow. I just wanted to get this over with. I knew Daisy couldn't really acknowledge who I was, but she'd asked me to stop by and say hello, just for good luck.

As I turned the corner into the shopping plaza, I stopped short and gasped. There was a line all the way around the block and an employee was shepherding people behind a rope.

"We'll be letting everyone in for the Dixson signing in just a minute," the harried employee called out to the restless crowd. "But please be patient and bear with us. I promise, we have copies for all of you."

I tried not to add up my royalty check just from the people in the line, but I couldn't help it. "Do you think all of the jobs will be like this one?" I asked Ben.

He laughed and kissed me. "God, I hope not." He smiled and winked at me. "What's the next guy's name?"

"Right now, I don't even care."

In fact, there was a next guy, and more clients after that. But that's a story for another time.

ACKNOWLEDGMENTS

Despite the single name on the cover, it takes an army of people to make any book (or movie) reach an audience, and *Absolutely True Lies* is no exception. My gratitude spreads far and wide, but most especially to:

Jennifer Weinbaum Ray, my talented manager at Principal Entertainment, for keeping me employed/sane and helping me grow as a writer. Joseph Weiner of Miloknay-Weiner, for watching my back (in the legal sense). Doug Stewart, from Sterling Lord Literistic, for believing in me and this little book. Lauren Spiegel, my fabulous editor from Touchstone, who saw something special in Holly, and guided me to create the best version of this book. Thanks to my husband and son, for more things than I can count—unconditional love, unwavering support, and story times with crazy accents. To Diddy Riese, for making inspirational ice cream sandwiches I can't stop writing about (and eating). And to my first readers, who suffered through endless drafts and self-doubt: Jamie Latta, Drew Weaver, Ann Sarnowski, Chrissy Bartz Brockman, Carol Gillis, and Lindsey McCann—your support means the world to me.

ABSOLUTELY TRUE LIES

RACHEL STUHLER

Holly Gracin has learned that living in Los Angeles as an entertainment writer doesn't come with any real perks. She makes little money and doesn't get to write any fun stories about celebrities or attend any swanky events. To top it all off, the fledgling magazine she's working for suddenly shuts down. Without a paycheck, a job, or a decent apartment, Holly is on the verge of moving back home to upstate New York.

Desperate and hopeful, Holly accepts a job to write the memoir of eighteen-year-old Daisy Mae Dixson, a Nickelodeon child star, blockbuster actress, and emerging pop star. As soon as Holly embarks on her ghostwriting duties, she quickly discovers that Daisy is not the sweet, wholesome girl that the public has lovingly embraced. Holly follows Daisy around the world as she travels on yachts, drinks heavily, is stalked by paparazzi, and fights with her own staff.

While accompanying Daisy around the clock, Holly struggles to write the memoir, a task made more difficult when she falls victim to the media's gossip mill and then becomes embroiled in a love triangle. When Daisy has a very public meltdown, Holly must figure out a way for the book to repair Daisy's image—without ultimately ruining her own.

FOR DISCUSSION

1. The title *Absolutely True Lies* is a contradiction. Discuss the meaning of this phrase. What is a "true" lie? Have you ever told one? Why did the author choose this as the title of the book?

2. After accepting her new job as a ghostwriter, Holly worries that she's in over her head. "I wasn't qualified to do this job, not in any way, shape, or form, and I guessed it was just a matter of time before Jameson discovered this and canned my ass" (p. 31). Why does Holly feel this way? Have you ever accepted a job that you felt unprepared for? What did you do?

3. Several characters refer to their jobs as "play." Why is that?

4. When Holly faints in a club, lies are immediately spread about her in the media. How would you react if a lie was told about you, especially one so public?

5. How does Daisy the person compare to Daisy the celebrity? Does her seemingly wholesome image remind you of any other famous pop stars? Which pop stars do you think may not be as innocent as they appear?

6. What do you think about Holly simultaneously dating Ben and Vaughn, although neither relationship is official?

7. When Holly first met the Dixsons, she thought they were the "quintessential American family" (p. 22). However, once she got to know them, her opinion changed drastically. She says, "As lovely and perfect as they seemed from the outside, in reality they had the market cornered on dysfunction" (p. 119). What

did she learn that changed her mind about the Dixsons? Do you agree with her? How did your feelings about the Dixsons change throughout the book?

8. Compare Ben and Vaughn. How are they similar? How are they different? Whose feelings for Holly seem more genuine? Are you on Team Vaughn or Team Ben?

9. How different would this book be if Holly could *actually* write about Daisy's reality? Would you maintain Daisy's good-girl image, or reveal her true self?

10. When Holly confessed to Ben that she was having trouble capturing Daisy's voice for the book since Daisy's real life is not the same as the one she portrays, Ben said, "That's part of Hollywood life, though. We're selling a celluloid dream, not reality. People don't want reality" (p. 180). What does Ben mean? Do you agree with him that people don't want to be sold reality? Do you think anything in Hollywood is real, or is it all manufactured for public perception?

11. When Holly is making her many wishes at the Trevi Fountain, she muses, "I know the popular wisdom is that voicing your wishes cancels them out, but I don't believe that. I think that all too often, we don't get what we want because we're too afraid to put it out there" (p. 183). Do you agree? Do you think Holly puts herself out there, or is she being hypocritical?

12. When Daisy disappears, Holly thinks to herself, "I know it sounds terrible, but [Daisy] was the architect of her own destruction and part of me truly felt like she needed to hit some kind of bottom if she had any hope of developing into a decent human being" (pp. 201-202). Why does Holly think that Daisy

needs a fall from grace in order to learn from her mistakes? Do you agree? Are there any celebrities who've had public breakdowns, and then ultimately made triumphant comebacks?

13. Jamie immediately turned his back on Daisy once she went to jail and her reputation in the public eye was at stake. When Jamie reaches out to Holly asking for money, he offers a warning about the Dixsons, saying, "They act like they care about you, but they don't. They'll use you and just throw you away. They do it to everyone" (p. 272). Were you surprised by Jamie's betrayal? Do you agree with his assessment of the Dixsons?

14. Were you surprised to learn of Vaughn's *real* intentions for dating Holly? Did you fall for his charm, too?

15. Describe what you learn about Daisy by the end of the book. Is she smarter than anyone gives her credit for?

ENHANCE YOUR BOOK CLUB

1. Holly hated being followed by the paparazzi. Look through issues of *US Weekly* or *People* magazine, or browse your favorite gossip blogs/websites. What kinds of celebrity pictures are published the most in the media? Would you want to be a celebrity? Could you handle the paparazzi following your every move?

2. *Absolutely True Lies* gives an insider look at the underbelly of fame and fortune. Read a tell-all celebrity memoir with your book club. Was it scandalous? Did you learn any juicy gossip? Anything about celebrity culture? Did the book capture "the voice" of the star? Try *Through the Storm: A Real Story of Fame*

and Family in a Tabloid World by Lynne Spears or *Facing the Music and Living to Talk About It* by Nick Carter.

3. Plan a European getaway to Rome! Visit the Trevi Fountain and make a wish. Like Holly, maybe yours will come true, too! If staying close to home is more your style, throw a Roman holiday–themed book club meeting with your favorite Italian foods, tiramisu, and lots of Italian wine.

A CONVERSATION WITH RACHEL STUHLER

Like Holly, you made a career out of ghostwriting a few celebrity memoirs. Are any of Holly's scandalous experiences based on your own from your ghostwriting days?

Absolutely True Lies is fiction, but a number of the crazy experiences Holly has are based on things I went through either as a writer or working on film sets. I've been forgotten about, and I've gone unfed and unpaid for long periods of time. I actually started writing the book as a form of catharsis after a particularly bad day, just needing to get out my frustration in some more positive way than drinking my way through a bottle of ready-made margaritas.

***Absolutely True Lies* is your first novel. How does writing a novel differ from ghostwriting a memoir?**

One is pure fiction and the other is a novel! I'm just kidding. Both have their own unique difficulties, but one of the bigger challenges with a memoir is that life doesn't happen as cleanly as it does in fiction. In a novel, I can come up with transitions and find plot points that work the best, but in a memoir, you have to smooth out a person's real experiences. And let's face it, life is bumpy and frequently doesn't make as much sense.

Besides Holly, are there any characters in the book that you can particularly relate to? Are any characters based on people you know or have interacted with in your own life?

Vaughn and Ben both have elements of my husband; the fun, talkative, funny guy I first met (Vaughn) and the smart, sweet, and insanely talented guy I came to know (Ben).

I also wrote in Axel and Sharla because I have a particular soft spot for the men and women of the "glam squad." I worked on film sets from nineteen years old to twenty-seven and grew to love the makeup and hair department. Those guys and girls get to set earlier than 90 percent of the crew and have the greatest energy. Most of my haircuts in my twenties came from a set hair stylist, in exchange for a bottle of wine!

What was your favorite scene to write in the novel?

That would have to be the two scenes where you really get a glimpse behind the facade of Daisy, first in the jail in Porta Maggiore and again at the party in New York. Daisy was a bit of a revelation to me as I wrote her. I had these ideas of who I wanted her to be and then she took on a life of her own, and both of those scenes are some of my favorite writing.

Hollywood seems to thrive on salacious, superficial stories that manipulate the truth. Do you find the portrayal of Hollywood in the book to be true to life or an exaggeration?

Hollywood IS an exaggeration. Actors are paid millions of dollars to tell big stories and that carries over into their real lives; to a lesser extent, this also happens to the people working with them. It's easy to get lost in the world of make-believe. Yes, salacious things happen here. But it's also true that just as often the gossip is false and used to either gain or deflect attention away from what you don't want people to talk about.

Let's talk about Daisy. Different layers of her character are uncovered throughout the book. Was she the most fun character to develop? Is she based on a specific celebrity?

Daisy is not based on a single person, or even a couple of people. Elements of Daisy come from quite a few performers I've worked with either as a writer or as a script supervisor. Of course it's fun to write a person who can literally say anything, but it's also a delicate balance. Daisy may be a little bananas, but it was important to me that she also be real. One of the major themes in the book is seeing beyond the facade, so I had to be careful to never dehumanize her.

Why do you think America is so fascinated with fame and celebrity life?

Part of it is innate, biological. I've read studies about how other species fawn over the alpha in their groups the way we do over movie stars.

I think that our current state of celeb worship has taken things to a different level. Reality TV has created a new sort of aspiration where you don't need to be an amazing actor or win an Olympic gold medal to become famous. So there's a level of personal identification we've never had before. What I have yet to understand is the desire to watch both the rise and fall of celebs. I know people who've been addicted to a show and nearly worshipped the stars only to giggle with glee when those same idols are arrested or cheated on.

You referenced *The Real Housewives of Beverly Hills* when describing Holly's introduction to the Dixsons' lifestyle. Do you watch reality television? What are your favorite shows? What do you think reality television reveals about America's celebrity culture?

Have you seen *RHOBH*? It's fantastic!

But seriously, I do watch a few reality shows. I'll be the first to admit I can't turn off *RHOBH* or *RHONJ*, and I was a devotee of *Dance Moms* until the end of season four (those kids are just too cute and talented). And the only two shows I have to watch live (as opposed to on DVR) are *Top Chef* and *Project Runway*, because I love food, fashion, and crazy talent (and I can't handle spoilers!).

I have a lot of industry friends who hate reality TV for changing the landscape of entertainment, but like anything else in life, I think it's both good and bad. Yes, we've made quite a few people famous for absolutely nothing, but I love that talented people from so many different disciplines are getting the attention they deserve. And sometimes it's educational; I'm a much better cook since I started watching *Top Chef*!

Was it intentional to name your main character *Holly*, as a play on words of "Hollywood"?

I'm particular about what I name my characters and I've always found "Holly" pretty. In terms of the Hollywood connection, I liked it only because I knew that it would drive someone like Holly crazy.

Holly constantly feels frustrated with Vaughn for failing to make concrete plans with her. "This is one of the many, many things I hate about men" (p. 172), she thinks to herself. Do you think women are more direct than men when it comes to relationships and their feelings?

I don't, in fact. I think what Holly's responding to isn't men in general, but "the rules" we're expected to play by in relationships. Wait three days to call, play hard to get . . . I've always hated any sort of pretense and Holly gave me an outlet for that frustration. She wants (as I always did, before I was married) a level of honesty that doesn't exist much in the dating game. Hell, we even call it a game!

Can readers expect a new book starring Holly Gracin in the future? Can you tell us anything about what you're working on now?

I loved every second I spent with Holly Gracin, and before I was even halfway through the book, I was already inventing new adventures for her in the future. So we'll see!

As for what I'm working on now, I'm mentally back in Italy, though this time it's a period piece, which is all I can say for now!

ABOUT THE AUTHOR

Rachel Stuhler grew up in Rochester, NY, so obsessed with movies and books that she spent as little time as possible in the real world. In her late teens, this obsession led her first to New York as a production assistant and then to Los Angeles. There, she spent four years working as a script supervisor (and pining after writing jobs) until one day an actor told her, "If you think you can do it better yourself, just do it."

Within a year, Rachel had sold TV movies to Lifetime and Hallmark and, because she doesn't know when to quit, began dreaming of writing a novel. After forcing countless crew members, family, and friends to read manuscripts, Rachel came to write *Absolutely True Lies.* She continues to work on TV movies and plot her next move in world domination, or writing about world domination, which is more fun and a lot less work.